A Dublin
Student Doctor

By Patrick Taylor

Only Wounded
Pray for Us Sinners
Now and in the Hour of Our Death

An Irish Country Doctor
An Irish Country Village
An Irish Country Christmas
An Irish Country Girl
An Irish Country Courtship
A Dublin Student Doctor
An Irish Country Wedding

A Dublin
Student Doctor

An Irish Country Novel

PATRICK TAYLOR

A Tom Doherty Associates Book

New York

This is a work of fiction. All of the characters, organizations, and events portrayed in this novel are either products of the author's imagination or are used fictitiously.

A DUBLIN STUDENT DOCTOR: AN IRISH COUNTRY NOVEL

Copyright © 2011 by Patrick Taylor

All rights reserved.

Maps by Elizabeth Danforth and Jennifer Hanover

A Forge Book
Published by Tom Doherty Associates, LLC
175 Fifth Avenue
New York, NY 10010

www.tor-forge.com

Forge® is a registered trademark of Tom Doherty Associates, LLC.

The Library of Congress has cataloged the hardcover edition as follows:

Taylor, Patrick
    A Dublin student doctor : an Irish country novel / Patrick
Taylor.—1st ed.
        p. cm.
    "A Tom Doherty Associates book."
    ISBN 978-0-7653-2673-7
    1. O'Reilly, Fingal Flahertie (Fictitious character)—Fiction.   2. Medical
students—Fiction.   3. Dublin (Ireland)—Fiction.   I. Title.
    PR9199.3.T36D83 2011
    813'.54—dc22   2011021543

ISBN 978-0-7653-2674-4 (trade paperback)

First Edition: October 2011
First Trade Paperback Edition: September 2012

Printed in the United States of America

0 9 8 7 6 5 4 3 2 1

To Dorothy

ACKNOWLEDGMENTS

This is book six in the Irish Country series, books that wouldn't exist but for the unflagging efforts of some very special people.

In North America

Simon Hally, who started it all.

Natalia Aponte, my agent, who acquired the first book for Forge, persuaded Tom Doherty to publish it and its successors, and who is a never failing support when the muse goes on vacation.

Rosie and Jessica Buckman, foreign rights agents. Their successes in placing my works lead me to believe they could persuade the Innu people of Nitassinan in Arctic Canada to buy blocks of ice.

Carolyn Bateman, my personal editor. Together we have been through the rough and smooth of nine books over fifteen years and are now working on book ten. Whenever my bicycle wobbles off course, she gently, but oh so firmly, puts me back on track.

Paul Stevens, my editor at Forge, for whom no question is ever stupid, no request too much trouble, and who likes Mrs. Kincaid's recipes.

Irene Gallo and the Art Department at Forge, and Gregory Manchess, the artist who renders the jacket art. No author could ask for a more sympathetic group of creative people who will accept authorial intrusion without complaint. Their efforts have made the Irish Country series instantly recognisable because the covers always reflect the contents of the work.

Patty Garcia and Alexis Saarela from Publicity. Much of their work goes unheralded, but without them, no one would know the books are out there.

Christina MacDonald, whose sharp eye in copy edit has rescued this book from its author's very personal style of touch typing and his persistent belief that George Gershwin wrote "Smoke Gets in Your Eyes."

"Old men forget." I wish I could remember who said that. So do old physicians. Once more, Doctors Thomas Baskett and Linda Vickars have freely provided their expertise on matters respectively obstetrical and haematological.

In The Republic of Ireland

Much of *A Dublin Student Doctor* was written while we were living in Ireland. My efforts to strive for authenticity would have been feeble indeed, but for the untiring support of:

The Librarian of the Royal College of Physicians of Ireland,

The Librarian of the Royal College of Surgeons in Ireland,

The Librarian of the Rotunda Hospital and her staff.

My limitless questions and requests for photocopying were dealt with by all of these experts with the grace of nobles and the patience of Job.

The people of Cootehall, County Roscommon, and Dublin City who allowed an Ulsterman to renew his feel for the life and the speech patterns in the Republic's rural and metropolitan regions.

To you all, Doctor Fingal Flahertie O'Reilly and I offer our most sincere thanks.

Author's Note

Like book four, *An Irish Country Girl,* this, the sixth book in the Irish Country series, is a departure from what for many readers will be the familiar rural Ballybucklebo and the eccentric population of the village. So why leave and how did *A Dublin Student Doctor,* a book set in cosmopolitan Dublin in the 1930s, come about?

Just as a constant gnawing in my mind led to the story of Mrs. Maureen "Kinky" Kincaid in *Country Girl,* so did a subconscious grumbling drive me to ask what forces shaped Doctor Fingal Flahertie O'Reilly. How did his early life turn him into the man he had become by the mid-'60s in Ballybucklebo?

In *An Irish Country Doctor* the Fingal Flahertie O'Reilly my readers know sprang to life fully formed like Athena from the head of Zeus, his physical character and his personality firm. But what of his past? I had decided that this book would start after Fingal, aged eighteen, left his public boarding school, an institution where his parents would have paid his fees, and follow his undergraduate days from 1931 to '36, the intervening years in Dublin, his assistantship in Ballybucklebo, and finally his Royal Naval service up to the time of his postwar demobilisation as Surgeon-Commander O'Reilly DSC, and his purchase of the practice in Ballybucklebo in 1946.

But by the point in the story when O'Reilly's medical studies still had one year to go, it was clear that the account of Fingal's war years, critical as they were in his life, would have to wait. I hope you will find his doings in '30s Dublin entertaining. His naval adventures will need a book of their own.

Young Fingal's story would be a venture into uncharted territory. I like to write gentle stories, but from time to time, as in my short stories and Provisional IRA thrillers, I need to expand into the grittier aspects of life in Ireland in the twentieth century.

This book is set in the Dublin of the '30s, for me a strange place and an unfamiliar time. It was a period of hiatus between two world wars, immediately following the Great Depression, and not a decade since England had granted twenty-six Irish counties partial independence and dominion status. Getting there had been bloody. All these events had left their scars in Ireland, nor could any adult alive in the '30s fail to be aware of ominous political developments on the continent of Europe, constant leitmotifs to daily life.

All that was before I was born. My first experience of the city was when, as a small boy, I was taken to Dublin in the '40s. I have three indelible memories: beggars, bicycles everywhere, and Sarah. She was the elephant at the Phoenix Park Zoo who gave children rides in a howdah and who for the bribe of a penny bun and on the command "Sing, Sarah," would raise her trunk and trumpet ferociously.

I spent a great deal of time in Dublin during a recent two-year sojourn in Ireland absorbing the atmosphere, the patterns of speech, the pubs, but I could not visit the tenements, the slums that were so much a part of that "Strumpet City" as Denis Johnston called the place in his play *The Old Lady Says No!* Thank God they are gone.

Those parts of Dublin were so unlike the rural Ulster of the 1940s and '50s where I grew up and which I may have idealised in my books. I have tried to capture the squalor and the existence of some of the tenements' denizens and was aided greatly by *Dublin Tenement Life: An Oral History,* by Kevin C. Kearns.

If the living conditions of the tenement dwellers were primitive, so was the medicine of the time. To ensure accuracy in matters medical I visited Trinity College, the Royal Colleges of Physicians and of Surgeons in Ireland, and the Rotunda Hospital, and have consulted their libraries. Sir Patrick Dun's Hospital was closed in 1987, but the hospital has been well described by others in the archives of the Royal College of Physicians of Ireland. The carved tabletops from the Dun's students' mess reside there. It was an eerie feeling to touch them and read the inscribed names of those who studied at the turn of the nineteenth to the twentieth century.

My efforts were helped enormously by Professor Peter Gatenby, author of *The School of Physic: Trinity College Dublin,* and Professor Davis Coakley, who among other invaluable pieces of information gave me *The Regulations of the School of Physic,* the timetable and curriculum of the medical school for 1930.

It is staggering to realise how powerless medicine was before the Second World War. No antibiotics, no CPR, no portable defibrillators, no CT scans; rampant tuberculosis, typhus, typhoid, rickets, syphilis. And no contraception; women routinely delivered twelve or more babies. And yet the patients were human beings with all the same hopes and fears as those of today, but with fewer expectations and a more fatalistic acceptance of suffering and death. The physicians did their best with limited resources, tending more to practise the art rather than the science of medicine, and perhaps with a more personal touch.

I have tried and, I hope, succeeded in portraying that accurately, and have been aided by reference to the slim 1935 first edition of *The Essentials of Materia Medica Pharmacology and Therapeutics,* by R. H. Micks. I used its 1961 eighth edition in my own studies and the book is still in my library.

As I have done in all the earlier works, I have appended a glossary. You will find it on page 475. Many readers say they find this helpful. I try to capture the speech and idiom of my characters and must warn my readers that some of the folks on these pages are blasphemous. I can only apologise to the offended, but I strive for accuracy in all things.

Any anachronisms in this work are mine, but they are not there for my want of trying to be true in all aspects to my characters and the periods in which they live.

I hope this short note will help you enjoy the next 480 pages.

Fingal Flahertie O'Reilly is waiting. Please enjoy his company.

PATRICK TAYLOR
Saltspring Island,
British Columbia,
Canada

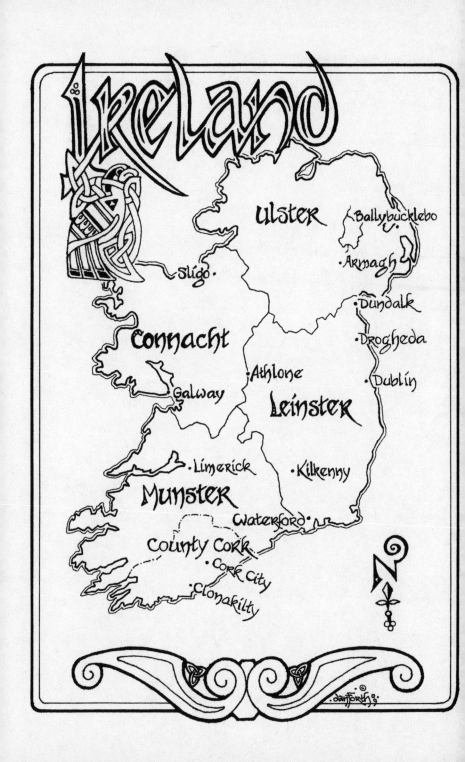

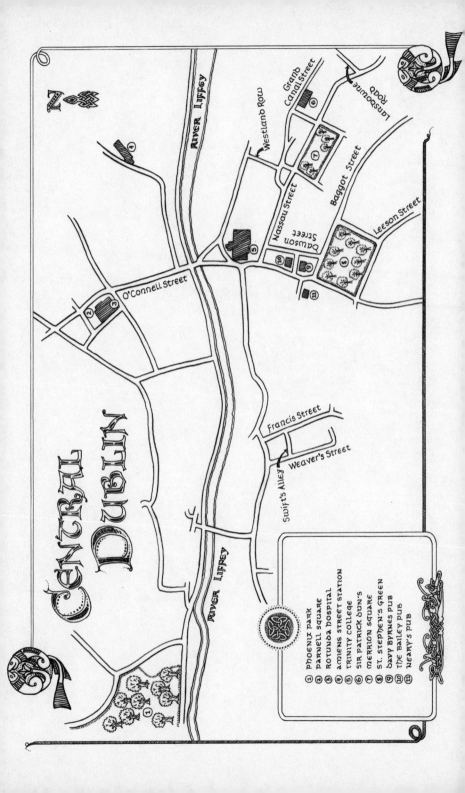

CENTRAL DUBLIN

N

River Liffey

River Liffey

O'Connell Street

Westland Row

Grand Canal Street

Lansdowne Road

Nassau Street

Dawson Street

Baggot Street

Leeson Street

Francis Street

Weaver's Street

Swift's Alley

① Phoenix Park
② Parnell Square
③ Rotunda Hospital
④ Amiens Street Station
⑤ Trinity College
⑥ Sir Patrick Dun's
⑦ Merrion Square
⑧ St. Stephen's Green
⑨ Davy Byrnes Pub
⑩ The Bailey Pub
⑪ Neary's Pub

1

It's a Long, Long Road from Which There Is No Return

Fingal Flahertie O'Reilly, *Doctor* Fingal Flahertie O'Reilly, edged the long-bonnetted Rover out of the car park. "Lord Jasus," he remarked, "but this twenty-fourth day of April in the year of our Lord 1965 has been one for the book of lifetime memories." He smiled at Kitty O'Hallorhan in the passenger's seat. "For all kinds of reasons," he said, "and now that the Downpatrick Races are over, it's home to Ballybucklebo." He accelerated.

Kitty yelled, "Will you slow down?" then said more gently, "Fingal, there are pedestrians and cyclists. I'd rather not see any in the ditch." The afternoon sun highlighted the amber flecks in her grey eyes. She put slim fingers on his arm.

"Just for you, Kitty." He slowed and whistled "Slow Boat to China." "All right in the back?"

"Fine, Fingal," said O'Reilly's assistant, young Doctor Barry Laverty.

"Grand, so." Mrs. Maureen "Kinky" Kincaid was O'Reilly's housekeeper, as she had been for Doctor Flanagan. Fingal had met Kinky when he'd come as an assistant to Thómas Flanagan in 1938. She'd stayed on when a thirty-seven-year-old O'Reilly returned in 1946 from his service in the Second World War and bought the general practice from Doctor Flanagan's estate.

They'd been a good nineteen years, he thought as he put the car into a tight bend between two rows of ancient elms. So had his years as a medical student at Dublin's Trinity College in the '30s.

"Jasus thundering Murphy." O'Reilly stamped on the brake. The Rover shuddered to a halt five yards from a man standing waving his arms.

O'Reilly's bushy eyebrows met. He could feel his temper rise and the tip of his bent nose blanch. "Everyone all right?" he roared, and was relieved to hear a chorus of reassurance. He hurled his door open and stamped up the road. "What in the blue bloody blazes are you doing standing there waving your arms like an out-of-kilter semaphore? I could have squashed you flatter than a flaming flounder-fish."

The stranger wore Wellington boots, moleskin trousers, and a hacking jacket. He had a russet beard, a squint, and was no more than five foot two. O'Reilly expected him at least to take a step back, apologise, but he stood his ground.

"There's no need for youse 'til be losing the bap, so there's not. There's been an accident, and I'm here to stop big buggers like youse driving into it, so I am. See for yourself." He pointed to a knot of people and the slowly rotating rear wheel of a motorbike that lay on its side.

"Accident?" said O'Reilly. He spun on his heel. "Barry. Grab my bag and come here." He turned back. "I'm Doctor O'Reilly. Doctor Laverty's coming."

"Doctor? Thank God for that, sir. A motorcyclist took a purler on an oil slick, you know. Somebody's gone for the ambulance and police."

"Here you are." Barry handed O'Reilly his bag. "What's up?"

"Motorbike accident." He spoke to the short man. "You'd be safer back down the road where drivers can see you before they're on top of you."

"Right enough. I'll go, sir." He started walking.

O'Reilly yelled, "Kitty. Kinky. There's been an accident. Stay with the car." Kitty would have the wit to pull the car over to the verge. "Come on, Barry." O'Reilly marched straight to the little crowd. Time to use the voice that could be heard over a gale when he'd served on the battleship HMS *Warspite*. "We're doctors. Let us through."

Ruddy-cheeked country faces turned. Murmuring people shuffled aside and a path opened.

A motorbike lay on the road, an exclamation mark at the end of two long black scrawls of rubber. The engine ticked and the stink of oil and burnt tyre hung over the smell of ploughed earth from a field and the almond scent of whin flowers.

A middle-aged woman knelt beside the rider. The victim's head was turned away from O'Reilly, but there could only be one owner of that red thatch. A duncher lay a few yards away. It irritated O'Reilly that Ulstermen wouldn't wear crash helmets but favoured cloth caps, worn with the peak at the back.

He knelt beside the woman and set his bag on the ground. "He's unconscious, he's breathing regular, his airway's clear, his pulse is eighty and regular, and he's not bleeding. There don't seem to be any bones broken," she said, and added, "I'm a first-aider, you know."

"Thank you, Mrs.?"

"Meehan. Rosie Meehan."

O'Reilly smiled at her. "Donal? Donal?" he said gently. Fifteen minutes ago he'd seen Ballybucklebo's arch schemer, Donal Donnelly, riding the motorbike from the car park.

No reply.

O'Reilly grabbed the man's wrist. Good. Mrs. Meehan was right; the pulse was strong and regular. "Donal," he said more loudly, "Donal."

Donal's face was chalky. He wore his raincoat reversed and buttoned over his back. It was the practice of country men when riding motorbikes. It stopped the wind of passage getting through.

O'Reilly was hesitant to move Donal. He could have a broken neck. Better to wait for the ambulance. The first law of medicine was *Primum non nocere*. First do no harm. O'Reilly bent lower. "Donal?"

Donal's eyelids fluttered. "Numuh?"

Better, O'Reilly thought. Donal might only be concussed. If that were the case he should start regaining consciousness. But you could never be certain about head injuries. The damage might range from a simple concussion with complete recovery through to serious brain injury leading to paralysis, permanent brain damage, and even death. O'Reilly gritted his teeth. Donal had a new wife and a wean on the way. O'Reilly's heart went out to the pregnant Julie Donnelly, née MacAteer. He heard the *nee-naw* of an approaching siren. O'Reilly leant over. "Donal?"

Donal's eyes flew open. "Doctor O'Reilly? What are youse doing here?" He struggled to rise. "I shouldn't be in my bed."

Donal recognised O'Reilly. That was a good sign even if he was unclear where he was. O'Reilly put a restraining hand on the man's shoulder. "Lie still. You had an accident."

Donal put his hand to his head. "I must have hit my nut a right clatter," he said. "It's pounding to beat Bannagher, so it is."

"Do you know what day it is?" O'Reilly asked.

Donal frowned. "Uh? Saturday. We made a wheen of money on the oul gee-gees at the races." He grinned like a small boy who had answered the teacher's question correctly. "And this here's the road to Ballybucklebo." A look of concern crossed his face. "Jesus, is Paddy Regan's motorbike all right? It's only on loan." Donal tried to rise.

"Stay put," O'Reilly said, and smiled. If Donal knew about events immediately preceding his accident it was probable he had suffered only a minor concussion. Even so, O'Reilly would never forget a footballer who'd been knocked out, recovered, gone back to finish the match, and died from a brain haemorrhage two hours later.

The *nee-naw, nee-naw* grew louder.

"I don't need no ambulance," Donal said. "I'm for going home, so I am."

"Sorry, Donal," O'Reilly said, "but you'll be spending tonight in the Royal Victoria Hospital."

"Och, Doctor—that's daft. I've a motorbike to get back to—"

"The Royal. For observation," O'Reilly said. "No arguments. I'll take care of the bike."

"But—"

"Donal, you're going to hospital," O'Reilly said as if speaking to a not overly bright child. "That's final." He stood and spoke to Barry. "I'll do a quick neurological exam once he's in the ambulance. Establish a baseline in case he gets worse. I'll go up to the Royal with him. Kitty's the senior nursing sister on the neurosurgical ward there. She'll want to come too. She can go with Donal in the back of the ambulance. God knows she's observed a hundred times more head injuries than you and I put together. She'll keep an eye on him and warn me if his condition deteriorates. You drive Kinky and the Rover home."

"I'll go and get Kitty." Barry started to turn as a yellow Northern Ireland Hospitals Authority ambulance drew up and its siren was turned off.

"In a minute," O'Reilly said. "Once the police have come and done whatever they have to do, measure things, take photos and statements, they'll have you fill in forms. When you're done, get them to give you a hand to load the bike into the boot of the Rover. At least Paddy Regan won't need to come all the way here to collect it."

"Paddy? I'll let him know," Barry said.

O'Reilly turned. "Do you hear that, Donal? We'll get the bike home for you."

"Thanks, Doc. But what about Julie? She'll go spare if I don't get home too."

O'Reilly frowned. "You've no phone, Donal, have you?"

"No, sir."

"I'll nip round and see Julie," Barry said. "Tell her what's happened. That she's not to worry."

"Thanks, Doc."

Barry turned to leave as two men approached wearing peaked bus drivers' caps, silver-buttoned blue uniforms, and carrying a stretcher. The bigger one, a burly, open-faced man, spoke to the first-aid lady. "What's the story, Rosie?" Of course he'd know her. They'd both be Downpatrick locals.

She nodded at O'Reilly. "Better ask your man there, Alfie. That there's Doctor O'Reilly."

The man turned to O'Reilly and grinned. "From Ballybucklebo, the wee village near Holywood?"

"That's right. How did you—?" He frowned. Alfie did look familiar.

"I met you at a rugby game, sir." He pointed at Donal. "What do you reckon about your man?"

"He came off the bike and hit his head. He was unconscious for a while but he's awake now. Concussion at least and I'd like him in the Royal for observation. You know head injuries can—"

"I do know. Too bloody well." The ambulance man frowned. "My brother, God rest him, got a smack on the nut with a hurley ball. He bled into his skull and died." There was a catch in Alfie's voice. "He was only nineteen."

"I'm sorry," O'Reilly said.

"Aye well." Alfie tugged at his tie. "Standing here both legs the same length won't get your man there to the Royal. What do you want us to do, Doc?"

"Before you move him, I'll give his fore and hind legs a once-over. Then I want you to take him, me, and Sister O'Hallorhan, she'll be here in a minute, up to the Royal. We'll radio ahead to arrange for him to be seen in casualty, get things rolling, then have him admitted to the observation ward."

"Right, Doc. Come on, Bert." The ambulance men aligned their stretcher alongside Donal as O'Reilly examined Donal's arms and legs through his clothes. "You're right, Mrs. Meehan. There are no bones broken," he said, and stepped back to let the attendants do their work. "Thank you, Mrs. Meehan," O'Reilly said. "You did a great job. Now go on home and get your tea."

She smiled, bobbed her head, and left.

O'Reilly climbed aboard the ambulance. "For crying out loud," Donal said, and tried to sit up. "This is daft, so it is. Going to all this trouble. Sure couldn't I just get the bike—"

O'Reilly made a noise like an enraged gorilla, one whose last banana had been stolen. "For the last time, Donal Donnelly, you're going to the Royal. This is not a bleeding debating society—so shut up, lie down, and let me examine you."

"I will, Doctor O'Reilly, sir," a clearly chastened Donal said—and did.

Fingal satisfied himself that Donal's reflexes were normal, that his pupils were equal in size and reacting to light, his pulse was strong and steady and his blood pressure was normal. The only worrying thing was a bruise over Donal's right temple. The parietal bone there was thin. There was a chance the skull was fractured. O'Reilly didn't need to reassure himself that getting Donal to hospital was the right thing to do. The middle meningeal artery lay beneath the parietal bone. O'Reilly climbed out to meet Kitty.

Barry was providing information to a uniformed Royal Ulster Constabulary officer. The man had a heavy pistol in a hip holster. Good for Barry, O'Reilly thought, one less chore for me, and frankly, the sooner we get Donal to hospital the happier I'll be. If his condition did deteriorate, speed of intervention was critical.

The second ambulance attendant climbed into the back and offered his hand to Kitty.

"Hop in," O'Reilly said. "All his baseline findings are normal, but please keep an eye on him. I'll be in the front, so if he starts to go downhill, let me know."

"I will," she said, taking the proffered hand.

He watched her climb in and as she did so her skirt rode up. God, but she had a well-curved calf, O'Reilly thought, but then, he grinned, she always had.

Barry finished with the officer. "Thanks for seeing to that, Barry," O'Reilly said. "You'll have to look after the practice tomorrow too because Lord knows what time I'll get home."

"That's all right."

"Off you trot." O'Reilly noticed his bag where he'd left it on the ground. "Take my bag to the car while you're at it. The ambulance will be fully equipped."

Barry paused. "How will you and Kitty get home?"

"Kitty lives only a short walk from the hospital. I'll get a train. Now go on. It's time we were off."

O'Reilly stuck his head into the ambulance. "Everything okay, Kitty?"

"No change."

"Good." As O'Reilly walked to the front of the ambulance, the last colours of the sunset flared and died. A straggling clamour of rooks flapped untidily across the dimming horizon and Venus rose, a glittering forerunner of the myriad stars that would spangle the sky's dark dome.

He climbed into the passenger side and shut the cab's door. "How's about ye, Doc?" Alfie, the driver, asked.

"Grand," said O'Reilly. "The lad in the back's a patient of mine." And, he thought, as close to being a friend as I'll let any of my patients be. "I think he'll be all right."

"Right," said the driver, "let's get going." He switched on his flashing lights, but not the siren, put the vehicle in gear, and started for Belfast.

"Can we radio ahead?" O'Reilly asked. "Let the neurosurgery people know we're coming?"

"Aye, certainly, sir." The driver lifted a microphone, depressed a button, and announced, "Ambulance despatch, ambulance despatch. This is delta alpha two sixer, over."

In moments O'Reilly had relayed the details to the dispatcher, who would contact the neurosurgery registrar on call. "Who is the senior neurosurgeon on call tonight?" Just in case, and the thought niggled at him, just in case that bruise at the side of Donal's head was a sign of more ominous damage.

"Mister Greer, sir." The voice from the speaker was distorted.

"Thank you, despatch. Delta alpha two sixer. Out." O'Reilly handed the mike back. "Thank you," he said.

Charlie Greer. He and O'Reilly went back to 1931, and that wasn't yesterday. He hoped Donal would have no need of Charlie's services, but if Donal did deteriorate he couldn't ask for a better brain surgeon.

"How long until we get to Belfast?" O'Reilly asked.

"About an hour and a half—and if you'll excuse me, sir, I'd better concentrate on driving. The road's twisty here."

O'Reilly said, "Pay me no heed." He sat staring through the window as rays from the dome flashers flickered and the headlights' beams picked out fluttering moths, the verges and hedges, and dry stone walls draped with straggling brambles. He wondered about Donal. O'Reilly knew that no amount of worrying was going to help anything. Kitty would let him know if anything changed, and if it did, Donal was well on his way to being in the hands of a bloody good neurosurgeon. Charles Edward Greer, M.D., F.R.C.S., from Ballymoney, County Antrim. A long time ago he had been a rugby-playing medical student like O'Reilly at Trinity College Dublin.

O'Reilly had met student nurse Kitty O'Hallorhan while he and Charlie, along with their friends Bob Beresford and Donald Cromie, and a nasty piece of work called Ronald Hercules Fitzpatrick who now practiced in the Kinnegar, had been working in Sir Patrick Dun's Hospital. Back in 1934.

He'd been twenty-five years old and had completed nearly three years of his medical studies at Trinity College Dublin.

Dublin had been richly described by the playwright Denis Johnston as, "Strumpet city in the sunset. So old, so sick with memories." The place had memories for O'Reilly, all right.

Trinity College with its Library's Long Room wherein resided the Book of Kells and the Brian Boru harp. The pubs, Davy Byrnes, the Bailey, Neary's, and the Stag's Head. Great broad O'Connell Street crossing Anna Livia, the Dubliners' name for the River Liffey. The tenement districts like the Liberties, the Coombe, and Monto, filthy, squalid, vermin-plagued, but with indomitable inhabitants. O'Connell Street and, halfway up it, Nelson's Pillar beside the General Post Office, from the steps of which Pádraig Pearse had read out the Proclamation of the Irish Republic at Eastertide 1916. Its façade and Ionic columns were still pockmarked with British bullets from the siege during the Rising.

O'Reilly was distracted by a sudden movement ahead and leant forward to see the bushy tail of a badger scurrying for cover and its home.

Dublin had become O'Reilly's home in 1925 when his father, young for the job at forty-five, had been appointed professor of classics and English literature at Trinity. O'Reilly had been born and brought up in Holywood, County Down, Northern Ireland, still part of the United Kingdom, but for eleven years had lived in the Irish Free State. Sometimes he thought he was neither fish, fowl, nor good red meat. He'd loved Ulster all his life, particularly Strangford Lough, where he and his older brother Lars had spent their winter Saturdays wildfowling. But he loved Dublin too.

The ambulance slowed then halted to give a large lorry right of way. O'Reilly turned and slid back a window between the cab and the rear of the vehicle. "Everything all right, Kitty?"

The lighting was dim and he had difficulty making out her features.

Kitty said, "Everything's fine. Donal's sleeping."

If the middle meningeal artery had burst, Donal would be deeply unconscious, not asleep, but surely a nurse with Kitty's experience—

"It's all right, Fingal. I've no trouble waking him up and there's no change in any vital signs."

O'Reilly exhaled. He hadn't realised he'd been holding his breath, and damn it, he should have known better than to doubt. "Grand," he said. "We'll be there soon." He closed the window as the ambulance began to move. Donal was going to be all right. Of course he was. O'Reilly looked out the windscreen to see the ambulance taking the left-hand fork of a Y junction.

Ireland was full of strange road confluences, the Six Road Ends in County Down, the Five Road Ends at Beal na mBláth in County

Cork where Kinky had grown up on a farm, and Michael Collins, head of the armed forces of the Irish Free State, had been assassinated in August 1922.

O'Reilly had come to a crossroads in his own life in '27. If he hadn't made his choice about which road to follow, he'd not have Charlie Greer and the others as friends, nor Kitty. Nor would he have been a rural GP, a life he loved, if he'd meekly caved in when Father had decreed over breakfast in the family house on Lansdowne Road in Dublin that no son of his was going to be a physician. The ambulance lurched over a pothole and a goose walked over his grave as he shuddered and remembered that day, September 17, 1927.

2

It Is a Wise Father that Knows
His Own Child

"So, Fingal," his older brother Lars said, refusing another slice of toast, "you're convinced Sir Malcolm Campbell can beat Major Henry Seagrave for a new land speed record?"

"Seagrave did 203 miles per hour," Fingal said, digging out the yolk from a soft-boiled egg, "but Campbell's tenacious. I admire that."

"I think," said Father, "you are forgetting that fragments of miles per hour can be critical. The major's actual speed was 203.841."

Fingal shook his head and looked across the table. Father was a professor at Trinity, a breed who tended to be inward-looking, but he had always been interested in the world around him and a stickler for accuracy. He was a tall, slightly built man with a neatly trimmed black moustache. His high forehead was scored with three horizontal lines, his nose aquiline. He wore a three-piece pinstripe suit, wing collar, and Old Harrovian tie.

Father looked at his watch. "Fascinating as speed may be, boys, I have to be in the college in fifty-three minutes, and, Fingal, I should like to have a word in my study." He rose.

Fingal glanced at Ma, who nodded encouragement. Lars rolled his eyes skyward. During their younger years, an invitation to the study from Father had always been a prelude to punishment or a dressing down. Father, with a capital *F*, never Daddy, Dad, or Da, had strict standards. Fingal had never been one for unquestioning obedience, so such trips to Father's lair had been frequent. As Fingal walked along the high-ceilinged parquet-floored hall he wondered, and not for the first time, if his contrary streak was a reaction against Father's standards.

Fingal went into the sanctum sanctorum, the holy of holies. He wasn't in trouble, but he wasn't looking forward to the interview. He knew they were going to replough a well-turned furrow and he was determined not to give in. He knew what he wanted from life and was not to be swayed.

"Please close the door and sit down." Father sat in a high-backed chair in front of an open rolltop desk. There were neat piles of papers, an open volume of Gibbon's *Decline and Fall of the Roman Empire*, and today's *Irish Times*.

Above the desk hung his M.A., 1904, from Queen's University Belfast and his D.Phil., 1907, from Oxford. Degrees befitting his position as professor of classics and English literature at Trinity College Dublin. He'd moved the family here from Holywood, County Down, when he'd accepted the post. The Victorian, sixteen-room, semi-detached house on Lansdowne Road was a short cycle ride from the college.

Fingal walked past floor-to-ceiling bookshelves. The room smelt of the dusty old books. Father wanted an academic career for his younger son, a life, as far as Fingal was concerned, that would be as dry as this library. He had other dreams.

He glanced through the window to where the stands of Lansdowne Road Rugby Grounds loomed against a soft autumn sky. One day, he told himself, he'd put on the green jersey with a sprig of shamrock embroidered on the left breast and play rugby football for his country. For now he'd better pay attention to Father because this conversation was going to concern Fingal's other, more important, aspiration. Since their last discussion of the matter, Fingal knew that Father would be expecting his son to have changed his mind. He bloody well hadn't. He sat and crossed his legs, aware of Father's disapproving look at his son's scuffed boots.

Father's own shoes were brightly polished. "It's September," he said. "Your school days are over. You've very good marks in your Leaving Certificate. It's time to make the decision about your university future."

Fingal said, "I'm going to register at Trinity next week. I have the five-shilling fee."

"Good." Father steepled his fingers. "You've thought about what I said? You'll be reading for a science degree?" He smiled and there was warmth in his brown eyes. "You're going to make me proud of you, son."

"I hope so, Father." Fingal sat erectly. "I truly appreciated your advice. I've given it a great deal of consideration." You're not going to like what's coming, he thought, but I will not back down.

"I'm delighted to hear it. You owe it to your forefathers. We O'Reillys go back a long way, descendants of the O'Connor kings of Connacht. Our name, Ó'Raghallaigh, is taken from the Irish, *ragh* meaning 'race,' and *ceallach* or 'sociable.'"

Fingal had heard it all before. He knew Father was, in rugby terms, kicking for touch, slowing the pace by putting the ball out of play to give himself time to formulate what he really wanted to say. Take your time, Father. I'm in no rush for the fireworks to begin.

"In mediaeval days we were renowned traders," he smiled, "so famous the word 'reilly' became a coloquial term for money."

"You're a grand man for the names, Father," Fingal said. "You gave me 'Fingal,' a fair foreigner, and 'Flahertie,' a prince."

"I did," Father said. "You were born in 1908, eight years after Oscar Wilde, Oscar Fingal O'Flahertie Wills Wilde, died."

"But Lars was born two years before me. If you thought so highly of the man why didn't you give Lars his name?"

Father frowned. "I thought hard about it. You do know Wilde had been imprisoned and died a disgraced man?"

"I know that he was homosexual. He and the marquis of Queensberry's son were—"

"Indeed." Judging by how Father's nose wrinkled he had not approved of Wilde's relationship with the poet Lord Alfred Douglas. "Your mother persuaded me that it was too soon after Wilde's imprisonment. She didn't want to cause a stir among our friends."

"I suppose people were a bit more—conservative back then," Fingal said. "I don't think it should matter what people do in that line, as long as it's in private."

"Good," said Father. "I should like to be able to agree, but old habits, the teaching of one's own parents, are hard to overcome."

But you can do it if you really try, Fingal thought.

"That is why I have tried to steer you and Lars along liberal lines."

"And we both appreciate the direction, Father." Fingal looked deep into his father's eyes. "In most things." He knew the real matter under discussion was going to cause a rift and now he wanted to get it over and done with.

Father was not to be sidetracked. "Instead we named your brother Lars Porsena O'Reilly, after—"

"The Etruscan king who went to war with Rome about 500 BC."

Father's eyes misted. "It seems like yesterday since I'd read the poem to you and Lars. The poet, Thomas Babington Macaulay, was the subject of my master's thesis."

Fingal smiled. He had fond memories of a much younger Father sitting in the nursery, one boy on either knee. "You named Lars for your thesis?" Fingal smiled. "Was your doctoral thesis about Oscar Wilde by any chance?"

"It was." He gazed out the window. "I wrote a dissertation on his children's stories."

"I remember them. *The Happy Prince, The Selfish Giant, The Remarkable Rocket.* You always made us laugh with that last one, and showed us how pride truly does come before a fall."

Father was nodding very slowly. "Those stories have a lot to teach about care for other people, self-sacrifice, selflessness. I think, no matter what his sexual proclivities, Oscar Wilde was one of the greatest masters of the English language—and one of the most romantic. I was proud to name you for him, despite what Mother believed people might think." He laughed gently. "I've always wondered if—remember I was still a young man when you were born—I didn't do it with a touch of mischief too. It certainly raised some eyebrows in the faculty common room."

Fingal sat back. Father? Dry old Father had had a mischievous streak?

The laugh faded. "It took me a while, Fingal, but I soon came to see that humour was all very well—in its place, but if you wanted to advance academically, and I did, it was better to be seen to be serious and not offend the establishment."

Like you want me to toe the party line, Fingal thought. He took a deep breath. "What about someone who doesn't give a tinker's curse for the establishment? Wants to go his own way?" If Father wasn't going to come to the point, Fingal wanted to, but that sudden glimpse of a different side to Father had weakened Fingal's resolve. "Father," he started, but it was as far as he could go.

Father sat forward, steepled his fingers, rested his chin on them, and looked directly at Fingal. "What are you trying to say, son? 'Wants to go his own way?' " He frowned.

Fingal hunched his shoulders and rocked in his chair, then steeled himself and returned Father's gaze. "I do want you to be proud of me, but I'm not as sure about having to preserve the O'Reilly name, and studying science is not what I want." It was out. Again.

Father pushed back in his chair. "You are still being stubborn."

"I know, and I really don't mean to be." Fingal didn't want this to grow into a row.

Father held out his hands palms up. "Then take my advice. Study science."

"Father, I want to be a doctor."

Father pursed his lips. "So you've told me, many times."

"Then why won't you listen? Let me go to medical school. Please."

"I am your father. It is my responsibility to advise you, and if you won't take my advice, I must do what I perceive as being the very best for your and your brother's futures."

"You didn't object two years ago when Lars wanted to study law."

"We are not discussing Lars. We are discussing your career." Father's voice was calm, the tones, Fingal thought, of a man who held all the trumps because he and he alone controlled the purse strings.

Fingal started to sweat. "I've wanted to be a doctor since I was thirteen in Holywood when Doctor O'Malley took out my appendix. When I was better he let me ride round with him while he visited patients at home, Father, you know that. I've been telling you for years. I told Ma—"

"I think you mean Mother." Father frowned. "Why must you let your language drop to the level of a street vendor?"

"Sorry," Fingal said.

Father's voice was cold. "I spent a great deal of money to have you properly educated. It was easy for a thirteen-year-old to be impressed by a rural GP who wore muttonchop whiskers and a frock coat and drove round in a pony and trap."

"He was kind. He cared about his patients. He was a real man, not a prince in one of Oscar Wilde's tales. You could see how he made a difference in the village. Father, I thank you for my education and for the time you spent teaching Lars and me about books, music, paintings. I know you're trying to give me good advice—I do know—but," Fingal put as much weight as he could summon into his next words, "I want to study medicine."

"You have a fine mind, Fingal. Don't waste it."

"I'd not waste it." Fingal felt his fists clench.

"I agree it's a respectable profession—"

"There *are* professors of medicine."

"And how many do research?"

"I don't know." And I don't care. Fingal uncrossed his legs and rubbed his thighs with the palms of his hands. I'd never get interested in research, he thought. I like people.

"Here at Trinity, medical research is done by Professor Bigger in bacteriology, Professor Jamieson in anatomy, Professor Fearon in biochemistry, and a few other basic scientists. Not very impressive."

"But I want to look after people, not laboratory rats." For God's sake listen to me. Hear what I'm saying. Try to understand.

"Fingal, you're only eighteen—"

"I'll be nineteen next month and I'm sorry, but why shouldn't a nineteen-year-old know what he wants?" He knew he was letting a sarcastic edge creep into his voice.

"Youth," Father said, and shook his head. "I've been around the groves of academe all my adult life. It is what I have tried to groom my sons for." He frowned. "Poor Lars. I don't think he'd have done very well," his smile reappeared, "but you, Fingal, you have exactly what it takes. Trust me." He leant forward and stared into Fingal's eyes. "You are special, Fingal O'Reilly. I'm a professor. Professors can make a difference too—but not in a small village like old Doctor O'Malley. In the whole world. Look at Einstein's work. He was awarded the Nobel Prize six years ago. Who can predict where his discoveries will lead—but you could be at the forefront of making new ones. You could go on and become a dean, a vice chancellor, because the subject of the future is—" Father's eyes shone.

"Nuclear physics. I know." Fingal's shoulders drooped. He rolled his eyes. He said, "But I've told you, God knows how many times—"

"Mind your language."

"Oh, bugger my language. I'm not doing nuclear physics." Fingal got to his feet.

Father pursed his lips. "Sit down."

Fingal shook his head. "What is so terrible about medicine?"

"Nothing, but it's not the best you can do." He stood and folded his arms. "It is the duty of every father to guide, yes, and if necessary force his children, particularly his sons, to do what they are best suited for—"

"And," Fingal knew his voice was rising, "for me that's medicine—not bloody nuclear physics. Can't you understand? For God's sake, Father, Queen Victoria died seven years before I was born. The old Irish tradition, first son gets the farm, second son into the church, third son Colonial civil service, stupidest son into the army, exactly as father dictates, those days are over. My friends have been able to choose their careers. Why in hell can't I?"

Father did not look remotely persuaded. He said, "Calm down and sit down."

"No."

"I can't force you to sit, Fingal—"

"No, you can't—" Fingal hesitated. If he carried on like this he might cause an irreparable rift.

"And I obviously can't force you to study nuclear physics."

"Good." Fingal smiled weakly. Thank the Lord he hadn't said what he wanted to say—that Father couldn't force him to achieve the goals Father hadn't achieved in his life. "I'm sorry," he said, "I came very close to losing my temper." It wouldn't hurt to offer the olive branch.

"I can't make you study nuclear physics, yet," Father said very quietly, "but I will not finance your medical studies. Perhaps when you've had time to give the matter due consideration we can reopen it. Students can enroll in April as well as in October. Six months really won't make much difference considering how long it takes to get a first-class Ph.D."

"What?" Fingal heard blood pounding in his ears, felt his fists clenching and unclenching. His breath came in shallow gasps. He felt the tip of his nose blanch. That was, and had been since he was sixteen, a sure sign that his temper was about to erupt. "No," he yelled. "No."

From somewhere inside a tiny voice told him, Control yourself. Get out of here. He's your father. He's wrong, but as Ma often taught, "Least said, soonest mended." "Thank you, Father. Thank you very much," Fingal said, trying to keep the sarcasm out of his voice, "I'm sure I'll find something useful to do between now and then."

3

I Feared It Might Injure the Brain

Something useful? O'Reilly was thoughtful as he stepped down from the ambulance into the brightly lit bay outside the Royal Victoria Hospital's casualty department. Young Fingal had found something very useful to do. He had, literally, run away to sea.

O'Reilly walked to the back of the vehicle and waited for the attendants. They'd gone to bring hospital orderlies to load Donal onto a trolley then take him inside. O'Reilly and Kitty would follow. If they'd been relatives they'd have been told to stay in the waiting room, but as members of their professions they'd go with Donal. And O'Reilly would not be a doctor today if it hadn't been for Lars and Ma, bless them both. Despite his bravado with Father, a young Fingal O'Reilly had thought things pretty hopeless after that morning discussion in 1927. He had stood in the dining room beside Ma and across from where Lars sat.

"Well?" she had asked, reaching up a hand to him, a faint smile on her lips, but tiny wrinkles on her forehead.

Fingal shook his head.

Her smile faded, the furrows deepened. "I'm so sorry, dear," she said. "I'm not sure what to advise. I had hoped after I'd had a word with your father—" She sighed. "Tell Fingal what you've been saying to me, Lars."

Lars pushed his chair back from the table and stroked his dark moustache. He cocked his head to one side. "I have a suggestion—"

"If it's to do what Father wants, don't bother," Fingal snapped, and immediately regretted it. "I'm sorry," he said. "Go on, Lars, I'm listening."

Lars looked at Ma. "Once Fingal has—and I hesitate to use the term—but once he has 'declared war' with Father, he won't be able to live here. He'll have to find a job and move into lodgings."

"I might be able to manage a little money," said Ma, "but—"

"Thanks, Ma. I understand. Go on, Lars. I'm listening." Fingal felt a lump in his throat. Ma simply could not have the resources to support him for the five-year medical course.

"It seems to me that you'd be able to save fastest if you had a job that gave you free board and lodge and no opportunity to spend."

After the interview with Father, the rising temper, and the disappointment, Fingal was in no mood for pie-in-the-sky suggestions. "I'd get that in the Mountjoy Gaol. But the wages are poor."

Lars lowered his head and regarded Fingal from under a set of bushy eyebrows. "Don't be facetious, Fingal, I'm trying to help."

"I'm sorry."

"How would you fancy going to sea?"

"Going to—?"

O'Reilly felt a hand on his shoulder that pulled him back to the present. "Excuse me, Doc. Could youse move back a wee ways?"

"Sorry, Alfie." O'Reilly stood aside to let the driver open the back doors, but his thoughts were soon back to 1927.

That suggestion by Lars and the twenty pounds Ma had given him from her own private nest egg had certainly opened the door for the young Fingal O'Reilly. He had enjoyed his three years at sea in the merchant navy.

When he'd joined the Royal Naval Reserve in 1930, he'd spent another year at sea, this time on the British battlecruiser HMS

Tiger as part of his training. He had made money in the peacetime auxillary branch of the British Navy and he'd made a good friend. A young sub-lieutenant named Tom Laverty. The Lord does move in a mysterious way, thought Fingal as the traffic noises rose to a crescendo on the Grosvenor Road outside the Royal Victoria Hospital. That Tom Laverty was the father of the young Barry who was now O'Reilly's assistant.

It had been a condition of RNR service that members would be called up for active duty in the event of hostilities, but it was only eleven years after the end of the Great War and he'd thought the risk small. The great powers had not seemed belligerent in 1930. The United States was following a policy of isolationism. The Fascist Mussolini in Italy seemed like a peaceful chap whose intention was to get the trains to run on time. Adolf Hitler couldn't even take his seat in the German Riechstag because he was an Austrian national. And Ramsay MacDonald, the British prime minister, was too busy trying to deal with the aftereffects of the Great Depression of 1929.

And Fingal O'Reilly had a lot more pressing business in mind. The sea had made him grow up, but he'd never wavered from his determination to be a doctor. As soon as he had saved enough he'd, in the naval parlance of the day, swallowed the anchor in '31 and enrolled at Trinity College Dublin. He might not have been as polished as some of his classmates—the sea could do that. Dealing with seamen didn't call for drawing room etiquette.

But at least he knew enough now to say, "Thanks, lads," to the ambulance crew as they handed Donal over to the hospital staff and prepared to depart. "Safe home."

Kitty climbed out. "No change for the worse, Fingal," she said. "Pulse, blood pressure fine. He's still asleep, but he'll wake up if you call his name."

He took her arm and followed the orderlies as they wheeled

Donal to the ambulance room, a part of casualty where patients were seen and assessed. The lights were bright, the floor tiled. The room was divided into cubicles that could be screened by closing curtains, and each contained an examining couch.

The smells were ones he'd known for more than thirty years, and those in Belfast differed not one jot from the ones he'd first encountered in Sir Patrick Dun's, a Dublin teaching hospital. He was barely aware of the niffs of disinfectant, floor polish, vomit. Sounds of retching came from behind curtains.

Donal was wheeled into the nearest cubicle, where a nurse would record his pulse, blood pressure, respiratory rate, and level of consciousness before a doctor came.

O'Reilly stopped near the front of the room at a tall desk that looked like something out of a Dickensian counting house. A young woman house officer leant against it. Her blue eyes behind rimless spectacles had dark bags beneath. He knew the hours these youngsters worked, could still recall the breaking dawns of his own junior years.

"I'm Doctor O'Reilly. I've come with the man with the concussion," he said, "and this is—"

"Hello, Sister O'Hallorhan," the young woman said. "I've just done three months on ward 21."

"Doctor Fleming," Kitty said. "Good evening."

The house officer pulled out a lined four-by-eight card. "I'll have to get a few details, Doctor O'Reilly."

"I'll give you them in a tick," said O'Reilly, turning to Kitty. "Why don't you go and sit down? Or head home? I'm going to wait until I see Donal settled."

He felt Kitty squeeze his arm. "I know you're worried."

"Och, not really," he said, "but—"

"I know you, O'Reilly. I still remember you sitting up all night with a patient when you were a student."

"Sergeant Paddy Keogh. Pneumonia. I remember him too." He smiled. "I just want to be able to tell Julie that Donal's fine."

"I understand." She looked down the room. "There's nothing for me to do," she said, "and the staff won't like having an off-duty sister breathing down their necks, but would you like me to stay and keep you company?"

O'Reilly shook his head. "Head home." He'd like to have kissed her, but not here. He lowered his voice. "You and I have to go shopping in the next week. I hear tell Sharman D. Neill's do a nice line in rings."

"I know," she said, and smiled. "I'll look forward to that, but I will run on now," she said. "I might see you tomorrow if you're still here at the hospital. I'll be on the ward in the morning."

"We'll see," he said, "but I hope Donal's well enough that I'll be able to get home soon."

"Good night, Fingal. Look after yourself—and Donal." She turned and left. It wasn't a long walk home and the hospital grounds were well lit.

O'Reilly turned to the house officer and gave her Donal's details.

He heard a voice behind him. "Doctor O'Reilly?"

He turned. "Yes?"

"I'm Mister Rajat Gupta, neurosurgery senior registrar." He held out a hand. O'Reilly shook it and appraised the young East Asian. His hair was glossy black, his eyes deep set and mahogany brown. His grip was firm. As the man's title was Mister, not Doctor, he had already passed the Fellowship examinations of the Royal College of Surgeons. It was one of the peculiarities of the British and Irish system of medical titles. Being a fully qualified general surgeon was a prerequisite for training as a brain surgeon.

"Thank you for coming," O'Reilly said. "It's probably just concussion, but I'm a country GP and there's no harm getting an opinion from an expert."

Mister Gupta smiled. "A trainee expert."

"You'd be surprised," O'Reilly said, "by how little brain surgery I practice."

"I understand."

"Donal Donnelly's in there." O'Reilly indicated the cubicle.

"Come in." The senior registrar held back the curtain and O'Reilly followed.

Donal lay on the trolley taking short, shallow breaths.

"Donal, wake up, you lazy bugg— so-and-so," O'Reilly said, moderating his language for the student nurse who was taking the patient's blood pressure.

Donal muttered something but did not open his eyes.

O'Reilly noticed the pallor of Donal's cheeks, that his breathing was shallow. "What's his pulse rate, Nurse?"

"One hundred, Doctor, but it's strong. His temperature is only ninety-three degrees."

O'Reilly was sure his own pulse had speeded up. Donal's condition had worsened, not dramatically, but he was concerned. "Mister Gupta?"

O'Reilly waited patiently until the senior registrar finished his neurological assessment. "I'm sorry," he said, "but your patient has a mild cerebral contusion. Nothing terrible, but I want him on the neurosurgical ward."

"Fair enough." Donal would not be going to the observation ward where he'd have spent the night if it looked as though he had suffered only a mild concussion.

Mister Gupta frowned. "I think there's a bit of relatively mild bruising of the cerebral cortex, but I can't completely exclude compression, squeezing of the brain because of bleeding."

"Go on." O'Reilly folded his arms across his chest and stroked his chin.

"He's got a bruise over his right temporal bone. That could mean a skull fracture and a possible tear to the—"

"Middle meningeal artery. Damnation."

Mister Gupta said, "I hope it's not, but to be on the safe side I'm going to arrange skull X-rays, the routine blood work and cross match in case he needs a transfusion, and we'll do an ultrasound once we get him admitted to ward 21. Unless you have some questions, Doctor O'Reilly, I'm going to get those tests ordered."

O'Reilly nodded. "Thank you, Mister Gupta." This young man clearly had everything under control and Donal was in good hands. O'Reilly looked at the unconscious face of Donal Donnelly, his freckles standing out against his pallid skin, the tips of his buckteeth barely visible. God, O'Reilly thought, he looks so young. He dropped into a chair beside the trolley and waited until the curtains parted and Mister Gupta reappeared. "Everything's organised, and I've had a word with Mister Greer. He's at home. He agrees with our plan—"

O'Reilly was flattered by the "our."

"He says to say hello."

"We were students together," O'Reilly said.

"And to call him if things get worse. Your patient might need surgery if they do."

"A craniotomy?"

Mister Gupta nodded. "Perhaps. If it's only a small bleed I can do a burr hole under local, drill through the skull, and let the blood out, but if it's a bigger bleed or doesn't stop, Mister Greer will remove more bone, drain the clot, and tie off the artery." He smiled. "I honestly don't think either will be necessary."

"Jesus," O'Reilly said softly, "I hope you're right. When I was a student, the mortality rate from brain surgery was fifty percent."

The senior registrar smiled. "We've come a long way, sir, and your friend Mister Greer is one of the people who's brought us to where we are today."

It was hard to imagine today's pillar of the medical establishment as the irresponsible young Charlie Greer of O'Reilly's student days. He shook his head. "How long before you'll have the tests done?" He took another look at Donal.

"About an hour."

"And you're sure—as sure as any of us can be—that Donal's not going to get worse?"

"Pretty sure." Mister Gupta stepped aside for two orderlies.

"All right if we take your man here 'til ward 21, sir?"

"Please," said Mister Gupta.

"Right," said the first orderly to his mate, "take you that end, oul' hand, and away we go." The rubber-tyred wheels squeaked as the trolley began to move. "Thon axle could use a wee taste of oil," he remarked.

O'Reilly put his hand on Donal's clammy arm. "You're going to be all right, Donal," he said quietly, and hoped he was right.

4

A Memory of Yesterday's Pleasures

O'Reilly carried a tray bearing a plate of steak and kidney, brussels sprouts, mashed potatoes, and a slice of apple pie. Its filling would taste like wallpaper paste, but he'd eaten a lot worse at sea and it could be a while before there was any further prospect of food.

He sat under pale yellow arches. The cafeteria had been built under two wards and was known as "the Caves." Smells of floor polish competed with an attar of boiled cabbage. A steady hum of conversation nearly drowned the clatter of serving spoons. He chewed a piece of steak and worried about Donal. Everything was under control. Mister Gupta clearly was competent. It would serve no purpose for Fingal to sit by Donal's bedside and he'd been in practice long enough to know that worrying never changed a damn thing. But head injuries were unpredictable.

What a terrible rent it would tear in the fabric of Ballybucklebo if anything happened to Donal Donnelly. Betting man, greyhound race fixer, poacher, pipe major of the Ballybucklebo Highlanders. Everybody in the village loved the little bucktoothed man. Well, maybe Councillor Bertie Bishop didn't, but everybody else did.

Fingal put down his fork. At least if surgery did become necessary, Mister Charles Greer, M.D., F.R.C.S., was the man for the job. Big Charlie, with shoulders like an ox and fingers like sausages, did not look like someone who could work with the delicacy his specialty demanded. But he could. After he'd qualified in 1936 he'd studied here at the Royal under Mister Purce and Mister Calvert, two of Ireland's pioneering neurosurgeons.

Fingal remembered Charlie as a student, a young man with a finely honed sense of irreverence and a shock of ginger hair to rival Donal Donnelly's ruddy thatch. Charlie's was greying now.

Fingal had met him in October '31 on the day they'd started their basic science studies and their lectures in French, English, logic, psychology, and Latin. The School of Physic at Trinity College Dublin, as the medical school founded in 1711 was known, demanded that fledgling doctors gain a Bachelor of Arts degree after three years of study.

As students, Fingal and Charlie had had something else in common. Rugby football. After a series of trial games, they'd been picked to play for the Trinity College first fifteen in the Irish Senior League. Fingal had hoped selection would be the first step to playing for his country, and that his four-year layoff while at sea hadn't made him too rusty.

And there was more to Charlie Greer than rugby football. It had seemed incongruous then that a man who enthusiastically thumped into opposing players during matches and boxed for fun, also regularly attended the university debating society, loved the works of Mozart, and sang in a choir. Even now, he was a member of the Belfast Philharmonic Choir.

O'Reilly picked up his fork and managed to swallow a soggy brussels sprout.

Charlie had attended Methodist College Belfast along with a short, green-eyed fellow student with prematurely thinning hair. The man played the bagpipes, the penny whistle, and raced yachts called "Waverleys" out of Ballyholme Yacht Club. Whenever Fingal and Charlie were getting themselves into mischief, the third man in the triumvirate was always Donald Cromie, who preferred simply to go by his surname. He was happy to explain why if anyone asked. He'd been born on September 6, 1914, the second day of the First Battle of the Marne. His father's only brother, Donald, had been killed that day. Cromie disliked feeling like a walking war memorial.

Today, Donald Cromie was a senior surgeon here at the Royal and two years ago had been knighted for his services to handicapped children.

The potatoes had the consistency of damp sawdust, but he'd eaten worse in his digs in Dublin, a damp, cramped bedsit on Westland Row. The three friends had surmounted the hurdles together: exams, lectures, and practical sessions. And they'd frequented Dublin's pubs, cinemas, and dance halls whenever time allowed. Charlie had once described those years as a time of pleasant relaxation punctuated by moments of intense panic.

Yet despite the panic, all three had passed and moved ahead. In October '33 in the beginning of third year, their little group had been joined by a man who had already spent seven years officially studying medicine. Robert Saint John, pronounced "Sinjin," Beresford was one of a number of students referred to as "chronics." These men, either by accident or design, kept failing examinations and in doing so had to repeat the courses they'd failed. They were said to be doing "the long course." Robert, Bob to his friends, was doing the very long course.

He was twenty-seven, stocky, and fair-haired. Piercing blue eyes looked out over a sharp nose and sardonic smile. A rich aunt had left him an allowance of two hundred pounds a year, which, as her will said, was to be "provided as long as he remained a student of medicine." It was a very handsome sum when a secretary might make fifty pounds and a lawyer two hundred and fifty a year. Bob had a flat in the upper-class Merrion Square and drove a 1929 Morris Minor.

The lads had taken to Bob and tried to encourage him to pass the next exam so the group of four could stay together. Perhaps a practical joke had persuaded him.

The four of them had been sitting in Bob's flat after class. Bob had a habit of inviting his friends for afternoon tea. Charlie Greer perched on one arm of a chair and, clutching a teacup that looked too frail for his big paw, said, "This afternoon you all heard our prof of physiology, Doctor Pringle, say, 'the human animal seldom if ever looks up unless its attention is attracted by movement or sound.'"

"So?" Fingal had asked.

When Charlie suggested a way to test the hypothesis, Fingal and Cromie laughed, but it must have hit Bob's funny bone. It took him a good minute to stop chuckling and say, "Let's do it." And they had—during the final applied anatomy class before the short holiday.

The learnèd professor had been right. For forty-five minutes not a soul in that lecture theatre had noticed anything unusual. They'd been too busy scribbling notes. Then a metallic jangling came from overhead.

The lecturer, Mister Chance, and all forty-one male medical students stared up. The women in the class had their own anatomy sessions. Every eye fixed on Gladys. The fully articulated human skeleton was usually stored in the rafters dangling from a pulley. Today she was resplendent in black brassiere, red knickers, suspender belt, and silk stockings. As the racket of the alarm clock lodged in her pelvis died away, the laughter started, first with a few titters building to a chorus of guffaws.

Mister Chance, widely regarded as a good skin, had not taken reprisals. "Gentlemen, as there are only ten minutes of class time remaining and your attention has been, shall we say, compromised, I suggest we bring today's class to a close. Good afternoon, and good luck." He swept from the theatre, his long, black academic robe billowing and making him look like an untidy crow.

Fingal made his way from the back row down wooden stairs worn concave by the countless boots and shoes of students like himself. A man waited halfway down. He was as tall as O'Reilly's six foot two, but in contrast to Fingal's nearly twelve stone would have been described by the locals as being as skinny as a wren's shin. He had a prodigious Adam's apple.

His voice was high and rasping. "I didn't find that schoolboy humour amusing in the least, O'Reilly. I know it was you and your infantile friends. You've been nothing but trouble since first year."

Fingal smiled. He wasn't going to let Ronald Hercules Fitzpatrick irritate him. Not on a sunny March afternoon at the end of term. Fingal shook his head, making his black, badly trimmed thatch flop over one dark brown eye. "Och sure, Hercules, life's too short to go round looking po-faced all the time."

"I should prefer not to be called 'Hercules'—" He was nudged aside by Charlie Greer. "Come on, Fingal," he said. "We're off to the pub. I'll let you buy me that first pint."

"Very decent of you," Fingal said with a grin. Now term was over he could even have found it in himself to invite Fitzpatrick to join them, but the man was a teetotaler, a Pioneer who had taken the pledge at thirteen. "Enjoy your week off."

"I shall study." He turned and left. "I want to be ready for next term. We'll be working in a hospital and sitting our BAs and Intermediate Two examinations in June."

"Indeed we will," said Fingal, "but all work and no play makes Hercules—I mean Ronald—a rather dull fourth-year medical student."

Passing the Intermediate Part II would mark the beginning of their study of real medicine. Examining patients, diagnosing illnesses, and learning how to treat them would become progressively more intense. And that was what Fingal had wanted to do since he was thirteen.

He and Charlie took the last few steps two at a time. Bob and Cromie were waiting at the door to the amphitheatre and together they walked two by two in the bright sunshine, Cromie and Bob leading. The sky was the eggshell blue of early spring as they crossed Trinity's forty-seven acres, an oasis in the midst of the bustling city.

Fingal felt a crisp breeze tainted with industrial fumes. The Provost's House was to their right. It had been built in 1759, thirty years before the rising of the United Irishmen and at the same time as the establishment of Guinness's Brewery.

On Nassau Street, outside the grounds, they were faced with a throng of pedestrians and traffic. "Come on," yelled Cromie, judging things nicely and nipping across the thoroughfare, Bob at his side.

Fingal and Charlie followed, dodging a fleet of bell-tinkling bicycles, a Morris Cowley motorcar, a laden Guinness dray, its iron-tyred wheels grumbling over the cobblestones, and a double-decker electric tram on its way to the suburb of Terenure. The air was noisome with exhaust fumes. Overhead, flocks of feral pigeons wheeled.

Charlie stopped, held up by a man pulling a barrow full of turnips. He was a tugger, a man who eked out an existence pulling goods in a rickety homemade two-wheeled cart. Two barefooted urchins had to jink like a pair of snipe to avoid colliding with him.

"Bob's heading to Davy Byrnes," said Fingal.

He preceeded Charlie into the long narrow room. The walls were of dark oak and a low hum of conversation rose among smells of stout and tobacco. Cromie had grabbed a table and Bob Beresford was halfway down the long, curved, wooden bar, ordering. The four of them knew each other's preferences. Bob looked smart today in a double-breasted grey suit and dove-grey spats over highly polished black shoes. He could afford to.

Fingal's scuffed boots clumped on the plank floor as he went to help Bob. "Come on," said Fingal, picking up two pints, "let's get these over to the table."

"Just in time," said Charlie, taking a pint. "My tongue's hanging out."

When everybody was seated, Bob lifted his whiskey. *"Sláinte."*

"Sláinte mHaith," came the reply.

The stout was smooth and bitter. Fingal sank one-third of the glass's contents in a single swallow. "Lord Jasus," he said, "but that hits the very spot." He wiped froth from his upper lip. "I'm not one bit sorry to see the end of applied anatomy."

Bob laughed, a deep rumbling for such a small man. "You're not sorry? I've sat through it three times." He grinned. "But this afternoon with Gladys? That was the berries. You three?" He shook his head.

"You don't have to repeat the courses again, you know." Fingal, who was conscious of his own limited budget, was not envious of Bob's money, but that anyone given the chance to study medicine should choose to squander the opportunity was beyond comprehension. "You could try to pass."

"Actually, I have been thinking that. Since I've drifted down into your year and met you lads the *craic*'s been ninety."

"Then why not pass your Intermediate II and stay with us?" Cromie asked.

"Wellll." Bob frowned. "There is the small matter—"

"Of your allowance?" Charlie asked.

"It does come in handy."

"But you'd make more as a doctor," Cromie said.

"I know," Bob said, "but," he wrinkled his nose as if inhaling a bad smell, "one would have to work."

Fingal was sure it was only by an effort of will that Robert Saint John Beresford avoided shuddering. "Come on, Bob," Fingal said. "We've twenty-seven months more to go, lectures, outpatient clinics, working on the wards, delivering babies." And how Fingal was looking forward to it all.

Bob smiled. "It would be grand sticking with you fellows and we'd still have two more exams to pass after Intermediate before we'll be finished. Lots of opportunity for me to fail one, stay a student for years more." He managed to look embarrassed. "You see, I really don't like responsibility. Life is such fun without it."

Bob offered Charlie a Sweet Afton cigarette. He refused on the grounds that he was trying to quit. He didn't want to ruin his wind for the rugby.

Fingal pulled out a pipe and lit it. He looked at his friends' glasses. It would soon be his shout and three shillings was all he could budget for this afternoon. He was relieved when he heard Bob call, "Same again please, Diarmud."

The barman said, "Right, sir."

Fingal looked at Bob. "And we're not asking you to stick with us just so you can pay the bills, Beresford. We enjoy your company."

Bob smiled. "I know that. We all know you're often short a bob or two, Fingal. You're the only one of us paying his own way through medical school, but you always pay your shout with us—"

I'd not have it any other way, Fingal thought.

"But term's over. I had a bit of luck on the horses at Leopardstown, so today's my treat—for you all."

"Bloody marvellous," said Cromie.

"Daddy Warbucks strikes again," Charlie said, and lifted his glass.

"And which one of you bowsies is Little Orphan Annie?" Bob wanted to know.

"Look, you lot," said Fingal, "I know your tongues are hanging out for another jar and we are grateful to you, Bob, but we've business to discuss too. Come autumn with our Intermediate and BAs behind us we'll be spending a lot of time working in teaching hospitals. I've asked around and heard that the system usually calls for us to pair off and work pretty closely together."

"Jasus, you and Hercules Fitzpatrick, Fingal. I can just see it." Bob grimaced.

Charlie laughed so hard he nearly spilled his pint.

"Exactly," Fingal said. "What a prospect, but how about us four in two pairs?"

"That makes sense," Bob said. "Bloody good sense."

"Another reason for you to pass the exams in June," Fingal said. "You'd be doing us a favour."

"Lord," said Bob, sipping his whiskey, "you, O'Reilly, will be having me Doctor Beresford before I know it."

That's right, Fingal thought, but held his peace. "Before we do anything we have to choose a teaching hospital. We can go to any one of ten in Dublin."

"Och," said Charlie, "the tyranny of choice. We're enchained by our freedom to pick."

"I haven't a clue," Bob said, paying for the fresh drinks. "I'd not been planning to go that far with my studies."

"I know exactly where we should go. It's a short bike ride from my digs, Bob's flat, or you two's rooms in Trinity to Grand Canal Street and Sir Patrick Dun's Hospital. It has just about everything we need." Fingal put a hand into his knapsack and pulled out the *Regulations of the School of Physic.* "Medical wards, surgical wards, a fever wing." He winked at Charlie. "And they have a home for student nurses nearby."

"Great," said Charlie, and lifted his glass. "I'll drink to that."

"They don't do obstetrics. Closed the unit in 1903, but I reckon the Rotunda up on Parnell Square is where we should do our five months of midwifery, but we've got to get medicine and surgery out of the way before we can." He lifted his new pint. "Thanks, Bob."

"My pleasure. You've really done your homework on this, Fingal."

"I have," said O'Reilly. "Now look. I'll arrange for us to see the Secretary of the Medical Board at Dun's and get signed up."

Cromie said, "So we'll stick together, the fearsome four, to do our clinical work at Sir Patrick's." His words were a little slurred.

O'Reilly smiled. Cromie was a tower of strength in many ways, but, unlike Fingal, had a weak head for drink.

O'Reilly lifted his glass. "To the next two years at Sir Patrick Dun's, may the work be interesting and the *craic* continuous"—he fixed Bob with a stare—"for all four of us." He drank to a chorus of "Hear. Hear."

"Damn right, and we'll start tonight," said Charlie. "When these are finished, let's get our tea and then go to the floating ballroom at Butt Bridge."

To which Fingal Flahertie O'Reilly had replied, "I'm your man, Charlie Greer."

5

The Fleeting Image of a Shade

O'Reilly looked at his watch and reckoned it was time to leave the cafeteria and see if Mister Gupta had good news. He climbed a flight of stairs and began to walk the length of the busy main corridor of the Royal Victoria Hospital. A couple of uniformed nurses passed him. A few folks in civilian dress, relatives of patients, no doubt. Medical students in bum-freezer short white coats. House staff in long white coats. A cleaner slowly advanced along the corridor pushing an electric floor polisher, known in Belfast as a bumper.

Once on the ward O'Reilly stopped at the nurses' desk. The young woman wore, beneath her starched white apron, a navy blue uniform that identified her as a junior sister. He thought she looked tired, with the typical pallor of night nurses, but her blue eyes were lively when she looked up and started to say, "I'm sorry, but visiting hours are—"

"I'm Doctor O'Reilly," he said. "Come to see Mister Gupta and my patient Donal Donnelly."

"Oh," she said. "Donnelly. The head injury. They should be back soon. Mister Gupta took the patient back to X-ray."

"Back?" In casualty he had understood that Donal would have his X-ray before being admitted.

"I'm afraid," she said, "the films weren't very clear and Mister

Gupta thought the ultrasound showed a possibility of bleeding, but he wants to be absolutely certain there is a skull fracture before he calls Mister Greer in from home." She shrugged. "He did a seven-hour surgery for an astrocytoma today."

"Brain tumour surgery's tough." O'Reilly could imagine his friend now in his big house on Harberton Park, sitting watching telly with his wife Noreen, probably dozing off in the middle of *The Avengers*. After an operation like that he'd be knackered. "With a bit of luck, we'll not have to trouble Charlie tonight," O'Reilly said.

Sister's eyebrow rose. "Charlie?"

O'Reilly laughed. She thought he was being too familiar with her chief. "Charlie Greer and I were classmates at Trinity. Back in the Stone Age."

"Oh," she said. O'Reilly could imagine the unspoken, "Well, that's all right then." Gupta wouldn't bring in a senior consultant unless there were serious grounds. That he hadn't done so immediately told O'Reilly that the young man was not unduly concerned, but by repeating the X-ray he was taking no chances. Sensible. The latest imaging techniques had failed to give clear answers. Until they did, the only way to decide how Donal was doing was still the old analysis of symptoms and signs. That way of assessing a head injury had not changed since Fingal had been a student at Sir Patrick Dun's. "Any change in Donal's clinical state?"

"I've his chart here," she said, and handed it to O'Reilly. The pulse rate was slower, the blood pressure stable, and the respiratory rate much slower. That was good. Patients who had suffered cerebral bruising, which was what Mister Gupta suspected, usually had a period of reaction when all those changes happened. O'Reilly sure as hell hoped that this was what was going on and that the next phase would be resolution with Donal regaining consciousness. He read on. Level of consciousness, unchanged, but the patient had spontaneously turned on his side. That too was a sign of the reaction period. Pupils equal and reacting to light. Good. Reflexes normal. Better. "When do we expect them back, Sister?" he asked.

"Twenty minutes—half an hour. We have our own X-ray department here in Quin House and the new Procomat automated film developer is a lot quicker than doing it by hand."

He chuckled. "When I was a lad we used to hold glass film plates over the patient."

She smiled and, he thought, tactfully refrained from comment.

"May I wait here?" he asked.

She beckoned to him. "Come round and have a pew. Can I make you a cup of tea?"

He smiled. Tea. Ulster's answer to anything from a laddered stocking to nuclear war. "Please," he said.

"I'll be right back." She rose. "Mister Gupta's really very good. Try not to worry too much." She left, heading for the ward kitchen. He had to smile. Usually it was him telling someone else not to worry. And, damn it, she was right. He should bide patiently. He looked at his watch. Ten past ten. It didn't seem like more than four hours since Donal had come a cropper.

It would be dark outside now and the curtains of the four-bedded wards were all closed. These rooms against the wall of the hexagonal Quin House abutted a corridor that separated them from the single-bed isolation wards forming the inner hub. All rooms were glass-fronted. The building had been regarded as revolutionary when it was opened in 1953.

Charlie had invited Fingal to the occasion. A much more serious Charles Greer than the young man who'd suggested going dancing at a floating ballroom back in '34. That had been a good night and yet Fingal had had no difficulty waking up the next morning. Youth, he thought wryly. He'd have more trouble nowadays getting his fifty-six-year-old bones out of bed at eight in the morning after a night of dancing.

O'Reilly crossed his legs at the ankles, locked his hands behind his head, and leant back in his chair. He could so clearly picture himself coming to in his digs, the sparsely furnished, linoleum-floored, ground-floor bed-sit at 23a Westland Row and remembering the night before. Charlie had been right about having fun. She'd been a pretty lass, that Finnoula—he had to struggle to remember her last name—Branagh. That was it. Branagh. Third-year botany student.

He'd taken her home by tram, kissed her goodnight, and had been pleased when she'd said she'd be delighted to go to the pictures with him on Saturday night. The Savoy Theatre on O'Connell Street had opened in 1929 and could seat three thousand. That was where they'd seen *The Barretts of Wimpole Street* with Charles Laughton and Maureen O'Sullivan. Now there was an Irish lass who'd done well for herself.

The springs of the single bed creaked as Fingal threw back the blanket. He felt the chill in the air. His stomach grumbled, but not in anticipation of the usual gruel accompanied by a pot of weak tea and a rationed two slices of bread and margarine that his landlady referred to as breakfast. No, once he'd showered and dressed he'd walk from here to his family home. Ma wasn't expecting him, but he knew bloody well she'd put on an Irish breakfast that would leave you ready to call the cows home.

He let himself out of the front door, pausing as he always did to lift his cap to the plaque on the wall of the terrace house next door. Oscar Fingal O'Flahertie Wilde had been born there at Number

21. And a young Father had bestowed those names, less the *O'*, on his second son.

With a bit of luck, Father wouldn't be home. He usually gave tutorials on Saturdays. Things between them had become very icy once Fingal had announced, back in '27, that he was going to sea. They'd thawed over the years, but only by a degree or two. Fingal had made a point of popping in regularly to see Ma and had loyally eaten Christmas dinner at home ever since he'd started his medical studies. But while Lars and Fingal got on well, he and Father were only able to maintain a surface civility, and the depth of his father's disappointment was palpable. Fingal strode on, humming "Lazybones." It had been a big hit last year for the American band leader Ted Williams.

"Excuse me, sir?" A short man stood on the footpath. He wore laceless army boots, ragged moleskin trousers, a dirty, collarless shirt, and a threadbare Ulster overcoat. Two bronze medals were pinned to its left breast. The right coat sleeve was sewn back because his arm had been amputated below the elbow. He wore a tweed duncher tilted to one side.

The man's pinched face was grimy, his cheeks blue, and Fingal saw that below a nicotine-stained moustache the upper two front teeth had gone. "Could you spare a penny, sir, so a poor, old sodger-man could get a cup of tea on a feckin' cold morning?" He held out his left hand palm up and shivered.

Christ, Fingal thought. Poor divil. There were more beggars per square mile living in the Dublin tenements than in the slums of Bombay. Some of the saddest cases were wounded ex-servicemen who had fought in the Boer and Great Wars. They were barely supported by meagre pensions from their now-departed Imperial masters and despised by their fellow countrymen for having fought for the British. For centuries the British Army and Navy had provided jobs and a steady income for many of Ireland's chronically unemployed, but a new Irish nationalism had burgeoned after the executions of the leaders of the Easter Rising and had made anything English despised.

Fingal thrust his hand into his trousers pocket. "Here," he said, "here's a florin. Get yourself a decent breakfast."

The beggar's eyes widened. "Holy Mother of God. Two whole feckin' shillings? Ah, t'anks, yer honour. T'anks." He snapped to attention and saluted with his left hand holding the shilling between his bent thumb and his palm. "Arragh Jayus, t'anks a feckin' million, sir."

" 'Breakfast,' I said. Not a wheen of jars." Fingal tried to sound stern.

Already the man had scuttled away in the direction of the alleys of the Liberties where the *poitín* and porter, the weakest ale brewed by Guinness, were cheap and plentiful. Och well, Fingal, he told himself, if the poor divil gets a bit of warmth in a shebeen and a few hours of drunken solace with his mates, a cigarette or two, why not? Fingal had lengthened his stride, eager to be home to see Ma, have his breakfast, and a nice cuppa.

"Here's your tea, Doctor O'Reilly." The nursing sister set a small tray on the desk. "What do you like in it?"

O'Reilly sat up. Uncrossed his ankles. Someone had dimmed the lights on ward 21. "Milk and sugar, please."

She poured. Handed him the cup and said, "And there are some McVitie's Rich Tea biscuits."

"Thank you, Sister."

"I'm going to have to leave you, I'm afraid," she said. "We've a full ward and it's time I made my rounds."

"Go right ahead," he said. "No word from Mister Gupta?"

"Not yet, but it won't be much longer. No news is good news. Enjoy your tea and biscuits," she said, and left.

No, O'Reilly thought, no news is exactly that. No bloody news. But he'd have to bide. He lifted a biscuit and dipped it in his tea. Ma, he remembered, had always served tea, McVitie's Rich Tea biscuits—no Dublin hostess would dare omit them—chocolate digestive biscuits, and Cook's homemade shortbread and chocolate éclairs when people had come for afternoon tea. Never mind afternoon tea, he thought, Cook always put on a hell of a breakfast at Lansdowne Road.

6

Mother Will Be There

Fingal climbed the stone steps to the front door, admiring the delicate wrought-iron railings and the Virginia creeper that clung to the house's red brick. The leaves were spring green. Come autumn they would be scarlet daubs of cheering colour among the sad leafless trees.

He stabbed the brass doorbell push and heard jangling in the hall, feet approaching.

"Master Fingal." Bridgit, the maid, opened the door. She looked smart in her black dress, white pinafore, and crimped white cap pinned to grey hair parted in the middle.

O'Reilly grinned. "Morning, Bridgit." To her, despite his twenty-five years, he was still "Master," not "Mister." Bridgit had been with the family for as long as he could remember. She'd probably helped change his nappies.

She led him to the drawing room. Fingal's mother sat in a wing-backed armchair in the bay of the bow window. The low morning sun put highlights in her blonde hair and cast her in shadow beneath a landscape in oils in the style of the French Impressionists. It was one she'd painted last year while Father had been fishing on a holiday to Ramelton in Donegal.

She turned from her *Irish Times* and smiled. "Thank you,

Bridgit. Fingal. What a surprise. How lovely to see you." She frowned. "Have you had breakfast?"

He shook his head. "Morning, Ma."

She tutted.

Typical Ma. Always worrying about her two grown sons. She probably thought that without food he'd be on the verge of collapse. He crossed to her and dropped a kiss on her head. As ever, her pearls were round her slender neck. "I've not eaten—yet."

"Is there anything special you'd like, son?"

He shook his head. "Not much," he said. "Something light. Porridge. Couple of rashers and two eggs please, Bridgit. Sausages. Bit of black pudding. Soda farl. Tomato. Maybe a couple of kidneys? Lamb chop?"

"Please tell Cook," Ma said to Bridgit.

"Hey bye, you always was a grand man for the pan, sir, so you were," Bridgit said as she left, her Antrim accent as strong as it had been the day she'd left the village of Portglenone and taken service with the O'Reillys.

"Father out?" Fingal asked.

"He's giving a tutorial."

Fingal blew out his breath. "How is he?"

She hesitated before saying, "Pretty much the same as usual. Perhaps he tires more easily. He'll be sorry to have missed you."

"Really." Fingal curled his left hand and inspected his fingernails.

Ma pointed to a chair, the twin of hers. "Come and sit down. It's lovely to have you here. It's been three weeks since your last visit." He thought she looked wistful when she said, "I just wish your brother could come as often as you do, son. I know sometimes when he drives up he's seeing that nice Jean Neely girl." She laughed. "No time for old fogies like us."

Fingal sat and crossed his legs. "Lars was down from Portaferry at Christmas," he said. "It's a three-hour trip in his motorcar."

"I know," she said, "and I'm delighted for your brother. He seems happy being a solicitor in that small town and Jean might just suit him well."

Fingal, not wishing to become too involved in a discussion of Lars's love life, said, "He always knew what he wanted for a career."

She touched his knee. "Both my boys did."

"And," he said, "thanks to you and Lars, Ma, I'm doing it. You've no idea how much I'm enjoying it."

"I think I do, and I'm delighted. I'm only sorry you had to go away for so long before you could get started."

"There was no other way." He caught her wistful look and knew it must have cost her. "I'm sorry too."

"Don't be." There was a tiny edge in her voice that Fingal had never heard before, not even at the height of his battles with Father. "Don't ever be sorry for following your dream. Of all emotions, regret is the most futile."

Fingal wondered what Ma had to regret.

She narrowed her eyes and tilted her head to one side. "I know what you're thinking," she said. "What could I have to regret? I have everything a Victorian wife could possibly want. A lovely home, a successful husband, two wonderful sons."

"Victorian? You make yourself sound old, Ma."

"Well, I was four in 1887 when Queen Victoria had her Golden Jubilee. And the attitudes of her era certainly didn't perish when I was growing up." She hesitated then said, "I was a girl once, Fingal. And I was lucky. Your grandfather had some advanced ideas. He believed girls should be educated—up to a point. When I was fourteen he sent me to Victoria College in Belfast and let me stay there until sixth form." She turned away and looked out through the window. "I was captain of hockey that year, 1901. I was eighteen."

"The year Queen Victoria died and a year after my namesake kicked the bucket," Fingal said, wondering why Ma was telling him this.

"Poor Oscar," Ma said. "I'd read his plays." She winked at her son before continuing, "Very risqué for a young lady then, but I loved *A Woman of No Importance*." She stood up quickly. "Come on. Let's continue this next door. I need coffee. There's a pot in the dining room. Have a cup with me while you wait for breakfast."

He followed his mother across the hall and into the formal dining room, admiring the stateliness of her carriage, the grace of her walk. She was a handsome woman. He could imagine her as a girl, lovely, spirited. He pulled out a chair and sat where Bridgit had set a place for one. The cut-glass chandelier overhead sparkled diamond and blue like moonbeams reflected from rippled water.

"Here." Ma handed him a cup of coffee and sat opposite with her own.

"That new hairdo suits you much better than your old chignon."

Ma patted her hair. "Lots of waves are all the fashion. I do try to keep up." She sipped her coffee. "I've always tried to keep up."

"With fashion?"

She shook her head. "With the world. When I was at Victoria College I read the *Belfast Telegraph* every day. I supported Lady Constance Lytton and Mrs. Emmeline Pankhurst and their campaign for votes for women."

"You were a suffragette? Good Lord."

"I was worse," Ma said, "I nearly gave your Grandpa Nixon heart failure."

Fingal sat forward, his coffee ignored. "How?"

"When I left school I told him that in 1899 the Faculty of Medicine of Queen's College Belfast had approved the admission of women."

Fingal pushed his chair back. "Ma—Ma, you wanted to be a doctor?" It was unbelievable. Ever since he was a nipper, it had seemed to Fingal that Ma had only one goal, to take care of her family. And yet all along, she had wanted what he himself so desperately did. "Jesus."

"I know. Shocking, isn't it?" Her smile was sad. "That's what Grandpa thought too."

"That's not what I meant. We have three girls in our class, and why not? I was just surprised about you, that's all. I never knew."

"I was going to tell you when you first told me medicine was what you wanted. Then I realised it had to be your decision, your dream, not mine, so I kept my counsel."

Fingal swallowed. It must have taken a lot of willpower for her not to say anything.

"Anyway," she continued, "Grandpa wouldn't hear of it. To be fair he did let me study English. Still, it's how I met your father so something good came of it. He was a postgraduate student working for his MA. He taught a series on the poetry of Oscar Wilde." She sipped her coffee and looked down at the tablecloth. "He was awfully handsome, and his voice when he read from Wilde's works gave me goose pimples."

Fingal looked at his mother.

"He was a socialist back then," she said. "Thought that Keir Hardie—the first Labour MP in the British Parliament—thought the man walked on water. I agreed. We were married in 1904 as soon as he got his MA. Grandpa was very pleased."

"And you've regretted not going to medical school ever since?"

She shook her head. "I told you, of all emotions, regret is the most futile."

Those, he thought, are her words, but he heard the catch in her voice.

"And that's why you helped me defy Father?"

"You remember we used to read Yeats together?"

He nodded.

" 'Tread softly, for you tread on my dreams'?" Fingal heard the edge back in his mother's voice. "No one should tread on anyone else's dreams. No one."

He felt his eyes prickle. "Thanks, Ma," he said very quietly. "Thank you very much."

For a while Fingal was content to respect her silence. His own thoughts bubbled. In 1927, he'd come close to accusing his father of wanting to live his life vicariously through Fingal. Instead he was living his dream all right—but Ma's too.

He heard the door open and turned to see his father standing in the doorway. He seemed to have lost weight since Christmas. Fingal noticed shadows under brown eyes. The darkness was new and somehow Father's skin seemed paler. His gaze rested briefly on Fingal, who stood so quickly he had to grab his chair to stop it toppling.

"Connan," Ma said, "I wasn't expecting you so soon. Look who's come to see us."

"Wretched student didn't show up, Mary. You know I always allow them ten minutes, but then they've had it."

Fingal's jaw tightened. He hoped his father meant the luckless student had missed his chance for a tutorial, but knowing Father he was pretty sure that unless a watertight excuse could be produced there was more severe retribution in store.

"It's all worked out nicely," Ma said. "Fingal popped in and now you're home early." She fixed her son with a glance. "You were disappointed that Father wasn't here. Isn't that right, Fingal?"

"How are you, Father?" Fingal asked.

"Well enough," he said in a clipped voice. "How are you, Fingal?"

"For goodness' sake, Connan, you're not addressing a class. Sit down. Have a cup of coffee," Ma said. "You sit too, Fingal."

Fingal sat.

Father walked round the table and took a chair beside Ma.

"I'm well too, Father," he said.

"And—um—how are your—um—medical studies going?"

"Well," Fingal said, "very well. You know I've passed all the exams first go so far. I'm ready for the next one in June."

"I would have expected that. And the arts courses?"

"Fine." Fingal smiled. "It's a good thing you and Ma—Mother— taught Lars and me to like reading when we were little. I'm really enjoying them, but I feel a bit of an eejit having to wear a gown to attend classes. It's so—so mediaeval. I'll be glad to be rid of the thing when I get my BA." He glanced at Father trying to gauge his response, hoping for a smile.

"Tradition should be respected." Father turned to Ma. "I'll have that coffee, please, Mary."

Fingal took a breath. A word of encouragement would have been appreciated. Fingal watched as Ma rose then he looked back to the spare man opposite. He sat, shoulders braced, back straight. His three-piece, pin-striped suit was perfectly tailored.

The Victorians, Fingal thought. This restraint, this self-containment. It was how they were reared. And yet his father's indifference was galling. It gnawed at Fingal. He knew he was breathing too quickly, suspected his blood pressure was rising. He was tempted to forgo breakfast here, there were plenty of cheap cafés, but he shook his head. There was no point making a scene.

Damn it all, Cook would, as always, serve up a right tightener and Ma would be terribly disappointed if he didn't eat every scrap.

And if Fingal hadn't realised by now he was never going to please Father, then perhaps it was enough to have pleased one of his parents. He looked at his mother, her lined but still radiant face turned to her husband. Perhaps it was enough.

7

Social Comfort, in a Hospital

The true beginning of Fingal Flahertie O'Reilly's immersion into clinical medicine started on a crisp Dublin morning. He strode from his digs under a sky that had the washed-out look of late autumn. Brittle brown leaves shared the gutters with fish-and-chip wrappers and discarded cigarette packets.

When Fingal arrived at the teaching hospital, Charlie Greer was waiting with a group of four other students. Fingal barely had time to bid them good morning when a small man came down the front steps and announced, "Good morning. I am Doctor Micks, deputy professor of materia medica and therapeutics and attending physician here at Sir Patrick Dun's Hospital."

He was slim with a pointed chin and narrow face that made Fingal think of Gladys, the classroom skeleton. Doctor Micks wore wire-rimmed spectacles and a long white coat over the waistcoat and trousers of a grey suit. "I'm here," he said, "to welcome you to the first day of your six-month clinical clerkship. You will be, as we call it, 'walking the wards,' working with general medical inpatients. You'll attend required outpatient sessions and prescribed lectures. Your surgery training will come later."

Fingal fingered the tubing of the stethoscope in his pocket the way an ancient Celt might have fingered a runic talisman. He'd

aced Intermediate Part II and collected his BA in June. Ma had
come to the graduation ceremony in the Examination Hall to watch
him and his friends, including a bemused Bob Beresford, receive
their degrees. She'd made an excuse for Father. Said he'd been a
bit under the weather. Now that those exams and the courses from
June to October were over, the real meat of learning medicine was
beginning.

"I should like to know your names," Doctor Micks said. "You
are, Miss?"

"Manwell, sir. Hilda Manwell."

"And you, Mister?"

"Fitzpatrick, sir."

Pity, Fingal thought, that the man had also picked Sir Patrick
Dun's. Hilda was an unknown. At least the other lads, Bob, Charlie, and Cromie, were here too.

"And you?" he asked, nodding at Fingal.

"O'Reilly, sir."

"O'Reilly? You, and I believe Mister Greer there, you play
rugby for Trinity, do you not?" He smiled. "I am led to believe
that one or both of you might be capped for your country."

Fingal blushed and glanced at Charlie, who said, "If it's anybody it'll be O'Reilly, sir."

"As long as it doesn't interfere with your studies, I wish you
both the best of luck. Your success will add lustre to Trinity and to
Sir Patrick Dun's."

Fingal swallowed. That had been generous of Charlie and it
wasn't true. Greer was the better player.

Doctor Micks turned to Bob.

"Beresford, sir."

"And you?"

"Cromie, sir."

"Thank you. Now, before I take you to the wards, I think it's important that you, as new junior medical staff—"

Fingal grinned. They were only students, but it was courteous to be treated like doctors.

"—know something of the history of Sir Patrick Dun's."

Fitzpatrick's hand shot up. He was so excited he was waving his hand. Fingal could picture him asking, "Me, sir. Me, sir. Pick me. Please, please."

"Yes, Mister Fitzpatrick?" Doctor Micks frowned. "You have a question?"

"No, sir." He adjusted the pair of gold-framed pince-nez. "I've read about Sir Patrick."

Fingal looked over at Charlie, who raised his eyes to the heavens. Fingal shook his head and inwardly cringed. This sucking up to teachers was taboo.

Fitzpatrick was tripping over his words. "He was born in Aberdeen, in Scotland in 1642. He treated King William of Orange for a shoulder wound on the day before the Battle of the Boyne. When he died, he left most of his fortune to found another medical school in Dublin. Some of that money went to building a hospital on Lower Exchange Street in 1792. The staff and patients moved here to Grand Canal Street in 1816."

A year after Waterloo, Fingal thought, and the victor of that scrap, Lord Wellington, had been born in Dublin. There was a dirty great monument to him in Phoenix Park.

"I see you've done your research, Mister Fitzpatrick," said Doctor Micks, and continued, "As you students will be spending the better part of two years with us in various departments I think it is important you understand your surroundings and develop a deep sense of pride in this institution." He pointed up. "Can anyone translate that gilt inscription on the arch beneath the clock?"

Fingal peered up and read, *Nosocomium Patr. Dun. Eq. Aurat. MDCCCXIV.* In full he knew it would be *"Nosocomium Patricii Dun Equitis Aurati"* and the date.

To Fingal's delight, Doctor Micks avoided Fitzpatrick and pointed at Charlie, who manfully translated, "The Hospital of Sir Patrick Dun, Knight, 1814."

"Well done, young Greer. That's the year this part of the building was completed, before it was opened, two years later." He removed his spectacles, polished, and replaced them. "But we must not dwell on the past," he said, "I want to bring you up to date with more recent developments."

Fingal leant forward.

"Since the original two wings on each side of this arch were built, one for men and one for women, Sir Patrick's has expanded. The upper floor of the east wing to my left became, and still is, a fever ward with twenty-six beds and a separate entrance. New operating rooms were built in 1898 and replaced in 1916."

The year of the Easter Rising, Fingal thought, and he knew that wounded rebels and British soldiers were treated here during the battle at the nearby Mount Street Bridge, which spanned the Grand Canal. One of the leaders had eventually come to Sir Patrick's and asked to be taken to British headquarters to arrange the surrender of the rebels.

Doctor Micks continued, "Those operating rooms were replaced again in 1924, this time in the rear of the building. There are student rooms when you are living in the hospital for the required periods of residence."

Fingal was looking forward to that. Every month spent practically *gratis* in the hospital was a saving of rent money.

Doctor Micks continued, "That structure in front of the east wing is the outpatients' department." He smiled. "It was opened last year. Thirty thousand patients a year are seen there, so you'll have plenty of opportunities to learn. And there is a home for student nurses on Lower Mount Street."

Fingal saw Charlie's grin. Perhaps Doctor Micks had seen it too. He continued, "The lady superintendent, Miss Northey, keeps a very close eye on her young ladies, so be warned."

Charlie's eyes narrowed. Fingal could almost hear him plotting how to bamboozle the redoubtable Miss Northey. Trust Charlie.

"The X-ray department is getting overstretched so the Board of Governors is applying for money from the Irish Hospitals Sweepstakes Fund for a new one. The massage department is next door to the lecture theatre, in which I'm sure, Mister Greer, you'll enjoy the weekly compulsory lectures delivered in Latin."

Charlie groaned.

"Now," said Doctor Micks, "that's enough about the place, unless there are questions?"

Fitzpatrick held up his hand.

"Yes, Mister Fitzpatrick?"

"Is it true, sir, that there's a memorial in the front hall, a brass table engraved with the names of the thirty staff and students of Sir Patrick's who fell in the Great War?"

"It is," Doctor Micks said.

Fingal shook his head. And it's true about you, Fitzpatrick. You're one of those people who only ever ask a question if they already know the answer.

"So," said Doctor Micks. "No more questions?"

Silence.

"Right. Follow me and we'll go and make ward rounds. Doctor Pilkington, the house physician, will be joining us."

Fingal trooped after the rest, through the front doors, past the War Memorial, and to the right of the splendidly named Grand Staircase.

"This," said Doctor Micks, holding open a door, "is Saint Patrick's Ward."

Fingal's nose was assailed by hospital smells. A low continuous moaning came from behind screens around a bed halfway up. Elsewhere someone was snoring, deeply and rhythmically. Nurses, their voices low and soothing, went about their duties.

Inside the door, a young man in a long white coat waited. Two student nurses, a staff nurse, and the ward sister accompanied him. She wore a neck-to-ankle white apron over a floor-length blue dress. A white starched fall, a headdress that was bound across her forehead below the hairline, drooped in folds at the back and sides like the head adornments of a pharaoh.

"Good morning, Doctor Pilkington, Sister Daly, ladies," Doctor Micks said.

The nurses bobbed, Doctor Pilkington said, "Good morning, sir," as did Sister Daly. Her accent was pure County Cork. She smiled, then her green-eyed gaze fell for a moment on the six students. She might, Fingal thought, be inspecting something she'd found on the sole of her shoe that wasn't to her liking. "Everything's ready. Shall we start?" she asked.

"Please."

Fingal looked around as he followed the entourage. He noticed that the walls were painted black. Someone called Nathaniel Hone had been resposible for the colour scheme, apparently believing that walls so coloured were easier to keep clean. High arched windows provided a great deal of light, and on good days were opened to admit fresh air. Light and air, it was believed, were two things critical to patients' recovery. In the children's ward, that recovery was helped along with liberal helpings of Bird's custard.

Along each side, beds were arranged with military precision, heads to the wall, feet to the central walkway. Every bed had a cane-backed chair at its foot and the case notes clipped to the bed-head. The twenty-five beds to each side were all occupied by men, some recovering from operations, others with medical conditions that did not require surgery.

Fingal recognised the painting hanging over a fireplace, a scene depicting Saint Patrick preaching to Oisín, a warrior from Irish mythology.

They arrived at a bed inside an oxygen tent. As the group arranged itself on either side of the foot of the bed, doctors to the right, nurses to the left, Fingal noticed a plaque on the wall. OTC COMMEMORATION BED. *Endowed by citizens of Dublin in recognition of the gallant defence of Trinity College. Easter 1916.* Dublin's history was never far away.

Through a wide celluloid window in the canvas Fingal could make out a man of about thirty propped up on pillows. The inflowing oxygen hissed and a fan whirred extracting carbon dioxide. Sister nodded to a student nurse who opened the zipper that gave access to the bed, and folded the material back. The man's cheeks were dusky, his breathing jerky and shallow, his head was turned to one side, and his eyes were closed. The jugular vein, running from his collarbone to the angle of his jaw, was distended.

The staff nurse handed Doctor Pilkington a chart. He glanced at it then started to give the patient's history. "The patient, Mister KD, aged twenty-nine, of Ash Street in the Liberties, was admitted last night complaining of weakness, shortness of breath, coughing and haemoptysis—"

Fingal had begun learning the language of medicine early. Patients were never referred to by name when they were being discussed. Only their initials. If a case were to be talked about in a public place, there could be no breach of confidentiality. Haemoptysis was spitting blood, as opposed to haematemesis, vomiting blood.

"He had no other symptoms. A diagnosis of acute rheumatic

fever was made five years ago when he was treated in Doctor Steevens' Hospital with bed rest, fresh air, and acetylsalicylic acid at a dose of two hundred and forty grains daily—"

"Aspirin," Doctor Micks added. "First introduced by MacLagan of Edinburgh in 1874 to treat rheumatic fever—"

Fitzpatrick interrupted, "But your book, sir, says it has now been proved that salicylates exercise no specific action in rheumatic heart disease." His grin was oily. "And you recommend only thirty grains daily for relief of symptoms."

Fingal looked at Cromie and crossed his eyes.

Doctor Micks inclined his head. "Thank you, Mister Fitzpatrick. Please carry on, Doctor Pilkington."

"He has been admitted on several occasions with congestive heart failure as a consequence of mitral stenosis and aortic incompetence."

Doctor Micks turned to Fingal. "Mister O'Reilly, what is rheumatic fever?"

"An infection with the bacterium beta-haemolytic *Streptococcus.* Given where Mister KD lives, a damp, filthy, tenement—"

Doctor Micks sighed. "Mister O'Reilly, we physicians cannot solve the difficulties of the whole world. Just tell me about the disease."

Fingal looked at the bed. That was a human being lying there, not just a disease, but he swallowed and continued, "The infection damages the heart valves. The mitral valve is narrowed so it's difficult for blood to get into the left ventricle—"

"Which is?" Micks asked Bob.

"The lower chamber of the left side of the heart that is responsible for pumping blood around the body, sir."

"Good. And aortic incompetence, Greer?"

"There's a valve between the aorta and the left ventricle. When the ventricle finishes pumping, the aorta contracts to boost the blood along and the valve shuts to prevent backflow. But—"

"But if the valve is damaged," Fitzpatrick leapt in, "blood goes back into the ventricle, the blood gets dammed in the system, pools in the lungs, and causes congestive heart failure—"

"Indeed." Doctor Micks cut him off and spoke again to O'Reilly. "And how is the diagnosis of valvular disease made?"

"From the previous history of rheumatic fever and by hearing the classic murmurs, sir." O'Reilly tugged out his stethoscope.

"Now," said Doctor Micks, "you've got your stethoscope out, O'Reilly, have a listen to his chest. Tell us what you hear." He nodded and said, "Sister, please."

Sister Daly said, "Nurse Kelly. Nurse O'Hallorhan. Please sit the patient forward."

A second student nurse joined the first. Together they bent over Mister KD and with their arms supporting his shoulders bent the man at his waist. The one on O'Reilly's side unbuttoned the pyjama jacket.

"Please, only describe the murmurs, O'Reilly," Doctor Micks said.

O'Reilly looked at the man's narrow, sallow face, at how he gasped for breath, at the fear in his sunken blue eyes. "You don't mind if I examine you?" he asked.

The man weakly shook his head.

"Get on with it, O'Reilly," Fitzpatrick hissed. "Don't waste time."

Fingal ignored Fitzpatrick. "Don't be frightened," he said to the patient. "I'm not going to hurt you." He plugged his stethoscope into his ears, placed the bell below the man's left nipple over the heart, and strained to make sense of what he was hearing. A fifteen-second glance at his watch told Fingal the heart rate was regular and ninety beats per minute. Superimposed on the heart's *lup-dup, lup-dup* beats was a bewildering series of clicks and whooshes. He knew he was meant to relate them to the lups and dups, but for the life of him could not. He looked up. "I'm not sure, sir."

"You're an honest man, O'Reilly. Very few people can at the first attempt. It takes practice. We'll make sure you get plenty."

Fitzpatrick, without waiting to be asked, provided a comprehensive description of what should be heard, larding his discussion with terms like opening snaps, diastolic murmurs with presystolic accentuation, and aortic diastolic murmurs.

"Very good, Mister Fitzpatrick. Have you by any chance got your eye on the prize for medicine?"

Fitzpatrick nodded.

Have you, by God? O'Reilly thought, made a mental note and glanced at Charlie, who slowly shook his head. There can be, Fingal thought, many a slip betwixt cup and lip.

"Treatment for congestive heart failure, O'Reilly?"

"Bed rest sitting up, oxygen, no-salt diet, small amounts of aspirin—"

"And the drug of choice is, Beresford?"

Bob shook his head. "Sorry, sir."

"Digitalis, sir," Fitzpatrick said. "Its active principle is the glucoside digitoxin, described in your chapter sixteen, sir."

God, O'Reilly thought, that man could give Dickens's Uriah Heep advanced classes in obsequiousness.

Doctor Pilkington said, "We gave him a loading dose of six ccs of tincture of digitalis on admission, sir, and he seems to be responding well. We have him on two ccs every six hours."

"Good," said Doctor Micks. He turned and for the first time spoke to the patient. "You're doing fine," he said.

Mister KD managed a weak smile.

"Now come out of the tent, please, and zip it up."

Fingal stepped aside and when the student nurse at the far side moved toward him, Fingal Flahertie O'Reilly found himself looking into a pair of grey eyes, eyes which had amber flecks in the irises.

When everyone was back in their place, Fingal closed the zipper of the oxygen tent. He tried to pay attention as Doctor Micks explained the classic murmurs associated with various kinds of heart valve disease, but his gaze kept straying to the face of the grey-eyed nurse. And when she caught him looking at her, she smiled. Fingal knew he should be listening to Doctor Micks, feeling sympathy for the young man in the bed. But those eyes.

There'd been a couple of other girls since Finnoula Branagh back in March. Fingal enjoyed the company of women, but he had no intention of starting anything serious until he was qualified. Nevertheless, come hell, high water, or the protective maternal instincts of the ward sister, he was going to get Grey Eyes's name.

8

City of the Soul

"Doctor O'Reilly?" Gupta was standing over him, his face grave. "I'm sorry to disturb you, but I knew you'd want to know. Your patient has got a fracture of the temporal bone."

It took a moment for O'Reilly to realize he was sitting at the ward 21 nurses' desk of Belfast's Royal Victoria Hospital, his tea cold, his heart still warmed by the memory of his first glimpse of Nurse O'Hallorhan's grey eyes.

"Clinically he's worsened. The bruise over his temporal bone is getting bigger. The ultrasound now shows an obvious shift in the *falx cerebri,* the connective tissue separating the two halves of the brain."

"Extradural haematoma?" O'Reilly asked, sitting up in his chair and giving himself a shake. There was blood between Donal's skull and the tough outer membrane, the dura mater, that surrounded his brain. Blast.

"I'm afraid so. I've sent Mister Donnelly straight to the operating theatre. I'll do a burr hole to release the pressure and let the blood out. Time counts," Gupta said.

"I know. Can I help?"

"Not in theatre. Drilling a hole in the skull is a one-man job, but would you please phone Mister Greer? Sister will give you the number. Ask him to come in. Burr holes are first aid. Your patient needs a craniotomy." Gupta left.

The nurse showed O'Reilly the phone number. He had trouble focusing his eyes. Damn. Damn. Damn. Poor Donal. O'Reilly wondered if he should be phoning Barry too. Ask him to tell Julie. No, best to let the hare sit until he had more news to report. He'd first learned in 1935 not to worry relatives unneccessarily until you knew all the facts.

"Dial nine to get an outside line," she said.

A well-remembered voice answered. "Greer."

"Charlie, Fingal. This patient of mine that's here with an extradural. Mister Gupta's gone to theatre to do burr holes—"

"I'll be straight in."

"I'd like to observe."

"Meet me in the surgeons' changing room in twenty-five minutes."

O'Reilly let himself into a brightly lit room. A row of metal lockers stood along one wall. Some had nameplates, Misters Alex Taylor, Colin Gleadhill, Derek Gordon. And there was Mister Charles Greer's. Several doors were ajar, the shelves inside piled neatly with white surgical trousers and short-sleeved shirts. He took a set from the LARGE pile and changed.

Donal was in there past double doors at the far end of this room. O'Reilly gnawed the inside of his cheek and recalled that the outcome for patients with Donal's kind of intracranial bleeding was dependent on how soon the pressure could be released. Mister Gupta could not have moved more quickly. There was still hope. There was.

He tightened the drawstring of his pants and selected a pair of white rubber boots. Knowing the man as he did, O'Reilly expected him to be here when he said he would be and sure enough Charlie Greer barged into the surgeons' changing room at the appointed time and went straight to his locker. "Fingal, you old fart. How the hell are you?"

"Good to see you, Charlie," O'Reilly said, and stood. "I just wish it was under different circumstances."

Charlie stripped off his overcoat and jacket as one and shoved them into his locker. "You worried about your patient?" He continued undressing.

"I am."

"You always were like that, O'Reilly," Charlie said. "Probably what makes you, by all reports, a damn good GP." He slipped into a theatre shirt. "Extradural haemorrhages can be tricky. No need to tell you that, but we'll do everything we can. You know that too."

"I do. I appreciate it." They'd be going into theatre soon and he didn't want Charlie to think that he, O'Reilly, was overly concerned. He'd noticed Charlie's pot belly. It was no longer flat and muscled the way O'Reilly had seen it in so many rugby changing rooms all those years ago. "I see you're putting on a bit, Charlie," O'Reilly said, and grinned.

Off came Charlie's shoes, and his trousers. "I'd say that was the pot—pun definitely intended—calling the kettle black." Charlie laughed.

"My housekeeper, Mrs. Kincaid, agrees. She keeps feeding me salads."

"How is old Kinky? I haven't seen her for months." Charlie tied his waist drawstring.

"And that, Charlie Greer, has not been for want of a standing invitation to visit. Particularly after what you offered to do for Barry last August."

Charlie shrugged. "The young man wasn't at fault. Of course

I'd have testified on his behalf. Damn it all, I did the surgery on your Major Fotheringham."

"Your offer was appreciated."

"Fine, now, come on. It's time to go and see what Gupta's up to."

As Charlie scrubbed and discussed the case with the gloved and gowned Gupta, a nurse stood nearby. She was the quaintly titled "dirty nurse." That meant she was there to attend to nonsterile tasks like fetching bottles of blood or mopping a sweating surgeon's brow.

The senior registrar briefed the consultant. O'Reilly thought they might as well have been chatting about laying courses of bricks, but on the table, beneath green sheets, lay Donal Donnelly.

"I did the burr hole," Gupta said. "He's still bleeding from it so at least the pressure's not building inside the skull."

O'Reilly could see Donal's head. His ginger hair had been shaved on one side and a small incision made in the scalp. A trickle of blood ran onto the towel, which appeared damply black under the brilliant overhead lights. The stain was slowly spreading.

"I'm sure the middle meningeal artery has gone," the senior registrar said, "that's why we're set up for a craniotomy, sir, and we have the patient anaesthetised for you."

"Two pints of blood cross-matched and ready, Charlie," the anaesthetist said from where he sat at the head of the table. His back was turned, but O'Reilly recognised the voice. The doctor was flanked by his Boyle's anaesthetic machine with its colour-coded cylinders of oxygen, cyclopropane, and nitrous oxide. Changed days, O'Reilly thought, since patients had been put under by chloroform dripped on gauze and held in place by a Schimmelbusch mask, a contrivance of metal bars that looked like something used in the old Bedlam lunatic asylum to muzzle dangerous inmates.

Tubing ran from the vapouriser on the machine to the breathing circuit where a concertina-like bellows inside a glass cylinder moved up and down feeding oxygen and the soporific gas mixture through a pair of black corrugated rubber tubes to a thinner tube in Donal's trachea. The whole apparatus was breathing for Donal while keeping him insensitive to pain.

"Fingal, if you stand beside Maurice, you'll be able to see better," Charlie said.

O'Reilly moved to the head of the table. No wonder he had recognised the voice. Doctor Maurice Brown, like O'Reilly, had served in the navy in the Mediterranean. Maurice's ship had been torpedoed, but he had survived. The man spun on his stainless-steel stool and said, "Fingal O'Reilly." He held out his hand. "How are things in County Down these days?"

O'Reilly shook the offered hand. "Maurice. Good to see you. County Down? Pretty quiet. It usually is."

Doctor Brown nodded his head to the table. "One of yours?"

"Donal Donnelly. He had a motorbike accident in Downpatrick."

"How did you know?"

"We were both at the races. I was first on the spot. Beat the ambulance to it."

"And I suppose you came up here in the ambulance with him?" Doctor Brown's eyes smiled over his mask. "Haven't changed, Fingal, have you? I remember when my ship was in Alexandria harbour. I was visiting a colleague at the base hospital and you arrived with one of your charges, a chief petty officer with a ruptured amoebic liver abscess." He chuckled. "Some Woman's Royal Navy nursing sister told you he'd have to wait like everyone else. Hang on," Maurice read a gauge and adjusted a knurled wheel. "Can't have him going too deep," he said, then continued, "I wondered did they use you on *Warspite* if they ran out of ammunition? I'd never heard an explosion like it. You wouldn't leave until you'd seen the man admitted and a senior surgeon commander hauled out of the mess to treat your patient. Pretty gutsy for a lowly surgeon-lieutenant."

O'Reilly grinned. "I shouldn't have yelled at a Wren sister, but my patient was a damn sight sicker than some of the malingerers there and a dose of the clap's not life-threatening. A ruptured liver abscess is. She should have known better."

Charlie Greer was speaking. "Ordinarily, Rajat, I'd let you operate, and I'd assist. You're here to be trained after all, but you do understand?"

"Of course," the senior registrar said.

"Thanks, Charlie," O'Reilly said quietly, "and thank you too, Mister Gupta. I remember how eager I was to do things when I was young."

"There'll be plenty more," Gupta said. "I've another year to go and Mister Greer's very generous in letting us trainees operate."

He would be, O'Reilly thought. Charlie Greer had always been a generous man when it came to letting others have opportunities to learn new techniques.

"Right, let's do it," Charlie said.

O'Reilly watched as his friend made an incision shaped like a reversed question mark in the skin in front of Donal's ear. He turned the skin flaps back to expose a muscle, which he incised. Gupta lifted a set of forceps with curved pieces at the end of each limb, which, when inserted, slipped under the muscle. He squeezed the handles and the limbs parted widely, pulling the severed edges of the muscle apart to expose a blood clot.

He swabbed the superficial clot away to reveal the bone beneath.

"That's a good burr hole, Rajat," Charlie said. "Right where it should be. Suction, please." He held out his left hand and the sister slapped a suction catheter into the palm. He slipped the soft tip of the tube through the hole in the skull.

The rhythmic sound of the anaesthetist's bellows now had to compete with a gurgling. O'Reilly could see dark blood from inside Donal's skull flowing through the plastic tube.

"Better an empty house," said Charlie as the blood flowed, "than a bad tenant."

Surgeons were adept at black humour. It was the nature of their calling. It took a special breed, O'Reilly recognised, to slice into a fellow human being. And in brain surgery, a mistake, a momentary lapse of concentration, could lead to permanent brain damage or death, and Charlie had already operated for seven hours today.

"See, Fingal?" He pointed to a dark line running along the white parietal bone. "That's the fracture and Rajat put the burr hole spot-on beside its edge. Bone nibblers please, Sister."

She handed him an instrument that looked like pliers but with sharp-edged circular steel cups inside the tips of the blades. "Gotta make room to get at the artery," Charlie said, and began to work.

O'Reilly heard the steady *crunch, crunch* as the blades of the nibblers bit out chunks of skull. Finally Charlie said, "There it is."

O'Reilly peered into the hole. A few feet before his eyes lay the membranes surrounding Donal Donnelly's brain, three pounds of tissue the consistency of porridge. It was the organ that made Donal who he was, moved his muscles, controlled his breathing, his heart rate, dreamed up his crooked schemes, and held his hopes and his fears, his love for Julie MacAteer and their unborn child. If, and O'Reilly's personal jury was out on the subject, if human beings truly did have a soul, it was here in the brain that it must reside.

He hoped with all his might that bruised and squashed as Donal's brain might be, it had suffered no irreparable damage. "You come back to us, Donal," he whispered, "that's an order." As if

Donal could hear or obey, but O'Reilly had felt deeply the need to offer up what in an earlier generation would have been a prayer of supplication.

He noticed how the shiny dura mater at the bottom of the wound was crisscrossed by dark pulsating blood vessels. Little gouts of blood spurted from one of the arteries.

"Suture." Charlie took a needle driver loaded with a curved needle, passed it under the bleeding point, and expertly knotted a stitch. The bleeding stopped as if a tap had been turned off. There was oozing from veins, but the real threat to Donal had been dealt with. Charlie placed a second stitch. "Our old friend Cromie, the sailor, would call that second stitch an arrester backstay. For the less nautically inclined, I prefer the expression belt and braces, but I don't want any chance that a stitch could slip without a backup in place." He handed the needle driver back to Sister. "Now," he said, "no sign of any other arterial bleeding, so we can conclude that the posterior branch of the artery is intact. All we have to do is stop that venous oozing. A bit of fibrin foam'll do the trick. Thanks, Sister." He used forceps to pack the blood-clotting sponge in place. "I think," he said, "it'll be safer to drain." Sister handed him a length of soft rubber tubing, which he laid on top of the dura. "That comes out in twenty-four hours," he said. He straightened. "Rajat, I'm banjaxed after today's surgery. Would you close?"

O'Reilly knew that it was customary for a senior surgeon to delegate the routine work of closing an incision. There were no doubts that Gupta would do a fine job.

"Come on, Fingal," Charlie said, stepping back from the table and pulling off his rubber gloves. "Thank you, Sister. Nurse. Well done, Rajat. See you tomorrow, Maurice. We've a meningioma to do at nine, or rather Rajat has. The intracranial pressure's going up. We can wait until tomorrow, but not until Monday. I'll assist."

O'Reilly was vaguely aware of the replies. He took one last look at Gupta working steadily away and at the object of his attention, Donal Donnelly. Good luck to you, Donal, O'Reilly thought. I'll see you when you get back to the ward.

"Come on, O'Reilly," said Charlie, turning his back so the dirty nurse could untie the strings of his gown. "Let's get changed. I'm sure you want to get home."

"I do," said O'Reilly, "eventually. But tonight I'd like to stay at the hospital. Barry had to drive my car home from Downpatrick and the last train'll have gone—"

"Good excuses. You'd fill your knickers if you believed for one moment that I thought you might want to stay because you're worried about Donnelly. Come on, Fingal, how long have we been friends?"

"Thirty-four years," O'Reilly said, "give or take."

Charlie grinned. "It wouldn't be the first time I've told you giving a damn for your patients is not a sign of weakness as long as you don't let it take control. If it's important to you and you want to stay here let me make a call before I go up to the ward. I want to take a look at this morning's case before I go home."

Ten minutes later, O'Reilly was sitting on a single, iron-framed bed. The room was spartan. Painted plasterboard walls, cheap bedside table, plywood wardrobe in one corner, an armchair and a sink with exposed pipes on one wall. Lighting was provided by a single sixty-watt bulb.

The rooms, housed in a small one-storey wooden building at the back of the hospital, were used by students or housemen. They were known as "the Huts" or, because they were situated between the tennis courts and the morgue, "Mortuary Mansions." Ordinarily O'Reilly would have found that funny, but tonight the morgue was a very tangible reminder that "Man that is born of woman hath but a short time to live." Still, Charlie had been adamant that Donal's prognosis was good because of the rapidity with which Mister Gupta had reacted.

O'Reilly moved to the tattered armchair and lit his pipe. He hoped Charlie was right about Donal. He certainly was about something else. You could get too involved with patients. It had happened to him, and with the first patient for whom he'd become responsible. Certainly there had been plenty of forgettable customers over the years, but the young man with the initials KD and the valvular congestive heart failure was indelibly marked on O'Reilly's memory.

9

There Shall Be Weeping and Gnashing of Teeth

"That's the last teaching patient for today," said Doctor Micks as the entourage left the final bed. "You've seen a valvular congestive heart failure, a recent heart attack, an epilepsy, tuberculosis, and a diabetes. A good sampling of what our work entails in general medicine."

Fingal recognised it was usual for doctors to refer to their work impersonally as cases, but now he'd got over his initial reaction to the young nurse with the beautiful grey eyes, he remembered the fear in the eyes of the first patient, Mister KD. He was a man, a scared human being with heart failure. "If you cut him, did he not bleed?" Fingal wondered if the man was single, married, had kiddies depending on him? Had he played Gaelic football before the bacteria had crippled him? Did he have a job or was he like the many unemployed men from the tenements consigned to hang out on street corners, grateful for the few shillings their working wives might allow them for a pint or two of porter. Come on, Fingal, he told himself, you shouldn't be getting too involved and you should be listening to Doctor Micks.

Doctor Micks continued, "This afternoon, four of you will be at outpatients, or any other classes you're scheduled to attend, and two will be working on the wards. Doctor Pilkington here will explain your duties as clerks before you leave this morning." He strode off, pursued by the ward sister, the staff nurse, and, to Fingal's disappointment, the student nurses.

"This is the first time for all of you at Sir Patrick's?" Doctor Pilkington asked.

"I think so, sir," Fingal said. Four years of maritime discipline, and Pilkington's thick head of grey hair, had led Fingal to mark the man's superior rank.

The doctor laughed as he took off a pair of tortoiseshell spectacles and pinched the bridge of his nose. "First of all I'm not 'sir.' I qualified this June. I'm only two years ahead of you. I want to be a specialist so I took this job as resident house physician. As a courtesy in front of patients, please call me Doctor, but otherwise I'm Geoff." He replaced his glasses.

"Right, Geoff," Fingal said, and saw the others nodding. One point to Geoff Pilkington. O'Reilly knew too many people who were overly conscious of their titles.

"As regards your work on the wards," Geoff said, "you will take the history from all admissions and examine them. You'll be expected to make a provisional diagnosis, or at least give a reasonable list of potential illnesses, what is called a differential diagnosis." Fingal was paying close attention until he noticed the grey-eyed nurse walk onto the ward carrying a basin. Even under her ankle-length dress that young lady had a delicious sway to her hips.

"You'll suggest any necessary tests or procedures and recommended treatment. Then you'll check with me or one of the consultants to see how accurate you've been. If procedures need to be done, like setting up an intravenous drip or taking blood samples, you'll learn how, and—"

"Who gets to see the first patient?" Fitzpatrick demanded.

Geoff Pilkington laughed. "You'll all get your fill, and more, of doing routine admissions. There are six of you so I suggest you team up in pairs."

Fingal and Charlie had already paired off, as had Bob and Cromie, just as they'd planned it in Davey Byrnes pub on that spring day in March.

"A different couple every day will come to the ward first thing in the morning to take any bloods and then to see admissions, day or night. All six will attend rounds in the morning. The rest attend outpatients or classes until it's your turn here. Off you go. Get your lunch and I want the first pair back here by one."

"That's us, Hilda," Fitzpatrick announced. He lowered his head and peered down over his pince-nez at her. "I don't mind working with a woman."

Hilda pulled herself up to her full five foot two and looked up at Fitzpatrick's six-foot frame. "Decent of you, Fitzpatrick," she said.

Fingal saw her roll her eyes. "Do you think a woman will mind working with Fitzpatrick?" he said to Charlie. "That's more like the question to me."

Hilda's smile was gratifying.

Damn you, Fitzpatrick, Fingal thought. I wanted to get back here this afternoon. I would have had a good chance to have a word with Grey Eyes. Now it'll probably have to wait until Thursday. He and Charlie were scheduled to receive instruction in the techniques of vaccination tomorrow afternoon. Each would pay a tuition fee of one pound one shilling, an archaic sum known as a guinea. Pity, Fingal thought. That much money would have bought twenty-five pints of Guinness. Still, it was in the good cause of increasing his skills. "Come on, lads," he said, "lunch," and headed for the door.

Before he could open it, the student nurse returned, now carrying two rubber basins. One was empty, but in the other several sets of dentures drifted in clear water like pink-and-white jelly-fish in a calm sea. He looked round. No sign of Sister. "Excuse me, Nurse," he said. "Excuse me."

She stopped. "Yes?"

"It's a silly question, but what are you doing with those teeth?"

She laughed, a throaty chuckle. "Paying for my sins." Her nose was a little too large, her lips a mite full. Her hair could be any colour, hidden as it was under her headdress.

"Sins?"

"You coming, Fingal?" Cromie called.

"In a minute. You three go on." He asked, "Sins?"

"Yes," she said, "and when I tell you, you're not to laugh."

"I promise."

"Before ward rounds, Sister sent me to wash some of the men's false teeth."

"I noticed quite a few gummy old boys."

"Fourteen," she said, "and I've thirteen to go."

"But there's more than one set in that bowl."

She laughed again and he knew, he just knew she was laughing at herself, a trait he admired. "That was my sin. I didn't think," she said.

Fingal looked again at the basin full of dentures and realised what had happened. He grinned.

"You promised," she said, and her eyes flashed.

"Sorry."

"I collected them all up at once to wash them. I thought it would be faster. It would have been if these things were inter-changeable, but of course they're not. Now I have to go to each man in turn and have him try every bloody set of dentures until he finds his. I put the dirty ones in this empty bowl and go back to the sink and rewash them. It'll get progressively easier as I get the right teeth matched up to the right patient, but it's still going to take all my lunch break."

"No it's not," said O'Reilly. "Not if you'll let me help you."

"Sister would kill me. We're not supposed to mix with medical students."

"Where is Sister?"

"At lunch."

"Och," said O'Reilly, "what the eye doesn't see the heart doesn't grieve over. Go on," he said, "try the next old boy and when you come back to the sink I'll wash with you."

She gave him a grateful look. "Thanks."

He turned into a room known as the sluice. In it was a device for flushing and washing bedpans, a steam autoclave for sterilizing instruments. It hissed and fizzled. Two stainless steel sinks had taps equipped with long handles that ended in flat expansions so they could be, if necessary, manipulated without using the hands. There was a distinct odour of faeces that a powerfully smelling disinfectant was trying to strangle.

Fingal took off his jacket and was rolling up his sleeves as she reappeared with a smile on her face. "I was lucky that time. Mr. Shaughnessy, a postop hernia, only needed to try three sets before he found his own." She handed him four pink, teeth-bearing dental plates. "Can you wash these?"

Fingal filled one sink. "Pop 'em in." He scrubbed. "Now, Nurse," he said, "I'm not much for formal introductions. I'm Fingal Flahertie O'Reilly."

"And by your voice I'd say you're from the Wee North."

"Holywood originally, but I've lived in Dublin since I was fourteen." He put the clean dentures in the bowl with water and the others.

"I'll be back," she said.

Fingal had trouble containing his impatience until she returned.

"Seven sets to do this time."

"Right." He scrubbed and waited until he could wait no longer. "You have me at a disadvantage, Nurse. You know my name—"

"And you want to know mine?"

And a damn sight more about you, he thought.

"Caitlin O'Hallorhan. My friends call me Kitty. I'm a first-year nursing student. My home is in Tallaght, South Dublin—"

"Tallaght means 'plague grave,' " O'Reilly said.

"Why yes, it does." She smiled. "The place is still a midden. I'm not sorry to be living in the Nurses' Home. They do let us out now and then and Dublin's quite the city."

"It is that. Here." He handed her the newly washed dentures. "Off you go."

Kitty. Kitty O'Hallorhan. That name had a ring to it, she could laugh at herself, and, those eyes. Fingal O'Reilly smiled. When she came back he was going to ask her for a date. He sang the old Irish air in a tuneful baritone,

> Kitty, me love will you marry me?
> Kitty, me love will you go?

"I heard that," she said. "You've a fine voice, Mister O'Reilly— and a quare brass neck. Marry a big lig like you?" She chuckled. "Not in a month of Sundays."

"Well," said O'Reilly, quite unabashed, "maybe it is a bit quick for a proposal—"

"Wash these," she said, handing him three sets.

He bent to his task. "But I could take you to the Savoy on Saturday night. *I Was a Spy* is on. Conrad Veidt and Madeleine Carroll."

"You're not a shy one, are you?" she asked.

"But he'd better start being one on my ward, Nurse O'Hallorhan."

Fingal looked round to see Sister Daly, brows knit, fists on hips. Her gaze was steely.

"I'll not have any hanky-panky on Saint Patrick's Ward—my ward. Is that clear?"

"Yes, Sister," they both said in unison.

"Good. Now get about your business, Mister O'Reilly, and leave Nurse to hers."

"Yes, Sister," Fingal said. Doctor Micks might be a consultant here, but the ruler of Saint Patrick's Ward was Sister Daly. It was not a good idea to have rubbed her up the wrong way on his first day, and it was his fault that Kitty looked as if she was in for it. One of the things Father had always insisted on was, "If you make a mess, you clear it up."

"Sister, I think you should know that this is all my fault. I thought Nurse O'Hallorhan was going to miss her lunch and so I offered to help her wash the dentures. She didn't approach me."

"Is that true, Nurse?"

Kitty nodded.

"And she'd no notion I was going to ask her out."

"I see." Sister Daly pursed her lips. "In that case, Nurse, I'll consider the matter closed. Get on with your duty."

"Thank you, Sister." Kitty started scrubbing with the focused concentration of a watchmaker.

"And you." She pointed a finger. "You can't sit for your finals without a certificate of good standing from Doctor Micks, so. Do not in the next six months give me any cause to have a word in his ear, bye. Am I clear?"

"Yes, Sister Daly. Perfectly. I'll be going." Fingal turned and left, not daring to take a backwards glance at Kitty. He could feel Sister Daly's eyes on him.

He knew where the lads would be eating and decided he had time for a quick bite. Damn Sister catching him like that. He was bloody sure if he'd been given another few minutes with Nurse O'Hallorhan she'd have accepted his invitation. Och well, at least he knew her name. He'd find a way to have another go. And, he reminded himself, it was all very well paying attention to pretty nurses. The real reason he was here was to learn about patients like the anonymous Mister KD.

And as for Sister Daly? He'd be at pains to tiptoe round her and mind his p's and q's. Because nothing, nothing was going to stop him sitting, and passing, his finals on time.

10

For This Relief Much Thanks

"Me?" Fingal spun on his heel. "Christ Almighty, I'm only a fourth-year student."

Nurse O'Hallorhan stood at the door to the ward. "Sister Daly says to come immediately. We've sent for Doctor Pilkington, but he's gone to lunch. The patient with valvular heart failure fainted. He looks awful." Fingal heard the tremor in her voice. "Sister wants to see if there's anything you can do until Doctor Pilkington gets back."

"What I can do?" Jesus. Fingal trotted to the ward, trying to remember what he'd learned about rheumatic heart disease. Mister KD had passed out. Not enough oxygen was getting to his brain because for some reason even less blood was being pumped by the damaged heart. Why? Why?

Fingal raced down the ward, pulling out his stethoscope. Perhaps atrial fibrillation had started. It was common in patients who had had rheumatic fever. The heart's electrical control system broke down and the muscles in the atria, the upper chambers of the heart that collected blood from the body and lungs, started working asynchronously. That meant each individual muscle fibre would contract as often as four hundred times per minute instead of the whole chamber at a rate of eighty beats per minute. That electrical chaos stimulated the ventricles irregularly and their ability to pump blood suffered.

Screens had been closed round the bed. He pulled one aside. Sister stood at the bedside. The oxygen tent was unzipped. She was taking Mister KD's pulse and looking at her watch.

Fingal saw how much more dusky the man's face had become. His lips were blue. His breathing was shallow and irregular. The great strap muscles of his neck stood rigidly every time he struggled to inhale through flared nostrils. He did not respond when Fingal spoke to him.

"He's fibrillating," Sister said.

"Thank you, Sister," O'Reilly said. "Can I listen to his chest?"

She opened the man's pyjamas. Fingal clapped his stethoscope over the heart and tried to count the beats, but the great muscle was wildly out of control, contracting rapidly, irregularly, and with hardly any ability to circulate blood to the lungs and brain. He could hear no air going into the lung bases, and higher up the chest there was clear evidence of fluid. Sister was right. The fibrillation and failure were going to kill the man if they couldn't be reversed. And quickly. Clearly the dose of digitalis was not enough. Should he be given more? Fingal remembered Doctor Micks's measured tones. "If any symptoms of overdosage are produced, sudden death is a possibility as the late stages of digitalis poisoning may be passed through very rapidly."

"How much digitalis has he had, Sister?" Fingal heard the uncertainty in his tone.

She lifted the chart. As she did, Fingal noticed that Nurse O'Hallorhan had come behind the screens. Her eyes were wide and a hand covered her mouth. If he was worried, she, as a first-year nurse, must be terrified.

"A total of twelve ccs since he was admitted last night." Sister's voice was calm.

"And it takes a whole day to get rid of about one cc, so he'll not have metabolised much," he said.

Sister nodded.

Fingal took a deep breath and looked at the man battling to breathe, listened to his wheezing gasps and the hissing of the oxygen. His eyes were open, pleading.

Standing here doing nothing, hoping to hell Geoff Pilkington would materialise, wasn't going to help Mister KD, but giving him more digitalis might kill him. Fingal exhaled and remembered one of Father's adages, "Never be ashamed to ask advice from an expert." "Sister Daly," he said, lowering his voice so the patient couldn't hear, "I'm very green. You must have seen hundreds of cases. Do you think more digitalis would kill him?"

"Mister O'Reilly, I don't know. You can never be sure—"

You're going to have to decide, Fingal. He could feel his own pulse hammering.

"—but, I think for a case like this, Doctor Micks would use quinidine sulphate, particularly as this patient has had digitalis already. He'd start with two grains to see how the patient tolerated the medicine."

He could have kissed her. "Could you not have given it yourself?" he asked.

"Only doctors and senior students under supervision can order medicines."

Fingal snorted. "That's ridiculous. With all your experience?"

She smiled and said, "Och, sure don't we know it does be ridiculous—but it's the rules, so."

"Can I prescribe it?"

"Only under supervision." She looked him directly in the eye.

"Bugger. We can't wait. Time matters. If I'm right, Doctor Pilkington will confirm it—when he gets here." And if I'm wrong, what the hell will Doctor Micks do? he wondered. "The sooner we get started—rules be damned—the better. Get some quinidine. You said two grains?"

"Come with me, Nurse O'Hallorhan," Sister said. "You can watch me prepare a quinidine solution."

The nurse looked at Fingal and whispered, "Good luck," before she left.

He turned back to Mister KD. To hell with rules and to hell with initials. Fingal picked up the chart and read "Kevin Doherty." The poor man did have a name; he wasn't merely a case of valvular disease complicated by fibrillation. O'Reilly sat on the bed and took a clammy hand in his own. "It's all right, Kevin," he said softly. "It's all right. We'll get you fixed," even though Fingal was not one bit sure they would.

Kevin Doherty managed to nod. He squeezed Fingal's hand. When Sister and Nurse O'Hallorhan reappeared, the student nurse held out a small glass of milky-coloured liquid.

Fingal took it. "Kevin," he said, "I want you to swallow this. I'll help you." He held Doherty by the shoulders, feeling the rise and fall of the man's chest. "Open wide." It was like talking to a child. "Wide." As soon as Doherty had opened his mouth, Fingal held the glass to the man's lips. He gulped, swallowed, and slumped back against Fingal's arm.

He lowered the patient to his pillows and took his hand again. A feeble grip was returned.

"Was that digitalis or quinidine?" Doctor Pilkington asked.

Fingal had not noticed his arrival on the opposite side of the bed.

Pilkington, without waiting for an answer, took Doherty's pulse. "Atrial fib. All right." He released the man's wrist. "Taking the pulse is all you need to make the diagnosis. Sorry, I asked you—"

"Quinidine."

"I'll confirm that order," he said to Sister. "Well done."

So it would not need to be reported that Fingal had acted without authority. "I can't take credit for the prescription. I asked Sister what she would suggest and she thought quinidine would be best," he said.

"And she's rarely wrong." Fingal heard the respect in the young doctor's voice. "It's a braver man than me who'll ignore the advice of a nursing sister and a fool who doesn't recognise that early."

"I believe," Sister Daly said quietly, "Mister O'Reilly is no *amadán*, so." She smiled at Fingal, who was relieved to learn that the ward sister believed he wasn't an idiot.

"Although his language could use some attention," she said.

Fingal remembered his intemperate "bugger" and "be damned."
"Sorry, Sister."

"Och," she said, "it is not unusual for a body to forget his manners when he's under the gun. It's more important he not lose his wits, and panic, so." She glanced at Nurse O'Hallorhan. "Perhaps it's not such a bad thing Mister O'Reilly was delayed going to his lunch."

Fingal swallowed. It sounded to him that Sister Daly was offering her forgiveness. "Thank you, Sister," he said. He noticed Geoff Pilkington inclining his head to one side and moving off, a signal he wanted to talk away from the patient. Fingal tried to remove his hand, but the grip tightened. He bent. "It's all right, Kevin. I'll be back in a minute." He looked at Sister. "He's scared skinny. Could maybe you or the nurse stay with him until I get back?"

"Nurse," was all Sister needed to say for Nurse O'Hallorhan to take the patient's other hand.

Sister turned to leave. "I have to deal with other matters. Please don't keep my nurse too long." She smiled and said quietly, "You did well."

Fingal inclined his head. He took a last glance at the patient, who was still struggling for every breath, then joined Geoff. "Yes, Geoff?"

Geoff's face was solemn, and he spoke quietly. "I'll not beat about the bush, O'Reilly. Have you had a patient of yours die yet?"

"No." Fingal shook his head then looked the houseman right in the eye. "But I did see two men who'd gone swimming taken by sharks when we were at anchor in the Red Sea while I was officer of the deck."

"Good Lord."

"Not pretty." Fingal could remember the screams, the blood in the water, his attempts to lower a boat. His self-recrimination that if only he'd got the boat away more quickly. He'd had nightmares for weeks.

"It never is. Look here, I heard you call the man 'Kevin.' "

Fingal narrowed his eyes and kept his counsel.

"I'm not recommending callousness, but patients do die."

"Will Kevin Doherty?"

"We all will."

"Jesus, Geoff, don't patronise me. I'm older than you, for Christ's sake." Fingal felt his nose tip start to blanch.

"All right. Calm down. It's going to take three hours for the quinidine to work fully. It might kick in earlier, but his ticker could pack up at any time before the medicine takes effect—or after for that matter."

"I see." Fingal looked back to where Nurse O'Hallorhan stood by the bedside. She was needed elsewhere. "Are family allowed in?"

"Sorry, no family allowed, and before you ask, I don't think things are bad enough to send for a priest—yet."

"But he shouldn't be left alone," Fingal said. "May I sit with him?"

"You should be getting your lunch then going to outpatients.

I'll ask one of your group who'll be on the ward this afternoon to sit with him."

That would be Hilda Manwell or Ronald Fitzpatrick. Hilda would be sympathetic, but leaving Kevin Doherty in Fitzpatrick's care didn't bear thinking about. "I'll do without lunch," he said.

"All right, but Fingal?" There was sadness in the houseman's eyes. "Don't take it personally if he goes. We've done our best. We can't save them all."

"I understand, but we can offer a bit of comfort."

"Go ahead." Geoff cocked his head. "I think, O'Reilly," he said, "you're big enough and ugly enough to take care of yourself."

"Balls," said Fingal gruffly, and blushed. "Go on, Geoff, and finish your lunch. I'm not hungry." Liar, Fingal thought, I'm always hungry. He felt the houseman's hand lightly on his shoulder, before Geoff repeated, "Do not, I mean it, do not take it personally if we lose him."

"I won't," said Fingal. He nipped out past the screens and brought in the cane-backed chair. "Off you go, Nurse O'Hallorhan. Sister needs you."

Her smile before she left was beatific. For the moment he was distracted from his concern for Kevin. He had to get to know this nurse better. He zipped up the tent then sat alone holding the hand of a very sick man.

Fingal lost track of time, only knew that he'd had to change hands twice because he'd got pins and needles, and his backside was growing numb. For most of the time Kevin Doherty was asleep or passed out, but every time Fingal took his pulse it was careering out of control. And there was less than the half of sweet bugger all Fingal could do about it. He felt futile. He wondered if Kevin Doherty even knew he was not alone.

The screens were pulled back and the tent unzipped. He looked up to see Caitlin O'Hallorhan. She carried a small tray bearing a cup of tea and a plate of buttered toast.

"I hardly think your man's ready for that," Fingal said, and smiled.

"Silly," she said. "Sister Daly reckoned a big fellah like you, your belly'd think your throat was cut. She sent me to make this in the ward kitchen."

"God bless you both," said Fingal. His stomach rumbled. "Pardon me," he said, but reached for a slice of toast.

"Sister says I can stay until you've finished." She sat on the bed and took Kevin's hand.

Teacup in one hand, toast in the other, he wolfed his snack listening to the rasping breathing, his gaze flitting from the face of the patient to the grey, amber-flecked eyes of Caitlin, Kitty to her friends, O'Hallorhan. He finished the tea, swallowed the last morsel of buttered toast, and said, "That was just what the sister ordered. Thanks, and thank her for me too, please."

The nurse rose and picked up the tray. "I know it's not the time or place," she said softly, "but I don't know if I'll get another chance to talk to you. I'm going to see my parents in Tallaght this weekend—"

Fingal turned to see her wide smile. The amber highlights sparkled.

"But I'll be off again in two weeks' time, on a Saturday, if you like."

"Jasus," said Fingal, wondering if he himself had suddenly experienced a bout of atrial fibrillation. "I'll be playing rugby at two thirty at the Wanderers' club on Parnell Road that day."

"I'll be off at noon. I'll come and watch. See you after the game." She slipped out and closed the tent.

Fingal's grin was from ear to ear when he turned back to Kevin and discovered that the man was staring at him. His breathing was less laboured. He had a glimmering of a smile on his face.

Fingal grabbed for his pulse. It was regular. He clipped in the earpieces. "Just going to listen."

Lup-dup. Lup-dup. The assorted clicks and whooshes were still there, but the beat was regular. Fingal concentrated and was convinced he could identify the classic snaps and murmurs that Fitzpatrick had described. More important than Fingal's having learnt something, the quinidine had worked in jig time. Kevin Doherty's wounded heart was beating more strongly. He looked at the man in the bed. "I think, Kevin," he said, "you're on the mend."

"T'ank you, Doctor, sir—"

"I'm only a student."

"Well you should be a doctor, or maybe get yourself made a feckin' saint. Sitting dere for ages."

Fingal frowned. "It's my job, that's all—"

"Bollix, Doc, wit' all due respect. I'll never forget w'at youse did for me. Your bum must be as numb as a feckin' plum."

Fingal blushed.

"And I've been awake for the last ten minutes. Dat wee mott in the uniform? She's a corker. Youse two have a good time, all right?"

He felt his face flush again; it must surely be the colour of beetroot. "I'm sure we will, Kevin. I'm sure we will."

As Fingal Flahertie O'Reilly rose to leave, he made himself a promise. He resolved that when he was in his own practice, he'd never think of patients or refer to them by their initials or as cases of whatever ailed them. And from now on, here at Sir Patrick Dun's Hospital, by God, he'd get to know his patients' names.

The iron bedsprings squeaked as O'Reilly rolled on his side. He sat up. He was glad he wasn't a houseman who had to make this cubicle in the Huts his home for twelve months. He rubbed the back he'd ricked on his way to a recent delivery of twins. Of course, housemen would have the advantage of youth. Perhaps it might be more comfortable in the chair?

He limped over to the armchair. A French epigram ran through his mind, *"Plus ça change, plus c'est la même chose."* The more things change, the more they stay the same. He'd never forget the day he'd stopped calling Mister KD by his initials. It was the day he'd started thinking of all his patients by their names. Imagine thinking of Donal Donnelly, arch schemer, dog racer, carpenter, husband, and soon-to-be father as DD? O'Reilly felt a familar tug of worry at the thought of Donal. How long would it be until he regained consciousness? Would he recover? O'Reilly's mind gnawed at the thought. Time would tell, but perhaps Geoff Pilkington had been right all those years ago. Better to stay detached.

And if he had been earlier tonight, he'd be in his own bed in Ballybucklebo. Donal, who had appeared perfectly lucid once he regained consciousness near Downpatrick, would have tried to ride the motorcycle home—and could well be lying in a ditch, far from expert help, under the bike that he'd crashed for a second time because he had continued to bleed into his head.

That decision, one he had never regretted, to treat patients as people not as ciphers, had been another crossroads for O'Reilly, no less important than the one back in '27 when he'd defied Father and refused to study nuclear physics.

Perhaps once he'd come back to live in Dublin, Fingal should have made a greater effort to heal the rift with Father. But only a saint—and he smiled at the thought because Ireland was said to be the Land of Saints and Scholars—only a saint could have withstood the scorn his father had regularly heaped upon his son's chosen profession. Father was a scholar all right, and his son was no saint. He had deeply resented how his entry to Trinity had been held up for four years by Father's pigheadedness. In 1801, when Vice-Admiral Horatio Nelson, he who adorned a column in the middle of Dublin's O'Connell Street, had fought the Battle of Copenhagen, the Danes had been described as being in "a state of armed neutrality." That pretty much summed up how things had been with Fingal and his father since 1931 and still were in October 1934.

11

Nazi Germany Had Become a Menace

"So, what do you think?" Lars pulled into the gravelled drive of their parents' house and sat back in the seat of his Morris Cowley. "It's secondhand, but the body's in excellent condition. Great engine too: 1548cc, side valve, straight four—"

"You know I'm not altogether wild, brother, about internal combustion. I still think fondly of Doctor O'Malley's pony and trap."

"Luddite," said Lars with a laugh. "One day you'll get your own car. Then you'll see."

"I think, Lars O'Reilly, you prefer cars to women."

"I do not," Lars said.

The two men ambled companionably toward the worn stone steps. The Virginia creeper had turned to its autumnal reds.

Whenever Fingal went to see Ma, he would skate tactfully round Father. Having Lars here would make things less strained.

They'd been close as nippers and had stuck together at boarding school, O'Reilly Major and O'Reilly Minor, as they had been known in an establishment where the use of Christian names was forbidden. One set of four brothers were collectively the Sintons: Maximus, Major, Minor, and Minimus. At a school where small boys were bullied, Lars had been a protective older brother until

Fingal had grown and discovered his vicious left hook. He felt he could never repay Lars for his support then, nor for his help back in '27 when he'd suggested Fingal go to sea. They hadn't seen as much of each other since, but they certainly kept in touch.

"So, if it wasn't you wanting to show me your new car that brought you down here, you must be in Dublin because you're taking Jean out tonight," Fingal said.

"I am." Lars smiled. "I'd never have thought two years ago when she was hosting the Irish Law Society dinner party for her father Judge Neely she'd even speak to me, never mind agree to go out with me."

"Your Law Society's like my Rugby Union, isn't it?" Fingal said. "Formed before the two Irelands split and happy enough to stay together since partition because the game is still the game and law is still the law."

"It is," Lars agreed with a grin. "Like Jean and me, still together, even though I have to roar up and down from Portaferry to go on seeing her."

"And I thought you did all that travelling just to give you an excuse to keep buying new motorcars like this one." Fingal laughed. "How many ccs?"

"Goat," Lars said, and threw a mock punch at his brother's head.

Fingal dodged it easily and said, "How is Jean, anyway?"

Lars blushed, but grinned. "Wonderful. I'm taking her to the Clarence tonight."

"The Clarence? On Wellington Quay? That place has been there since 1852." Fingal whistled. "It's not cheap." He looked right at Lars. "Getting serious about her?"

"Yes. Yes I am."

"Going to propose?"

Lars stopped. His blush deepened. "Why do you ask?"

"I believe it's what's usually done if a young man is sufficiently—" He hesitated over the words "in love with" and said, "fond of a young woman."

"I—that is—"

"Come on, Lars," Fingal said, "it's me, remember?"

Lars laughed. "Oh, damn it all, Finn—you know how embarrassed I get. You're right, of course, but it's been tricky carrying out a romance at long distance. I'd like to get married, but—I get so bloody tongue-tied around women. Most women. Jean's different."

Fingal clapped his brother on the shoulder. "Don't worry. You'll do fine if it's meant to be and when the time's right. I'm glad you've found someone who suits you so well, Lars. You deserve happiness."

"Thanks, Finn." Lars started up the steps and Fingal followed, wondering when the time and place might be right for him.

Lars stopped. "How's your love life?"

Fingal laughed. "Oh, well, I love 'em and leave 'em. You know us sailors. And getting qualified's a damn sight more important."

"Footloose and fancy free?"

"Something like that. I'm seeing a student nurse, after the game today. She's got amazing eyes."

Lars smiled and started to climb. "Careful you don't get hooked."

"Me? Not likely. I've exams to pass, profs to impress, poor and unsuspecting patients upon whom to inflict my stumbling efforts as a student doctor, and a big brother to tease about his swanky motorcars—" Fingal rang the bell as Lars took another playful swing.

Fingal grappled with Lars, his laughter drowning out his brother's protests.

Bridgit opened the door. "Dear God," she said. "Have youse two taken leave of your senses? Mister O'Reilly, Master Fingal. I—"

"It's all right, Bridgit," Lars said, disentangling himself and stepping into the foyer. "The folks in the drawing room?"

She nodded. "You two," she said, wagging a finger. "Youse was always acting the lig when youse was weans. It takes me back a wheen of years seeing grown men acting the eejit, so it does."

"I promise we'll behave," Lars said with a grin. "Now, please tell Cook there's one more for lunch. I'm expected, but this one isn't," he said, pointing to Fingal.

Bridgit giggled, nodded, bobbed, and withdrew.

Together they went into the big familiar room. "Father. Mother," Lars said. "See who I've brought."

They were sitting in armchairs that flanked a fireplace where a coal fire glowed. Ma was working on her embroidery. "Fingal, what a lovely surprise," she said, turning and smiling at them both, "and wicked of you, Lars, not warning us that you were bringing your brother. Now," she said, "pull over a couple of chairs."

"Boys," Father said, glancing up from papers that Fingal assumed he was correcting. A grey woollen cardigan, open-necked shirt, and flannel trousers replaced his usual three-piece suit. "Do as your mother asks."

Fingal brought over an easy chair and set it close to Ma. Lars pulled his closer to Father.

"No tutorial today, Father?" Lars asked.

"My assistant's taking it."

Unlike Father to delegate. Fingal was going to ask why but decided against.

"Fingal, you will be staying for lunch," Ma said.

"Indeed I will, Ma." Father fixed him with a steely gaze. "I mean Mother. Lars has asked Bridgit to tell Cook, but I'll have to go at one thirty. I've to walk to Parnell Road. Kickoff for the game is at two thirty."

"You'll take care, son, won't you?" Ma asked. He noticed her frown.

Fingal laughed. "I think it'll be Wanderers who're going to need your advice, M— Mother."

"I should have thought," Father said, "you'd have outgrown that schoolboy game by now."

Fingal shook his head. "I enjoy it."

"It's good exercise too, Father," Lars said. "You always taught, *mens sana in corpore sano.*"

A healthy mind in a healthy body, Fingal thought, and, hoping to change the subject, said, "I read in the *Independent* that the German army is now three hundred thousand strong."

Father sat forward. "That is three times," he wagged his finger, "three times the level allowed by the Versailles Treaty." He pursed his lips. "I'd hate to see another war."

"Surely," Lars said, "the League of Nations will prevent that."

Father shook his head. "I'm not so sure. Remember, Hitler withdrew Germany as a member last year because the League disapproved of his treatment of a Jew. He argued that Jews were not protected by the League's minority clause because Jews were not fully human."

"That," said Ma, "is reprehensible. Despicable. I do try not to dislike people, but that Herr Hitler—" She pursed her lips and frowned. "And his ministers, Herr Doktor Goebbels and Herr Goering, are no better."

Father said, "Those Nazis are a belligerent lot. I'm worried. I truly am."

"Still," Lars said, "even if the worst happens, you should be all right here. I can't see de Valera letting Southern Ireland be anything but neutral."

Ma frowned. "What about you, Lars? You live in the north. It's a part of the United Kingdom. Could you be conscripted?"

"I don't think so," he said. "After the sacrifice of the Ulstermen at the Battle of the Somme we were promised no conscription in Ulster—ever."

Fingal did not mention his own liabilty for involvement because of his naval commitments. He didn't want to worry Ma. Indeed on such a lovely autumn day with the whole family together he was regretting introducing the topic in the first place. He turned to Ma.

"Did you know," he said, "that I'm a fully qualified vaccinator now, with a certificate to prove it."

She smiled. "Good for you."

"I still think it's a waste," Father joined in. "You've a very agile mind, boy. Too swift for a country quack."

"A what?" Fingal's voice rose and he felt his fist clench, but he took a deep breath and said in as calm a voice as he could muster, "I think that agility may be because you spent so much time teaching Lars and me when we were little, Father."

"To produce what? A jolly jack tar who's going on to be a rustic sawbones when he could have—"

"Connan," Ma said, and Fingal heard the edge in her voice. "Fingal's made a special effort to visit. Lars is here. Don't spoil it."

"I am sorry, Mary," Father said. He sighed. "I suppose you're right, but—oh, never mind."

Bless you, Ma, Fingal thought.

The silence was broken by Bridgit's appearance. "Please ma'am, Cook says the Mulligitawny soup'll be ready in ten minutes. She knows Master Fingal's here so she put in extra potatoes and vegetables to go with the leg of lamb."

"Thank you, Bridgit, and please thank Cook." Ma set aside her embroidery as the maid left. Father rose. "I'd like to wash my hands," he said, and walked slowly to the door.

Mary O'Reilly watched her husband go, then turned to Fingal. "Thank you for holding your tongue. That took a great deal of self-control," she said. "You've changed. A year ago you'd have stormed out when Father called you a rustic sawbones."

Fingal gritted his teeth. "I think," he said, "what I'm seeing has changed me. The hospital's full of people with diseases none of our potions or our operations can cure. The patients suffer. Their families suffer. The average Dubliner puts up with it, makes the best of it, accepts things, even cracks jokes. It's humbling. Having an intransigent father as the worst of my troubles is not a killing matter," he said, but inside he wished that Father could bend, could try to understand.

She stood and touched his arm. "Thank you, son. I couldn't have stood another row."

Fingal sighed. "I just wish he'd let the hare sit, Ma. I'll be qualified in another twenty months. I'm not turning back now—for anyone. I wish Father could come to terms with it."

She stood and pecked his cheek. "He will, and I'm proud of you," she said, "very proud."

Fingal Flahertie O'Reilly blushed to the roots of his dark hair.

"So am I," Lars said. He rose and put his hands on Fingal's shoulder.

"Thank you, big brother," Fingal said, and smiled.

"Now," said Ma, "before lunch, Father and I have a little something for you, Fingal." From a nearby coffee table she picked up a small, gaily-wrapped parcel and an envelope. "You'll be twenty-six on Monday. We know you'll be working so won't expect you here, but many happy returns. Don't open them now," she said. "Pop them in your pocket."

"Thanks, Ma," he said, and wrapped her in a hug. "Thanks."

She disentangled herself and smiled at him.

"I imagine this might come in handy." Lars handed Fingal a plug of Crow Bar pipe tobacco. "Many happy returns," he said, "although why you insist on smoking this stuff is beyond me."

"I like the taste," Fingal said. And it's the best I can afford, he thought. "You're a sound man, Lars Porsena O'Reilly," Fingal said as he released Ma. "A sound man. Thank you."

Ma said, "It's wonderful having my boys together, but Cook gets a bit put out if we're late for meals."

"After you, madam," Fingal said, bowing and making a leg like an eighteenth-century courtier.

Ma laughed. "Fingal, behave yourself. You're going to be a doctor soon. It's time you started to develop a bit of *gravitas*."

Fingal's stomach rumbled. "Never mind *gravy*-tas," he said, "I'd rather get stuck into Cook's gravy."

Ma and Lars laughed. And Fingal thought, Cook's Mulligitawny soup was always a thing of beauty, and a leg of lamb? Just the job to fuel a rugby player for a big game.

Fingal's breath burned in his chest. The referee had blown his whistle for a scrum in Trinity's favour twenty-five yards out from their own goal line. There were two minutes left to play and the game was tied. Now sixteen forwards, one eight-man "pack" from each side, would vie to see which team could get possession of the ball and a chance to mount a game-winning attack.

Trinity's front row of three men was ready. As second-row forwards, Fingal and Charlie stood side by side behind the front row and put their near arms round each other's backs just beneath the armpit. Fingal could smell the sweat, feel his partner's muscles tense.

The two front rows locked their heads together forming a tunnel in the middle of the sixteen men, who from a distance looked like a many-legged turtle because of the way the supporting forwards held on to each other to form opposing human battering rams.

Fingal heard his man tossing the ball into the tunnel. "Coming in left, Trinity—now."

The Trinity pack drove their legs against the ground. But no matter how he and his teammates strove, Fingal, purple of face, muscles standing out in his neck, felt himself being driven back. "Ball's lost." That was his captain's voice, but Fingal also heard a stranger call "Bananas." That was code for some unusual play. He let go of Charlie. Immediately ahead, one of the Wanderers' players lay flat on the ground. He must have made a flying pass because now the whole of the Wanderers' back line was rushing forward in echelon in a standard attack. Fingal hesitated. He couldn't see who was carrying the ball.

He sensed a movement to his right. A Wanderer, ball under one arm, was running like a whippet towards the Trinity goal. Fingal took off. On the command "Bananas" the attacker must have picked up the ball. The elaborate movement of the opposing backs had been a diversion. Fingal put everything into it and after four strides launched himself in a headlong dive. His shoulder crunched into the man's thighs. The runner fell and his boot clouted Fingal's cheek, but Fingal ignored the pain as he scrambled to his feet, grabbed the loose ball, and started running.

Ahead he saw two of his own players coming at the charge. As he passed them, they ran in support of him off to his side, but slightly behind. Passing the ball forward was not allowed. Fingal's nearest opponent tried to tackle but was thrust aside by a brutal straight arm. Now the last Wanderers defender in striking distance must tackle Fingal, who ran straight at his opponent, making no attempt to avoid the tackle, and at the last moment passed the ball.

As he got to his feet and stood, hands on knees gasping for

breath, he saw his teammate sliding across the goal line immediately under the crossbar of the goalposts. Bloody marvellous. Trinity twelve. Wanderers nine, and the kicker should have no difficulty adding another point by hammering the ball between the uprights.

"That result, I think," Charlie said to Fingal in the dressing room as he shrugged into his jacket, "was very satisfactory."

Fingal shoved his muddy togs and boots into his hold-all and zipped it shut. He laughed. "So do you reckon," he pointed to the bruised swelling under his slowly closing left eye, "that it was worth getting this?" He opened the door. "And me with a nurse to woo?" He'd spotted Caitlin among the spectators.

"Och sure," Charlie said, "can't you always play the wounded warrior?"

"Come on," said Fingal, "let's go and see Bob and Caitlin." He stepped out into the autumn sunshine.

"Fingal. Fingal O'Reilly." She stood with Bob Beresford, who often came to support the team.

Cromie wasn't here today. He and Hilda had decently agreed to work for Fingal and Charlie so they could be free to play. Charlie would repay Hilda tomorrow. Cromie said he'd settle for a pint or a return favour in sailing season.

"Bob." Fingal's friend looked very dapper in his camel hair overcoat and rakishly worn bowler hat, an ivory-headed ebony walking stick in his left hand.

"Caitlin." Fingal smiled at her. He'd barely been able to speak to the girl, had only exchanged a few smiles in the past two weeks. She wore a tartan tam. Her hair, usually hidden under her nurses' headdress, cascaded down to below her shoulders. It was blacker than his own, had a sheen to rival Bob's cane, and rippled in the light breeze. Those eyes sparkled. Her lips pursed, and she tutted. "That's a nasty shiner." He heard the concern in her voice.

Before Fingal could shrug it off, Bob said, "Great tackle, Fingal, and brilliant run." He lowered his voice. "I saw T. J. Greeves, one of the Irish selectors, watching."

Fingal, who had been focussing all of his attention on Caitlin, gasped. "Really? Honestly?" One of the men who'd pick the national team? They only came to a match if they were interested in a particular player.

Bob nodded. "We'll keep our fingers crossed."

Fingal saw Caitlin looking expectantly at him. "Och," he said, "they're probably here to watch Charlie, not me. There's only room for two second-row forwards on the team. They'd not pick both players from the same club."

"We'll see," Charlie said. "Right now, Bob, I'm more interested in a post-game pint."

"You go on, boys, Caitlin and I are going to the flicks." Fingal looked straight at Bob, who must have taken the hint. Bob turned to Caitlin, took her gloved hand in his, bent his head, and raised it almost to his lips. "It has been a great pleasure to make your acquaintance, Miss O'Hallorhan," he said, "I do hope we shall meet again." He released her hand.

You'll bloody well not, Fingal thought. Not unless I'm with her. His vehemence surprised him. He barely knew the girl.

"Thank you, Mr. Beresford," she said, and smiled.

At least, Fingal thought, it's not "Bob" and "Caitlin" yet. He wondered why he was feeling so possessive.

"You played well, Fingal," she said. "It's not often you see a second-row forward running with the ball. You handed off that Wanderer beautifully."

Fingal frowned. "I'd have thought a girl would know more about field hockey or camogie." Rugby football was a boys' sport.

She put one hand on her hip. "Just because girls don't play doesn't mean we can't understand the game. That's about as sensible as saying because men have never been pregnant they can't deliver babies."

"Point taken," Fingal said, and laughed.

"My father's a fanatic for the game," she said. "He's taken me to matches for years."

"Och," said Fingal, impressed by her knowledge and by her willingness to stand up for herself, "seeing how you understand the game you'd not expect a forward to run and think at the same time, do you? Our man was in the right place to collect the pass. That's all."

She looked at him appraisingly, her right eyebrow arched. "You got all covered in confusion a week ago when Kevin Doherty was discharged and he tried to thank you. Are you trying to pretend you didn't set up that try perfectly? Are you by any chance one of those Irishmen who get all hot and bothered if he's paid an honest compliment?"

He swallowed. "Caitlin, it's nearly five o'clock. We don't want to miss the start of the big picture." It was a cheap night out when admission cost four pennies each. "Why don't we get a tram to O'Connell Street?"

"You *are* one," she said, and laughed deep in her throat. "All right. Let's get a tram. And never mind the Caitlin, Fingal O'Reilly. It's Kitty." Then surprisingly she reached out her hand and took his.

12

Even My Lungs Are Affected

"Your left hand holds the barrel of the syringe," Geoff Pilkington said to Fingal and Charlie. "Put your index and middle fingers through these stainless steel rings at the top end with your thumb through the central ring on the plunger."

It was the week before Christmas, and Fingal and Charlie were being taught how to tap a pleural effusion, a collection of fluid between the two layers of the membrane that sheathed the lungs. Geoff was demonstrating with a large syringe. "This," he said, indicating a device between the syringe and the hub of a wide-bore needle, "is a two-way tap. When you have the handle parallel with the axis of the syringe, fluid can run in or out of the needle. When you put the handle at ninety degrees and shove on the plunger, the fluid in the barrel will come out here." He pointed to an open tube on the side of the valve.

This was the trickiest procedure he'd learned in three months. He and his friends had become adept at collecting blood from the patients, or setting up intravenous drips. Well, most of them had. Bob Beresford seemed to be cursed with two left thumbs and sometimes took as many as three attempts to find a vein. Cromie had confessed to Fingal over a pint that, for the sake of the patients, Bob was letting Cromie take all the bloods since the patients had started calling Bob "Count Dracula."

Fingal had even done two cut-downs for patients in such degrees of shock that their veins were too collapsed to find. For them it had been necessary to freeze the skin beside the inner ankle bone, make a small incision, expose the long saphenous vein, incise it, and slide in a narrow tube through which blood or saline could be infused. It had been very gratifying to feel that in a small way he'd helped when both patients recovered and were discharged.

Fingal watched Geoff repeat the actions for a second time. It looked straightforward, but Fingal glanced back at the big needle. "Geoff," he said, "that looks like something Captain Ahab would have stuck in Moby Dick." He didn't like the look of it one bit, nor fancied using it on living flesh. Particularly today's patient.

"Maybe," said Geoff, "but it's what you or Charlie is going to drain that pleural effusion with."

Fingal looked at Charlie and started to say he'd rather not, but Charlie beat him to the punch. "Me," he said. "I'm from a farm. I've had to help my da often enough to geld bullocks."

Fingal exhaled. He knew he would need to learn the technique, but not today. He was happy to watch Geoff walk Charlie through the steps again.

Fingal was surprised at his own discomfort. The repetition of doing procedures and the knowledge that they were of benefit had helped him conquer his natural aversion to inflicting pain. Gradually he was becoming inured, but not completely. Today he simply did not want to pierce this particular fellow human with a bloody great skewer the size of a knitting needle. He'd grown fond of the man.

"And that's it, Charlie," Geoff said. "You'll do fine. We'll get the gear sterilized." He put the instruments, including a smaller hypodermic, into the water of the sluice's autoclave, shut the lid, and flicked a switch to heat the water to boiling. "You'll not be using Big Bertha until you've put in some procaine two percent. That's what the little syringe and its fine needle are for."

Thank God for local anaesthetics, Fingal thought, taking a deep breath. By now he barely noticed the smells in the bedpan washing room.

"That'll take twenty minutes to cook," Geoff said. "Come on. We'll go and see the patient."

They followed Geoff out of the sluice onto the, as ever, full Saint Patrick's Ward. Sister Daly straightened up from speaking to a patient, tugged her apron straight, and walked toward Fingal's group. She graced them with a smile.

Fingal returned it. He was convinced that the faster their skills improved the more useful she considered them, and the wider her smile grew.

"We're going to tap the pneumonia in bed 51's pleural effusion, Sister," Geoff said.

"Grand, so. I'll send a nurse with the trolley. I imagine the instruments are being sterilised?"

"They are," Geoff said, and led the way to bed 51. The plaque read *Gascoigne Bed. Supported by Colonel Trench Gascoigne. 1898.*

This bed was inside an oxygen tent like the one that had helped the long discharged Kevin Doherty. This patient was a man of thirty-four. He was skinny as a rake, his upper front two teeth missing, his Old Bill moustache nicotine-stained, and his right arm ending in a stump below the elbow. Fingal had admitted him so it was his job to keep up the daily progress notes and present the case, when required. Fingal had spent quite a bit of time with the little man. "Good afternoon, Sergeant Paddy Keogh," he said. As many male patients did, the man was wearing a tweed duncher. "How are you today?"

"I'm not altogether at myself, Mister O'Reilly, sir," he coughed and winced, "but I'm mending, t'anks."

Dubliners, Fingal thought, could never manage the *th* sound. In the north, folks had trouble with *thr* so instead of "three" they'd say "thee."

"Always glad to see yourself, sir." Paddy Keogh tried to smile. His breathing was laboured, his lips and cheeks cyanosed. Even without a stethoscope, Fingal could hear the wheezing of the little sergeant's lungs. Fingal had admitted the patient at one A.M. four nights ago. One disadvantage of living in students' quarters was that they were easily called at night. Still, it increased the number of patients they saw and so their experience grew.

On that night it had taken Fingal a moment to recognise the beggar he'd given two shillings to last March. Sergeant Pádraig, "Paddy," Keogh—febrile, sweating, suffering violent pain with every breath, coughing, wheezing, and shivering as he was—had no difficulty recognising Fingal. "Jasus," he'd gasped, "it's yourself, sir, w'at gave me a whole feh—" He must have seen the nurse and corrected himself in time, "sorry, a whole two shillings, sir."

"Och," Fingal had said, "sure and amn't I only an eccentric millionaire? Now let's get you seen to."

Fingal had busied himself with the admission history and physical examination. Address, 27 Francis Street; age thirty-five; religion, Roman Catholic. He'd recorded the symptoms and signs. The diagnosis was simple, particularly as it wasn't the man's first bout of pneumonia. Fingal cursed the Dublin tenements.

With Geoff's advice, tests had been ordered. A chest X-ray confirmed that the man had left lobar pneumonia and pleurisy: inflammation and infection of his left lung and the membrane surrounding it. Treatment was prescribed; oxygen, sponge baths to try to relieve his temperature, and the drug that had been in vogue since the late 1800s to reduce temperature, acetylsalicylic acid—or aspirin. It might help the pain a little, but morphine was out of the question because of its known suppressant effects on respiratory function. He was going to be in pain for a while.

Fingal had already heard that one of Hilda's patients, a young woman, had died of pneumonia. Some days after the onset of the disease, the crisis had come heralded by a dramatic rise in temperature. They'd all hoped for an equally dramatic fall in her temperature, followed by a gradual recovery. But at the height of the crisis the woman had died. Victorian novelists like the Brönte sisters and Wilkie Collins had loved to use pneumonic crises for dramatic effect. The course of the disease and its treatment weren't much different in 1934. What was needed was a medication that killed bacteria, but according to Doctor Micks, in 1930 a Doctor Fleming had abandoned attempts to use a derivative of a fungus called *Penicillium notatum* for such a purpose. The substance was known to stop bacterial growth in the lab but couldn't be collected and purified well enough for human use. Patients had to rely on their own resistance to fight off the infection.

Fingal lifted the notes and scanned the temperature chart. The graph covered the eighty-four hours since admission. Thirty-three hours ago the spidery, black line had ripped upward to an acute spike then plummeted to where it wandered along rising above and falling to the normal level of 98.4 degrees Farenheit before rising again. Even though he'd not been on duty, Fingal had taken it upon himself to sit with the sergeant that night until the crisis passed.

Fingal could still hear Fitzpatrick's nasal whining. "You're not on duty, O'Reilly. I want this case. I've never seen a pneumonic crisis."

"You'll get your chance."

"I don't care. I want this one. It's my turn."

"For God's sake, Fitzpatrick," little Hilda Manwell said, "Fingal's particularly interested in the man. You met him before he got sick, didn't you, Fingal?"

"I did."

"Suit yourself." Fitzpatrick stormed off muttering, "Serve you right, O'Reilly, if he snuffs it."

It had been all Fingal could do to restrain himself from charging after Fitzpatrick and belting him. Instead he'd sat by the bedside willing the sergeant to pull through. That had been a day and a half ago.

Geoff had abandoned his attempts to make Fingal treat patients dispassionately. The house officer didn't even shrug when Fingal said, "Your fever's getting better, Paddy."

Perhaps because of the old soldier's dogged refusal to give in to the pain, to try to get a laugh if possible, Fingal felt so protective of the man, so unwilling to do the procedure and hurt him. "You are on the mend," Fingal said.

He was rewarded with a weak smile and a hoarse, "I hope so, sir. I was sick two days at home now four days in here. I'm gasping for a fag."

Fingal shook his head. "You light a cigarette next to that oxygen and you'll be giving an impression of a *flammenwerfer.*"

"A German flame thrower? Jasus."

"Oxygen is very flammable."

"I'd not want dat, but sure how could I anyway? Didn't the nurses take me gaspers away?" He sounded aggrieved.

"Paddy, you eejit, you're not well enough to smoke."

The sergeant grunted.

He was recovering, but not fast enough. A repeat X-ray this morning had shown a dark shadow, a collection of fluid at the base of the left lung between the twin layers of the pleura. This morning at rounds Doctor Micks had instructed Geoff to drain the fluid to reduce the patient's suffering and shortness of breath.

Fingal saw the trolley being wheeled along the ward and smiled. Sister had sent Kitty. He winked at her. Her eyes smiled at him from over her mask. Turning to the patient, he said, "All right, Paddy. You've a spot of fluid on your lung—"

"Jasus, sir, I was never gassed." He held up his stump. "Losing me arm was bad enough, but I saw chlorine gas in the trenches and w'at it did to a man's lungs."

Fingal put a hand on the man's bony shoulder. "We know you weren't gassed, Paddy. The bug that felled you has made your lungs raw and your body's tried to soothe it by making fluid. That fluid's squashing your lung. Making it harder for you to breathe."

"Aye, and sore."

"So," said Fingal, "Doctor Pilkington and Mister Greer are going to remove the fluid."

"You mean they're going to stick a feckin' great needle into me back?"

"I do."

He coughed and held the left lower side of his chest. "I had that done once before. It stings like bejizzis." His bony hand sought Fingal's and the sergeant looked up into his eyes. "Would you do me a favour, sir?"

"If I can."

"Would you do it yourself, like?"

"Me?" Fingal recoiled. "I've never done one before." And I don't want to do this one, he thought.

"Ah, but—" He coughed again. "I know you'll be gentle, sir."

Fingal looked at Charlie, who said, "Fine by me." He'd be disappointed to be deprived of the opportunity to add to his growing armoury of skills, but he'd have another chance.

"I'll help you," Geoff said. "Come on, we'll go and wash our hands." He turned to Kitty, who stood at the bedside with her instrument trolley. "Can you and Mister Greer get the patient sitting up?"

"We can, Doctor."

"We'll only be a minute, Paddy," Fingal said.

He and Geoff soon returned, gloved and masked, and stood by the instrument trolley. While they'd been away, the screens had been closed.

Charlie and Kitty had the sergeant sitting on the far side of the bed. His skinny legs dangled over the side. Charlie stood facing him with a hand on each shoulder to support him. Kitty moved to Fingal's side.

He glanced at the instruments. Big syringe, he shuddered, little syringe, stainless steel kidney dish, small gallipot with antiseptic solution, cotton wool balls, sponge holder. He loaded several cotton wool balls into the jaws of the holder. "Just going to wash your back, Paddy. It'll be a bit cold." Fingal couldn't understand why when the antiseptic was diluted they didn't use warm water. A little thing, but important to the customers.

Fingal daubed the left side of the man's back over the spot where the X-ray had shown the fluid.

"There." Doctor Pilkington pointed to a space between two of the lower ribs, halfway between the chest's edge and the spine.

Fingal nodded and picked up the smaller syringe. "Local please, Nurse."

Kitty lifted the bottle of procaine. Fingal filled the syringe's barrel. As he withdrew the needle from the bottle, his glance caught hers over her mask.

In the three months since the Wanderers game he'd been seeing her as often as their duties permitted, which wasn't one hell of a lot. Even a few stolen words and glances on the ward were risky. Sister Daly had her rules about student nurses and medical students.

Even so, after only five dates they had grown closer. He was able to read some of her moods by looking into her eyes, and he sensed she was encouraging him. Bless her. She was quite the girl, but this was not the time for those kinds of thoughts. They'd have to keep until the New Year's Eve Ball at Trinity unless he could arrange to see her sooner.

He turned to the patient. "You'll feel a little jag, Paddy."

"All right, sir."

Fingal slipped the needle under the skin and began to inject, raising a blanched wheal.

"Now, Mister O'Reilly," Doctor Pilkington said, "gradually advance the needle tip, injecting as you go to infiltrate the intercostal muscles and the pleura."

Fingal took a deep breath. The pleura was exquisitively sensitive. He knew when he'd hit it because he heard the patient sucking in air through clenched teeth. "Sorry, Paddy," he said.

"It's all right."

"We'll give the local time to work," Doctor Pilkington said as Fingal withdrew the needle and laid the little syringe beside Big Bertha. That was a powerful needle all right. Fingal hoped the local would be very effective.

He stretched out his hand for the larger syringe.

"Give it a minute or two," Geoff said.

Fingal waited, then, remembering something he'd learnt in outpatients, picked up the small syringe. "What do you feel, Paddy?" He gently pricked the target area with the fine needle.

"Not a t'ing, sir."

"Right," Geoff said.

Fingal took a deep breath, picked up Big Bertha, and held it the way he'd seen Charlie being shown.

He heard a very quiet whisper from Kitty, who was standing closer to him, studiously staring into space. "You'll do a great job, Fingal."

He exhaled, thought, thank you, girl, thank you. He looked at Doctor Pilkington, who nodded and said, "Go in at a right angle to the skin and advance slowly. Keep pulling with your thumb on the plunger's ring. As soon as you start to see fluid in the syringe's barrel, stop advancing. You're in the cavity and you don't want to go too far."

Too bloody true, I don't, Fingal thought. On the left side of the chest, less than an inch from the needle's point of entry, was Paddy's heart. "I'm going to start now, Paddy. All right?"

"Go you right ahead, sir." He began coughing. Fingal had to wait until the paroxysm had passed. "I suppose," Paddy managed, "you'd not want to shoot at a moving target. I never did meself unless the Hun was coming over the top." He collected himself. "I've stopped coughing now. You carry on."

"You're a tough man, Paddy Keogh," Fingal said, his confidence increasing. "A tough man."

He put the needle tip against the red mark where the local anaesthetic had been injected and followed Geoff's instructions. It took an effort to advance and it was awkward trying to pull back with his thumb. His efforts were rewarded when a dirty brown fluid flowed into the barrel. He immediately stopped advancing and slowly filled the syringe. "Could you hold the kidney dish please, Doctor Pilkington?"

Geoff put the stainless steel receptacle under the out-spout of the syringe.

Fingal turned the two-way tap and thrust on the plunger. A jet of brown blood-tinged fluid spurted into the dish.

He had emptied eight and a half syringefuls before more suction refused to produce any fluid. "Just about all done, Paddy."

"T'anks, sir."

"Needle out, and I'll dress the puncture," Geoff said.

As Fingal removed the needle, Geoff clapped a dressing over the entry wound. "Well done," he said.

There was a whispered, "Well done, Fingal," from Kitty.

"Well done, Paddy," Fingal said, and realised he was grinning. He wiped sweat from his forehead with the back of his gloved hand. "Come on, Charlie," he said, "let's get Paddy here back on his pillows." Fingal was amazed to see how the man's colour had already improved. "Are you all right?" he asked.

"I'm sound, sir. Sound—and it doesn't hurt as much."

Fingal smiled. "I'm delighted," he said, and for the life of him he couldn't be sure whether his pleasure was in the reassurance he'd been given by Kitty, the "well done" from Doctor Pilkington, the fact that he himself had been able to stifle his squeamishness, or the fact that his work had helped to improve Sergeant Paddy Keogh's condition.

"You, Mister Fingal Flahertie O'Reilly, have a quare soft hand under a duck," Charlie said.

"I'd drink to dat meself—if I could get me hands on a feckin' gargle," said Paddy.

Fingal said, "Sister gets one-third-pint bottles of Guinness free from the brewery for tonics for our patients. Do you think, Doctor Pilkington, Sergeant Keogh could benefit from one?"

"Two a day," said Geoff, "until he's discharged."

Fingal grinned. "Och," he said, "I'd go a celebratory pint myself, but we're on duty tonight and have outpatients tomorrow afternoon, but after that I'll be in the snug in Neary's pub at seven if anyone would care to join me." He didn't need to look at Kitty. He just hoped she could find some excuse that would allow her to leave the Nurses' Home in the middle of the week. Three months ago, when his brother had warned that he might get hooked, he'd replied, "Me? Not likely. I've exams to pass, remember?" But, damn it, the New Year's Eve Ball seemed like an eternity away, and Fingal Flahertie O'Reilly wasn't a monk who'd taken vows of chastity.

13

We Will Go into a Public House

Fingal stopped on Grafton Street and listened to a ragged man playing "The Irish Washerwoman" on a penny whistle. Oblivious to the busker, well-dressed folks Christmas window-shopped on the brightly lit thoroughfare. The power for the streetlamps and storefronts came from a hydroelectric plant at Ardnacrusha on the Shannon River near the city of Limerick. The generator, Fingal knew, had opened five years ago.

The man switched to "The Wind that Shakes the Barley." Fingal thought the musician a deal more adept than Cromie on his whistle and chucked a couple of coppers into a cap on the pavement where the man's mangy dog sat, its tongue lolling, a grin on its face. "Lummox," Fingal said, and patted its head.

"Lummox, yourself," a familiar voice remarked.

Fingal turned and saw Bob Beresford, dapper as ever.

Bob lifted his bowler. "Evening."

"What the hell are you doing here, Bob?"

"Looking for a little Yule gift for Bette."

"Bette? Not Freda?"

Bob smiled. "Bette."

"Don't tell me you're dating Bette Davis. I'd not put it past you, Beresford."

Bob laughed. "Bette Swanson, and no, she's not related to Gloria. You'll meet her at the New Year's Eve Ball," he said, and winked. "What brings you to the bright lights?"

"I'm hoping Kitty'll show up in Neary's snug," Fingal said.

"Neary's? On Chatham Street?" Bob grabbed Fingal by the arm. "Brilliant notion. Come on. I'll buy you a jar. You're probably broke. I saw you giving that old boy money."

"Pennies," Fingal said, and hesitated. He wanted Kitty to himself, but Bob was such a good-natured chap.

"Don't worry, Fingal," Bob said. "One drink and I'll be off. I'll not play gooseberry."

Fingal, laughing at the thought of Bob intruding on a friend's assignation, fell into stride.

In no time he was sitting in the familiar small room. The snug was open to ladies and their escorts. A curtain across the arch leading to the men-only public bar was closed, but he could hear the sounds of conversations, the clink of bottle neck on glass.

Bob came back clutching a Jameson and a pint. "Here you are," he said. "Cheers."

"Cheers," Fingal said, and drank. "Begod, that hits the spot. Thanks, Bob."

"My pleasure."

Fingal said, "I hope Sergeant Paddy Keogh's enjoying his one-third-pint bottles back at Sir Patrick Dun's."

"The fellah with one arm and a pleural effusion? You like that wee man, don't you?" He sipped.

"He's a terrier." Fingal savoured the bitterness of the stout. "Never complains. Do you know where he's from?" Bob shook his head.

"Francis Street."

"Should I know it?"

It was Fingal's turn to shake his head. "Not if you can help it. It's in the Liberties."

"The tenements? I've heard about them."

"I've seen them." Fingal pursed his lips. "We take all this," he waved an arm round the brightly lit snug, "for granted. But there'll be no electric light in Paddy's place. Just tallow candles or a reeking paraffin lamp." Don't get involved with your patients, Geoff Pilkington had said. But why not? Fingal took another pull.

"I remember Doctor Micks telling us way back we couldn't change the world," Bob said. "I'm not heartless, Fingal, but the tenements of Dublin have always been there."

Fingal sat back. This wasn't the place to give his friend a lecture, and yet. And yet perhaps happy-go-lucky Bob Beresford should have his eyes opened. Just a bit. "Actually they haven't," he said. "They're relatively recent."

Bob frowned and stopped his glass before it reached his lips. "Go on then. You have my attention."

Fingal set his pint on the table. "My mother is committed to slum clearance. She's told me that in 1802 after the Act of Union of Ireland with the rest of Britain and the dissolution of the Irish Parliament, the Anglo-Irish upper classes decided life would be better in England and started leaving Dublin."

"Silly of them. It's a great city," Bob said.

"They didn't think so. It certainly wasn't politically stable then. Irish Nationalism was rampant. They might indeed have been safer getting out."

"I suppose." Bob sipped.

"So did they. They flooded away. Do you know that by 1840, a Georgian house that would have sold for eight thousand pounds in 1791, just before the United Irishman rose in 1798, was worth perhaps only five hundred?"

"I've always said it's safer putting money on the horses than speculating on property," Bob said. "It's over quicker." He laughed.

Fingal chuckled. "Can you not be serious about anything, Bob?"

"Not if I can help it." He finished his whiskey.

Fingal took a small pull on his pint. "Think about this. Once the prices had fallen, whole terraces were acquired by profiteering landlords who crammed as many as fourteen people into one room."

"How many?" Bob's eyes widened.

"Fourteen."

"Good God. I didn't know." Bob frowned, looked at his empty glass. "One more for the road," he said, rose, and inclined his head to Fingal's pint.

"Not for me." He didn't want to have too many before Kitty appeared.

Fingal glanced at his watch. Seven fifteen. It wasn't like Kitty to be late, and the later it got the less likely it would be that she was coming. Her punctuality, a trait she shared with Charlie Greer, was one of the things he'd come to admire about the twenty-two-year-old from Tallaght. That and her understated pride in looking after her patients. He took a pull on his pint and was struck by a thought. He didn't want to move on to another girl as he usually did. They had had such fun on the few nights they'd been out together, and he knew he really wanted to see Kitty this evening. And if they kept on walking out? He was curious about what their future might hold. Not that he had any immediate plans for anything permanent with Kitty O'Hallorhan. But, and the thought surprised him, if things did progress, who knew what might transpire? Certainly, and the unromantic, practical nature of the idea amused Fingal, a GP could do worse than having a nurse for a wife. At this stage he should be thinking less about domesticity and more about what great legs she had and how they would feel above her stocking tops, not what might happen two years from now.

"They're quick on the pour here," Bob said as he reappeared with a whiskey. "Sure I can't get you another?"

Fingal shook his head. "But thanks."

Bob sat. "Makes you think," he said. "Fourteen in one room." He drank. "Still I imagine there weren't too many like that."

"You'd be wrong. One-third of Dublin's population is living in at least six thousand tenements. My ma's a friend of Eamon Donnelly. He's a member of the Dáil. She quoted his speech to the House to me over tea one day. 'To pass through O'Connell Street with all its brilliant lights . . . one would scarcely think that only some yards away the slaughter of the innocents was going on.' He had been referring to disease-ridden Gardiner and Dominick streets."

"Good God. They're just up the road from here," Bob said.

"Where we're enjoying a warm pub and a drink." Fingal sipped. "Did you know a Housing Bill had been passed in 1931? Dublin's finally started slum clearance."

"Actually no. I didn't. I don't pay much attention to politics, but it sounds like it's about time."

Fingal finished his pint. "We started this conversation talking about Paddy Keogh and Francis Street. It's still there. Not cleared yet. No rehousing for Paddy. Don't you think, Bob, there should be more for him to look forward to when he gets discharged from Dun's than a damp slum with one outside privy to serve sixty or more people and slop buckets that have to be emptied every morning stinking up the room at night? The man was a hero of Passchendaele, for Christ's sake. Surely he deserves better, but the government of the Irish Free State has no obligations to British ex-servicemen, and the British government barely gives pennies to their old Irish soldiers. So he's like the man with the penny whistle. He has to beg."

Bob stared into his glass then looked Fingal squarely in the eye. "I've wondered about you, Fingal. I know you take great satisfaction from working with patients. I can see an attraction to medicine in that. I've envied you, but looking after patients isn't enough for you. You want to change the world too, don't you?"

"No, Bob." Fingal shook his head. "No I don't. Just a little corner."

Bob nodded. "I'm beginning to understand. Tell me. How do you think a doctor could help? I'm not cut out for looking after patients. I'm too bloody ham-fisted."

"You don't have to see patients. We've been doing courses in hygiene. They're all about public health." He smiled. "Changing little corners of the world by making sure people have sanitation, clean drinking water, get vaccinated."

"Sounds dull," Bob said, "but I see what you mean."

Fingal was struck by a thought. "Bob, will you make a bet?"

Bob grinned, ear to ear. "Is the Pope Catholic? Try me."

Fingal finished his pint. "I'll bet you that if that Scottish fellow, that Doctor Fleming that Doctor Micks was talking about, finds a way to purify the stuff from the mould *Penicillium,* doctors will be able to put an end to infections."

Bob laughed. "That's a fine bet, Fingal, but we'll be waiting for years to see who won."

"True, but it would be exciting finding out." He waited.

"Do you know, Fingal. I agree. It would." Bob grinned. "It bloody well would. That's just like a horse race. You speculate, then wait for the outcome, and I love that."

It was Fingal's turn to smile. "I think the 'finding out' is called research, Bob. And the payout is possibly helping thousands, maybe even millions of people. Something to think about, my friend?"

"Indeed." He looked pensive. "I suppose going into research could be a reason to pass my exams."

The curtain was drawn back.

As was expected of gentlemen when a lady entered, they stood. Fingal knew he was grinning like the Cheshire cat.

"Sorry I'm late," Kitty said, propping her umbrella against the wall, pulling off her head scarf, and shaking her black mane loose to shine in the light from the overhead fixture. "Hello, Bob."

"Kitty." Bob raised his hat, took her hand, and lifted it to just below his lips. "Delightful to see you. May I buy you a drink?"

Kitty O'Hallorhan was a very different woman out of her austere uniform. And it wasn't the first time Fingal had wondered what she'd look like out of her ordinary clothes as well.

"Well—" She glanced at Fingal, who nodded. "Glass of Shooting Sherry, please."

Bob had said he'd not play gooseberry. Fingal glanced at his friend. Handsome, beautifully dressed, manners of an English "Milord," pots of money, women round him in swarms. For a second Fingal wondered if he should be worried.

"Fingal? You sure?"

Fingal laughed. "All right, but just one." He held Bob's gaze.

Bob nodded, lifted Fingal's empty glass, and left.

"I'm sorry I'm late, Fingal," Kitty said. "I'd things to finish on the ward." She opened her raincoat then laughed. "I told the superintendent it's my father's birthday. Sometimes she's not a bad old stick. She's let me out until ten."

Good for you, girl, he thought. He smiled. "Och, but sure absence makes the heart grow fonder." Fingal hugged her and gave her a chaste kiss.

She sighed. "I just wish our schedules weren't quite so full. It's been three weeks since you took me to the Abbey Theatre to see that wonderful *Pygmalion* and it'll be nearly two more until New Year's Eve."

He shrugged. "I know, but what can we do? I'm on call every third Saturday. I have to study, and—" He hesitated. He didn't want her to think she was coming second to it. "And then there's the rugby."

She shook her head. "I'm perfectly happy to come and watch you play." Her lips curled into a smile and her eyes sparkled. "Your friend Bob Beresford is such a marvellous escort."

Fingal coughed and frowned. "I'm sure he is. He'll be leaving soon."

"Now don't be getting jealous, Fingal O'Reilly. You look like a grumpy old bear."

"I'll accept grumpy, but not old. I just turned twenty-six." His kiss was less than chaste. "And that's to prove it. Now," he said, pulling out a chair. "Sit you down."

"Thank you," she said.

"Here we are," Bob said, returning with the drinks. He gave each theirs, but remained standing. He lifted his glass and drained it. "Fingal, thank you for explaining to me about the tenements."

"I hope I didn't bore you."

"Not at all. And you're right. There are more ways a doctor can help than in the clinic."

"Think about it, Bob."

"I will. Now, Miss Kitty, fairest of the fair—"

Fingal saw Kitty smile and blush.

"'Parting is such sweet sorrow,' but I've to see a man about a dog."

Kitty laughed. "I thought men said that when they needed an excuse to go for a drink."

Or for a pee, Fingal thought.

"They do," Bob said, "but in this instance the man in question has a great lummox of an animal and he plays the penny whistle for pennies." Bob glanced at Fingal. "I reckon two shillings would buy them both supper."

"You," said Fingal to Bob's departing back, "are a sound man."

14

Have Felt My Soul in a Kiss

"What," asked Kitty, "was that all about?"

Fingal laughed. "I met Bob on Grafton Street. I was patting a dog's head. Its master was playing the penny whistle."

"And I'll bet you gave him money, then, you big softie."

He shrugged.

"You are, you know, and I like that." She sipped her sherry and stared into the glass, then turned to him, a smile replacing the pensive look of only a moment before. "I wish I got more than Saturdays out of that Nurses' Home or could finagle more special dispensations like tonight." She tossed her hair. "They call it the Nurses' Home, but it's more like a bloody nunnery." She laughed and took another sip. "And just because the senior nurses are referred to as sisters doesn't mean they're nuns. Some of them just act that way. They seem to think anything pleasant is sinful. We even have to turn off the radio at nine o'clock and I love listening to good dance bands like Duke Ellington and Joe Loss."

Fingal nodded. "Mantovani. Billy Cotton." He moved closer to her. "If Glenn Miller ever comes to Dublin, I don't care what the rules are, I'm getting you out of there and we're going to the concert even if I have to tunnel under the wall and borrow the money from Bob."

Kitty laughed. "I'd love that, but if the lady superintendent was in one of her better moods, like tonight, you could save yourself a lot of digging." She frowned. "Most of the time the way she goes on you'd think that men, students in particular, were one step down from the devil." She screwed up her face.

"Old Nick himself, bye," Fingal said in a stage Cork accent, "we're the divil's own when it comes to girls. Indeed we are, so. Mashers to a man."

"You're not one of those women chasers, are you, O'Reilly?" she said. "You've told me about your years at sea."

"You know what sailors are. Girls in every port."

Her smile was broad as she finished her sherry. "And am I your girl in the Port of Dublin?" And yet he heard a plaintiveness in her voice.

Fingal gathered her in an enormous hug, kissed her again and tasted the sweetness of her, felt the tip of her tongue on his. For a moment he allowed his hand that was inside her raincoat to slide along the firmness of one breast. He felt her shudder.

"Fingal." She was breathless when she pulled away. "You haven't answered my question. Am I—"

"My girl in the Port of Dublin? By God, Kitty O'Hallorhan, you are. The only one." He meant it. He kissed her again.

She moved closer and made no demur, but trembled as his hand caressed her breast through her wool dress.

She pulled away, closed her coat, and yet her smile was gentle as she said, "We have until ten tonight," she inhaled deeply, "before I've to be back." She put up one hand to smooth her hair. "So would you get me another drink, please?"

He picked up her glass and his own, now empty. "Just be a tick." He could still imagine the softness of her and her delicate musk lingered with him. If she'd worn that on the ward, Sister Daly would have had a purple fit. No jewellery, no perfume was the order of the day.

Begod, no wonder. If that perfume of hers had the same effect on the male patients on Saint Patrick's Ward as it had on him it would be like the miracle at the pool of Bethesda. Half of the men would rise, take up their beds, and walk and the other half would have envied the hell out of them. Quite the girl, all right.

He went to the bar. "Brendan, a glass of Shooting Sherry and a pint."

The barman, a young lad of eighteen who stood five foot and had healed acne scars on a face like a potato, sucked a hollow tooth, started a pint, picked up a bottle and poured. "Shooting Sherry? Same young lady after t'ree months? Not like you, Fingal O'Reilly. It's usually more like a couple of nights den dey're gone." He tutted, winked, and handed over the glass. "Mind you, she's rightly fit." He described an hourglass shape in the air with his hands.

"I'm glad she has the Brendan Mulcahey seal of approval, you gurrier."

Brendan laughed. "Takes one gurrier to know another—sir."

"Go 'way," Fingal said with a smile. Good head that Brendan. He always enjoyed a bit of good-natured slagging and could give as good as he took.

The barman topped off the pint. "One shilling and six pence, please."

Fingal paid, took the drinks, and went back to where Kitty was sitting. "Here you are." He sat beside her and raised his glass.

She took the glass. "Thanks." She sipped and crossed her legs with a whisper of silk on silk.

He admired her well-curved calves and the way her patent leather belt accentuated the thinness of her waist, the hint of cleavage at the V-neckline of her green wool dress. Kitty O'Hallorhan was on the generous side there, but Peter Paul Rubens wasn't the only man who liked his ladies well endowed. And Kitty's were full, and firm he now knew. He sat beside her and lifted his pint. "Cheers." He took a long pull.

"Cheers."

"You, Kitty O'Hallorhan," he said, "are looking particularly lovely tonight," and moved closer.

"Thank you, sir," she said, and leant to him, but sat back as a man opened the curtain and ushered his lady in and seated her at a table.

"Dirty night out," he said. "It's feckin' chucking it down out dere now."

Fingal smiled. "But it's snug here in the snug." He wished they'd go away.

"True on you, sir." The man asked his date, a faded blonde, what she'd like to drink, and went through the curtain.

Fingal knew Kitty'd been going to kiss him, but now propriety forbade any overt displays of affection.

She lowered her voice. "So what are the plans for this night of wild hedonism to celebrate a successful pleural tap?"

"Seeing it's been so long since I saw you last how'd you like me to treat you to dinner?"

"Can you afford it?" He saw her frown, open her mouth and start to say, "If you'd like I could," then bite off the word "pay." It would be unthinkable. That was the man's responsibility and he was grateful for her consideration of his feelings. She didn't need to know he'd been going out less for his pints with the lads and walking a lot rather than taking trams so he could afford to take her to the upcoming ball.

"Course I can," he said, "but it won't be the Gresham or the Shelbourne Hotels."

She laughed. "Goat."

He felt warmed by her easy familiarity and slid closer.

"Interesting place the Gresham," he said. "Did you know Percy Shelley and William Thackeray have stayed there?"

"No. I did not," she said. "You like poetry, don't you?"

"I get it from my father. He's a prof—"

"Of English. You told me. Have you forgotten?"

"Kitty," he said, leaning nearer and speaking softly, "in that dress you'd make me forget my own name." She would and he knew he was growing to like her. A lot. He pulled out his briar. "All right?" he asked.

She nodded. "I've told you before, I like the smell. Dad smokes a pipe."

He lit up.

"May I see that?" She held out her hand and he gave her his new Ronson lighter. "'To Fingal on his twenty-sixth birthday. Eighth October, 1934. From his parents with love,'" she read. "That's sweet." She gave it back.

Bloody thing should really read, "From Ma," he thought, but kept it to himself.

"My folks gave me a new easel for my birthday."

"An easel. You never told me that you were an artist. My ma paints."

"I love it," she said. "I went to the National College of Art and Design when I left school, but—" He heard how wistful she sounded. "I do sell a few. One went last week. That's how I bought this new dress, but there's no real money in it so I decided to nurse."

"I'm bloody glad you did," he said. "And I'm glad I went to medical school or I might not have met you."

"Thank you," she said quietly. "I think you made the right choice."

"To meet you?"

She laughed and punched his arm. "No, you eejit. To study medicine. You're going to be good at it."

"Well, I—"

"I thought you tapped that pleural effusion well."

Inwardly Fingal glowed.

"He's a nice wee man, Paddy Keogh," she said.

"Funny," he said, "Bob and I were discussing him before you arrived, and what a terrible place he'll be going home to." Fingal was glad to have something else to talk about, something to stop his gaze constantly returning to Kitty's cleavage. He shook his head. "As my old family doctor in Holywood, Doctor O'Malley, used to remark, 'It's ill divid,' meaning the money in the world is not well divided." He thought of tonight's window shoppers and how Paddy, back in October, had thought two shillings, half an old-age pensioner's weekly stipend, a full day's wage for a cleaner, was a king's ransom.

She looked at him, her head cocked to one side, eyes slightly narrowed. "You've not been listening to Bertrand Russell on the wireless, have you? That's a pretty socialist idea."

"Do you mind that?" he asked, and waited.

"Not one bit," she said. "I've a few of those notions myself. When I realised I wasn't going to support myself by painting and needed another job I'd no difficulty choosing nursing. It doesn't pay worth a damn, has little social standing, but," she glanced down, back at Fingal, and said quietly, "I've always liked to help." She looked sad. "There's so many poor people in Tallaght. It's unfair."

"I understand," he said, and he did. "Doctor Micks told us on our first day at Sir Paddy's that we physicians can't change the world. Bob's just quoted him. Some people are trying to, but I'm not sure I like what I hear is going on with socialism—they call it Communism, in Russia. Stalin's trying to change his country in a big way."

"We don't hear much about Russia in the newspapers or on Raidió Éireann."

"One of my father's friends was an attaché to the British embassy in Saint Petersburg. They call it Leningrad now. I was at home last year when he was visiting. My ma thought a great deal of Lenin and Stalin. I think what Father's friend told her rocked her."

"Go on." Kitty laid her forearms on the table.

"It seems that Stalin's idea to modernise Russia is to collectivise the farms."

"Collectivise? I've never heard that word."

"Neither had I. Apparently Russian agriculture was millons of small private farms run by people called Kulaks. Stalin's amalgamating them into a relatively few, huge, state-owned operations."

"I don't imagine their owners were impressed."

"They were not. So far about twenty million of them have been forcibly retrained as industrial workers. Thousands of Kulaks have even been sent to prison camps or shot."

"God, that's awful. Twenty million?" her voice cracked. "Twenty million. That's about seven times the whole population of Ireland. And the ones that resist get imprisoned or shot? That's appalling."

He thought her near to tears and admired her for it. "Not much news gets past the Russian censors these days," he said. "I don't like censorship and, like you, I sure as hell don't like to hear of people getting imprisoned and shot." Fingal stood and took a deep pull from his pint. "There's two more like Stalin in Europe now, Mussolini and Hitler. They all want to make Utopias, at least what they think of as heavens on earth. A lot of people admire them for bringing order. I think all dictators are bloody monsters. They don't give a tinker's curse who they trample on."

He remembered the first time at school he'd fought back against the bullies. "You only have to stand up to them once and they'll slink off. One day somebody's going to have to say, 'enough's bloody well enough,' and rear up and fight those three."

He took a deep breath. "I'm sorry, Kitty. I didn't mean to get worked up, but dear God, it must be hellish living in Russia or Germany." He lowered his voice. "I don't think people should try to change the whole world all at once, not the way the dictators are doing it. They don't really give a damn about improving things. They want power and position. Do you know Lord Acton's dictum?"

She shook her head.

"He said that power corrupts, and absolute power corrupts absolutely. He was right. All my old GP did was to try to make changes on a small scale in our village. Not in a big city, but I'm damn sure in a country practice a good doctor could get involved in the community. Make things better." He took a huge puff on his pipe. "I just wish we could do a bit more for Paddy Keogh here."

She'd nearly finished her sherry and was looking at him strangely, quizzically. There was softness in those grey eyes. "I've never seen you like this before, Fingal. Golly. You have a serious side? When we've been out with your pals and their girls, or even alone with me you hide your feelings by acting the lig—"

"I'm sorry," he said. "I didn't mean to get carried away." He could feel the presence of his father breathing down his neck. "By all means feel strongly, but don't let it show. It's common." Fingal inhaled deeply. Go away, Father. I'm a grown man now and I don't have to live by your values. I'll say what I need to say. "Paddy Keogh gave his right arm for what was then his country and what that man needs now is a decent place to live or a job or both. I've no notion how I might get him one, but, by God, I'm going to try."

To Fingal's surprise, Kitty ignored the other couple in the snug, wrapped her arms round him, and kissed him long and hard, her tongue flickering on his. He was breathless when she pulled away and said huskily, "I'm getting to be very fond of you, Fingal Fla-hertie O'Reilly. Very fond indeed."

He was at a loss for words. He knew he was starting to care. The very thing he'd told Lars that he was going to avoid was happening. He pulled hard on his pipe. He knew he wasn't ready to confess to deep feelings, yet every time he was with her things happened inside him, and tonight more than ever. His usual banter had gone into hiding. She was right. He did hide his feelings by acting the lig. All he could manage was, "I like you a lot, Kitty."

She pursed her lips and said, "I mean it, Fingal, very fond."

Now what should he say?

She spared him. "Enough seriousness for tonight. What about that dinner?"

Fingal was relieved that the subject had been changed. "I have," he said, "enough for one more round here then I know a great wee chipper over on Drury Street—"

To his surprise, in a soft contralto she sang a snatch from a Dublin song, "Anna Livia,"

> —we got a whiff of ray and chips
> and Mary softly sighed,
> "Oh, John won't you come for a one-on-one
> "Down by the Liffey's side."

They both laughed. "Why the locals call the cheapest order of fish-and-chips 'one-on-one' is beyond me, Fingal," she said, "but I'd love some—although I'd prefer codfish to ray."

"Done," he said, "and when we've eaten I'll walk you to the Nurses' Home and get you back before ten o'clock. With a bit of luck the rain'll have stopped." There were dark places on the way there for a bit of a cuddle, he thought. He could still feel the firmness of her breast under his fingers.

"Lovely," she said, "now go and get those new drinks."

As he left to do as he was bid, he wondered, had he been too reticent? Should he have told her how he was feeling? But how in the name of the wee man could he when he wasn't sure himself? Maybe later tonight? Maybe at the New Year's Eve Ball?

And maybe not until much later, thirty-one years later to be exact, thought O'Reilly as he stretched in the tattered armchair, massaged his leg, and stood. He'd had enough of the Royal Hospital's Huts, damn it, and he wanted to know about Donal Donnelly. It was time to go up to ward 21, see Donal, and perhaps drop into the cafeteria on his way back. He smiled ruefully. Pity the kitchen didn't do a good one-on-one.

15

'Tis the Season to Be Jolly

"They just brought him back, Doctor O'Reilly," the night sister said. "He's unconscious. We have him in a single-bedded ward." She rose from her desk. "Mister Greer popped in before he went home," she said as they walked. "Told me where you were. Asked me to let you know if anything happened to your patient. I phoned, but you must have been on your way here."

"Thoughtful of Charlie," O'Reilly said, "and thank you, Sister."

"How are you finding the Huts?" she asked.

"Pretty basic," he said.

Mutterings and snores came from the darkened wards. One room was brightly lit. A staff nurse sat in a chair beside the bed where Donal lay. She was using a suction catheter to clear saliva from his mouth and throat. His head was swathed in a gauze bandage. He had no pillow.

"This is Doctor O'Reilly," Sister said.

The nurse turned off the sucker and smiled.

"How's Donal?" he asked, looking down on the man and the array of tubes that surrounded him. You poor bastard, he thought. A tube in your nose into your stomach to remove any gastric secretion, getting fluids from an intravenous drip, having your bladder emptied by a catheter, and judging by the stain on the bandage, still leaking blood from the injury. Charlie had been right to put in a drain.

"He's doing well." She handed him a clipboard.

O'Reilly read the observations. Donal's temperature, pulse, blood pressure, and respiratory rates were all normal. "Good," he said. The man had surmounted the first hurdle and it gladdened O'Reilly. How completely Donal would recover remained to be seen, but the next step was for him to regain consciousness. Come on, Donal, fight, O'Reilly thought, although after years of practice he knew Donal had no control over the next hours. But damn it all, he wanted Donal to get better. Completely better.

O'Reilly returned the clipboard. "Thank you, nurse. Please take good care of him." He regretted the remark, smiled, and said, "I know you will." He turned to Sister. "Thank you both." He yawned. "Oh Lord, it's been a long day." He looked at his watch. One twenty. The last train to Ballybucklebo had gone hours ago. "I'll try to get some shut-eye."

"If anything changes with your friend I'll give you a ring," Sister said.

The word "friend" wasn't lost on O'Reilly. Come to think of it, all his patients in the little village and townland were his friends, and he liked it that way. "I'd be grateful," he said. "Good night, Sister?"

"Hoey. Jane Hoey. I'm a friend of Kitty O'Hallorhan."

"So am I," said O'Reilly. He saw how she was looking at him. "I suppose you already knew that."

She smiled. "She has spoken of you."

"She'll be pleased about Donal too," he said, not wishing to discuss himself and Kitty. Not at this hour of the morning. "I'll get a cuppa, then bed. Good night, Sister Hoey," he said and left.

It was a fair walk back to the cafeteria. He thought of Jane Hoey and how, with his life and Kitty's coming together, this woman might become a part of a new set of friends. And it lifted his spirits, the thought of new friends and old. Old friends like Cromie, Beresford, Hilda Manwell, Charlie. And Donal Donnelly.

O'Reilly considered phoning Barry asking him to go and see Julie to give her the latest information, but, he shook his head, what was the point in disturbing both of them, even though the outlook at this point was good? Julie would be worried enough, and the news, while comforting, wasn't good enough to soothe her fears. The morning would be fine, and Donal might be even better.

O'Reilly sat in the Caves finishing a tea that could have given Maggie MacCorkle's corrosive cuppas a run for their money. Very few diners were in the place at this hour of the morning.

He didn't want anything to eat. The apple pie he'd had hours ago still felt like sludge in his stomach, or perhaps was it his concern for Donal that was slowing his digestion? He shook his head. It took a lot to put Fingal Flahertie O'Reilly off his victuals. As a student he'd once had to eat not one but two Christmas dinners on the same day and it hadn't troubled him at all. Well, not too much.

He pushed back his chair, crossed his arms, let his head rest on his left shoulder, and closed his eyes.

Fingal could hear church bells, their bronze voices strident, their cadences ragged. Each, it seemed, was trying to outdo the others. As Christmas services and masses ended, the joyous pealing rang over the districts of Dublin. Over Ranelagh and Rathmines, Ballyfermot and Bluebell, the Phoenix and Blackrock. The bells brought their message, ". . . and on earth peace, good will toward men," to the homes of the well-to-do on Lansdowne Road in Ballsbridge, and to the tenements of the Liberties, Monto, the Coombe.

Paddy Keogh and Kevin Doherty were not at home, but here on

Saint Patrick's Ward. Kevin Doherty's breathing was regular and his cheeks were pink. Paddy Keogh must have tired of his Old Bill. His moustache was neatly trimmed. Fingal winked across at Paddy and was rewarded with a left-handed salute. The old soldier was sitting at attention.

They weren't sick, but two of the lucky winners of an annual lottery. It was a tradition of Sir Patrick Dun's that only seriously ill patients were admitted for the three days preceding Christmas Day, and every effort was made to clear as many beds as possible. On Christmas Eve morning, messages were sent to the homes of a number of men and women. They were some of the poorest ex-patients who lived nearby. They were invited to attend for admission that afternoon. Each would be treated to a Christmas dinner the next day. A list had been compiled over the year by Sister Daly and names drawn from a hat.

Saint Patrick's, the men's ward, was decorated with holly over the picture frames, coloured crêpe paper ribbons wrapped around bed-head frames. A tree resplendent in tinsel and coloured glass balls stood in the centre aisle. Beside it was a low table heaped with wrapped gifts. Each patient had a Christmas cracker on his bedside locker.

The sounds of "Hark the Herald Angels" came from the horn of a windup gramophone on a table near Fingal. He'd been given the job of musical director. He thought the record sounded scratchy. Time to change the needle. He removed a triangular piece of bamboo from a little box on the gramophone's top and a pair of clippers. One cut and the bamboo, sliced on the bias, was ready. He lifted the arm from the record, unscrewed the worn needle, and replaced it with the new bamboo. He wound up the machine and put the needle in the groove. Better. Much better.

It was de rigueur for every fourth-year student to be here to serve the patients and to have their own Christmas dinner. Senior staff supervised the proceedings in both the men's and women's wards.

"I wish," said Cromie, who was standing near Fingal with the three other juniors and Geoff Pilkington, "I wish Doctor Micks would hurry up and get here." Charlie was not on the ward. He was preparing a surprise.

Fingal sipped a sherry. They all had one except Ronald Hercules Fitzpatrick, who clutched a glass of orange juice. "Once we've fed the customers and had a bite ourselves, we're free," Cromie said. "I'm meeting Virginia today. It's too far to try to get to Bangor. My folks understand." Cromie had started seeing Virginia Treanor ("Virgin for short, but not for long," as Bob had once muttered, sotto voce), a classmate of Kitty's.

Fingal was getting fond of that girl. He'd recognised it in Neary's. Trouble was, could he afford to get involved at this stage of his studies? He'd meant what he'd told Lars about not getting hooked, and yet— He looked across at her where she stood. Sister and her staff nurses and students were lined up along the other side of the table. They too held full glasses. God, Kitty was gorgeous and if anyone would understand a medical student's life who better than a nurse?

Doctor Micks arrived. Fingal's naval discipline asserted itself and he came to attention.

The senior consultant carried a large hold-all. "Merry Christmas, all."

"Merry Christmas, Doctor Micks."

He put the bag on a trestle table near the centre of the ward between the ranks of beds. On it stood plates in piles, cutlery, serviettes, large bone-handled carving knives and forks, and places set for the staff. "To business, Sister."

She despatched a student nurse. "Tell the kitchen we're ready to serve dinner."

"Doctor Pilkington, if you please," said Doctor Micks.

"Right, you five," Geoff said. "Follow me." He led the students to the table under the tree. "I want each of you to grab half a dozen presents. They're labelled with bed numbers. Go and give one each to the patients. Sister's arranged for tobacco or cigarettes for the smokers and mickeys of Jameson for the nonsmokers."

Fitzpatrick sniffed then said, "I don't think small bottles of whiskey or tobacco are very healthy. I'd have thought New Testaments or psalters might have been more appropriate."

"Och, sure," Fingal said, "don't half the doctors in Dublin recommend tobacco to settle the nerves? And a wee tot never did anyone a bit of harm. The worst a few cigs does is stunt your growth if you start smoking too young."

"Nevertheless, I do not approve," Fitzpatrick said.

Hilda Manwell fixed the man with a stare that would have done justice to Balor the mythical Fomorian whose gaze could kill. Her voice was low and controlled. "It's the season to be jolly, for God's sake."

Fingal thought Hilda was going to tear a strip off Fitzpatrick, but a commotion at the end of the ward attracted everyone's attention.

"Ho, ho, ho," a deep voice boomed.

That was Fingal's cue. He lifted the arm, spun the windup crank, removed the record and replaced it with Guy Lombardo's Royal Canadians' "Winter Wonderland."

—In the lane snow is glistening—

"Ho, ho, ho." A red-suited, white-bearded Santa Claus bounded along the ward. If his red hair hadn't been sticking out from under his white cotton-wool-trimmed hat Fingal wouldn't have recognised Charlie Greer. He made a beeline for Sister Daly, stood in front of her, and from behind his back produced a sprig of mistle-toe. He held it above Sister's head.

"Merry Christmas, Sister," Santa yelled.

Every eye was on the couple.

Fingal stole a glance at Doctor Micks. The ordinarily reserved senior physician was smiling broadly and when Santa bent and planted a wet kiss on her forehead, Doctor Micks burst into laughter and began applauding. Soon everyone was joining in.

—gone away is the bluebird—

Sister Daly blushed to match Santa's coat, but said, "It does be the festive season, Mister—"

Fingal was sure she was going to say "Greer," and perhaps demand retribution, but she continued, "—Claus, so little liberties are permitted, so." She returned the kiss quite forcibly, it appeared to Fingal. The applause deafened him.

"But," Sister continued, as Santa tried to hug her, "only shmall little ones. You students—keep away from my nurses." And yet, Fingal thought, as he watched Sister's gaze flit from Kitty to himself, there was a kindness in the Cork woman's eyes. She spoke to Charlie. "Go you now and have a sherry and give Doctor Micks's helpers a hand with the presents."

Charlie joined the group at the tree and grabbed a handful of gifts.

"Well done, Charlie," Fingal said quietly.

"Begod," said Charlie, "that sister is a ferocious kisser. I wonder what she gets up to on her nights off?"

Fingal laughed, ignored the question, and whispered, "Give me the mistletoe."

He'd accepted the sprig when he felt a tug on his sleeve and turned.

Bob Beresford smiled and proffered a gift. "It's for your sergeant pal in bed 65. I thought you'd like to deliver it."

"Thanks, Bob." Fingal wondered what it was about Bob Beresford that intrigued him so. He made a point of seeming not to care and yet he was considerate, looked after his patients well, and had a quick mind. Surely he didn't keep failing simply to hang on to his inheritance? That conversation they'd had in Neary's about public health and research would be worth following up.

Fingal took the gift, picked up the remaining few that were left on the table, and went to distribute them. When he passed Kitty he showed her the mistletoe, inclined his head toward the sluice, and grinned.

He kept Paddy's gift for last. "Merry Christmas, Sergeant Paddy," he said, and handed over the parcel. "Glad you're looking well."

The neat moustache went up as Paddy Keogh grinned and said, "T'anks, sir. T'anks a whole lot for the present and even more because I'm well because of you and your feckin' great skewer. Jasus, I t'ought the first time I seed it, it was a French bayonet."

"Och, sure it's only my job," Fingal said, but he smiled. "Thank you too, Paddy. I've done another pleural tap since." But I learned on you, he thought.

"Ah well, fair play to you, sir. Merry Christmas." Paddy pointed across the ward. "Jasus, Mary, and Joseph, would youse look at dat?" His eyes were wide.

The kitchen staff were setting steaming platters on the table. Roast stuffed turkeys surrounded by roast potatoes and chipolata sausages. Hams, their skin studded with cloves, gave off tantalising scents. Tureens of carrots jostled with dishes of brussels sprouts and more dishes of mashed potatoes. There were sauceboats of gravy, bread sauce, cranberry sauce. From where he stood the aromas made Fingal's mouth water.

"Mother of God," Paddy said, his eyes even wider. "I've niver seen the likes in me whole feckin' life. Is it the five t'ousand you're for feeding?" He shook his head and his smile vanished. "Here I am in dis place wit' all you learnèd folks waiting on us hand and foot and serving us a feast. I'll tell you, Mister O'Reilly, sir, it beats the bread and dripping pieces my two sisters and brother'll be having in our wee room."

Three people in one room with nothing for Christmas but bread spread with bacon grease. Fingal felt a prickling behind his eyelids.

"Mind you, we've a lot more space dan we had a couple of years back. Two of me sisters got married and left . . ." The man's voice trailed off and Fingal waited. "I don't mind telling you, sir, you're feckin' near family yourself, you know so much about me." Paddy shrugged. "The ould ones passed along wi' me baby brother, Aidan, not long after. Feckin' fever. Daddy Nagle, the chemist on Meath Street, made them up powders but—och."

Fingal shuddered. "The fever" that had taken Paddy's mother, father, and brother had probably been typhoid. It was endemic in the Dublin slums due to poor sanitation and contaminated drinking water or milk. The tenement dwellers had great faith in their pharmacists. Mister Nagle would have administered a "powder" of ground-up herbs, perhaps a bit of strychnine. Ipecacuanha was a popular ingredient because of its foul taste. Everyone knew that the worse a medicine tasted the stronger it was.

"Is there no way you and your family could move out?"

"Where to? Me sisters have work as charwomen. Barry's a messenger boy. I beg to add to me British pensheen."

Fingal knew the addition of the Irish *sin,* pronounced "sheen," was used to diminish something. It was Paddy's way of saying "tiny pension."

"On what we make combined we'll not be moving into Dublin Castle in a hurry, sir. We get by, but we're like most people. You live where you get born unless you're a girl and some fellah takes you off to his place." Paddy pushed himself further up the bed. He managed a smile and lowered his voice. "At least my ones'll have a couple of bottles of stout apiece. Sister, she's a good skin, she give me an extra bottle every day I was here. For to take home for me family, like. We've saved dem wee bottles up for Christmas."

Fingal glanced over to Sister Daly. She was indeed a good skin. She had no authority to hand out extra Guinness. He admired anyone who clearly believed rules were for the obedience of idiots and merely for the guidance of wise folks.

"Aye," said Paddy, his smile returning, "and Dicey Duggan, her w'at has a fruit barrow at Mason's Market on Horseman's Row, her w'at the lads call, 'the tart wit' the cart,' she give me half a dozen oranges for treats."

Fingal had heard how the people of the Dublin tenements pulled together. Even those who recently had been rehoused by the City Council's new building program pined for their old neighbourhoods and wanted to return. It wasn't that they missed their dilapidated surroundings, but vibrant communities had been torn apart. Neighbours of years' standing had been separated by bureaucratic fiat. A family of fourteen might have shared one room across the staircase from their longtime friends. After rehousing, even the family might have been broken up and placed in separate, distant flats, with their former friends and neighbours a dozen streets away.

Because of their friend Dicey Duggan, Sergeant Keogh's family would each get two oranges as their Christmas treat. Fingal remembered that he and Lars would always find an orange at the bottom of the pillowcase full of Santa Claus presents. It had been one of Ma's family traditions. He looked at Paddy. Damn it, Fingal, he told himself, you told Kitty a week ago you'd try to find the man a place. And what have you done? Sweet Fanny Adams.

Sister said to the patients, "Now gentlemen, Doctor Micks will carve and my nurses and the medical staff and students, and Saint Nicholas himself, will serve you." She grinned at Charlie. "Hope you're not too hot in there under all that red serge," she said.

Charlie grinned and wiped the back of his hand over his glistening forehead.

She lifted a bottle of Jameson. "All of you who wish will get a glass of this after you've had your Christmas pudding and pulled your crackers."

The patients applauded.

A voice yelled, "It's a life of feckin' Riley. Can we stay tomorrow too, Sister?" That provoked laughter and cheers.

Fingal, wondering how he might get a glass of the Jemmy instead of this sticky sherry, crossed the ward and joined the line of students and nurses waiting to be handed loaded plates. Quite a reversal, he thought, for members of the upper class to be acting as servants for the workers. Maybe the fellah whose birthday they were celebrating today had it right when he washed the beggars' feet.

Before the staff sat down to dine Doctor Micks opened his hold-all and distributed gifts. He coughed. "Seems a bit odd me giving you a present, Santa."

Charlie laughed. "It's Greer, sir, and thank you." He accepted a gift.

"Here you are, O'Reilly," Doctor Micks said. "Try this Murray's Erinmore Flake. It doesn't stink like that Crow Bar stuff you smoke."

"Thank you, sir."

Fingal did justice to the meal, finished the last of his Christmas pudding, got up to say good-bye to Kevin Doherty and Paddy Keogh. He caught Kitty's eye where she sat at the nurses' side of the table. This time it was her turn to nod toward the sluice.

He showed her five fingers and hoped she understood. He needed a few minutes before he could be there.

He went and sat on Kevin's bed. "How've you been, Kevin?" he asked.

Mister KD, the "heart failure because of rheumatic valvular disease" smiled. "Not so dusty, sir. I'm off quinidine now. Dat digitalis stuff—is it true it's made from foxgloves? It's doing its trick all right."

"I'm delighted to hear it," Fingal said, "and yes. From a foxglove called *Digitalis purpurea*. I hope it keeps up the good work. We don't want to see you back in here, do we?"

"I hope you're right, sir, but it's happened before."

And it probably will happen again, Fingal thought, but said, "We must hope for the best." He rose. "You look after yourself, Kevin, and have a happy New Year."

"And to you, Doc—and t'anks for all you done. By the way." Kevin Doherty raised one eyebrow. "You don't mind my asking, sir? But how did t'ings go with dat pretty wee mott over dere?"

"Ah," said Fingal, glancing over to where Kitty was walking to the end of the ward. "I'm taking her out to bring in the New Year."

"Fair play to you, sir. Fair play."

Fingal could see that Kevin's smile was one of pure pleasure. Although his own life had been limited by poverty and ill health, he wasn't bitter about someone else's happiness.

"Thanks," Fingal said, glancing at his watch. "You look after yourself, Kevin. I'd better be running. I'm expected at my folks' for Christmas dinner."

He made sure Sister Daly was deep in conversation with Doctor Micks, then slipped into the sluice, where Kitty was waiting. He stood beside her, held the sprig over her head, encircled her with one arm, and kissed her long and hard. "Merry Christmas, Kitty O'Hallorhan," he said. "A very merry Christmas and a happy New Year."

16

We'll Keep Our Christmas Merry Still

Ma asked, "Has everyone had enough? Are we finished?"

Father, from his place at the top of the long mahogany dining table, said, "Marvellous, Mary." The yellow silk cravat Lars had given him added a festive touch to his otherwise sober suit.

Lars wiped his mouth and folded his napkin. "It was wonderful, Mother. Thank you." His words were formal.

Ma glanced at her son. "Are you sure you're all right, Lars? You've eaten very little."

"I'm fine. Honestly."

Was Lars fine? Fingal pursed his lips. When he'd arrived, his brother had seemed subdued. The man wasn't normally boisterous, but he usually exuded an air of rural contentment. They'd not had a moment alone, but the minute they did Fingal was going to find out why his big brother had fidgeted through the meal and barely eaten his turkey.

Fingal hadn't done Cook's efforts justice either. He swallowed, stifled an urge to burp, and wondered if he might undo the button of his waistband. The answer was no. Ma and Cook would both be devastated if they thought he'd had to struggle to eat what they didn't know was his second Christmas dinner of the day.

The light from the chandelier glanced off the facets of a Waterford cut-glass bowl where the remnants of a sherry trifle clung to the sides and bottom. The Christmas pudding lay in ruins.

"You may clear, Bridgit," Ma said.

"Thank you, Ma'am." Bridgit moved from where she'd been standing and began piling plates onto her tray.

"That meal," Fingal said as she took away his dessert plate, "was the bee's knees." He knew his remark would be relayed to Cook.

Father's brow wrinkled and he asked, "The what?"

"Bee's knees," Fingal said. "Just a step down from the cat's pyjamas and much better than the eel's ankles."

Ma chuckled. "Eels don't have ankles, Fingal."

"Perhaps not, but bees do have knees. I've seen 'em," Fingal said and was relieved to hear Lars's dry laugh.

Father shook his head. "I despair. American slang, I suppose?" He pursed his lips, and tutted. "Our American cousins will be the ruination of the English language." He sipped a little wine. Surprisingly he was on his second glass of claret.

Here we go, Fingal thought. Another of his sermons. Surely not on Christmas Day?

"Bee's knees indeed," Father continued. "As your namesake remarked as long ago as 1882, 'We have really everything in common with the Americans nowadays except, of course, language.'" He smiled broadly. Fingal's mouth opened when Father laughed and said, "Who can identify the quotation?"

Fingal beat Lars. "*The Canterville Ghost*," he said, then realised that his brother didn't look as if he'd tried to answer.

"I'm glad you remembered," Father said.

Fingal said, "You made us act it out one Christmas. You and Mother took all the grown-up parts and Lars and I were the Otis twins, known as the 'stars and stripes.'"

Ma laughed, but Fingal heard a wistfulness when she said, "It was fun when you two were young. You were the show-off, Fingal. I often wondered if the stage might not have been in your stars."

He shook his head. "You know what I've always wanted." I wish, he thought, I hadn't said that, because I know I've given Father a cue to start a discussion I'd rather avoid.

"As for your career, Fingal—"

Here it comes. Fingal sat back and folded his arms.

"I think after seven years," Father leant forward, "I am becoming reconciled to your decision to study medicine."

What? Fingal's eyes widened. Reconciled?

"Father and I have talked about you a lot, son," Ma said, and smiled at him.

I'll bet you have, Ma. "Thank you."

"We have," Father said. "We only have one point of disagreement now."

Ma turned to Father. "I wonder if today is the right time, Connan?"

"To discuss it? Of course it is. It's for Fingal's own good. It's because we worry about him, Mary."

Fingal wondered what was coming but decided that he would not rear up no matter what Father might say.

"We have some medical friends who move in literary circles. Doctor Victor Millington Synge is a nephew of the playwright the late J. M. Synge and Mister Oliver St. John Gogarty is a poet in his own right."

"Mister Gogarty is also an ear, nose, and throat surgeon and can charge as much as three hundred pounds for one operation," said Fingal. That was probably more than Father made in one year. He wondered what Father was coming to and continued, "Mister Gogarty has a primrose Rolls-Royce, his own aeroplane, and a mansion at Renvyle on the west coast." He frowned. "I'm not quite sure what he and Doctor Synge have to do with me."

"They are specialists," Ma said, "and Father, having met them both several times, is very impressed by them and how they do their medical work."

And he can't quite bring himself to say it, Fingal thought, but he's on the verge of telling me to specialise.

"Your mother is absolutely right," Father said. "I may just have been wrong forbidding you to go your own headstrong way about university, Fingal."

Glory Hallelujah, he may just have been wrong. He had been. Totally wrong. Then Fingal recognised the thought as ungenerous and said, "Thank you, Father. Thank you very much."

Father coughed. "Our Christmas present to you, Lars, is a trip to the French Riviera this coming February or March—"

"Thank you. Thank you both," Lars said. It looked forced to Fingal, but Lars finally did smile after having taken a deep breath. He stood, shook Father's hand and hugged Mother. "That's most generous. Thank you both. So much." No wonder. Usually gifts from the folks were things like Fingal's birthday lighter. And if Lars was getting such an expensive present what was coming next?

"And yours, Fingal, is fifty pounds annually for the next two years. You should be qualified as a doctor in 1936."

Fingal pushed his chair back. Fifty pounds? Manna from Heaven. No more scrimping and saving, long walks instead of tram rides, no more fish-and-chips unless he really wanted them. And, the realisation dawned, a bridge had been thrown over the chasm between father and son.

Fingal stood. He too shook Father's hand. "Thank you, Father. Thank you very much, and not only for the money. I was pigheaded. I'm sorry." That was as close to a complete apology as he could get without being hypocritical. If he'd not been stubborn he'd be a nuclear physicist by now, and hating it. He looked at Ma and saw her smiling, nodding, and with brightness at the corners of her eyes. Lord knew how hard she must have worked to bring this to pass. "Thank you, Mother," Fingal said. "Bless you." He enfolded her in a bear hug.

Bridgit reappeared with an empty tray and began clearing the last of the dinner things.

Ma inclined her head toward the maid and said, "We've had a lovely meal, but Christmas is such extra work for the servants."

"Tell Cook, Bridgit," Father said, "how very much we enjoyed our dinner. And thank you both for all your efforts."

Bridgit bobbed. "Thank you, sir, ma'am."

Ma rose and picked up her plate. "I'm coming with you, Bridgit," she said. "I'd like to thank Cook personally." She followed the maid.

Fingal, still hardly believing his father had come around, picked up his glass. "Will we go through to the lounge?"

Father said quietly, "You boys go ahead. I'll finish my claret then Mother and I'll join you." He smiled. "Seeing we've something to celebrate I might just open the Napoleon to complement the coffee."

Fingal understood what his father was trying to say and was searching for the right words when Lars said, "Thanks again for the trip to France."

"When it came to finances, Mother and I have always tried to treat you boys equally," Father said.

"You have, Father," Fingal said, "you really have. Thank you."

"We'll go through," Lars said.

"Don't be too long, Father," Fingal said, smiled, and moved toward the drawing room, but, he thought, give me enough time to find out what's bothering my brother.

Lars plumped himself down in an armchair, one of four arranged in a semicircle around a low table in front of a blazing fire. He crossed his legs.

Fingal sat in another armchair, set his glass on the table, and pulled out his briar and the unopened pouch of Erinmore Flake tobacco, his present from Doctor Micks. "Right, Lars," he said, "come on. What's eating you?"

Lars shrugged. "I'm letting it show, aren't I?"

Fingal nodded.

"I'm sorry. You remember telling me I'd know when the time and the place were right?"

Fingal had to think for a few seconds then remembered the day back in October. They'd been climbing the front steps after Fingal had dutifully admired Lars's new car. "Jean Neely?"

"Last night. Dinner at the Gresham, a drive in Phoenix Park, the moon four days past the full." He lowered his head onto his locked hands.

Fingal waited.

Lars pulled a velvet-covered box from his pocket and opened it to show a ring, a diamond solitaire flanked by smaller sapphires. His voice trembled. "She said no. She couldn't bear living in the country." He sighed. "And I know I couldn't take big city living. I should have seen it coming. I know how she loves Dublin. She said she was actually planning to break things off, but was waiting until after Christmas."

"Lord." Fingal stood. He put his hands on Lars's shoulder and squeezed. "I'm sorry, Lars. I really am." He could imagine what it must have cost the man to open himself completely. How he must be hurting. Fingal wanted to hug his brother, but that was something men did not do. Pity, he thought. About as humane as not calling patients by their names, but Lars would be embarrassed. "Is there anything at all I can do?"

Lars shook his head. "But thanks, Finn." He rose, stood by the mantel, and took a deep breath. "I've always had a lousy sense of timing." He managed a wry grin. "I'll get over it," he said. "In time."

"Course you will." But Fingal wondered if his brother would. He knew several of his father's friends who were confirmed bachelors. Would Lars become one too?

His brother returned to his seat. "Sit down, Finn." Lars took a deep breath. "It hurts like hell, but life has to go on. It's been a big day for you. I don't want to spoil it."

"Thanks, Lars, but your news. You're right," he tried to make Lars smile, "you do have a lousy sense of timing. I don't suppose you've said anything to the folks?"

"I didn't want to spoil Christmas. Ma would be upset and Father?" Lars stared up. "I didn't need his 'importance of marrying well' lecture today."

Fingal laughed. "Nor me. Mind you, I'm safe so far. No ladies on the horizon."

Lars shrugged. "Men have been rejected before. They recover."

"I hope so," Fingal said. "I really do."

Lars inclined his head. "Let's not make a song and dance about it. It happened. What's more important is that I never thought the old man would back down over you choosing medicine. Never. How do you feel?"

"Flabbergasted," Fingal said.

"I think," Lars said, "the pair of us have misunderstood him. Mistook a deeply held sense of having to do what he sees as right for sheer bloody mindedness."

Fingal lit his pipe. He stared into the fire then back at Lars. "You're right," Fingal said, and lifted his glass. "To our Father," he said, then grinned and continued, "which art in Lansdowne Road. Professor O'Reilly be thy name. Thy will be done."

"Unless your younger son runs off to sea," said Lars, and managed a smile. "Which was a bloody good thing too."

Fingal inclined his head to one side and looked long at Lars. "You suggested it back then, big brother, and now look what's happened." He sipped his wine. "Lord, Lars, I'm tickled pink, and not only about the money."

"Because Father has bent, is willing to accept your decision?"

"Right. You know how strained things have been. It's going to be a lot more pleasant coming home in future."

"I really am delighted, Finn." Lars stared out of the window then back to Fingal. "And speaking of visiting, when are you going to come up to Portaferry?"

"Maybe in the spring. Once the rugby season's over." Fingal let go a mighty puff of tobacco smoke. "You still wildfowling?"

Lars smiled. The wrinkles at the corners of his peat-brown eyes deepened and his moustache curled up to reveal straight white teeth. His smile had always been slow, lazy; perhaps, Fingal thought, like the man himself who if rumour be true had scraped through law school with a minimum of effort and the lowest marks compatible with passing. "I'll be in a wheelchair before I stop." He leant across and tapped Fingal's knee. "It's time you came up for a day out. A breath of fresh air would do you good."

Fingal hadn't taken his shotgun out of its case since he'd started at Trinity. It was a matter of priorities. The duck-shooting season would close before the rugby was over for the year, but he would have enjoyed a day in the wild solitude of Strangford Lough. The place had been important to Fingal ever since he was thirteen and living in Holywood. His brother, nearly three years his senior and at the time seeming like one of the ancients, had loaned him a light gun and brought him out along the banks of the stream at Lisbane. Fingal smiled at his brother. "You're right," he said. "It would. I will if I can make time. I miss the place."

"Aye," said Lars softly, "it's beautiful there. I miss it already."

His eyes brightened. He inclined his head. "I'd never want to be far from Strangford. It has a pull all its own. It's somewhere I can go if I'm worried, hurt—"

"Like now," Fingal said quietly.

"Yes, Finn. Like now. I'll go to the shore as soon as I'm home. Lick my wounds." He sighed. "If my clients could hear me, the fellah they think is a dry old stick of a lawyer, saying how much of a hold the lough can have over a man, they'd think I'd taken leave of my senses, but it is a place I love dearly."

"I envy you, Lars," Fingal said. "You've found your spot." He wanted to take the words back, suddenly aware that it was Lars's love for the lough that had ended his romance with Jean Neely.

But Lars's face was composed. "And what about you, Finn?" he asked. "Any closer to finding yours?"

"Yes and no. Medicine certainly, but general practice or specialise? I'll cross that bridge when I come to it, Lars. I don't have to choose right away. I'll probably do what a lot of people do. Qualify, be a GP for a few years, then decide whether to stick with it or change course and specialise. But so far medicine's everything I ever wanted." He glanced over his shoulder. "I'd be qualified, but for—"

"Father's certainly turned up trumps now." Lars stretched his legs to the fire and leaned back into his chair. "God knows what it's cost him to admit he was wrong."

"Good old Ma." Fingal puffed contentedly and said, "However she did it I'm damn glad my personal state of hostilities is over."

"I'm pleased for you too," Lars said.

"And you're not alone," Ma said. Fingal hadn't heard her coming in.

"I'm in your debt, Ma," Fingal said. "Deeply."

She wagged a finger at him. "You repay me by working hard, passing all your exams, and being the best doctor you can be."

"I will," he said.

"You had better, Fingal Flahertie O'Reilly," Father, who had just entered, said, "and if you'll take some advice—" He held up a hand. "—not mine, Mister Gogarty's. Don't settle for being a GP. Specialise."

It's Christmas, Fingal thought. Father has just made a massive concession. Humour him. Don't say, "that's my decision." Instead he smiled and said quietly, "I've the next eighteen months to get through first, Father. I enjoyed my time in internal medicine, but I still want to see how I like surgery and obstetrics. I'll be doing them later this year and early next." He pointed his pipe stem at Father's chest. "The whole field of clinical practice so far has been exciting, but I must try it all before I make up my mind."

"And I," said Father, "have no doubts whatsoever that you will." He walked over to the sideboard and lifted a decanter. "Now. Who would like a brandy?"

"I'll not," Ma said, "but I'm sure the boys will." She took one of the vacant chairs and smoothed her cerise silk dress over her knees. "Now," she said briskly, "I want to hear what both of you are planning for 1935. You first, Lars."

17

Why He a Wauling Bagpipe

". . . For the sake of auld lang syne." The discordant singing ended and a drum roll accompanied the cheers of the students and their partners welcoming 1935. Fingal tootled on his party horn and chucked a coloured paper streamer to tangle with the myriad others that arced through the air. Spotlights picked out balloons released from an overhead net.

"Happy New Year, Fingal," Kitty yelled in his ear. "Happy New Year."

He picked her up off the floor and whirled her in a circle. The train of her floor-length backless dress trailed out behind her. He set her on her feet. "Happy New Year, Kitty O'Hallorhan," he roared, and kissed her. "When we come to this dance—" He'd been going to say, "next year, you'll be a staff nurse and I'll only have six more months to go to be qualified," but he realised there was no guarantee he and Kitty would still be keeping company twelve months from now. What had happened to Lars on Christmas Eve was evidence of how fragile love affairs could be. But that wasn't it. Fingal knew he just wasn't ready to tell her he loved her. Not yet. He'd too much invested. Four years at sea. Paying his own way for three and a half years at school. A newly healing seven-year rift with Father. And he'd invested it all for one reason. He wasn't like Bob studying to please a deceased eccentric relative. Fingal yearned to be a doctor. It was perfectly simple.

He tugged at his wing collar and hoped she'd not heard him. His naval jacket, blue waistcoat, and gold laced trousers were in gaudy contrast with the other men's subfusc formal attire. He'd kept the mess dress from his days on HMS *Tiger*. Even with Father and Ma's Christmas present, Fingal did not want to waste money buying clothes. He smiled at Kitty. He'd been willing to wear the damn monkey suit because she'd been so keen to come to this dance.

Cromie was squiring Virginia Treanor, a petite blonde wearing a short crepe de chine evening frock. At the start of the evening he had taken one look at Fingal and said, "Good Lord, a salty sailor man. Come on, O'Reilly, dance the Sailor's Hornpipe."

"Listen, you heathen haggis," Fingal had said to Cromie, "seeing you're in full Highland dress, Glengarry bonnet, jacket with silver buttons—and isn't that a lovely skirt—"

"Kilt, you eejit." Cromie pointed to a dagger stuck down the leg of his sock, "and that's a *skean dhu,* a black knife."

"And that yoke hanging down your front like a dead cat with tassels is a sporran. I know, but why the Highland regalia? You're not Scots."

"Actually Great-grandfather Cromie was from outside Aberdeen. The name of his village in Scots Gaelic, *crombach,* means 'the crooked place.' The family had been there since at least the tenth century. He moved to Bangor in 1870."

"I'll be damned."

"And it may have escaped you, I do play the pipes. I've to play after midnight. Pipe in the New Year."

"Indeed," said Fingal. "Well, you pipe away and I'll give you a hornpipe—after you've danced a Highland fling."

"Sword dance more likely," Bob Beresford said from where he stood with Charlie and their partners.

Cromie had laughed and suggested they have a warm-up drink.

Now, four hours later Fingal wondered if letting Cromie start so early had been a good idea. His friend was being helped onto the stage by Charlie Greer.

"Do you think he'll be all right, Bob?"

"Och aye." Bob Beresford stood beside his own partner, Bette Swanson, a honey blonde with a winter rose that Bob had given her pinned close to her décolletage. It kept company with her Christmas cameo that Bob had told Fingal had been bought after he'd left Neary's and given the whistle player not two but five shillings. "I'm told pipers play best when they're half cut." He shot a cuff with diamond cuff links that matched the studs of his white waistcoat. "Charlie'll keep an eye on him. Don't worry."

"I hope so." Cromie did not hold his drink well and after a couple of beers could start to sway. "We should have made him take it easy on the grog."

"Ladies and gentlemen," the emcee announced in a fake Scots burr, "ladies and gentlemen, please welcome Angus MacHamish MacAngus Auchterlony, Laird of the Tattie-bogles, Thane of Pitten-weem, Master of Ballantrae, and Commander of the ancient Caledonian Order of the Thistle, twelfth class. Angus will now play 'MacReekie's Lament.'" He handed Cromie a set of bagpipes.

Fingal laughed and said to Kitty, "Did you ever hear such fake Scottish gibberish?"

"Sure, it's only a bit of *craic*," she said, and chuckled.

He put his arm round her waist and pulled her to him. "You're right, but I'm still worried about Cromie. He's had quite a skinful. He doesn't usually drink much. I should have kept an eye on him or persuaded him not to go onstage. I don't want him to make an ass of himself."

"Don't worry your head about it, Fingal. You can't be responsible for everyone. And look," she said, pointing to the stage. "Big

Charlie's up there with him. He'll make sure Cromie's all right. You heard what Bob said about pipers and the drink."

"I hope he knows what he's talking about."

Cromie tucked the pipes under his left arm, the drones sticking out in front of him, took a couple of unsteady steps, and teetered near the edge of the stage. Fingal started forward, but Charlie grabbed the back of Cromie's jacket and hauled him away from the drop.

Someone yelled, "Scots wha' hae," over the cheering of the crowd.

Cromie blinked in the footlights.

Get him off the stage, Fingal thought, clenching his teeth.

Cromie slammed to attention and in three stacatto movements, thrust the pipes out to arm's length, hauled them back to tuck the bag under his left arm, and set the drones on his shoulder. He put the blow-pipe in his mouth. His cheeks swelled and reddened. The bag only swelled. Cromie thumped its tartan cloth covering with the flat of his right hand and immediately placed his right fingers beneath those of his left hand to cover the holes of the chanter, which hung down from the neck of the bag.

A sonorous roaring came from the drones and underpinned the harsh melody that Cromie's flying fingers wrung from the chanter. Fingal recognised "Pibroch of Donal Dhu." He felt the hairs on the nape of his neck tingle and could envision the clans being spurred into battle by the martial music.

Cromie marched across the stage, kilt swinging, pipes blaring. No wonder the American troops in their War of Independence had called the Scottish regiments, "The ladies from hell."

On the dance floor undergraduates and their partners were forming themselves for Scottish dancing. Fingal turned to the four women and Bob. "Come on, we'll make a set." Everyone would know the dances. Young ladies and gentlemen were instructed in the art as part of their senior school curriculum at Protestant public schools, and Trinity was a Protestant university. He remembered his physical training instructor, a retired sergeant-major from the Gordon Highlanders, trying to teach the sixth-form boys a hornpipe saying, "Put yer left foot in—the bloody left one, left one, O'Reilly—like a nice young gentleman."

They formed two lines. Fingal faced Kitty and Bob stood across from Bette while Virginia and Charlie's date, a quiet, dark-haired country lass from near Maynooth, made up the final pair. Despite her shyness earlier in the evening she had shown remarkable proficiency dancing both the old Lindy hop and the brand-new college shag.

The noise from the stage stopped and the emcee announced, "Ladies and gentlemen. Our piper will now give us a reel, a jig, and a strathspey."

The hall rang with whoops and cheers, and the air was split asunder by the voice of the great highland bagpipe, *an pib mhór*.

Cromie played four sets. Fingal was perspiring from his exertions. He'd had to work hard remembering the intricacies not only of the manouevres but also of the steps required, the *pas de basques,* the common *schottisches.* As the last notes rang out, Fingal put his arms round Kitty. She fitted there as if she'd always belonged. "Having fun?" he asked.

"It's been wonderful, Fingal." She looked up into his eyes and he saw the amber flecks in the grey.

Again the pipes began. This time the song was slow, soulful. Fingal recognised "Lord Lovat's Lament." The notes soared, faded, rose again, a keening for a loss, a fitting requiem for the year 1934.

"That's beautiful," Kitty said. "So haunting."

"You're beautiful," Fingal said softly, "and you haunt me." He bent and put his lips to hers.

"Thank you, Fingal," she said. "You are fond of me, aren't you?"

He swallowed and came close to saying more, but the pipe music changed to a rattling rendition of an Irish song, "The Minstrel Boy." Perhaps, he thought, the interruption was not a bad thing. It wouldn't have taken much for him to tell her he was falling in love, but he had another mistress and he must stay with her for eighteen more months until he graduated as Doctor Fingal O'Reilly. He kissed Kitty then took her hand.

He looked up at the stage. Cromie finished playing, pulled the drones from his shoulder, and tucked them and the bag under his arm. He stood at attention. A man wearing a waiter's white jacket offered a silver tray to the sweating piper.

He stretched out his hand, lifted a small silver goblet, and held it at arm's length. *"Sláinte,"* he bellowed, put the vessel to his lips, and tilted his head back. To a roar of approval Cromie held the goblet upside down over the tray to show every last drop of whiskey had been swallowed.

"Happy New Year," he yelled, wobbled, and sat firmly on the bag of his pipes, which shrieked as it deflated. Cromie stayed on his bottom, legs asplay, knobby knees shining in the lights.

"Oh, Lord," said Fingal as he watched Charlie Greer bend over Cromie, who was starting to topple sideways. "Come on, Bob, we'll have to give Charlie a hand to get Cromie back to his room."

"Don't worry," Bob said. "I have my car. You and Charlie and your ladies stay on. Bette and I'll run poor old Cromie home, tuck him in, and be back here in no time."

It didn't take long for the three friends to put the now-snoring Cromie in the back of Bob's car. When they returned to the ballroom Kitty was alone. "Your partners, boys, have gone to powder their noses," she said. "They'll be back in two shakes of a lamb's tail."

Fingal saw how the light was reflected from her hair. "Come on. One last dance." He took her hand, warm in his, led her onto the floor, took her in his arms, and together they danced.

The band's singer, a countertenor, crooned,

. . . something deep inside cannot be denied . . .

Kitty laid her cheek against his and he felt the softness of her, inhaled her musk.

. . . when a lovely flame dies, smoke gets in your eyes.

He felt her move back and heard her whisper, "You won't let it die, Fingal, will you?"

"No," he said, "I'll not." And he knew he meant it.

18

Heal What Is Wounded

"I'm bollixed." Cromie walked into the Dun's students' mess. He yawned, flopped into a chair, and heaved his legs up on a low circular table.

Fingal, who had been sitting, absently tracing the names of generations of resident students carved into its wooden top, stopped, and looked up.

Bob Beresford arrived and yawned mightily. "We'd a bad night last night," he said. "Hardly slept a wink. A few more like that and never mind the pleasure of sharing call with Cromie and having you two here to greet me in the morning. I'll be rethinking my plans for Finals Part I in June. And I'm bloody well not going on rounds this morning."

This from the man who before Christmas was seriously considering passing his exams. "Balls," said Fingal. " 'Go to the ant, thou sluggard; consider her ways and be wise.' We can manage without sleep for the odd night. It was two A.M. when we packed it in on New Year's Eve. Didn't seem to bother you back then, Bob."

"That was two months ago," Bob said, "Cromie's not Bette Swanson, and don't you quote Proverbs at me, Fingal Flahertie O'Reilly. The ant and her constant working be damned." He lit a Gold Flake.

"All right, Bob, you're tired," Fingal said, "but you're not seriously thinking of giving up." Fingal was convinced that the more Bob learned about all aspects of medicine, understood how satisfying it was, the more he'd want to be a doctor. Perhaps not a clinician, but he'd seemed to have had his interest piqued in research that evening before Christmas.

Beresford grunted.

"Look," Fingal said, "June's four months away, and we've only to pass pathology and microbiology, materia medica and therapeutics, and medical jurisprudence and hygiene. It's not a whole hell of a lot."

"It sounds like a whole hell of a lot right now. That's six bloody courses, Fingal." Bob rubbed his eyes and yawned again. "We'll see. Right now I don't even feel like passing wind."

Fingal laughed. "The three of us'll keep nagging at you if you don't keep studying. Right, lads?"

"I don't care. I'm going to bed."

"Doctor Micks won't be pleased," Charlie said.

"Don't worry, Bob," Fingal said. "I'll tell him you've got a rare blood group and are donating blood, or you were bitten by a rabid badger."

"Fingal, don't be daft," Bob said, but at least a small smile flicked across his lips.

"I'll come up with some excuse for you," Fingal said, "provided that tonight we review the pathology of cirrhosis of the liver together. I know you cut the lecture to go to the races."

"I'd planned to see Bette tonight and—" Bob must have seen how Fingal was glaring at him. "Oh, all right."

"And Charlie will be with us too," Fingal said.

"Aye," Charlie said. "It's a pest that those Thursday pathology and microbiology lectures clash with rugby practice. Fingal and I missed hearing about cirrhosis too."

Conflict between important classes and rugby was indeed a pest. The last international match this season would be played between Ireland and Wales in March at Ravenhill in Belfast. They'd no chance of selection, but there was always next year. Both he and Charlie were doing everything in their power to improve their game, but they had to study too.

"Cirrhosis of the liver. Sounds about as exciting as watching bubbles float down the Liffey," Bob said, and looked at Cromie. "Jaysus, lad, by the way you threw up outside my car on New Year's morning I'd say it's a subject you should be studying with us."

"I must," said Cromie with a straight face, "I must have got a bad bottle."

Fingal laughed. "You want to work with us, Cromie?"

"Not tonight, thanks."

"We do need to catch up," Fingal said. He and Charlie would never miss a practice now and would work on staying fit throughout the summer too. Fingal could practically taste that place on the Irish side, but he had to attend seventy-five percent of all lectures or repeat the course. He was meeting the target, just, by attending every class on Monday and Tuesday.

Bob stubbed out his smoke. "I'm off." He paused. "By the way, Fingal, we admitted an old friend of yours this morning. Mister KD. In failure again."

"What? Bugger." Fingal clenched his teeth. "Thanks for telling me, Bob. We'll see him on rounds." He glanced at his watch. "And we'd better not be late for Doctor Micks." He stood. "Come on, lads." Fingal wondered just how sick Kevin Doherty was.

"Very" had been the answer. He'd managed a smile when he recognised Fingal, but had lapsed into semiconsciousness. His heart failure was worse and he was having another bout of atrial fibrillation. Doctor Pilkington had restarted treatment with quinidine.

Fingal determined to go back to Saint Patrick's Ward as soon as he had finished his afternoon work.

"Suture duty, you and me, Charlie," Fingal said, as they walked to outpatients. "And Cromie and Bob, now he's rejoined the ranks of the living after his nap, are doing skin diseases, aren't you?"

"We are," said Cromie. "I always feel itchy after a session there. All those rashes. Still, the treatments are pretty simple, 'If it's dry, wet it; if it's wet, dry it.' That's what Doctor Wallace says."

"When he's not lecturing on medical jurisprudence," Bob said. "I'd rather listen to someone reading a laundry list."

"But a subject we've to pass in June," Fingal said, "and he's a damn good teacher. By the way, Bob, Doctor Micks accepted my explanation that you had migraine, but he delivered a homily about his having difficulty issuing certificates of good standing to students who missed too many sessions."

Bob shrugged.

The outpatients department was a long, narrow room with two side aisles and a single central aisle. Ranks of plain, wooden, backless benches marched from the rear to the front arranged in blocks with dividing passages separating the seating. Each block was outside the door to an area dealing with a particular branch of medicine. Patients came, went to a desk, and were directed to wait outside the section where their needs could be met.

Bob and Cromie left to go to dermatology. Fingal and Charlie headed for the suture room. The waiting hall was packed.

"I think," Charlie said, "Doctor Whiteside, the consultant in charge of outpatients, was understating the case when he told us, 'In these halls you may see scabies, fleas, lice, tapeworms, diarrhoea, tonsillitis, conjunctivitis, galloping consumption, syphilis, boils, blains, sebaceous cysts, eczema—"

"And all the other ills that afflict us humans. We'll be seeing tons of that and more in general practice," Fingal said. "It's tough on the customers here, but it's a hell of a place to learn."

He strode on past the mass of huddled humanity aware of a low hum of conversation punctuated by nurses' cries of, "Next, please," and hacking coughs. Chronic bronchitis and pulmonary tuberculosis ran rampant in the crowded damp rooms of the slums.

Fingal and Charlie entered a small room with a bright overhead light. The smell of disinfectant was overpowering. A middle-aged man, his hand wrapped in a blood-soaked rag, sat on a wooden chair. He wore dungarees and a duncher, from under which poked tufts of grey hair that seemed to have been starched. He had one eye and a leather patch over what was probably an empty socket. A student nurse stood beside the chair. Charlie winked at her. Fingal knew that under Elizabeth O'Rourke's fall, her thick hair was copper-coloured. In the last month she'd succeeded the dark-haired country lass from Maynooth as Charlie's companion. As Fingal had predicted, Charlie Greer had found a way to circumvent the strictures of the lady superintendent, Miss Northey.

"Hello, Nurse," Charlie said. "What have we got?"

"You've got feckin' nuttin, mate," the man remarked, dolefully. "It's me what's got a chisel slice as wide as the Grand Canal in me right palm. Me whole feckin' hand's cat." He curled his lip.

"Did you say, 'cut'?" Charlie said.

The patient snorted. "By your accent, son, I'd say youse is from the wee north?"

Charlie nodded.

"Us Jacks say t'ings different here. We say 'cat.' Youse'd say 'bollixed,' or 'banjaxed.' 'Cat' means feckin' useless."

"Oh," said Charlie, "I'll remember that, Mister—?"

"Duggan. Willy Duggan, builder by trade. At least I was 'til I bollixed me hand," the man said with a sniff. "I'd be better with a hook."

Fingal started to fill in the emergency card. Name, age, address, occupation, religion, complaint. "Will you do Mister Duggan?" he asked Charlie.

Charlie shook his head. "Your turn."

Times had changed from six months ago when the pairs of green students had had to work out a fair system for doing procedures. Hilda and Fitzpatrick had practically come to blows when he kept hogging cases. Every one of them had been keen as mustard. Now they were all blasé about routine tasks.

"Could you get the things ready please, Nurse?" Fingal asked as he washed his hands, put on gloves, then swabbed the man's injured hand and peered at the gash. "It's going to need stitches," he said.

"Ah sure, dat's all right," said Willy Duggan, builder by trade.

Fingal kicked a wheeled stool close to a stainless steel table that was now covered with a towel. He sat on the stool, asking Willy Duggan to place his injured hand on the table. Fingal disinfected the wound and covered the hand with a green towel with an elliptical gap through which the calloused flesh and red gash were visible.

He and Nurse O'Rourke prepared an injection of local anaesthetic.

"Right," he said. "Just a little jab."

It had been months since Fingal had flinched when he slipped a needle home, but he still recognised he was injecting a human being.

"I'm going to start sewing in a minute," he said.

"Dat's all right. Go ahead."

Fingal stitched away with little fuss, a far cry from his first clumsy attempt when they'd started attending here.

"Finished," he said, removing the green towel. In the middle of the area of disinfectant-stained skin stood a row of neat black silk stitches. "Come back in seven days and we'll take them out."

Willy scrutinised the work. "Dat's very neat," he said, "t'anks." He grinned. "You'd make a bloody good carpenter with hands like yours. I don't suppose you'd want to switch trades?"

Fingal shook his head. "No thanks, but why do you ask?"

"Jasus," said Willy, "wit' all this slum clearance and rebuilding I'm up to me arse in work, but I can't get tradesmen for love nor money."

"I'm surprised to hear that."

"It's true. Men who've served their apprenticeships are rare as hens' teeth. I can't even get lads with no skills to carry a hod or stack bricks."

"Why not?" Fingal asked. "I'd have thought with all the unemployment, men would be delighted to earn a wage."

Duggan made to spit but stopped himself. "Most of dem bowsies would rather hang around street corners and play pitch and toss for pennies."

Fingal knew the game. Any number of players, coat collars turned against the damp, stood a fixed distance from a wall and threw coins. That was the pitch. Whoever landed closest to the wall collected all the other coins, threw them up in the air, the toss, and yelled "Heads" or "Tails." He kept all those coins displaying the emblem he had specified. The player who was second nearest repeated the process and so on until all the coins had been claimed. What a soulless way to kill time and perhaps win enough to buy a pint.

"Mind you," the builder said, "I've heard it said if a man's out of work for two straight years he'll never work again. It breaks him." He fixed his eye on Fingal. "You're gentry, probably don't need a real job."

Fingal laughed. "Oh, but I do."

"Well den, you're a lucky lad to be gettin' an education."

"I think so."

"I wish," said the builder, "I could even get a half-learned man who could read, and write, and cipher. He could keep track of my inventory, free me up to build, once me feckin' hand's better."

"I'm sorry I can't help you there," Fingal said as he dressed the wound. Then he wondered. Paddy Keogh had been a sergeant. Would he have needed some education to rise to that rank? Possibly. In the Royal Navy, petty officers, the nautical equivalents of sergeants, were literate. It was worth bearing in mind. He'd not say anything yet, but if he could find out, he could always contact Duggan by pulling his emergency card and getting his address. "I'm afraid all I can do is tell you to try to keep that clean," Fingal said.

"I will, sir, and t'anks again. Back in seven days?" He rose.

"Seven." Fingal stood. That might be the time to mention Paddy Keogh, if Fingal could get a chance to talk to the little man, but for now Fingal had more pressing business with Kevin Doherty. "Any more for us to see, Nurse O'Rourke?" he asked.

"No," she said. "It's been one of those odd days where not everyone in Dublin seems bound and determined to slice themselves open."

"Makes a change." One which Fingal welcomed. "Right, Charlie," Fingal said, "if you can hold the fort I'd like to nip over and see how Kevin Doh—" He realised that Willy Duggan was still within earshot. "Mister KD's getting on."

"Off you go, Fingal," Charlie said. "I'm sure your patient will be on the mend by now."

"I hope so." He stripped off his gloves. "If you get busy, call the ward and I'll come back."

19

The Heart No Longer Stirred

Hilda Manwell gave Fingal a tired smile when he arrived on Saint Patrick's Ward. She'd come out of the sluice. "Busy day," she said. "We've admitted an epilepsy and a diabetic. Thank God for insulin. Doctor Micks says that up until it became available, diabetes was an automatic death sentence." She sighed as she pulled a hand through her hair. "At least insulin is specific. The body can't produce the hormone—replace it. Miracle cure. Not like treating the other admission."

"Which is?" Fingal asked.

"A case of tertiary syphilis who's being given neoarsphenamine supplemented with mercury. From what Geoff says, it's probably doing as much good for the poor divil as rubbing him with vegetable marrow jam."

Fingal had to laugh, then said, "I know we can't cure syphilis when it's so advanced, but perhaps we can slow the progress. It's worth a try."

"It amazes me that a drug that's mostly arsenic is any good for anyone," Hilda said.

"Seems odd using a couple of poisons to try for a cure," said Fingal as he moved out of the way of a passing trolley. Two porters were bringing a case back from the operating theatre. "I suppose the causative bugs are more susceptible to them than the patient is. It's not that long ago that doctors were actually giving patients with syphilis a dose of malaria hoping the high fever would destroy the spirochaetes. It'll be an interesting patient to follow. Your case, Hilda?"

"Not at all. Ronald Hercules snaffled the patient. He only wants the exotic ones."

"I did not 'snaffle,' as you put it, Miss Manwell." Fitzpatrick appeared from behind screens around a bed. "You and I agreed to see new admissions turn and turn about."

"Indeed we did," she said. "Pity I was looking in on Mister KD when the syphilis arrived and you happened to be free and didn't want to interrupt me even if it was my turn."

Fingal did not want to be embroiled in a dispute. "Is Mister Doherty any better?"

Hilda sucked on clenched teeth. "No, Fingal. I'm sorry. He's not responding to digitalis, quinidine, and hydroclorothiazide and he's been on the quinidine for a lot more than three hours."

"Huh," said Fitzpatrick, "his ticker's so badly wrecked the sooner he's out of his misery the better if you ask me."

Fingal stiffened. He took two paces forward. "We didn't bloody well ask you, you gobshite. For once in your life have some pity."

Fitzpatrick sniffed. His Adam's apple bobbed. He snatched off his pince-nez and took a pace to the rear. "I've listened to his heart, examined his ankle oedema. I'm glad I did. I've never seen such swelling. The man's finished."

"That," said Fingal, very levelly, "that's as may be, but he'll be scared. He's drowning himself in his own fluids. He shouldn't be written off like a spavined old horse."

"Well put, Fingal," Hilda said. "You really are a heartless bastard, Fitzpatrick."

"Rubbish," Fitzpatrick said. "Anyway, I've no time to be standing round. You can admit the next case, Hilda." He strode off.

"Dear God," said Hilda, "and that man's got his sights set on the prize for medicine? He should be a pathologist. Examine tissue specimens. Look after the dead. Those patients don't need sympathy. Or in basic research—no patients at all."

"And," said Fingal quietly, "he doesn't need a prize either." He saw how Hilda was looking at him, her head tipped to one side like a thrush looking for a worm. "Aye," he said, "we'll need to see about that later, but not now. Now I'm going to see Kevin."

"You go ahead, Fingal. There's yet another case of tuberculosis over on the women's side. I need to reexamine her. It's pitiful. All we can offer them is fresh air, bed rest and a good diet, and gold injections. Ye gods. Gold injections. What the hell are they supposed to do?"

Fingal sighed. "Things haven't changed much for hundreds of years," he said. "A sixteenth-century French surgeon, a man called Ambroise Paré, did battlefield amputations. He was famous for saying 'I dressed the wound, but God healed the patient.'" Fingal shook his head. "Pretty much the same for TB patients today." He remembered the bet he'd offered Bob about a germ-killing drug. If ever one was needed, it was for TB.

"You go and visit your patient," she said softly, "everything that can be done has been." He heard the sympathy in her voice.

"Thanks, Hilda." Fingal headed off to the bed where, behind screens, Kevin Doherty struggled to breathe. "Kevin," Fingal said.

Kevin lifted one bony, blue-veined hand. Inside the oxygen tent his eyelids drooped, his nostrils flared. His legs were on top of the bedclothes. Fingal could see that Fitzpatrick was right. From toes to knees the legs were massive. Serum had collected in the tissues despite the fact that Kevin's legs were elevated on pillows to assist their drainage. In Biblical times swelling like that was called "dropsy."

Fingal could visualise the page of the textbook. *"In desperate cases of congestive failure, as a last resort, multiple punctures of the lower limbs can be essayed. The oedematous legs are flexed and made dependent. Multiple small stab wounds are made in the oedematous tissue and the resulting effluent allowed to drain. In some cases, there will be amelioration of the patient's pulmonary congestion."* Fingal slipped a hand inside the tent and squeezed Kevin's. "Back in a minute," Fingal said, forced himself to ignore the pleading in the man's eyes, and left. Hilda thought everything had been done? Not yet it hadn't.

Sister Daly was at her desk. "Mister O'Reilly?"

"Sister, where can I phone Doctor Pilkington? About Mister Doherty."

"He's very sick. I'd be surprised if he's with us in the morning, the poor lamb, so."

Fingal remembered Geoff remarking that it was "A braver man than me who will disregard the advice of a nursing sister." He hoped she was wrong. "You're probably right, Sister," he said, "but I want to ask Doctor Pilkington if he thinks multiple punctures might help."

"Do you now?" she asked. Fingal heard respect in her voice. "Do you now? I've only ever seen it done twice. It might just." She pointed to the phone. "Go ahead. He's in the clinic."

"Sure you want to do this, Fingal?" Geoff Pilkington asked.

Fingal nodded.

He did not, but he must. He knew if he hadn't done everything in his power and Kevin died Fingal would have to go through the same self-inflicted persecution he'd suffered six years ago because he thought he'd been too slow getting a boat away in the Red Sea.

"You all right, Fingal?" Geoff asked. "You look pale. I'll do it if you like."

"I'm fine."

"I don't mind you going ahead, even if it is our team's turn to learn procedures," Hilda said. She'd come back ten minutes earlier from the female ward. "I know this patient is important to you." She glanced at the door from the ward. "Pity Fitzpatrick's not here. He'll be livid when he finds out he's missed seeing this." There was the hint of a smile on her lips. It faded. "May I watch?" she asked. "I may never get to see another one."

Fingal looked at Geoff, who nodded and said, "Of course, Hilda." He turned to Fingal. "You scrub. Put on gloves. I'll get the gear organised, and, Fingal?"

"Yes?"

"I know it sounds pretty brutal what you're going to do, but because the oedema has stretched the skin so much, it'll've disrupted nerve transmission. The patient will feel practically nothing."

"Thanks, Geoff." I hope so, Fingal thought, as he headed for the sluice, I certainly hope so. He put on a full-length rubber apron, the kind butchers wore, and started to scrub.

Bloody sharks, he thought. He'd been on the poop deck of a freighter that morning in 1928, smoking his pipe and sheltering under a canvas awning. The heat was palpable. He was sweating and could see the air shimmering as it rose above the hot iron deck. As officer of the deck he'd granted permission to swim in groups of four and a companionway had been lowered. He could hear laughter, splashing, and a cry that made the hairs of his neck stand upright.

"Sharks."

"Shite." Fingal hadn't wasted time looking. He bellowed, "Boat's crew," and tore down to the boat deck. They were well drilled and already the lashings had been cast off and the davits were swinging outboard. As soon as the lifeboat's gunwales were level with the deck he piled aboard, accompanied by four lascar seamen. His commands to the men on the davits came smoothly, "Marry the falls." The men handling the ropes that lowered the boat brought the lines together so each would be paid out at exactly the same rate and neither the bow nor the stern would hit the water first.

"Lower away."

The falls rushed through the blocks. These men understood the urgency.

"Handsomely," Fingal roared. He wanted the men lowering the boat to slow down. It would be no help to anybody if in their haste it was capsized. "Handsomely, for Christ's sake."

A shriek. Silence save for the splashing of men in the water and his calling the stroke of the oars.

He hauled two terrifed seamen onboard. The water round the boat was pink. A grey reef shark swam near the surface and in its eye he saw the mindless stare of death.

Maybe if he'd let the davit men carry on lowering the boat at breakneck speed. Maybe if he'd stationed a lookout with a rifle or lowered a guard boat? He'd not make the same mistake twice.

When he returned and went behind the screens, Geoff, Hilda, and a staff nurse were ready. Kevin sat sideways on the bed propped up on pillows and supported by Hilda and the nurse. His head was slumped forward on his chest and his swollen legs hung over the bed's edge on top of a red rubber sheet. Its free edge was folded into a bucket.

"Ready, Fingal?" Geoff asked.

"As I'll ever be." Fingal took a deep breath.

"Right. The disinfectant's in the gallipot."

Fingal picked up sponge holders, loaded them with cotton wool balls, soaked them, and said, "I'm going to wash your legs, Kevin."

No response. Fingal painted the discoloured skin. He discarded the sponge holders and stared at the trolley. The only instrument there was a stainless steel scalpel. Its blade was triangular and pointed. He looked at Geoff, who said, "Start above the ankle and work half-round each leg. Go about a quarter of an inch deep. Space your incisions two inches apart. Once you've done a row at the front of both legs, move up a couple of inches and do the same thing over again. We don't need to stab over the calf muscles."

Fingal lifted the scalpel. It was cold. He faced Kevin and squatted. "This may sting a bit," he said, hoping to God Geoff was right about the nerves being stretched and insensitive. Fingal put his left hand behind Kevin Doherty's right ankle to steady the leg. The skin was warm and the flesh doughy. Fingal shuddered.

He took a deep breath, held the scalpel as he had been taught months ago when for the first time he'd lanced a carbuncle. "Sorry, Kevin," he said, closed his eyes, gathered all his resolve, opened his eyes and made the first wound.

Fingal had no sense of the passage of time. Kevin had tried to writhe away twice, but had been restrained. Still holding the bloody scalpel, Fingal stood. "I'm finished, I think."

"Well done," Geoff said.

Fingal gave him a weak smile. Hilda and the nurse were pale. He could feel sweat trickling down his brow. He dropped the scalpel onto the instrument trolley, bent, and put his mouth close to Kevin's ear. "All done, Kevin." There was no reply, only laboured breathing and the sounds of rasping and wheezing in the man's chest.

Fingal glanced down at the row of cuts, each draining blood-tinged straw-coloured serum onto the rubber sheet and into the bucket. Work, he thought, please work. Give Kevin Doherty back his breath.

"Nurse, please get him into his oxygen tent," Geoff said. "Stay with him until we come back. We'll take the trolley."

"Yes, Doctor Pilkington."

"Come on, Fingal, you need to get those gloves off and wash your hands." Geoff set off pushing the trolley.

Fingal put his mouth beside Kevin's ear again. "I'll be back in a minute."

"You," said Hilda, "'are a better man than I am, Gunga Din.'" She shuddered.

Although Fingal's hands had been steady while he worked, they now shook and his breathing was shallow and rapid. Reaction, he supposed. It wasn't every day that he went round stabbing people. "I was scared silly," he said. "I hope it helps."

"You're a soft-hearted man, Fingal O'Reilly, for all your bluff and your acting the lig with your friends," Hilda said. "Us girls heard about the skeleton in her undies last year and who dressed her. The fearsome four."

"Och, that was just a bit of fun. We all took life lightly," said Fingal. "It's getting serious now. Maybe I was soft when I started, but doing all the things to people we've had to since we came to the hospital, I think it's built in as part of the training. Not just learning the techniques, but having to do them over and over. You learn, but it hardens you too. I think it's meant to."

She gave him a knowing look. "I'm not convinced it's working with you, Fingal O'Reilly. Now hang on," she said. "Your gloves are bloody. Let me open the door."

Fingal went in, crossed to the sink, stripped off his gloves, and washed his hands. He knew there was truth to what he'd said, but Hilda was right too and he hoped, no, he resolved that he would not let himself become too hard. Ever.

"We should send for the Catholic chaplain," Geoff said.

Fingal rounded on the houseman. "For the last rites? Extreme unction? You've given up, haven't you? Damn it, I haven't. Not yet."

Geoff shrugged, but said, "I don't think KD's going to make it and he is a Catholic. It is the proper thing to do."

Fingal lowered his head. "You're right," he said. "Of course you are." He dried his hands and turned only to see the staff nurse standing there, the glint of tears in her eyes.

"Come quick," she said. "I think he's got ventricular fibrillation."

"Christ." Irregular contractions of the ventricles would stop the heart. Fingal barged through the door and pounded down the ward, pursued by Geoff and Hilda. He tore one of the screens from its rail as he ripped it back. The oxygen tent was open.

Kevin lay limply, tilted to one side on his pillow. His jaw hung open, there was no rise and fall of his chest, and his eyes stared. To Fingal they looked exactly as had those long-ago shark's eyes.

He grabbed for Kevin's wrist. The skin was clammy. There was no movement in the radial artery at the base of the thumb. Fingal lowered his head and put it immediately in front of Kevin's mouth, but there was no gentle current of air moving back and forth.

Fingal stood. "I think he's gone." He felt the lump in his throat, but swallowed it. Damn. Damn. "Can we try the Silvester or Holger-Neilson methods of artificial respiration? I learnt them in the navy." He knew how high-pitched his voice must sound.

Geoff shook his head. "They're for drowning victims. If the heart has stopped nothing can restart it." He shone a pencil torch into each of Kevin's eyes in turn. "No reaction," he said. He put his stethoscope on the patient's chest, listened, and shook his head. "Too late for the priest now," he said. "This'll have to do even if I don't have oil sanctified by the bishop and I'm neither

Catholic nor ordained, but I've seen it often enough." He made the sign of the cross over Kevin Doherty's forehead and intoned slowly, "To this through his most tender mercy may the Lord pardon thee whatever sins thou hast committed. *Ego te absolvo.*"

And Fingal O'Reilly, his hands trembling, his own heart bruised, said, "Amen. *Requiescat in pace,* Kevin Doherty." He leant over and closed Kevin's eyelids. "Thank you, Doctor Pilkington," Fingal said. "I'll remember those words. At least we can tell the family he didn't die unshriven, even if it's not entirely true. It'll comfort them. And I may need to do it myself in the future."

Geoff Pilkington put a hand on Fingal's arm. "I know you're upset," he said, "but if you can think of the relatives and your future patients, you're going to be all right, Fingal O'Reilly."

Fingal himself was not so sure. All the training seemed pointless. By the time he was finished he would have spent five years learning masses of facts, trying to believe he was a learnèd man, but for what reason? Patients still died all the time. Yes, perhaps it was better that he understood the mechanism of the sickness that had killed Kevin Doherty. His forebears, from the Greeks right up to the doctors of the eighteenth century, would have attributed the condition to an incorrect balance of the four "bodily humours." His immediate seniors had given up leeching, cupping, and bleeding, so less harm was inflicted in the name of healing. But at the heels of the hunt, Kevin Doherty had died because medicine had virtually no truly effective cures. Arsenic and mercury for syphilis? It was little better than witchcraft.

"I hope you're right, Geoff," Fingal said, "I really do," and wondered if Father could be right? Could a career in basic medical research benefit thousands? Was wanting to see the effects of your efforts in a small community and reap the satisfaction as your reward a high form of selfishness?

Fingal O'Reilly left Saint Patrick's Ward and stumbled past the

Grand Staircase, out into the daylight. He paused, took in lungsful of fresh air, barely noticing clouds scudding across the sky, raindrops on his cheeks. He looked into his heart and asked, "Are you really cut out for treating patients, Fingal O'Reilly? Are you?"

20

The Feathered Race with Pinions
Skims the Air

"Excuse me, Sister Daly?" Fingal hoped she'd be sympathetic. "Would it be possible for me to make an outside phone call?" He knew personal calls were forbidden, but this once Fingal needed someone. He wasn't going to be able to cope alone.

She looked up. "Who to, bye?"

That informal "bye" was promising. Sister usually called him "Mister." "My brother in the North."

She smiled. "I'll not ask what about, but if you don't tell, I won't." She nodded at the receiver. "Lift the phone and ask the exchange to put you through." She winked. "Whatever your brother works at, call him 'Doctor.' That way it sounds like business. One medical man to another."

Fingal lifted the receiver, identified himself to the operator, and gave Doctor Lars O'Reilly's number, "Portaferry, 57."

Fingal heard Annie, one of the operators, say, "I've a call for yiz from Mister O'Reilly in Dublin. Would yiz two be related, sir, seeing youse is an O'Reilly too?"

Pause.

"Dere's a t'ing now. A doctor and a goin'-to-be doctor in one family. Lord be praised."

Fingal surmised that Lars had understood and had gone along with the deception.

Despite his sadness over Kevin Doherty, Fingal couldn't help smile. Was there a more inquisitive breed than telephonists?

"Here yiz are, Mister O'Reilly, sir."

"Thank you, Annie," Fingal said. "Lars?"

"Fingal? What's the 'Doctor' Lars business about?'"

"Sister's letting me use the ward phone—"

"I understand."

Lars wouldn't want to waste time on explanations. Calls were charged by the minute and Fingal was being granted a privilege. "I've a bit of bother." Fingal hesitated, but if he couldn't tell Lars, who could he confide in? Not his friends, who knew he'd been warned about getting involved with patients. Not Ma. He was far too old to run to Mummy with a grazed knee, and not Father. Certainly not Father. Kitty? She'd understand, but he couldn't see her until Saturday night. Lars was different. Lars would listen. "We lost a patient yesterday. One I'd grown fond of. It has me a lot more rattled than I expected. I didn't sleep much last night. I'd like your advice. I'd like to come up to Portaferry."

"Right now? I'll drive down and get you, Finn."

"Not tonight, Lars. I appreciate it. I can manage until Friday, but thanks for being worried."

"You're sure you're all right?"

"Not altogether, but I will manage. I'll be in Belfast at three off the last Dublin train. We can have a good blether, shoot the dawn flight at the stream at Lisbane on Saturday, and then if you don't mind running me up to Belfast, the train's at twelve and gets in here at four so I'll be back in time to—" He glanced at Sister Daly, who was studiously minding her own business. "—go out on Saturday night, and be on duty on Sunday."

"I'll be there."

In more ways than one, Fingal thought, and blessed his brother. "Friday it is, and thanks, Lars." He put the phone down. "I hope I wasn't on too long."

"Och, sure there's times we all need family, Mister O'Reilly," Sister said. "Dun's finances can stand one phone call to the North."

Lars was waiting at Central Station and drove Fingal the thirty miles from Belfast to Portaferry. Fingal didn't want to talk about his troubles until they were at Lars's home. Instead as the car swung onto the Newtownards Road he said, "I hesitate to ask, but it's been a couple of months since Christmas. Have you heard anything at all from Jean Neely?"

Fingal heard how flat his brother's voice sounded. "No. It's over, Finn. I try not to think about it too much."

Fingal wasn't sure how he'd feel if Kitty were to say good-bye. Deeply hurt certainly, but he hadn't got to the stage of proposing. Not like his brother. "I imagine it still stings. You must miss her," Fingal said.

"I do, Finn." Lars swung into a tight bend. "Very much. I only went out with a few girls when I was a student and you were away." He grinned. "Five years at an all-boys' boarding school may get you through puberty, but it hardly prepares you for encounters with the opposite sex."

"True," Fingal said. It had taken his seagoing years and lessons in the school of life to let him become more comfortable with women.

"Most of the girls in Portaferry are farmers' daughters, fishermen's lassies, shop assistants. Nice girls, but Fingal, we've nothing in common, nothing to talk about, and you've no idea how tongues wag in such a wee place, particularly as the single women have only one goal. Marriage. I wasn't sure I was ready for domesticity until I met Jean. I knew from the first night she was different. She was so easy to talk to. She made me laugh."

Hadn't he felt that way about Kitty since their first date? She was certainly easy to talk to and they did laugh a lot. Like the way Lars described Jean, but he wasn't opening up completely. And that was his privilege. But Fingal knew that if his brother had proposed marriage, his feelings for Jean went beyond fun and laughter. Far beyond.

"Jean was worth driving down to see as often as I could. I felt I'd known her all my life. And, Finn—" Lars's voice dropped to a whisper. "She was wonderful to hold. To kiss. I wanted a lot more." Fingal saw his brother's face in profile and his cheeks were red.

"I know what you mean." Fingal thought of the walk back from the fish-and-chip shop after he'd taken Kitty to Neary's, her body warm in his arms at the New Year's Eve Ball.

"And you know that means marriage."

"I do." It was what had been drummed into young men. No intimate relations out of wedlock. The horrors of venereal disease, he thought of the case of incurable syphilis, the utter disgrace of getting a girl pregnant. Ah, but the girl in Bali in 1928 and the one in Penang in '29. Somerset Maugham had been right in his portraits of the East.

"It's not to be," Lars said. "And don't tell me there are more fish in the sea."

"I won't." But there are, Fingal thought, and wondered again if his brother, twenty-nine years old now, was on the road to bachelorhood.

They lapsed into silence for the rest of the journey.

"I'll help you with that," Lars said once he'd parked at his shoreside home, a grey, pebbledashed, two-storey pile overlooking

Strangford Lough and the demesne of the eighteenth-century stately home Castle Ward on the far shore. He picked up Fingal's suitcase. "You bring your gun."

They left the baggage in the hall and went into the lounge. Fingal sat back in an armchair and stared across the lough's narrow mouth to the ferry dock in Strangford town on the other shore. He looked beyond to where the Mourne Mountains, dusk dark against a robin's egg–blue sky, stood as ramparts against the salty waters of the Irish Sea.

"Here." Lars handed Fingal a Jameson. "We'll have to manage on our own for the next couple of days. I've given Myrtle, my housekeeper, a few days off."

"*Sláinte.*" Fingal watched phalaropes, long-billed, dun-coloured birds, dancing on stiltlike legs over wrack caught in a tide rip. Eddies and whirlpools formed and spun away only to form again. "The Narrows certainly boil when the tide's running," he said, and looked straight at Lars sitting in an armchair opposite. "I've been in a bit of turmoil myself, Lars." Fingal pursed his lips, frowned. "I didn't think losing a man called Kevin Doherty would get to me." Through the window he could see that the evening was closing in. Fingal looked down into his whiskey, back to Lars. "I didn't think it was going to hit me as sorely, but I can't stop thinking about him."

"It's your first?" Lars asked.

"Yes, he was." Fingal refused to think of Kevin Doherty as "it." "Other patients have died since we started, but he was the first one I'd got to know. He was a young man, your age. He should have had his life ahead of him. It's so bloody unfair."

Lars nodded. "And you're feeling John Donne-ish, 'No man is an island'?"

Fingal forced a smile. "I remember Father reading that to us, his tone when he said, 'Any man's death diminishes me, because I am involved in mankind. And therefore never send to know for whom the bell tolls; it tolls for thee.' " He shook his head. "Donne had a point."

"Finn, I'm sure you've been told this, but not all patients get better."

"The first time Kevin was admitted, we nearly lost him." Fingal sipped his drink. "Geoff Pilkington, the house physician, tried to warn me then. He said, 'Don't take it personally if he goes. We can't save them all so don't let yourself get involved.' "

"Do you think that was good advice?"

"It's perfectly sound. You can't help notice how experienced specialists have become remote from their cases. I told another student, a woman called Hilda, that I thought there was an un-written agenda to make us do procedures on folks, over and over, until we become inured, toughened. I used to shake before I took a blood sample. Now?" Fingal shrugged. "Wee buns."

"Perhaps there's a point to professional distance. My barrister colleagues say they have to keep at arm's length from their clients so if a case is lost in court there's no need to take it personally."

Fingal sipped. "I don't want to get hardened, but I don't want to get so worked up either," he said. "I know, I absolutely know every-thing possible was done. There's no reason to blame myself." Fin-gal had no trouble picturing the pointed scalpel cutting into Kevin's swollen, waterlogged legs. He stood and paced across the room. "Maybe I was wrong not talking to my friends? Telling them my troubles."

"You'd have found that difficult, Finn," Lars said quietly.

Fingal turned to Lars and frowned.

"I'm no Sigmund Freud, no Carl Jung," Lars said, "but you and I have the same father. Stiff upper lip and all that. Never tell a lie.

Big boys don't cry. Keep your troubles to yourself. We went to the same public boarding school. The ethos there was straight from *Tom Brown's Schooldays* or *Stalky and Co.* Don't tell tales, play up and play the game. Remember Kipling's poem 'If'? 'If you can keep your head when all about you are losing theirs . . . And yet don't look too good, nor talk too wise.' And most of all never wear your heart on your sleeve and always keep your troubles to yourself." He drank. "Despite all that indoctrination, Finn, you didn't give in. And you're still finding it hard to bury your humanity. If you can keep it up, you'll make a bloody fine doctor. I just think, I *know,* you're going to have to find a way to care a tiny bit less."

Fingal held his glass in both hands and hunched forward, head lowered. He was at a loss for words.

"Mebbe," Lars continued, "mebbe school would have worked, we might have become cold, insulated, and unhurtable, but for Ma. She taught us both to care," Lars said levelly. "You know that as well as I do. You remember after Christmas dinner how she went to thank Cook personally? How much work she does raising money for charities, all the rallies she goes to to agitate for better housing for the poor? She's forever doing things like that and giving folks their due. She practised what she preached about how every person mattered. How everyone is entitled to respect and I don't mean deference or subservience, but treating everyone with common courtesy. She made us learn that."

Fingal looked at his older brother with a new appreciation. "You're right. And Ma's bloody well right, too. People should count."

Lars nodded. "So what are you going to do about how you feel before the next patient comes along? Start building a carapace or get to know them?"

Fingal swallowed a mouthful of whiskey. "First, I'm going to try to make myself believe, really believe, it wasn't my fault we lost Kevin."

"Good idea."

"I'm not going to stop feeling sorry that he died—"

"It's trite, brother, but the hurt will fade with time."

Fingal nodded and inside he prayed it would for Lars too after Jean Neely. Fingal had every intention of marrying, one day. He'd hate to see his brother stay single, wither up. Fingal made a promise to himself. Even if he was laying himself open to more hurt, he was damned if he was going to stop caring, and yesterday's flirtation with the idea of moving into a research career? It might suit Bob Beresford. Not Fingal. "I thought about giving up clinical medicine once I'd qualified. Going into research."

"Father would be delighted."

"I know, and I'd like to please Father, but, Lars—"

"Go on—"

"I've always wanted to be a people's doctor."

Lars laughed. "You won't remember, but you told me that the first time I took you shooting. You were thirteen."

"Honestly?"

Lars nodded and said, "I thought you'd grow out of it, like playing with Meccano sets, reading *The Boy's Own Paper,* Boy Scouts."

Fingal laughed. "Once in a while I think I'd still like to build a gantry or a steamboat from perforated metal strips and nuts and bolts, and I can still tie a bowline and a sheepshank. Came in handy at sea." He finished his whiskey. "I've only wavered this once about being a doctor. I'll not anymore. Thank you, big brother, for helping me see it is what I want."

Lars smiled.

Fingal glanced out of the window. It was slack water in the Narrows, that moment at the turn of the tide when all turbulence ceases. The surface was glassy, the islands of wrack motionless. The phalaropes rose as one and flew away, a little dun cloud that jinked, turned, and vanished by blending with the gauze of the evening's soft mist.

"Out," Lars said. It was pitch-black when he parked in front of a farmhouse where Davy McMaster, an old friend of the O'Reilly brothers, lived, farmed, and operated a small public bar from what had been his living room. Fingal obeyed. He could barely see for a few yards, but he knew that a hundred yards up the road from Portaferry to the Six-Road-Ends, a stream chuckled under the Salt Water Brig, so called because on a rising tide the sea flowed upstream past the brig, the locals' word for bridge. He inhaled the tang of decaying seaweed and the smell of turf smoke. Davy's wife was an early riser.

Lars strode through a gate into a churchyard. Fingal tucked his gun into the crook of his arm and followed. He'd tramped through here as a boy when he and his brother had come down from Holywood or travelled together up from Dublin. Before Lars had moved to Portaferry the boys had stayed with Davy when they'd come up from Dublin to shoot. Their love of the lough was something else they shared. Fingal was sure that love had drawn Lars back to Portaferry.

Ma's brother Hedley had introduced Lars to wildfowling when he was thirteen and he'd done the same for his brother when Fingal was old enough.

They passed three-hundred-year-old headstones and a moss-grown Celtic cross, a dark mass too old now to stand straight so taking support by leaning against the sky. The familiar landmark triggered a memory of Lars's hand in his the first time they'd come here, and his brother's voice reassuring him that nothing in the graveyard could hurt them. Fingal smiled. He'd not been so sure then that Lars was right.

His brother's springer spaniel, Barney, quartered the paths between the graves.

Fingal climbed over a stile in the seawall. Ahead, a grassy stream bank was pitted with brackish pools. Clumps of ben weeds stood like tattered flags, their dried leaves rustling in the breeze. To his right the bank ended and the mud flats began. At full tide the water would flood up to the edges of the bank, and spring tides flowed over the grass.

A splash and hoarse craking ahead told Fingal that Barney had startled a teal from a pool.

Lars stepped off the bank and crossed the mud heading toward the mouth of the stream. The ribbed soles of his waders left water-filled impressions that glittered in the starlight. The shore gave off an earthy aroma, mingling with the air's salty tang.

They stopped beside a large rock near where the stream flowed on to meet the waters of the ebbing tide. Not long to slack ebb and the dawn. They'd have three hours before the rising waters pushed them off this part of the shore. Fingal leaned his shotgun beside Lars's weapon propped against the rock. "I'll give you a hand," he said, bending to gather armfuls of bladder wrack to construct a low semicircular rampart behind which he, Lars, and Barney would crouch to wait for the morning flight. The weed was cold and numbed his fingers.

The false dawn began to grey the eastern sky and send shy pinks to the belly of a narrow bank of low clouds. Fingal's breath made vapour jets. Those parts round his eyes and lips that were not covered by a balaclava helmet felt the nip of the southerly breeze.

"That should do," Lars said, stooping to spread an army surplus gas cape on the muddy floor so they could kneel, but stay dry.

The camouflaged material was waterproof and mustard-gas-proof, a relic of the trenches. Fingal hoped others like it would remain unused, but under Adolf Hitler, Germany was rearming and Mussolini's troops had sailed to be ready for the invasion of Abyssinia.

He moved his gun closer to hand and knelt beside where Lars crouched to the right of the hide. It wouldn't be long until dawn and the birds began to fly. Getting here and building the hide had kept Fingal's mind occupied. Now as he waited, his thoughts ranged freely. He'd meant what he'd said about persuading himself he could not have done any more for Kevin. Was he ready to accept that now? He thought so. Face it, Fingal, in truth all any doctor can do is their best.

And considering that, Fingal had to ask himself, what, for all his earnestness to Kitty in Neary's pub, had he done for Sergeant Paddy Keogh? Bugger all. Perhaps he'd be better taking care of the living patients instead of berating himself over the dead. Fingal had had a notion to put Paddy, if he could read and write, in touch with the builder Willy Duggan. Kevin's death had driven the idea out of Fingal's mind. He'd try to remember once he got back to Dublin.

He looked inland over the Ards Peninsula where life was coming to a new day. The band of low cloud was changing from timid pink to screaming yellows and raucous scarlets. Under the cloud and above the hills, the sun's upper limb, a convex sliver, peeped into the sky as if a sudden noise might make it jerk away. But then, gaining confidence, it swelled, grew, and blazed.

The day lightened. Rocks cast shadows over the glistening mud. Patches of sea wrack changed from charcoal to shiny brown. Dull hills to his left wrapped themselves in clothes of green spangled with yellow gorse flowers.

He knelt, lost in the solitude of dawn on the shore, a time and place where he could find solace, put his worries away, try to see things clearly.

Inland, a cow lowed and the crowing of a rooster nearly made him miss the whickering of pinions. Fingal crouched, swung to face the sound, and slipped off the safety catch.

"You take left," Lars whispered.

Five mallard tore toward them. Fingal picked a drake, stood, lifted his gun to his shoulder, and covered the bird. The ducks flared, wings beating. Fingal swung, squeezed the trigger of the right barrel, felt the butt slam into his shoulder, and heard a double roar. Lars had fired at the same time. A split second was all that separated the "thumps" as two drakes hit the mud. Fingal smelt the acrid tang of burnt smokeless powder.

"Hi lost, Barney."

The liver-and-white springer tore across the mud.

"Nice shot, Lars," Fingal said, "and thanks again."

"For bringing you here?"

"That's part of it, but thanks for yesterday evening. For listening." Fingal stretched out his chilled right hand and was warmed inside by the firmness of his brother's icy handshake.

By the time the flooding waters nudged the wall of the sea wrack hide and forced them out, Fingal had shot another mallard and Lars had his first mallard and a brace of widgeon. They retraced their steps of the early morning, cased their guns, stripped off their muddy waders, and loaded the ducks in the car's boot.

"We'll get you to Belfast in plenty of time for the train. Hop in," Lars said, putting Barney into the back. Lars cranked the starting handle until the engine fired. He joined Fingal, slowly closed the choke, and put the car in gear.

Fingal sat back in his seat as the car rose and fell over the humpback bridge where the stream flowed on as it must have done from time immemorial and would do long after the O'Reilly boys had put away their shotguns for the last time. They left the little estuary behind and his last view of it was of the pale lough waters drowning the silver mud flats.

"I can see, Lars," Fingal said, "why this place has such a pull on you. I'd—"

The engine made a ferocious *bang,* followed by a grating screech. Smoke spurted from under the bonnet and the engine rasped and fell silent.

Fingal looked at Lars, who said, "Oops," and brought the car to a halt.

They got out and Lars opened the bonnet.

Fingal could see where oil was dripping through a crack in the crankcase. Blue buggery. "Your crankcase is banjaxed and there's probably a big end of one of the piston rods gone," he said.

"I thought you once told me you didn't know about engines."

"I don't," Fingal said, "well, not much, but I had to learn a bit at sea. I reckon that's a garage job. You'll have to get a tow."

"There's a garage with a mechanic in Kircubbin. That's not too far," Lars said. "Davy McMaster'll give me a tow with his tractor, but I don't know about getting you to Belfast in time for your train."

21

Too Late, Too Late

"Thanks a lot," Fingal said as he climbed down from the trap.

"I hope you catch your bus, so I do," the farmer said, clucked his tongue, and turned the pony into a lane halfway to Kircubbin. It was a start on the road to Belfast. There were still two hours before the twelve o'clock train and Fingal had only twenty miles to cover. No need to panic. Overhead a flock of green plover crying *pee-wit, pee-wit* tumbled across a gunmetal grey sky. Leafless blackthorn hedges flanked the road. Sheep in a nearby field huddled under the far hedge to shelter from a bitter wind blowing in from the lough. He heard rumbling and a lorry stacked with metal milk churns appeared round the bend. Fingal waved to the driver in his open cab.

"Could you give me a lift to Kircubbin?"

"Och, aye. Hop in," the man said. "We're no very fast, but we're steady and I'm going 'til Greyabbey if that's any good 'til youse. It's about six miles, so it is."

"Wonderful," Fingal said as he climbed aboard.

Half an hour later, chilled to the marrow and having been passed by faster vehicles, Fingal wasn't so sure it was wonderful, but he arrived in Greyabbey in time to catch a bus for Newtownards, where he waited two hours before boarding the Belfast coach. He'd missed the noon train, but there was time to get the three fifteen.

He'd be late for Kitty, but he'd be there and she'd understand. Since New Year's Eve when he'd damn nearly told her he loved her, they'd managed four Saturdays out. Neither had talked about deeper feelings, but he knew they were there.

There was time to think about Kitty and any other subject that came to mind. The bloody vehicle had stopped not just at the marked stops, but for passengers who flagged it down along the way. At the Holywood Arches on the outskirts of Belfast, a collision between a motorcar and a tram kept the bus waiting for the police to finish and clear the road. By the time he got to the railway station the Dublin train was long gone and it was the last one until tomorrow.

He'd have to let someone at Sir Patrick Dun's know and try to get a message through to Kitty.

The Crown Liquor Saloon was across Great Victoria Street. He'd get a bite there and perhaps they'd let him use the phone. He crossed and stopped to admire the ornate mosaic tile work, the stained-glass windows that had been installed by Italian craftsmen in the last century. The men had been brought to Ireland to install stained glass in churches and worked for the publican on their days off.

Fingal went straight up to the red-granite-topped bar.

"How's about ye, sir?" the barman asked as he polished a glass with a tea towel. "What'll you have?"

"Pint please, and a menu, and I'm in a bit of a pickle. Could I use your phone?"

"Where do you want to call?" He stopped polishing.

"Sir Patrick Dun's Hospital, Dublin."

"Dublin?" The barman started to shake his head. "You're joking me."

Fingal remembered Sister Daly's trick for fooling the hospital switchboard. "I'm Doctor O'Reilly," he said. "It's urgent. I'll get time and charges from the operator and pay you for it."

"Doctor? Right enough? And you'll pay? 'At's different." The barman pointed to a relic from Alexander Graham Bell with a separate earpiece hanging from a forked clip. "Thonder's the phone, sir."

"Thanks." After a brief conversation with the Belfast operator asking her to ring him back with the cost of the call and giving her the Dublin number, Fingal found himself talking to Alice at Sir Patrick Dun's switchboard.

"And did yiz have fun at dem ducks wit' your brudder, Doctor O'Reilly, Mister O'Reilly?"

"I did, Alice. Can you give me Saint Patrick's Ward?"

A female voice said, "Saint Patrick's Ward. Nurse McVeigh."

He remembered her. From County Donegal. "Ellen," he said, "it's Fingal O'Reilly. I'm in Belfast. Would you do something for me?"

"If I can."

"Cromie and Charlie Greer are on duty. Is either one on the ward?"

"I think Cromie is. Hang on."

Fingal waited, until, "What's up?" Cromie asked.

"I'm stuck in Belfast. I can't get back in time to take call tomorrow. Can you or Charlie or Bob—"

"Jesus. Charlie was on with Hilda yesterday. They've both gone for the weekend. Bob's invited me down to Conlig tomorrow. Some big family do."

"Bugger." For a minute Fingal wondered about hitchhiking.

"Hang on a minute," Cromie said.

Fingal heard indistinct voices then, "Geoff says he'll help out. Don't worry and thanks for letting us know. Just get here as quick as you can."

Praise be. "Thank him for me, will you? One last thing. Can your Virginia let Kitty know? I'm meant to be seeing her tonight."

"Do what I can."

"Thanks, pal." Fingal hung up. That was a load off his mind. Now it was time for a pint, a meal, and if the barman was willing to let him, make a local call to see if an old school friend who lived on Camden Street could offer a bed for the night.

"It's unconscionable, O'Reilly." Fitzpatrick stood near Sister's desk. "You promised to take Hilda's turn because she'd taken your call on Friday. The fact that you spoke to Cromie last night doesn't make up for your absence. Doctor Pilkington had to assist at some major surgery because the surgical house officer is sick. I've been single-handed since eight o'clock." His Adam's apple bobbed. "It's three o'clock in the afternoon. There are two admissions I've not been able to see yet. Doctor Micks is *not* pleased and I wasn't having him blaming me. I told him this morning I was on my own. I told him you'd let us down." He pulled off his pince-nez and polished the lenses with a handkerchief.

"You didn't tell him I'd phoned? Tried to make arrangements?"

"Phoning's not the same as being here. Of course I didn't."

There was no excuse for not showing up as promised, but there was an explanation and he had tried to arrange cover. There'd been no need for Fitzpatrick to drop Fingal in the dirt and put his clerkship in jeopardy.

He inhaled. No point fighting with Fitzpatrick. "I've already apologised," Fingal said. "I came to the ward straight from the train. I'll go to work the minute I get back from my room, dump my gear, and get my white coat."

"Get a move on," Fitzpatrick said, pinching the bridge of his nose. "I'm tired."

"Leave the charts at the desk for whoever you want me to see." Fingal turned and left. Bloody Fitzpatrick, he thought.

Five minutes later, Fingal was trotting back from his room in the resident student quarters. A staff nurse at the desk handed him sets of clinical notes. "Mister O'Reilly, Mister Fitzpatrick asked for you to admit two patients on the women's ward."

He glanced at the social details of the first. Mrs. Roisín Kilmartin, aged thirty-six, married, mother of eight, youngest six months, address Swift's Alley. Fingal knew the place. Narrow, cobbled, two-storey terraces. He read on. Occupation, cleaner. Religion, Roman Catholic. Complaints: Fatigue. Severe shortness of breath.

Fingal wasn't surprised she was tired. In the tenements most of the men were chronically unemployed. The women who did menial tasks were the breadwinners and they were the ones who reared the chisellers too. She had eight. Shortness of breath. Fingal flinched. Paddy Keogh had been short of breath. So had Kevin Doherty. Fingal left Saint Patrick's Ward and crossed to the west wing. The structure, furnishings, and smells of the women's ward were identical to those of the men's. The sounds were softer, but for a high-pitched keening coming from behind drawn screens.

"Your case, Mrs. RK, is in bed 12," a staff nurse told him, "and the racket is because a patient, God rest her," she crossed herself, "has just died of TB and the family's saying good-bye, God love them."

"Thanks, Nurse." Fingal made his way along the now familiar ward. He smiled at the woman in the bed and closed the screens. "Hello, Mrs. Kilmartin," he said. "I'm Mister O'Reilly, a student. I've been sent to examine you."

"Ah sure," she wrinkled her nose, "dat's all right."

He sat on the side of the bed. She was a small woman. Her bright green eyes were sunken and had bags under them. Her lips were pale. Her chestnut hair was long and lustreless, but it was clean and well brushed. She must take pride in her appearance. Not an easy task in the slums.

"What brought you to the hospital?" he asked. The students had been taught never to ask leading questions; let patients tell their own stories.

She thought then said solemnly, "A tram."

Fingal smiled and tried again. "What are you complaining of?"

"Huh." She pulled in a breath. "Just about every feckin' t'ing."

Fingal waited, but eventually had to prompt, "Such as?"

"Such as? Me room at home's too small. It's damp. Dere's bedbugs. Me wages as a cleaner, two shillin's a day, twenty-four pence, wouldn't keep a feckin' slave when a stone of spuds is sixpence and Woodbine fags are tuppence for five. Himself, Brendan, my oul' one, he's not workin'. He'd not work to warm himself. He spends most of his time on the piss—and a pint of porter's tenpence. Add dat up. If I spend dat in one day I've sixpence left, and the rent's six shillings."

"I'm sorry."

"Ah sure, it's not your fault, son." She inhaled deeply.

"I'm trying to find out what's making you sick."

"I'm waitin'."

Fingal frowned. "Waiting?"

"For youse to find out w'at's wrong wit' me."

How to get her back on track? "When did you first feel sick, Mrs. Kilmartin?" he asked.

She puffed out her cheeks and gasped. "When did I not? Ever since I married that great bollix Brendan Kilmartin." She blew her breath down her nose. "I must have been out of my feckin' mind when I said yes. And me up the builder's every bleedin' year since." She leant forward. "That eejit of mine, all the bugger has to do is hang his trousers on the end of the bed and I'm poulticed again."

And yet for all her apparent bitterness Fingal heard affection in her voice. For a moment he marvelled at the number of Irish euphemisms for being pregnant. But no matter what you called it, repeated pregnancy depleted a woman's iron stores, and the odds of a tenement dweller having a diet sufficiently rich in liver, green vegetables, and egg yolk were remote. He'd pursue that line. Fingal leant forward and said, "Look up. I want to look under your eyelids."

"I never knew your eyeballs could make yiz short of breat'," she said, gasped, then holding her head steady stared up at the ceiling.

Fingal leant forward and put a thumb on each of her lower eyelids. He pulled down and everted the lids to look at their inner surfaces where tiny capillaries could be seen. Those conjunctival vessels should be rich with blood cells, and scarlet in colour. Hers were carnation pink. She was anaemic. The condition's symptoms included tiredness and shortness of breath. Step one. The next step would be to define the severity of the anaemia and detect the cause. Fingal smiled and said, "I think you're anaemic."

"I am not one of dem Neemicks," she said abruptly and crossed herself. "I'm a good feckin' Catholic. Just you ask Father O'Regan. Sure amn't I at confession every Sunday? Jasus, Mary, and Joseph. Neemick indeed?"

O'Reilly released her eyelids and chuckled. He was unsure who or what a "Neemick" might be, but he said, "No. I'm sure you're not. I'm sorry. I should have explained that I think your blood is very, very thin. And thin blood, what doctors call anaemia, can't carry oxygen from the air, and that makes you breathless."

"Is dat a fact?" She narrowed her eyes. "And would a few pints of Mister Arthur Guinness's best be a cure? My granny, her dat lives wit' us, she's a quare one for building up the blood wit' porter—the oul' bowsie."

So husband Brendan wasn't the only one in the household with a strong weakness for the drink. "It might," he said, "but we need to find out what's causing the blood's thinness. I'm going to ask you questions and then examine you, Mrs. Kilmartin."

"Ah, sure," she said with a grin. "It's Roisín. Mrs. Kilmartin's Brendan's ma."

By the time he'd finished Fingal was certain she was anaemic, but not because of blood loss. She was too young for bowel cancer and had no symptoms suggesting other intestinal diseases that might bleed. She hadn't had periods often enough, being so frequently pregnant, for heavy menstruation to be a cause. She wasn't jaundiced so it was unlikely that she was breaking the haemoglobin in her red cells down too quickly. The most likely cause was poor dietary intake or something amiss with the haematopoetic system that made red blood cells.

"Roisín," he said to her, "we'll need to do some tests."

"Fire away."

"And I'll need to discuss it with a senior doctor, but I reckon we'll have answers for you in a couple of days. We'll keep you in here."

"Grand," she said. "I'll postpone me trip to Monte Carlo." She chuckled and Fingal saw she was toothless.

Dubliners. They'd make a joke of anything. "I'll go and make the arrangements for your tests."

"Doctor, can I ask you a question?"

"Of course. And I'm not a doctor, only a student."

"Is you the fellah as looked after Paddy Keogh, him w'at was round at our place wit' Brendan when the doctor sent me here?"

Fingal nodded and was struck with guilt. "I am. How is he?"

"He said if I met a big fellah called O'Reilly I was to be sure to tell you Paddy Keogh, himself late a sergeant in," she curled her lip, "His Britannic Majesty's Royal Army Ordnance Corps, to tell you he's doing fine."

"Thank you, Roisín. I'm pleased to hear that." And annoyed with myself that I was full of great boasting to Kitty about trying to find Sergeant Paddy a house or a job; and doing nothing about it. Kevin's death had driven a lot of thoughts from Fingal's mind, but it was no excuse for having forgotten about Paddy. Now, thanks to Roisín Kilmartin, he knew the sergeant was a man with technical skills, and of a high order at that, otherwise he'd not have risen above private in the RAOC. It was almost certain that Paddy would be able to read and write, and wasn't that what the builder, Willy Duggan, had been looking for? Fingal would deal with that later. "Right, Roisín. I'll get your tests ordered. I'll see you tomorrow."

"Ah sure," she said, "dat's all right."

But it wasn't. Doctor Micks was coming onto the ward as Fingal neared the nurses' desk. "O'Reilly," he said. "I'm glad you could find time to show up."

"I'm sorry, sir."

"Is that all you have to say?"

Fingal nodded.

"No extenuating circumstances?"

Fingal hesitated. Father and his, "Never explain. Never complain. Take responsibility for your actions. Don't make excuses." All very well, but Doctor Micks would decide if Fingal, indeed any student, would be regarded as satisfactory or would be expected to repeat the whole clerkship.

"I think," said Doctor Micks levelly, "or rather, I hope, there are. You've been doing well, O'Reilly, but a doctor must be totally responsible. Reliable. Are you certain you have no good reason for being so late? I'd have thought at least you'd have phoned to let us know. Give us a chance to find a replacement. Behaviour like yours makes it very difficult for me to certify satisfactory performance. I certainly considered refusing it this morning regardless of your subsequent explanation."

Disaster. Fingal felt chilled. He tensed. Sorry, Father, he thought, but sometimes explanations were called for. "I swapped ward shifts, I was to do today, and went to Portaferry on Friday. To see my brother. He was running me to Belfast on Saturday morning when his car broke down. I missed the Dublin train. I couldn't get one until today."

Doctor Micks tapped his upper teeth with his right thumbnail and scrutinised O'Reilly. "I'll accept that. You arranged cover on Friday. Cars do break down."

Fingal's hunched shoulders began to ease until his senior asked, "But why didn't you call? Surely you had access to a telephone?"

Fingal hesitated. "I did phone, sir. I spoke to a friend who was on duty. I thought I'd made arrangements for someone to cover for me today until I could get back."

"Was it by any chance Mister Fitzpatrick you spoke to?"

"No, sir."

Doctor Micks stroked his chin. "That might explain why he didn't tell me this morning."

"It might, sir." Fingal thought it would be petty to say that Fitzpatrick had known bloody well and had no reason not to inform the senior doctor.

"Very well, O'Reilly. I will accept your explanation—this time. But understand, I'm not pleased that even inadvertently you left this ward understaffed. Medicine is a serious business. You'll get no thanks from a pregnant patient if you fail to show up for her delivery."

"I am sorry, sir."

"I'm sure you are." The consultant frowned, crossed his arms, and drummed his right fingers against his coat. "So, I won't withhold your certificate—this time—but one more lapse, O'Reilly, and I'll have to consider how willing I'll be then to attest to your good standing. You have one more month with us. Put it to good use."

Fingal swallowed. The relief. "Yes, sir," he said, "thank you."

"See there are no more slipups," Doctor Micks said. "Now, tell me about the patient you've just admitted."

Fingal started the classical litany of patient presentation. "Mrs. Roisín Kilmartin—"

"Mrs. RK. I thought you'd have learned that by now."

"Sorry, sir." Another gaffe. He took Doctor Micks through the history and physical examination, his differential diagnosis, and suggested blood tests.

"I see," said Doctor Micks. "Very well." He scratched his chin. "You're probably right that it's some kind of anaemia. Did you consider one of the leukaemias?"

"Yes, sir, but they are more common in men, she has no enlarged lymph nodes, no cough, so it's unlikely that her chest is affected."

"That's usually a late symptom."

"Yes, sir. And her spleen's not enlarged."

"Fine. So what tests will we order?"

"We need a full blood count, sir, and a full white cell count in case I'm wrong about the leukaemia."

"Chest X-ray?"

"No sir. Not unless the white count's abnormal. Her chest is clear to percussion and auscultation. She's a smoker, but then everybody in the Liberties is."

Doctor Micks nodded.

"And smoking's not known to cause any diseases," Fingal said. "She's no history of bronchitis, asthma. We can't completely exclude TB, but I think we should hold off on the X-ray until we see what her blood tests show."

"Well done, O'Reilly," Doctor Micks said. The deputy professor looked at his watch. "Arrange for the bloods to be done in the morning and we'll discuss the case again on Tuesday rounds. I'll be off," he said and added, "Now, keep up the good work between now and the end of this clerkship." He strode from the ward, a dapper man in a raincoat and a grey trilby hat.

Fingal exhaled. He hadn't realised he'd been holding his breath. One bloody thing after another, he thought. Those had been anxious moments when it looked like Doctor Micks had been going to refuse Fingal's certificate. He still might, but that was in Fingal's control. He'd make bloody sure there were no more slipups. The senior man was right. Doctors should be reliable. Fingal had not been with his promises to Kitty about Paddy Keogh. He would nip round to outpatients as soon as the opportunity presented and get Willy Duggan's and Paddy Keogh's addresses. Perhaps Bob could drive him to see Willy as soon as class was over tomorrow. If that went well, he'd pay a call on Paddy. A promise was a promise.

22

In Poverty, Hunger, and Dirt

The stench on Francis Street was something new to Fingal. He swallowed, wrinkled his nose, and wound up the car's window. It was as if he'd been transported to seventeenth-century London where the aristocracy walked the thoroughfares with handkerchiefs doused in perfume crammed against their noses. Physicians making home visits then wore grotesque masks with long artificial birds' beaks stuffed with aromatic herbs to prevent the inhalation of foul airs, miasmas, the supposed causes of disease. The bizarre duck-billed facial coverings gave the doctors their nickname "quacksnifter," which became shortened to "quack."

He inhaled and shuddered, but putting up with a bit of a pong was going to be worth it. Half an hour ago, Willy Duggan, initially surprised to see the student who'd sewn up his chisel cut, had agreed that he certainly could use a clerk and if Paddy could do the job it was his.

"Jasus," Bob said, pulling past a pile of refuse and parking under a pole full of washing sticking from a fourth-floor window, "the stink here would gag a maggot, and it's dark as bedamned."

No sun's rays could filter past the five-storey buildings. No wonder, Fingal thought, that rickets due to lack of exposure to ultraviolet light was so prevalent.

Fingal and Bob got out. Immediately they and the car were surrounded by a throng of kids, little boys in ragged short pants, hand-me-down shirts, threadbare woollen pullovers, battered caps; girls in ankle-length dresses worn under grubby grey linen pinafores. Not one child, as far as Fingal could tell, wore shoes, and their feet were black from the filth on the cobbles. All the youngsters' eyes were oversized for their pinched faces. Their shouts filled the air like the babbling of a flock of starlings.

"It's Lord feckin' Muck from Clabber Hill come for to see us," a boy said.

Fingal felt a tugging at his coat and looked down at a girl of about six. Her bare toes were turned in and her cornflower-blue eyes stared up at him. "Could yiz spare a couple of bob, yer honour?"

A boy yelled, "If it's a mott yiz is after, mister, ye'd be better off in Monto."

Fingal smiled. Monto, a corruption on the name Montgomery Street near Amiens Street Station, had been the biggest red-light district in Europe, reputedly employing 1,600 prostitutes. It was said that the Prince of Wales, later King Edward VII, had lost his virginity there. It was closed down in the mid-'20s, but its reputation lived on in folk memory.

Someone else called, "Would yiz give us a ride, mister? Me and me little brudder? We could go up 'til the Phoenix like toffs."

Bob picked the biggest boy, a lad of about fifteen. "You, son."

The boy pointed at his chest, hunched his head into his shoulders, and narrowed his eyes. "Me, sir? I done nuttin' wrong."

"I know," Bob said, "but would you like sixpence?"

"By Jasus, sixpence?" His eyes narrowed. "What would I have to do for it?"

"Guard my car while I'm away."

He held his head up, cocked it to one side. "If you'll give me ninepence, sir, a tanner for me and t'ruppence for Jockser over dere," he pointed at a gangly youth standing smoking at the front of the crowd, "we're your men." He spat on a grimy hand and offered it to Bob, who grinned, shook it, and rummaged in his pants' pocket. "Here's fourpence on account," Bob said, "and if you and Jockser clean the windows while we're gone I'll take it up to a shilling when we come back."

"Fair play to you, sir. Jockser, get your ragged arse over here. You're going to get rich."

Fingal watched Jockser approaching, scratching his head. Probably he had what the locals called "mechanised dandruff," head lice. Fingal felt the tugging again. "Even sixpence, sir?" The blue eyes bored through to his soul.

He squatted. "What's your name?"

"Finnoula," she said, "and dat means fair shoulders."

"Well, Finnoula of the fair shoulders," Fingal said, "you take me to where Paddy Keogh lives and you'll get your sixpence."

"Don't you do no such t'ing, Finnoula Curran. Your man here could be a Peeler in plain clothes." An older boy stood between Fingal and the little girl. Even though Fingal towered over them both, the lad stood with his legs apart, feet firmly planted. Loathing of the informer had been a thread woven through Irish history since the English had come eight hundred years ago. Fingal stood and faced his accuser, a skinny youth with bad teeth and a bent nose. "I'm no policeman, son. I looked after Paddy when he was in Sir Patrick Dun's Hospital last year. I just want to see him, that's all."

The youth squinted at Fingal, looked him up and down. "Are you—are you de Big Fellah?"

Fingal laughed. "I suppose so. How do you know?"

"Sergeant Keogh told my ma, Missus Kilmartin, to keep an eye out for a big lummox called O'Reilly when she went into Dun's yesterday."

"I'm Fingal O'Reilly, and your ma's doing well, she's going to get better, and she'll be home soon, son. What's your name?"

"Declan. Declan Kilmartin." The youth turned and yelled to the crowd, "It's all right. De Big Fellah here—"

Fingal was flattered to be given the same sobriquet, the Big Fellah, as Michael Collins, a hero of the Irish War of Independence, martyred during the Irish Civil War.

"He's a doctor. He fixed Paddy Keogh and he's looking after me ma, so youse w'at was going to feck the car battery when the minders weren't looking? Leave the car be." He bent to Finnoula. "Take you your man and his friend to see Sergeant Keogh. He lives at number twenty-one. Top back—"

Fingal knew the terms for the different tenement rooms. Top back was one of the cheaper. It would cost six shillings weekly and would be a single room at the back of the upper storey. Not nearly so grand, if the term could be used, as a front parlour or a two pair front.

"And youse two," Declan pointed at Jockser and his friend, "youse gurriers give dem windows a good polishing as well as a wash."

"Jasus, sirs, I'm sorry to have yiz find me like dis." Paddy Keogh spun round. He was sitting on a wooden crate wearing nothing but a collarless shirt, the waist of his pants undone, and his trousers rolled up to his knees. His feet were in a basin of liquid, which to Fingal had a familiar bitter smell. "Me granny swears by mustard for me corns." He was smoking a cigarette and tried to rise.

Stale tobacco mingled with odours of fried onions and boiled cabbage. Underlying these was a musty aroma of damp coming from torn mildewed wallpaper behind which the plaster had crumbled. Fingal could see bare laths.

He clapped a hand on the man's bony shoulder. "Don't get up, Paddy. We'll only take a minute—"

"Would yiz like a cup of tea?" He smiled. "It's good of youse to call."

"No thanks," Bob said, "we only popped in."

"You're looking well, Mister O'Reilly, or is it Doctor now, sir?" Paddy said, and coughed.

"Still Mister for a while, Paddy." He nodded at Bob. "And you'll remember Mister Beresford?"

"I do, sir, from Saint Patrick's Ward. Good day, sir."

"Good afternoon, Sergeant," Bob said.

"W'at brings youse two here?" Paddy asked, and held up his hand to embrace the single-windowed plank-floored room.

Two more crates served as chairs. A table with one short leg resting on a house brick took up space in the middle of the room. A metal basin was piled with chipped plates. The water would have to be hauled upstairs from a pump in the courtyard. A print of the Bleeding Heart of Jesus hung beside a crucifix on one wall above a soot-stained brick fireplace. The back third of the room was hidden behind a curtain. Fingal guessed that was the sleeping end.

One splash of colour brightened the place. A small, long-tailed, redbreasted bird in a wicker cage trilled a song of joy.

"Och," said Paddy, "isn't the oul' linnet in grand voice?"

Fingal had heard that captured wild songbirds were in great demand as pets in the tenements.

"I suppose yiz needed a bit more luxury for a change." Despite Paddy's sarcasm there was no bitterness in his voice, and his grin was broad. "Welcome to Dublin's answer to the Taj Ma-feckin'-hal." He lifted his feet out onto a worn towel. "And in case youse is wondering, I've seen dat place. I was stationed at Jaipur before the war. De oul' white tomb was only a couple of hundred miles away." He dried his feet. Fingal could see the corns.

"That's what we've come about, Paddy."

Paddy frowned. "The Taj or the war?"

"Partly the war." Fingal had been worried about asking a grown man if he could read and write. Such a question could be taken as a mortal insult so he would try to find out without enquiring directly. "You were RAOC?"

"I was, sir. I was learned a trade." He straightened his shoulders. There was pride in his voice when he said, "I was a bloody good mechanic. I t'ought it would stand me in good stead on civvy street when I was demobbed, but," he waved his right arm stump, "a feckin' great shell in the motor repair depot in 1917—" He shrugged, put the towel on the floor, nipped out his cigarette, blew through it, and put the butt in a small tin. "For later." He lifted one of his old boots and bent to put it on. "Fair play to the army, sir. Dey didn't chuck me on the rubbish heap when me stump healed. Dey kept me on for a while."

It was Fingal's turn to frown. What could a one-armed man have done?

"You'd be amazed, sir, by how many spare parts an army needs for its lorries, motorbikes, and dem new tank things. Dey kept me on as a store-man—at least until '19. Den the army let me go and when I came back to Dublin nobody in Ireland was giving work to an old English soldier wit' only one flipper." He waved the stump again.

"A store-man?" Fingal wanted to cheer at this news and berate himself at the same time for not following up months ago with Willy Duggan. "Did that mean keeping lists?"

Paddy started to put on his other boot. "If I'd a penny for every feckin' list I wrote, me and the rest of the family would have a mansion in Blackrock wit' the other swells."

"Paddy," Fingal said, "how would you like a job as a store-man on a building site?"

The clatter of a boot hitting the planks startled Fingal as Paddy dropped it and sat bolt upright. He peered up at O'Reilly. "Youse isn't codding me, sir?"

"I am not."

"Jasus," Paddy said, "I'd give me feckin' right arm for work." He rubbed his stump with his left hand and laughed. "Dat's if I'd one to give."

"No need, Paddy," Fingal said. "There's a Mister Duggan re-building after tenements are torn down. He's been looking for months for someone to keep tabs on his materials. Mister Beresford here and I spoke to him today, didn't we, Bob."

"We did," Bob said. "Mister O'Reilly told him all about you, Sergeant. We didn't know then you already had inventory-keeping experience."

Paddy sat forward. His hand clutched the edge of the crate. "And?"

Bob inclined his head to Fingal, who said, "He told me to bring you round to meet him this evening—"

"Now?" Paddy plucked at his shirt. "Jesus Murphy, I've no de-cent clothes."

"Never worry, Paddy," Fingal said. "There's very few men in top hats and tails on a building site."

Paddy bent, grabbed his boot, and stood. "I'll get me cap and coat." He headed for the curtain.

"Hang on," Fingal said. "Don't you want to hear about the job?"

Paddy turned. "Please, sir."

"If Mister Duggan likes the look of you—and he's bound to,

good trained list makers are hard to come by—he'll start you tomorrow."

"Tomorrow?" The word was whispered.

"The pay's four shillings a day for a six-day week."

"Holy Mother of God, that's—one pound and four shillings a week, more than fifty quid a year." Paddy looked round the room and Fingal saw him curl his lip at the grimy window that looked down into a sunless yard. "I'll tell you, sir, me and the other Keoghs'll be out of here by week's end."

"Good," Fingal said, blessing the chisel cut that had wounded Willy Duggan, but was going to bring a new life to Paddy Keogh and his family. "Go on, Paddy. Mister Beresford will run us over in his car to see Mister Duggan, so get your coat." He looked straight at Sergeant Paddy Keogh, who was grinning from ear to ear while tears coursed unchecked down his cheeks.

"I don't know how to thank you, sir," he said.

Fingal looked away. "Go on," he said gently, and looking round took in the peeling plaster, the curtained-off sleeping area, the stench. A thought struck him. It was something he'd said to Lars. Fingal O'Reilly would be better looking after the living than grieving for the dead, and a doctor who did, could make a difference, even if only in a small way.

23

Eating the Bitter Bread of Banishment

"Mister O'Reilly, your patient," Doctor Micks said.

"Yes, sir." Fingal accepted the chart from Sister Nancy Henry. She was in charge of the women's ward, a tall, hawk-faced woman from Cootehall, County Roscommon, who, as far as Fingal could tell, had been born lacking a sense of humour and had failed to acquire one in fifty years of living. He moved to the head of the bed.

He laid a hand on Roisín Kilmartin's shoulder. "I'm going to tell these other doctors and nurses all about you."

She smiled and said, "Ah sure, dat's all right."

Fingal gave a summary of her case, then waited for Doctor Micks to start.

"Miss Manwell. Your differential diagnosis?"

Hilda listed her suspicions.

"Good," said Doctor Micks.

"Excuse me, sir," Fitzpatrick peered over his pince-nez, "but she's breathless. I think we should consider tuberculosis too. The tenements are riddled with it." His lip curled.

A look of horror crossed Roisín Kilmartin's face. Damn you, Fitzpatrick, Fingal thought, you've scared her silly. He was relieved when Doctor Micks turned to the patient and said, "Please do not concern yourself, my dear. I've had a look at your tests. You do not have TB, I promise you."

She managed a weak smile. "Ah sure, dat's all right den, sir."

"For those of you who do not know, TB terrifies the working class of Dublin. So much so that I've had more than one woman tell me her husband was in gaol rather than admit he was in hospital with tuberculosis. Furthermore," he stared through his wire-framed spectacles at Fitzpatrick, "there are certain diseases we simply do not mention in front of patients. Am—I—clear?"

Fitzpatrick whipped off his pince-nez and polished them.

"Now," said Doctor Micks, "let us continue. Mister Cromie, how would you investigate this patient?"

"Lord Jasus," said Roisín Kilmartin, "investigate? I dun nuttin' wrong. Is your man a Peeler?"

"No, Mrs. Kilmartin," Fingal said, "Mister Cromie is not a policeman. By 'investigate' we mean what tests does he think should be done? Remember when we took your blood yesterday?"

"Blood tests? Ah sure—"

Dat's all right, Fingal thought.

Cromie made a good reply and included a differential white cell count, "In case of neoplasia of the blood system."

"Well done, Cromie," said Doctor Micks. "Neoplasia. Absolutely right." He glanced at Fitzpatrick.

Fingal knew that neoplasia, taken from the Greek and meaning "new growth," was a euphemism for cancer, which, like TB, was another disease that should not be mentioned in front of patients. In Fitzpatrick's case, Doctor Micks was rubbing the message home. "Now, Mister O'Reilly, please tell us what the tests showed."

"The haemoglobin level is low, the red blood cell count is down, and mean corpuscular volume and diameter are elevated. The cells are oversized or macrocytic." He added, "White and platelet counts are low so I don't think we need worry about neoplasia." Or leukaemia, he thought. "Many of the enlarged red cells are immature or megaloblasts."

Doctor Micks asked, "And that degree of megaloblastic activity means? Mister Beresford."

"I'm sorry, sir."

It wasn't the first time Bob had been unable to answer a straightforward question.

"Mister O'Reilly?"

"Pernicious anaemia, sir. And after eight gravidities," Fingal wasn't going to risk saying "pregnancies" in front of the consultant, "I'd be pretty sure there will be iron deficiency as well."

"Correct."

"And the treatment? Miss Manwell?"

"For pernicious anemia, sir, either intramuscular injections of liver extract containing antianaemic substance—"

"The equivalent of half a pound of raw liver daily that until recently the unfortunate patients had to consume orally," Doctor Micks added.

Fingal shuddered. The thought of having to eat raw liver every day. Revolting. A cure from the Stone Age, but little by little the science of biochemistry was making advances. They hadn't identified the factor in liver, but he was confident they would. The outlook for people with sugar diabetes had been powerfully advanced since insulin had been discovered in 1921 by those Canadian doctors Banting, Best, and Macleod. Trinity had appointed the first professor of biochemistry last year, Robert Fearon, a man Fingal admired enormously, a polymath who introduced literary quotes into his lectures, had written a play about the Irish patriot and martyr Parnell, and who played the organ. Research certainly suited some folks. It, nor any other branch of medicine, wouldn't suit Bob if he didn't pull his socks up and study more.

"And you were going to say, Miss Manwell?" Doctor Micks asked.

"Or desiccated hog's stomach or gastric juice from a healthy subject—although the latter is hard to come by."

"Good. The anaemia is caused by the body's inability to absorb a substance found in liver because a factor in normal gastric juice is absent from the patient's stomach." He turned to Bob. "Beresford? How do we treat iron deficiency?"

Bob shook his head.

Fingal sighed. Fingal wanted his friend to pass Finals Part I, and the examinations were only three months away. Time to have a word in his delicate shell-like ear.

Fitzpatrick butted in, "Inorganic salts of iron, either a ferric one, but they can cause gastrointestinal disturbances, or ferrous ones, although they are hard to keep and tend to oxidize to ferric ones." He smiled.

Oily bugger, Fingal thought. He's practically quoting verbatim from Doctor Micks's textbook.

"Correct." Doctor Micks turned to the patient. "You're a lucky woman," he said, "and these young doctors have done a fine job of finding out what ails you. Thin blood, and we'll treat it, and have you home in no time."

"T'anks very much, sir, and t'anks to you too, Mister O'Reilly, sir."

Fingal shrugged, but inside he glowed. Eeyore was right. It was "nice to be noticed." And it wasn't only the thanks. Knowing he'd been part of helping a patient, a patient called Roisín, recover, gave an intense sense of satisfaction. Even if getting to know the patients could cause great pain, as it had with Kevin Doherty, it was worth it. Hadn't seeing Paddy Keogh being taken on by Willy Duggan yesterday been worth, as Ma would have said, all the tea in China? And that sort of thing only happened if you continued to think of the customers as people, not sterile "cases." "My pleasure, Roisín," he said.

"Excuse me, Professor, sir, can I ask a question of Mister O'Reilly?"

"Certainly."

"Yiz knows how much it rains in Dublin?"

"I do."

She frowned and ran a reddened hand through her chestnut hair. With her head cocked she asked, "If I've to take all d'at iron can I go out in the rain?"

"Now why on earth shouldn't you?" Fingal asked.

"Have you seen w'at water does to iron? It feckin' well rusts."

Fingal smiled. "It's all right," he said, "your skin's waterproof. It's like having iron galvanised to prevent rusting."

She laughed. "Wait until Brendan hears his oul' one's galvanised. He'll shit a feckin' brick."

Everyone chuckled. Even Sister Henry managed a smile.

"All right," said Doctor Micks. "One more patient to see. We'll start your treatment today and I'll see you in six days after we've repeated your blood tests, Mrs. Kilmartin."

"Ah sure," she said with a smile at Fingal, "dat's all right."

"O'Reilly, a word."

Fingal moved beside Doctor Micks.

"You did well with that patient."

"Thank you, sir."

"But there are good reasons for maintaining a certain professional distance. You will not call my patients, indeed anybody's patients, by their Christian names. Names may be used, but surnames only. Your calling her Roisín was patronising in the extreme. Is that clear?"

"Yes, sir."

"Excuse me, your honour." Mrs. Kilmartin looked at Doctor Micks. "Don't be too hard on young Mister O'Reilly," she said. "Didn't I ask him to use me Christian name?"

Doctor Micks cleared his throat. "Indeed. Thank you, Mrs. Kilmartin." He turned to the entourage. "Next patient please, Sister."

They moved down the ward until Doctor Micks stopped, bringing his entire party to a standstill. "I want to draw an important matter to your attention," he said. "In the last week of March a group will be visiting Sir Patrick Dun's. They are called the Pilgrims because they travel to different centres, even to the Continent. The travel club is made up of professors, of whom Professor Victor Millington Synge, the playwright J. M. Synge's nephew, is one."

Was he indeed? Fingal thought. He'd seen *Playboy of the Western World* at the Abbey Theatre and thoroughly enjoyed it. And Professor Synge was an acquaintance of Father and Ma.

"I want you to make a good impression. To that end I will be presenting a patient with valvular heart disease. That much I will tell you. The specifics of the diagnosis, which valve or valves are affected and in what way, I leave up to you to discover."

Fingal swallowed. Not another one.

"To let you see him in advance would be cheating, but I intend to ask one of you to examine him in front of the visitors. I hope the individual I ask will make an accurate diagnosis and bring kudos for the standards of teaching in this institution."

Fingal's eyes narrowed. He remembered on their first day here how knowledgeable Fitzpatrick had been about the murmurs of valvular heart disease. An idea began to germinate. He'd need to talk it over with the lads. If they accepted the notion, he was certain Hilda, who had no great affection for the man, would come onside. If it worked it would take the wind from the sails of that bloody know-it-all.

Fingal savoured the idea but then focused his attention on Hilda as she presented a case of cirrhosis of the liver. Even from where he stood he could smell the ketones on the patient's breath because her failing organ could not process the breakdown products of proteins. Poor woman. Unless somebody found a way to give her a new liver, and that was about as likely as capturing a unicorn, she'd not be long with us. Not long at all. Geoff Pilkington and Lars were right. Not all patients get better.

"By God, Fingal," Cromie said as the friends ambled past the Grand Staircase. "If we can pull it off, Fitzpatrick's going to have a canary. He hates being laughed at."

Charlie chuckled and said, "He needs to be put in his box. Self-righteous bollix. You're right—and I see no reason why we can't set him up to make an ass of himself when those senior profs—what did Doctor Micks call them?"

"The Pilgrims," Fingal said. "It won't take much." He explained exactly what he had in mind.

"Bloody ingenious," Bob Beresford added. "I can hardly wait."

"I—" said Fingal, and stopped. Approaching from the nurses' dining room was Kitty O'Hallorhan. "I'll catch you up."

"Right," Charlie said.

"Kitty," Fingal said as she drew near, "Kitty, I'm sorry about Saturday. Please let me explain."

She stopped and faced him. "Go ahead, but I already know," and she smiled. "Virginia gave me your message. I knew you were stuck in Belfast and I knew you were on call on Sunday. I was disappointed, but I did understand."

"Thank the Lord. I'd not have wanted you to think I'd run off with someone or got steamboats with the lads."

She chuckled. "Steamboats? You're starting to sound like a real Dubliner." Then she said, "I'd never have thought that of you, Fingal O'Reilly. You're not the kind of man to be thoughtless. But

I would have been worried sick if I hadn't known where you were. I'd've had you dead after a car crash or a train derailment."

"I'm sorry," he said, "I wanted to have a morning's wildfowling. I—" He looked down at his boots then back up at her. "I needed to get away—just for a little while."

She touched his sleeve. "Mister Doherty?"

He nodded.

"I had a good cry for him," she said softly. "He was such a nice man." She looked straight at him. "I love the way you care," she said.

O'Reilly took a deep breath. "I love the way you care." That's what she'd said. "I took it hard. Too hard." He spoke softly. Inside himself, in quiet moments, he was still mourning. "Portaferry's on Strangford Lough. Strangford's always been special to me—a place I could go to if I was hurting."

"Go on."

"Lars and I talked things through on Friday then went wild-fowling on Saturday morning. We left the shore and set off in his car for Belfast in plenty of time to catch the Dublin train and be with you that evening. His car broke down. I missed the train. Spent the night in Belfast with a friend. I'm sorry."

She inclined her head. "Fingal, it's all right. You did let me know, and we'll be able to get together—"

"Mister O'Reilly. Nurse O'Halloran." Sister Daly had come round the corner. "You two know the rules. You, Nurse. Back to the ward. At once. You're late. I'll speak with you later."

Kitty fled.

Fingal sought for anything he could say to protect Kitty from the wrath of Sister, but she forestalled him.

"I warned you, Mister O'Reilly. I warned you when you started here. Doctor Micks will not be pleased."

Was there any point pleading now? He shook his head. All he could do was say, "I am truly sorry."

There was iron in her voice. "I've watched you since you started. You are gentle with your patients and you care—perhaps too much. You are developing good diagnostic skills. I've seen generations of students. I know how to judge them. One day, when you've grown up, you will make a fine physician."

Fingal held his peace.

"I will think about you for the next two weeks and I will decide whether or not I believe my suggesting to Doctor Micks that an extra six months repeating this clerkship might help you achieve the maturity that you currently lack."

"Thank you, Sister."

"But you will not be seeing Nurse O'Hallorhan during that time. I shall arrange for her to be transferred to the children's ward and I will be having a word with the lady superintendent to ensure Nurse O'Hallorhan is confined to barracks for the rest of March."

24

And Great Was the Fall of It

"Are we certain we want to go ahead?" Charlie asked, sprawled in a chair in the students' common room. He nodded to where Fitzpatrick had hung his white coat.

"Bloody right I am," said Fingal. "In twenty minutes we've to be in the lecture theatre with Doctor Micks, the patient with valvular disease, and the learnèd professors of the Pilgrims. It's a brilliant opportunity to prick Ronald Hercules's balloon."

"Hear him," Cromie said, and ran a hand through his thin hair. "Hear him."

"I know it's what we've planned," Charlie said, "but, Fingal, so far you've been on your best behaviour. It'd be a shame to spoil it just to put one over Fitzpatrick."

In the last two weeks Fingal had done everything possible to appease Sister Daly and impress Doctor Micks. Today, with a bit of luck, Sister would agree not to report Fingal after all, and in one more week he'd get that certificate of good standing from Doctor Micks.

"I think the risk's worth it," Fingal said. "We've put up long enough with Fitzpatrick's arrogance, his disregard for other people's feelings."

"But Charlie has a point," Cromie said. "Our three months in psychiatry starts next month and we want you with us. And for the surgical dressership in July."

"After Finals Part One," Fingal said, looking straight at Bob Beresford. "We all have to pass in June."

"Well, actually, no," Bob said. "We don't. As long as we have our certificates we can continue our clinical studies and repeat Part One six months later. The *Regulations* say so. I should know. God knows how many cracks I took at Intermediate Part Two."

"And," Fingal asked, "how many goes at Finals Part One were you thinking of having, Bob?" Fingal had had a heart-to-heart with Bob two weeks ago, but it clearly had been as much use as farting into a force-ten gale.

Bob reddened. "Well I—that is—"

"Haven't been studying quite as hard as you might?"

Bob looked away, then smiled and said, "You all know I'm in no rush to qualify, which is why I have a suggestion to make about our plan for the downfall of Fitzpatrick."

"Go on," Charlie said, glancing at the coat again, "but I reckon if we all confess—if we have to—Micks won't hold us all up."

"I've a better idea. I know getting qualified as quickly as possible is important to you three." Bob shrugged. "I've all the time in the world." He lit up.

"What are you suggesting, Bob?"

"I don't believe Doctor Micks is going to be too enthralled when we pull this off. We'll embarrass Fitzy all right, but we'll embarrass Doctor Micks too."

"Come on," Fingal said. "Our chief's not going to treat us like schoolkids. He'll see the funny side."

"If he doesn't?" Bob asked.

Silence.

"I'll tell you," Bob said. "We act as planned, but if Micks demands to know the perpetrator, I'll be happy to own up."

Fingal said, "A regular Sydney Carton, 'It is a far, far better thing I do now—'"

"*Tale of Two Cities,*" Charlie muttered. "Dickens."

"I'm not so sure I want you going to the guillotine for us, Bob."

"Facing Doctor Micks is not facing beheading. He might let me off." He hesitated then continued, "And you're right, Fingal. I haven't been working as hard as I should. I'm not sure repeating the medical clerkship would necessarily be a bad thing for me."

Fingal said deliberately, "All right, but on one condition if the other lads agree."

"Which is?" Bob asked, and blew a lazy smoke ring.

"Which is, Bob Saint John Beresford, you make a solemn promise here and now—"

"To what?" The smoke ring collapsed.

"To use the next three months to get stuck into the books and bloody well pass Part I with us. We'll help, won't we, lads?"

Both grinned and their heads nodded. "Indeed we will," Charlie said.

Bob's jaw dropped. "That's blackmail."

"Yes," Fingal said with a grin, "but it's in a good cause." He held out his hand and eventually Bob shook it. "It's a promise, Fingal Flahertie O'Reilly," he said to the applause of the other two. "But you're one crafty devil. You're the Wily O'Reilly, by God."

"Wily O'Reilly," Cromie echoed. "I like that."

"Och sure," said Fingal as he stood and removed Fitzpatrick's white coat from its hook. "Dat's all right."

Fingal and the rest stood round a trolley upon which lay a young man with sandy hair, blue eyes, and a narrow nose between plum-coloured cheeks. He was propped up on pillows and his pyjama jacket was unbuttoned.

The trolley was positioned head toward a blackboard, feet to the semicircular tiers of benches and the members of the Pilgrims. Fingal scanned the faces of the soberly dressed men. Victor Millington Synge, physician to Baggot Street Hospital and recently appointed King's Professor of the Practice of Medicine at Trinity College, sat in the centre of the front row.

"Pilgrims, welcome to Sir Patrick Dun's," said Doctor Micks. "We've a full day arranged where you can visit our new facilities, observe a new surgical procedure, and, of course, the banquet in the Royal College of Physicians this evening. But first we'd like you to see our students in action. Mister SH here is used to his trips to Sir Patrick's. He is a willing volunteer when we need to demonstrate his condition and has often been used as a case for our students to diagnose in the medical part of their Finals Part II practical exams. How often?" he asked the patient.

"I've bin an exam case turteen times, sir." He grinned. "It's a great day out for me. Gets me away from herself and the feckin' chisellers. And the hospital gives me a grand lunch. And I've learned a fair bit of medical lingo."

"Quite," said Doctor Micks.

Fingal saw Professor Synge smiling broadly at Mister SH's last remark. The professor was in his midfifties and bore a striking resemblance to the pictures of his famous uncle. His hair had receded as far back as his ears and from there a central patch of shiny pate was surrounded by a rim of hair. He wore spectacles and was paying attention as Doctor Micks said, "And the net result of his condition has been damage to the heart's valves."

Fingal glanced at his classmates. Hilda had been let in on the plot. She and the three others looked innocent. Fitzpatrick was staring eagerly at Doctor Micks, who said, "Here at Sir Patrick Dun's we take pride in our students being well grounded in the finer points of cardiac auscultation.

"We have here today six typical, late-fourth-year Trinity students. I should like one to examine the patient."

Fitzpatrick nearly tripped in his haste to step forward.

"Very well," Doctor Micks said.

If the swelling of a pigeon chest was ever accompanied by an explosion, Fingal thought, the attendees would have been deafened.

The assembled professors leaned forward.

Fitzpatrick, a supercilious smile on his lips, fumbled in the pocket of his white coat, produced his stethoscope, plugged in the earpieces, stepped forward, and without a word to the patient clapped the instrument on his chest.

By the way Mister SH flinched, the bell must have been cold.

"There is a—" Fitzpatrick frowned, moved the bell a couple of inches. "There is a—" He blanched. Beads of sweat appeared on his forehead. He pulled out the earpieces, stuck a finger in each ear in turn, replaced the earpieces, stared at the bell, and put it on the patient's chest. He remained immobile, then shook his head. "I can't hear anything," he said hoarsely. "Nothing. Nothing at all."

Fingal didn't dare look at the lads.

A muted murmuring arose from the audience.

"Well," said Doctor Micks, "anyone can have an off day."

"Excuse me," Professor Synge asked. "May I see that stethoscope?"

Fitzpatrick crossed the well of the theatre and handed over the equipment in question.

Meanwhile Doctor Micks, with a scowl like thunder, said, "Miss Manwell, please."

Hilda approached the patient. "Hello," she said, "I'm going to examine you."

"Ah sure, grand," he said, "and such a pretty wee mott, yiz can be my doctor anytime."

Hilda smiled and bent to her work.

Fingal snatched a glance at Professor Synge, who had removed the bell from Fitzpatrick's stethoscope and was fishing up the rubber tubing with a narrow propelling pencil.

Hilda said, "I'm pretty sure I can hear an opening snap—" her brows knitted, "a low-pitched rumbling diastolic murmur, and—and presystolic accentuation." She straightened and looked at Doctor Micks.

Fingal hoped she was right. He had learned that there were many combinations of sounds depending upon which valve or valves of the four in the heart and blood vessels were damaged.

The patient said, "You take the prize, miss. Dat's w'at all the professors say."

Doctor Micks smiled. "Well done, Miss Manwell. Very well done." He addressed the audience. "I can assure you she is absolutely right, gentlemen."

"That's impressive, young woman," Professor Synge said. "And Robert—"

Fingal realised he was addressing Doctor Micks.

"Don't be too hard on the young man. It would be impossible to hear anything," he held up the offending objects, "when the tubing of your stethoscope is stuffed with cotton wool."

The laughter began slowly, but soon everybody was laughing—everybody but a red-faced Fitzpatrick.

Doctor Micks cleared his throat. "Very well. Now Mister O'Reilly?"

"Yes, sir."

"You heard Miss Manwell. Those murmurs are diagnostic of?"

"Mitral stenosis, sir."

"Sure it's not mitral incompetence?"

"Yes, sir. The systolic murmur of that occurs when the ventricle contracts in systole, not when it relaxes in diastole."

"Good."

There was a small round of applause. Doctor Micks smiled and inclined his head to the audience.

"If you'll excuse me, Robert?" Professor Synge said.

"Of course."

"I think I can speak for all of the Pilgrims when I say we are impressed with your last two students and have sympathy for the first."

There was a muttering of assent.

"You have every right to take pride not only in the skills of your students, but in their sense of humour. That's only the second time I've seen the cotton wool trick. The first was when Edgar there," he pointed at another Pilgrim, "did it to me in front of old Professor Purser."

To a man, the Pilgrims chuckled.

"Thank you, Victor," Doctor Micks said. "Most understanding."

"I take it," Professor Synge continued, "these youngsters are near the end of their clerkship?"

"They are," Doctor Micks said. "They have one more week to go. Sister's reports earlier today on them are all favourable." He glanced at Fingal.

What? I love you, Sister Daly, Fingal thought. The minute I'm out of here I'm off to the ward to thank you.

"And unless one of them commits a felony in the next seven days they'll all be getting their certificates of good standing."

Fingal wasn't sure—but had Doctor Micks actually winked at him?

"In view of Professor Synge's intercession I shall ignore the recent—um, incident."

"I'm delighted to hear it," Professor Synge said. "It's not so long ago we were students ourselves. Good luck to you all." He looked at Fitzpatrick. "Don't take it too hard, son. We all had a good laugh."

The look Fitzpatrick gave O'Reilly might have been lethal. So what? Fitzpatrick had been punished and the dark cloud hanging over Fingal had blown away. He'd have no difficulty persuading the lads to head to the Bailey for a few pints.

He'd miss Saint Patrick's Ward and Doctor Micks's regular teaching sessions, but it was time to move on to new aspects of the trade. And they'd be back on the old ward with its black walls and painting of Saint Patrick and Oisín in July to start their surgery.

25

That Where Mystery Begins

"Life as a medical student," observed Cromie, from his seat in Davy Byrnes pub, "as I have before remarked, is one of long periods of relaxation punctuated by short spells of intense horror." He took a pull from his pint.

"Horror as in the Finals Part One exam in sixteen days," Fingal said, swallowing a mouthful of Guinness then emitting a puff of smoke. He could afford Erinmore Flake these days. The better tobacco was pleasant and so was the restoration of diplomatic relations with Father.

"Indeed," said Charlie. "I hope we're all well read."

"We bloody well ought to be," Bob said. "Fingal here's been keeping everyone's nose to the grindstone for the past three months since he wrung that promise out of me back in March."

"I have medical jurisprudence and materia medica coming out my ears," Charlie said. "What I don't have is the fresh pint I need. Anyone else?"

"I'm fine," Cromie said. "I'm seeing Virginia later and meeting Fingal and Kitty in the Stag's Head off O'Connell Street tonight. I'd better heel tap."

Finally, Fingal thought, Cromie was learning to handle his drink. "Kitty's going with her sister and nephew to the zoo this afternoon. I'm meeting her there in Phoenix Park, but we'll see you two at seven."

"I'm not waiting until seven for a jar. It's Saturday," Bob said. "Jameson, please, Charlie, then I've a date with the horses at two thirty over at Leopardstown. Want to come?" He lit a cigarette.

Charlie shook his head. "No thanks, Bob, I'm going to buy some trousers, and put my feet up tonight. Listen to Raidió Éireann. Fingal? Pint?"

"Not for me. I'm heading home." Earlier this week Ma had dropped him a note practically demanding he visit today. It wasn't like her. She usually made her invitations informal. Fingal had written to say he'd drop by this afternoon and had tried not to worry.

He watched Charlie rise and amble over to the long bar, stopping to greet a nonmedical acquaintance. Byrnes was a friendly place. No wonder James Joyce had spent so much time in here writing *Ulysses*.

"So, Fingal, how goes the studying?" Bob said. "Are you and Charlie catching up with Cromie, and much as it hurts an old chronic to say it—with me?"

"I think so."

Bob cocked an eyebrow at Fingal. "You've missed a fair number of pathology and bacteriology lectures on those Thursday afternoons you've gone to rugby."

"I know, but I am making up," Fingal said, hoping it was enough.

Bob leant forward and tapped his glass. "I was disappointed there was no Irish selection for you or Charlie this year."

So was Fingal, but he didn't want to let it show. "Always next year, Bob. And I'm in top condition."

"So," said Charlie, "is my pint." He set it on the table. "Here, Bob." He handed Bob his whiskey. "*Sláinte.*"

"Cheers," said Bob. "Here's to July first and the end of those three bloody awful months of psychiatry."

"I'll drink to that," said Fingal, raising the last of his pint. "I don't think I saw a single patient improve. Sedating folks with chloral hydrate or barbiturates is about all doctors can do. You feel so bloody useless."

Bob sipped from his glass, Charlie raised his pint, and Fingal puffed on his pipe.

"Begod," said Fingal, "I wonder if they'd not do better with a jar or a smoke or two?"

"I'll drink to that," said Charlie.

"At least Jameson's tastes better than chloral hydrate," Bob said. "I tried it." He grimaced.

The friends looked at each other and burst into laughter.

"Fingal." Ma rose from her chair in the living room and hugged her son. "It's been a while."

"I'm sorry, Ma," he said, "life's pretty hectic."

"Perfectly all right," she said, "now come and sit down."

Fingal thought she looked pale.

"I'm so glad you could come."

"What's up, Ma? Something's bothering you."

"I wanted to talk to you alone. Father's gone to see an exhibition at the Royal Hibernian Art Gallery," she said. "Percy French watercolours." She made a little moue. "I let him go alone. I don't like watercolours. Much prefer oils."

"I know," he said, thinking of the Yeats in the dining room and the veritable gallery in heavy gilt frames that adorned the rooms, halls, and staircase walls.

She leant forward and her pearls swung away from her throat. "That's why I asked you to come today. Lars was here yesterday." She smiled. "He's still got some of the tan he got in Villefranche. I think the time away did him good."

The last time Fingal had been home in March, Lars, recently returned from France, had been tanned and seemed to be feeling less hurt by Jean Neely.

"I think you're right." Fingal frowned. "I didn't know he'd been in town this week."

"No," she said. "He was only able to get away yesterday and I wanted his advice before I spoke to you. Father was in Trinity Library when Lars popped in. He did agree it was a good idea to seek your advice." She fiddled with the loop of the necklace. "I worried about writing to you earlier, but I did want to see you, son."

"About what?"

"Father." Her voice was flat.

"Father?" What in the world could he, Fingal, advise about Father?

She looked straight at him. "He's not well, Fingal, and he refuses to admit it."

"Not well?" Fingal leant forward. "How exactly is he not well?"

Ma's fingers plucked at her skirt. "He tires so easily. He's getting very short of breath. You remember when you and Lars were here last year and Father'd let his assistant take the Saturday tutorial?"

"Yes." Fingal had noticed that.

"He confessed to me he'd been feeling run down."

Fingal started to work out a differential diagnosis. On those two symptoms it was a long list. "Has he seen his doctor?"

Ma shook her head. "He gets angry if I even hint at it. I thought you might have an opinion about whether he really needs to see someone. If you do, I'll find a way to make him go."

Fingal heard the iron in her voice. Despite his worry he smiled. "Have you," he asked, "noticed anything else?"

Ma's eyes glistened. "He's—that is, I think he's losing weight and—and he looks terribly wan."

Losing weight was always worrying. Cancer patients lost weight. Tired, short of breath, pale? Ma could be describing Roisín Kilmartin, she of the pernicious anaemia. It would be a coincidence if Father had the same condition, but it certainly sounded as if it might be some kind of anaemia.

"Lars thought that as you are almost a doctor you'd have some ideas." She touched his knee. "I do hope so."

Having strangers as patients could be upsetting, but your own father? "I'm certain," Fingal said, "that someone needs to examine him. That might be enough, but if it's not, some simple blood tests, perhaps an X-ray, might tell if anything's wrong."

She smiled. "Thank you, Fingal. Lars was sure I was right to want to ask you."

"Perhaps," he said, "but you'll have to persuade Father to go. I can't examine him." He grinned. "They say a doctor who treats his own family has idiots for patients."

Ma nodded. "I understand, but I will find a way to get him to go," she said, "and I want him to see a good doctor—a really good doctor."

"I know the one," Fingal said. "A consultant who taught me for six months. Doctor Micks. He was our clinical clerkship supervisor. I don't see much of him now we've moved on to studying other branches of medicine, but I'm sure he'd be willing to do one of his old students a favour. I'll ask him on Monday."

"If he agrees, Father *will* keep his appointment."

Fingal had no doubt about that.

"I'd be so very grateful, son. It would take a great load off my mind."

Fingal could hear the pleading in her voice. He struggled not to let his concern show. "First thing on Monday I'll see my old chief and I'll phone you. I'm sure Sister Daly won't mind."

She smiled. "You're a good lad, son. But then, you always were."

Fingal smiled back. "Och," he said, "the last time I heard tell you only get issued with one ma. You're meant to keep an eye on her."

She chuckled and sat more straight, her hands clasped in her lap. "Now," she said, "now that we've got the unpleasant business out of the way, tell me about everything else in your life."

Fingal sat back. "Let's see," he said, "at work things are chugging along nicely. I should be qualified in twelve months. Only two more exams to go, one this month. No rugby until September." He could tell by her smile she was perfectly happy that he was unlikely to get injured for a while. He winked at her. "This evening I'm going for a walk in the Phoenix with a young lady. Her name's Caitlin O'Hallorhan. Her dad's an accountant and she's a nursing student."

"Is she indeed?" Ma asked, and smiled. She cocked her head to one side. "And is she the kind you might like to bring home to meet us?"

Fingal laughed. Typical of Ma never to enquire about her sons' romantic lives, but if they volunteered information she'd come to the point, but not directly. She was really asking was he serious about Kitty. "Not yet, Ma. Not yet, but in a while? You never know what might happen. You never know at all." If he did bring her, which was tantamount to telling his parents he was thinking of proposing, it wouldn't be until after Finals Part II next year, and the more he saw of Kitty O'Hallorhan the more he hoped she'd be happy to wait. She'd been almost as jubilant as he in April when he'd finally been able to tell her face-to-face about Paddy. He still remembered the soft way she'd looked at him and said gently, "You are a gentleman, Fingal O'Reilly, and I admire that," then she'd kissed him and he could taste it yet.

"And you're seeing her this evening?" Ma opened her handbag and took out her purse. "Here," she said, handing him a pound note, "buy her a nice tea."

He tried to give it back. "Ma, I can't—"

"Oh yes you can, Fingal O'Reilly. Now put it away. The workman is worth his hire. That's your consultation fee." She smiled. "And see you have a good time tonight."

26

The Stag at Eve Had Drunk His Fill

Fingal loosened his collar. The tram was crowded, hot, and humid. He got off in Phoenix Park near the Wellington Monument, a massive obelisk on a square plinth. It had been erected two years after the Battle of Waterloo as a tribute to the Duke of Wellington, who had been born Arthur Wellesley in 24 Baggot Street Lower. Of Anglo-Irish stock, when accused of being Irish, the Iron Duke had icily replied, "Being born in a stable does not make one a horse."

Fingal spotted Kitty sitting on the steps at the monument's base. She was waving at him, hatless, and ignoring the fashion dictate that young ladies should wear gloves.

She hugged him. "Fingal." She held him at arm's length. "It's been forever."

"It has." He'd seen her only three times since her restriction to the Home had finished at the end of March and here it was, the first week in June. "But I don't see what else we could do. We can't meet on the ward. You've been in paediatrics, I've been in psychiatry. And the work's been heavy."

"At least now that my first year's over, I'm out of that Nurses' Home and sharing a flat with Virginia. That should make things easier."

"After Finals Part One," he said.

"Of course, after Part One. I know it's important." He felt her against him, firm and warm, and he inhaled her gentle musk. The perfume was mingled with a hint of fresh perspiration. He found the combination arousing. He gave her cheek a quick peck. The Phoenix was crowded and modesty forbade public displays of affection.

"Come on," he said, taking her hand. "Let's walk up as far as the zoo, across to Ashtown Castle, then head down Chesterfield Avenue to the tram stop." It was great just to hold her hand. He'd missed her company sorely. Fingal, content to be with her, felt no need to make conversation as they strolled. He wanted to put away his concerns for Father and bask in the company of the young woman who for him was living proof that, as he had once told her, absence did make the heart grow fonder. He hoped Kitty was enjoying the afternoon sunshine as much as he, the springiness of the grass underfoot.

The sticky buds of horse chestnuts had long since burst to free the multifingered leaves. Under the trees a mosaic of emerald brightness and bottle-green shade dappled the lawn where sparrows hopped and starlings strutted. Phoenix Park on the north side of the River Liffey was a rustic refuge in the gritty, workaday capital city.

Horse-drawn open carriages carrying top-hatted gentlemen and ladies sheltering under lacy parasols and wide-brimmed hats rolled through the park. The air was filled with the clop of hooves, the clatter of motorcar engines, the high-pitched squeals of children, and, from the zoo, the piercing cry of a peacock.

"Where are we going tonight?" she asked.

"The Stag's Head."

"Stag's Head," she said. "Where's that?"

"On a street off O'Connell Street. We're meeting Cromie and Virginia. It was his idea."

"Oh. She told me this morning she was to meet him at Nelson's Pillar, that was all."

"She's been a good friend to you, hasn't she?" he said. "And she saved my bacon when Lars's car broke down and I wasn't able to make it to Dublin that night back in February."

"Ginny's a lamb," Kitty said. "She didn't believe the stories the girls in the Nurses' Home were telling me. Told me to ignore them."

"What about?"

She squeezed his hand. "It's funny," she said, "when I was confined to barracks they told me I'd better get used to not seeing you anymore. You know what kind of cats young women in residence can be."

He stopped. "Why on earth not see me?"

She laughed. "You have a bit of a reputation, you and Bob Beresford."

"As what?"

"I think the word is Lotharios."

Fingal blushed. "Well I—that is—"

She laughed. It was a rich sound. "Eejit. I knew that before our first date. Why shouldn't a student see lots of girls? And you two aren't youngsters like Cromie and Charlie. Heavens," she said, "you don't think you're the first boy I've kissed, do you?"

Kitty kissing another man was an image he preferred not to dwell on. He said nothing.

"Course you don't, but, Fingal?"

"Yes?"

"You're the first I've wanted to go on seeing."

He took a deep breath. A phrase from his medical jurisprudence course, *res ipsa loquitur,* sprang to mind. The thing speaks for itself. He'd not looked at another woman since last October. "Me too," he said.

"I knew on New Year's morning when that nice countertenor sang, 'Smoke Gets in Your Eyes.' "

And he remembered telling her he'd not let the flame die. He didn't regret it. Perhaps he should be asking her home to meet his folks as Ma had suggested and yet, and yet he wasn't ready to declare his love. "I know," he said, "we've not seen a lot of each other in the last nine months—"

"I'd imagine it's much the same for a busy doctor's wife," she said.

Fingal took a deep breath. "I suppose it would be. GPs are on call twenty-four hours a day." He looked into her eyes. "Would you want to be a GP's wife?"

"I might—if the right GP asked me." Her tone was serious.

"Kitty, I—" He was unsure how to respond.

"It's all right, Fingal," she said, "I know at the moment you can't see much further than your exams, your rugby, but maybe one day—?"

Her voice was firm, not pleading, but there was a wistfulness. "Maybe," was as far as he could go and he hurried to say, "but you're right about the exams. I have to put them first. I won't make any promises until I'm Doctor O'Reilly." It was the truth. How would she respond?

"It's all right," she said, "I understand." She let his hand go and strode off toward the zoo.

Oh Lord. Now what? Women. They were such complicated creatures. If Charlie was annoyed with Fingal he'd tell him straight out. Bob and Cromie behaved exactly the same, but all the years he'd watched Ma handle Father? She always approached serious matters obliquely, never head on, and she usually got her way. He'd better chase after Kitty and try to find out what she wanted, although inside he was pretty sure he knew, and couldn't give it to her. Not yet. "Hang on a minute," he called.

Kitty only shortened her stride.

He hurried after her. "Hang on, Kitty."

She stopped and turned to face him. There was no hint of a smile.

"Look," he said when he caught up, "I'm sorry. Honestly." He took her hand and looked into her eyes.

"There's nothing to be sorry for," she said. "I understand. Sometimes I don't know what I see in you. You're about as romantic as a sack full of spuds."

What had Ma said last year about Father? "He has great difficulty in expressing affection, that's all." He grabbed her hand, forcing her to stop and face him. Modesty be damned. He pulled her to him and kissed her.

She was breathless when they parted. He smiled at her and was pleased to see her smile back. "There now," he said. "Is that romantic enough for you?"

"Fingal Flahertie O'Reilly," she said, and shook her head, "you're an *amadán* of the first magnitude."

"Och sure, wouldn't any man make an idiot of himself round you, Kitty?" He lowered his voice. "You make it very hard for a fellah not to get very fond of you. Very fond indeed." Face it, he thought, you're more than just fond of her, but you have one more year of studies and rugby, and nothing, nothing is going to distract you. And she knows that now.

"Thank you, Fingal," she said, "because I'm very fond of you too." She pecked his lips, turned, and called over her shoulder, "I'll race you to the zoo gates."

Fingal and Kitty left the Dublin United Tram Company vehicle at the base of Nelson's Pillar on O'Connell Street. From his pillar, the cocked-hatted, one-armed Lord Nelson stared down with his single eye. He'd been there since 1808, a memorial to a British hero, and the recipient of a century and a quarter's worth of Irish pigeon droppings. There had been a great deal of talk in the wardroom about "fostering the Nelson spirit" when Fingal had served on HMS *Tiger* in 1930.

He took Kitty's hand and guided her across the broad street where trams ran up the middle and horse-drawn and motor traffic the outer lanes.

Once on the footpath he walked slightly ahead to bulldoze a way through the Saturday crowds. Barefoot women in shawls, gurriers in ragged short pants. Men in cloth caps with clay dudeens between their lips stinking of cheap tobacco rubbed shoulders with gents in top hats, morning coats, and spats. How could they stand to be so overdressed in this heat?

As they passed the General Post Office, still bullet-pocked from its occupation by the Rebels and the siege during the 1916 Easter Rising, he had to raise his voice. "Cromie said the Stag's Head Pub is near the column."

"It would be lovely to stop and have a drink. My feet are killing me in these half-heels and you look parboiled."

He laughed. "We'll go up to one more cross street, then I'll ask," he said. Fingal O'Reilly had always hated having to seek help. With anything. He ploughed ahead until he was pulled up short at the junction with Prince's Street.

Model A Fords jostled with Austins. He saw a Beauford convertible nearly brush against an open Rolls-Royce tourer. Over the hum of voices, motorcar engines burbled and iron wheels rumbled on tarmac as a pair of Clydesdales hauled a Guinness cart stacked with barrels. And there were bicycles. Everywhere cyclists jingling their bells. Sweat, car exhaust, and the whiff of a recently dropped pile of horse apples stung his nose. A man approached wearing a buttonless woollen suit one size too small. The jacket was missing a lapel and laceless boots shod his feet. "Buy my sheet music, sir?" He had a Northside, nasal Dublin accent you could cut with a knife. "For the lady, like?"

"How much?" Kitty asked.

"Och, Jasus, lady, only a penny. One penny."

"Go on, Fingal," Kitty said, "and ask him about the pub."

O'Reilly laughed, rummaged in his pocket and produced two pennies. "I only want one sheet."

"Lord bless you, your honour," the man said, and handed O'Reilly a green paper.

He glanced down and saw, printed in smudged typeface, the music and lyrics of "The Star of the County Down."

"Ask him, Fingal," Kitty said.

"Excuse me," O'Reilly said, "but would you know where the Stag's Head is?"

"Stag's Head?" He grinned and exposed a set of stained upper teeth. "The Stag's Head? I do, by God. The Stag's Head is exactly where you'd expect it to be, sir."

"And where is that?"

The man laughed then said, "The stag's head is always, always, invariably—about six feet from the stag's arsehole, sir."

He was long gone by the time O'Reilly and Kitty stopped laughing.

He noticed a policeman approaching, probably a former member of the Dublin Metropolitan Force which had been amalgamated with Garda Síochána after partition. The uniformed man was very tall and wore a large spiked helmet. The Metropolitans had been known as the "giant police." They had all been at least six feet.

O'Reilly approached him. "Excuse me, officer."

"Yes, sir?"

"I'm looking for a pub called the Stag's Head."

The constable smiled. "Turn right on Abbey Street," he said. "You can't miss it, but if you do dere's another pub next door, the Vincent van Gogh."

"Thank you very much. Come on, Kitty." He led her through the crowd and in minutes had found the pub.

Cromie and Virginia were inside sitting at a circular table. "Come on over," Cromie called. Fingal noticed how the sunlight coming through a clear glass window highlighted Virginia's copper hair.

Fingal and Kitty were soon seated and had placed their orders. He couldn't wait to tell Cromie the story of the sheet music seller. Virginia was a broad-minded young woman. She'd not mind the punch line.

". . . The stag's head is six feet—"

"Away from the stag's arsehole," the barman who had arrived with the drinks said. "Sorry to spoil your line, sir—" He set the drinks on the tabletop as the laughter subsided. "—but," he continued, "we all know dat crack round here and dat's why the boozer next door, the oul' Vincent, is called the Stag's Arsehole by the locals."

Fingal paid the man and lifted his pint. *"Sláinte."* He swallowed and savoured the Guinness, the summer day, the company. He glanced at Kitty. He didn't have to choose between his studies and her. He never thought she'd insist on that, but it was good to know and he considered himself a lucky man. A very lucky man. "Och Jasus," he said aloud, even if momentarily nagged by a thought about Father, "God is in His Heaven, and all is right with the world."

27

The Fever and the Fret

Fingal stood in the bay window while his mother aligned the lace-bordered antimacassars on the backs of the sitting room chairs. She moved to a vase of roses, rearranged them, and glanced at the ormolu clock on the mantel.

"Please, Mary," Father said, "come and sit down. We're not receiving royalty."

"But we are expecting Doctor Micks and I can't have the house looking untidy."

"It is unnecessary," Father said.

Fingal wondered if Father meant the tidying or the doctor's visit.

"I'm just a bit under the weather, that's all," Father said. "A strong tonic or Cook's beef tea is all I need, not a visit from a specialist."

"You promised," Ma said. She stood behind his chair and dropped her hand on his shoulder. "You know what a worrier I am. That's why I persuaded Fingal to speak to his senior." She glanced down. "I should have asked you first, Connan, but when Fingal was here on Saturday I thought the opportunity too good to waste. We're doing this for my peace of mind, remember, dear?"

Fingal heard the rain rattling on the panes, the thrashing of the trees. Mid-June and a summer gale was howling. He hoped Doctor Micks wouldn't be soaked getting here. On Monday he'd listened to Fingal's request, smiled, and said, "I'm sure it's nothing to worry about. I'm busy for a couple of days, but I'll make a domiciliary visit at two o'clock on Thursday."

"Thank you, sir. Very much." Fingal felt comforted knowing that soon there'd be some answers; worries, he hoped, laid to rest. "I'll let them know to expect you."

"Your father's probably simply tired—it happens to men in their fifties. I suspect he needs a warmer climate for a while, perhaps a cruise."

Fingal smiled. " 'My mother would enjoy that. Father might be harder to persuade."

Doctor Micks looked over his spectacles. "You are familiar by now with the expression, 'Doctor's orders,' O'Reilly?"

"Of course, sir."

"If I believe it to be necessary, he will go."

Fingal stifled a grin. Poor Father. He'd certainly find it difficult to stand up to both Doctor Micks and Ma. The medical profession put great store in the curative properties of lots of fresh air. Of course the less well-off had to make do with the Dublin variety, tainted as it was with dampness, chill in the winter, and chimney smoke. The upper classes were sent on a cruise or to a spa like Bath or Baden-Baden.

Ma had been grateful on Monday night when Bob had run Fingal over to tell her to expect Doctor Micks this afternoon. "Could you be there when he comes, Fingal? Sometimes doctors' talk can be so confusing. Perhaps you could be my translator?"

"Of course." Another Thursday pathology lecture missed to add to the ones he'd skipped for rugby practices. Sarcoidosis was the topic. All he knew about the condition was that it was some kind of rare chronic inflammatory condition that could affect any body system. Ah, well. He could always borrow someone's notes. He knew that pathology, the study of how damage to the body's systems caused illnesses, was important to a doctor's understanding, but it was bedside medicine that enthralled him. Once the exam was passed, he would be done with basic sciences forever.

Bridgit ushered in the visitor. "Professor O'Reilly. Ma'am. Doctor Micks."

Father stood and Ma dropped a tiny curtsey. "Good of you to come, Doctor," Father said, "and on such a filthy day." He offered his hand, which Doctor Micks shook. "May I introduce Mrs. O'Reilly. I believe you know our son, Fingal."

Doctor Micks nodded at Fingal. "How do you do, Mrs. O'Reilly?"

"How do you do, Doctor Micks? Please have a seat." Ma indicated an armchair and said, "Would you care for some tea?"

"Thank you, no," Doctor Micks said.

"You may go, Bridgit," Ma said.

"Perhaps a sherry when we've finished?" Father said.

"Perhaps, but now, if there is somewhere private?"

"Of course," Father said, moving toward the door. "Please come with me."

Ma had tried to make small talk with Fingal, but she kept glancing at the drawing room door. He knew she was willing the consultant to return, and to return with good news. She sat forward the second the doorknob started to turn.

"Your husband will be with us shortly, Mrs. O'Reilly," Doctor Micks said when he entered. "I have completed my examination. We'll wait for the patient and I'll tell you together what's in store." He smiled. "Ordinarily I'd consult with your GP and have him explain, but under the circumstances—"

"We'd both like you to talk to Fingal," Ma said, "I'm sure he'll understand more than us."

Fingal waited.

Doctor Micks frowned. "It's irregular. We usually don't discuss adult cases with family members other than husbands or wives."

And then only if the news is bad. How many times, Fingal wondered, had he heard a husband being told that his wife had cancer, but under no circumstances was she to be told. The adage was that next of kin should know the worst, but patients should always be allowed to cling to hope. In his opinion they'd be a damn sight better off knowing the truth.

"The trouble is, Doctor," Ma said, "my husband is very much a man of letters, not at all scientific, and I'm just—" Her smile was dazzling. "Fingal is nearly qualified. I know he'll understand."

The usually austere Doctor Micks smiled. "Of course, my dear Mrs. O'Reilly. If that is what you and your husband wish."

"It is."

"In that case, if you'd come with me, Mister O'Reilly? You'll excuse us, madam?"

Fingal followed the senior man into the high-ceilinged hall. Before either could speak, Father passed them on his way back to the drawing room, smiled, and spoke to Doctor Micks. "Talking about your patient, I see. I seem to remember a quotation from George Bernard Shaw; he said that, 'all professions are a conspiracy against the laity.'"

"On the contrary in this instance," said Doctor Micks. "Mrs. O'Reilly wanted your son to be informed so he could explain matters to you if I became too technical."

"We appreciate that. Don't let me hold you up." Father closed the door behind him.

"This is irregular, O'Reilly," Doctor Micks said, "but your mother is right. You are practically a doctor."

"Thank you, sir."

"I'll not beat about the bush." Doctor Micks pursed his lips. "Your father is not well. He is anaemic, and I noticed bruises on his wrist and left shin although he cannot recollect having injured himself."

"I see." Doctor Micks was implying that there was not only a lack of red blood corpuscles, but some defect in the clotting process. Not good.

"I found enlarged lymph nodes in his left anterior triangle."

Fingal's trained mind said, "The space bounded by the neck, the shoulder, and the outer edge of the trapezius muscle that runs from the base of the skull to the shoulder tip." He thought, I don't like the sound of this.

"The spleen is also enlarged. There are no other clinical findings." He smiled but there was sadness in his look. "Please understand, I am not using your father as a teaching case, O'Reilly, but would you care to offer a differential diagnosis?"

Fingal swallowed. "It's got to be one of the blood diseases, but I'm not sure"—or I'd rather not face the possibility of—"which one." While he had a vague notion of those disorders, he wished to hell he'd not cut those classes to play rugby.

Doctor Micks nodded. "Or it could be a virus infection. Glandular fever, the Americans call it 'mono,' short for infectious mononucleosis. It was first described in 1887 by Doctor Nil Filatov. It can be associated with your father's findings, anaemia, bruising, and enlarged lymph nodes."

"I hadn't thought of that, sir."

"Of course, usually in infections the patient is febrile." Doctor Micks frowned. "Your father's temperature is normal."

The patient, Fingal thought. Somehow it was less personal to think of Father as "the patient."

Doctor Micks smiled. "It'll be easy enough to sort out. We'll arrange a complete blood analysis. If the number of lymphocytes is massively increased we'll have a diagnosis of glandular fever."

"Because their function is to fight viruses," Fingal said, although he realised that his senior colleague was trying to sidestep the critical question. He took a deep breath and looked Doctor Micks in the eye. "Sir, could my father have leukaemia?"

"I'm sorry. It is a definite possibility. If so, and we won't know until we have the results, we must pray it is one of the chronic varieties."

"Why, sir?"

Doctor Micks frowned. "I should have thought you'd know that by now."

"Sorry, sir."

"Their prognosis is very good. Remember that."

"I will." Fingal wanted to ask Doctor Micks to explain about the other kinds of leukaemia, the ones with the not-so-good prognoses. He knew vaguely about them, every fourth-year student did by now, but not only had he missed the lectures on the subject, but disorders of the blood was a topic he'd not yet read up. He asked, "How long will it take to get the results, sir?"

"The blood for tests will be taken tomorrow. I'll arrange to have the slides read first thing Monday morning. Come to the ward at eleven after rounds. We'll have an answer by then. I'll set aside time on Monday afternoon to talk to your family. I assume you'll want to be there?"

"Thank you, sir." Fingal glanced down, then back at his teacher. "I do appreciate all you're doing. May I ask another question?"

Doctor Micks inclined his head.

Fingal said, "Doctor Pilkington taught us that patients should be told why tests were being ordered and what results might be expected." Earlier Fingal had been convinced patients should always be told the truth. They were the ones with most at stake. "What will you say to my folks, sir?"

"There's no point giving them reason for concern until there are clear answers," he said, "and as an old teacher of mine used to say, 'some questions are better left unanswered.' In this case if your parents don't accept my explanation of a probable virus infection, I'll prevaricate—until I know for sure, and I will expect you as a junior colleague to support me." That wasn't what Geoff Pilkington had taught, but Doctor Micks was the senior.

"You don't think they'll be more worried by uncertainty? Could they blame you, sir, if the diagnosis isn't glandular fever?" Fingal asked.

"They could, of course," Doctor Micks said, "but that is a risk every doctor must accept. We try to cure, but we can't always, so we must spare our patients as much suffering, and I include mental anguish, as possible. If we become less than loved by a disappointed patient, but have spared them grief, it's a small price to pay."

"I see." Fingal did see the kindness of the approach. It also answered his own question of what to tell Lars. Fingal would phone, tell his brother that Doctor Micks wasn't worried, but was doing tests next week.

"Good," Doctor Micks said. "Shall we go and talk to them?"

"Please."

Fingal thought his parents looked as if they were posing for an old daguerreotype. Father, one arm flexed across his chest and the other hand on Ma's shoulder, stood behind her chair. She sat erectly, hands clasped in her lap.

"Please have a seat," Father said.

Ma's gaze went from Doctor Micks as he took a chair to Fingal who remained standing, and back to Doctor Micks when he said,

"You were right asking me to discuss the case with your son. He is going to make a fine physician."

Father and Ma both smiled.

Nicely done, Fingal thought, starting on a cheerful note.

"He has asked me to explain, and with respect to your wishes, Mrs. O'Reilly, I have given him permission to interrupt if I become too technical."

"Thank you, Doctor."

"I have examined the professor thoroughly and can find little obvious. You are anaemic, I am sure, and bruise easily. There are lymph nodes enlarged in your neck."

Fingal saw his mother frown. "We all have lymph nodes, Mother. They're part of a system that fights infection. Father's are swollen and it could be a sign of infection."

"I see." Ma smiled up at Father. She covered his hand with her own.

"Precisely, and I suspect we may be dealing with one. All the signs are compatible with a diagnosis of glandular fever," Doctor Micks said.

She frowned, and said, "Glandular fever? Connan, is that what your nice young colleague had last year?"

"Arthur? Yes, I believe it was." He smiled. "It took him a while, but he did get over it."

"Sometimes the patient doesn't show much of a fever. I'm afraid in older patients it can be slow to resolve, with the nodes staying enlarged for quite some time," Doctor Micks said.

"And the tiredness?" Father asked.

"Can be slow to resolve, but complete recovery is the usual outcome."

"I see."

"I'm sure you'd like to know exactly what is going on," Doctor Micks said. "So, Professor, if you can attend the outpatients' laboratory at Sir Patrick Dun's, they'll be expecting you at eleven to-morrow. We'll take some blood and have an answer early next week." He smiled. "Now, you did mention sherry?"

Neatly done again, Fingal thought. Without saying as much, Doctor Micks has given the impression there wasn't much to be worried about and by accepting the offer of a drink has signalled that the consultation is over.

"Of course," Father said, rose and walked to a sideboard where decanters and Waterford glasses sat on a silver tray. "Mary? Fingal?"

"Please," Ma said. "And if it's only an infection that's going to get better I think a little celebration is in order, don't you, Fingal?"

"I do indeed," he said, following his senior's lead and keeping his concerns to himself. "A small one for me, Father. I must be running on soon." Fingal accepted the glass. He wanted to leave before there were any more questions. "I'd like to phone Lars before I go. Let him know not to worry," he said. "My brother," he explained to Doctor Micks.

"The one in Portaferry whose car broke down?" Doctor Micks said.

And Fingal was relieved to see that his senior was smiling.

28

These Things into My Ear

"What did Sir Robert Woods, honorary professor and laryngolo-
gist to Sir Patrick Dun's, say was the golden rule?" Bob Beresford
asked, as Fingal and a nurse held the wriggling child of six. Bob
was trying to remove something the boy had shoved in his ear. His
mother had a girl of four by the hand and a baby of a few months
wrapped in the folds of her tartan shawl. Beneath the ragged hem
of a long skirt, her bare legs vanished into a pair of mildew-speckled
boots.

"Would youse feck off, yuh big fecker," the child yelled, then
spat at Fingal, who smiled back, ignored the spittle on his trousers, and tightened his grip. He could understand how scared the
youngster was, and Weaver's Street where he lived wasn't a finishing school. "They get their language in their mothers' milk," he
said quietly to Bob. "Pay no heed, but get a move on."

Friday morning was oto-rhino-laryngology outpatients, known
more understandably as ear, nose, and throat, ENT for short. They
had been a regular fixture in Fingal's and his friends' calendar for
the past three months. They'd seen their share of earaches, deaf-
ness, sore throats, nose bleeds, nasal polyps, and several throat
cancers.

"Come on, Bob." Fingal knew his friend wasn't adroit at procedures but believed the more he practised the better he'd become. "You can do it." Fingal was now adept at packing bleeding noses, removing foreign bodies from ears and nostrils, and clearing out earwax. He felt a ferocious blow to his shin. "Aarrgh." Bedamned. The little bugger had landed a kick that would not have ashamed a rugby fullback. Fingal, still with the boy gripped tightly, bent, and making sure the mother couldn't hear, applied Geoff Pilkington's advice to speak to patients in language they could understand. "Do that again, you wee gurrier, and I'll kick your arse from here to the Dodder River. Now hold still."

The child stiffened, stared at O'Reilly, and burst into tears, but he didn't move and in a few moments Bob was holding a pea between the tips of his forceps. "Got it," he said. He grabbed an otoscope. "Keep holding his head please, Nurse." Bob popped the illuminated instrument's hollow tip in the ear canal. "Drum's a bit inflamed," he said, and turned to the mother. "I'll give you a note to go to the hospital dispensary and get some drops."

"Can I come back for dem tomorrow, sir?"

Fingal, still holding the boy, understood. Either she'd not come back or she'd have pawned something to pay for the medicine.

Bob clearly understood too. "Or," he said, "make up salt in warm water, a tablespoon to a pint, and put a few drops in Enda's ear three times a day. If he's not better, still says it's sore, in five days bring him back."

"I will, sir." She managed a small smile.

Fingal turned his attention to the patient. "You can let him go, Nurse." He gradually lessened his own hold, squatted, and looked at the little lad. Tears ran down his cheeks, snot glistened on his upper lip. "You're all better now, Enda, so dry your eyes and blow your nose. Here." Fingal handed him a cloth from Bob's instrument table. The boy snatched it and did as he was told. O'Reilly produced a paper bag of brandy balls. "Go on," Fingal said, "take a couple."

The boy sniffed, looked in the bag, then at Fingal. "Can I have six, mister?"

Fingal laughed. Greedy wee divil, he thought.

"Nah," Enda said, "only two for meself," he nodded to where his mother sat, "and two for Emer, me sister dere, and two for Brid w'ats at home minding the dog."

Fingal swallowed. "Here," he said, "take the bag." Replacing the ha'penny's worth of boiled sweeties he always carried in case he had to deal with children would hardly bankrupt him.

"Honest?" Enda looked suspiciously at Fingal. "Honest?"

"Cross my heart."

The boy snatched the bag. "T'anks, mister."

"And," Fingal said, feeling guilty for his outburst and leaning closer to the boy's good ear, "I'd not have kicked you. Not really."

It was the kid's turn to laugh. "If you had, you'd not have been the first, but," he looked Fingal over from head to toe, "even if you are a big fecker, you're not strong enough to kick anyt'ing as far as the Dodder. Dat river's all the way to Ballsbridge."

"Take him away, mother," O'Reilly said. "Take him away." He was still chuckling after they'd gone, then he turned to Bob. "And to answer your first question, the prof's golden rule was, 'Never, never, *never* put anything in your ear smaller than your elbow,' and by God, he was right."

Fingal was no stranger to Bob's flat on Merrion Square on the ground floor of a yellow brick Georgian terrace. Since he'd extracted the promise from Bob that he would study, Fingal had changed partners and instead of Charlie had worked with Bob in outpatients and spent a lot of time here making sure Bob studied too.

The drawing room was carpeted, the walls papered, and on them hung framed prints. Old masters and Van Gogh's *Starry Night* kept company with several of Stubbs's horses.

"I've always liked your pictures, Bob," Fingal said, opening his knapsack and taking out a tome. "Particularly the Van Gogh."

"I'm not that interested," Bob said, "except in the horses, but I've been living here for eight years and bare walls aren't very cheerful so I borrowed these from home."

"You and your horses." Fingal set the textbook on the table and opened it at "Disorders of the Haematopoetic System." "Blood today, Beresford. I missed the lecture for rugby and you were—"

"At the horses. I won twenty quid that day too." He opened a sideboard. "I know we're supposed to be studying, but I could use a drink. Fancy something?"

Fingal shook his head. "After we've done a few hours. We need to catch up on these blood disorders."

"Anaemias, leukaemias—"

Fingal flinched. This morning Father's blood samples would have been drawn.

"—thrombocytopaenias, polcythaemias, that sort of stuff?"

"Right." Fingal put a notebook beside the text, set his bag on the floor, and pulled out a chair. "Come on, Beresford, get your idle arse over here." He was used to working alone, but for three months had developed a system of studying with Bob. This was for Bob's benefit, Fingal could take in information quickly by reading and making notes by himself, but he did enjoy the man's company, perhaps because he was more of an age with Fingal than the younger Charlie and Cromie.

"Idle arse," Bob said, as he sat opposite. "Not exactly an elegant expression. You still think you're at sea, O'Reilly. Do you miss it?" He offered Fingal a cigarette, smiled when it was refused, and lit one himself.

"Not really, although I enjoyed my time on HMS *Tiger*. Did a bit of boxing." He'd won the fleet championship for his weight division, but was not going to boast.

"Did you, by God." Bob looked sideways at O'Reilly. "I'd not like to go three rounds with you, you big lump. Did you ever think of boxing for Trinity? I think our friend Charlie goes to the gym."

"He does," Fingal said, "he likes to spar, but rugby, Kitty, and studying fill enough of my time, and studying is what we came to do. Here." Fingal opened the text and slid it across the table. "You read. I'll make notes."

"Jasus," said Bob as he picked up the book, "was it a cargo ship or a slave galley you were on?" He took a deep pull on his smoke. "Before we start, tell me a thing, Fingal. Nothing to do with pathology."

"You're hopeless, Beresford," Fingal said. "I'm surprised the thought of working doesn't bring you out in a rash." Fingal was sure that the more Bob learned the less scared he became of the subjects and the more he seemed to want to pass after all. "What do you want to know?"

"You mentioned Kitty. How are things going with you and her?"

Fingal hesitated. He didn't like discussing his private life, but this was Bob Beresford. "Things, as you put it, are fine. She's a great girl. I'd like to see more of her, but you understand, her schedules, mine, work."

"Are you in love with her?"

Fingal sat back. "God, Bob," he said, "a policeman wouldn't ask you that."

"I'm not a Peeler, Fingal, and we've been friends for a while now. I'm only asking because I don't want to see you hurt."

Fingal frowned. "Hurt? How the hell could I get hurt?" He thought of Lars. If he'd not let himself fall for that Jean Neely girl he'd not have been wounded. Kitty was fun, beautiful, but Fingal wasn't ready to buy her a ring. Not quite yet.

Bob crushed out his smoke. "Three years ago, before I met you and the boys, I walked out with a girl from Cultra." His voice softened. "It wasn't until she'd married an army captain, Lord John MacNeill, next in line to be the Marquis of Ballybucklebo, that I realised I'd let a gem go. Your Kitty's a jewel. She cares for you and it shows. Don't make my mistake if you feel for her. Don't lose her."

Fingal sat back. "Thanks, Bob," he said quietly. "I appreciate the advice. I didn't know about the girl from Cultra. I'm sorry for your troubles. Thank you for telling me."

Bob shrugged. "Water under the bridge."

Look in your heart, Fingal told himself. Bob's giving you good advice. You are in love with Kitty O'Hallorhan. "I'll tell her—after the exam."

Bob inclined his head. "Good man. I don't think you'll regret it."

"You're right." Fingal took out his fountain pen. "Now. Read the bloody book."

Bob began, *"The leukaemias are a family of blood cancers—"* Fingal's fingers tightened on the pen, *"first described by Rudolph Virchow in 1885 who reported a large number of white blood cells in a smear of a sample taken from a recently deceased patient. He coined the term from the Greek* leukos, *white and* aima, *blood. Ten years later Franz Neuman noted that instead of being red the bone marrow of a leukaemia patient was 'dirty-green-yellow—'"*

"So medicine's only recognised the disease for fifty years," Fingal said.

"Looks like it." Bob read on—and on until he closed the book and announced, "Here endeth the lesson."

"Right," Fingal said. "Let's see what you've learnt."

Bob sighed. "I love the way you can switch from slave driver to grand inquisitor, O'Reilly. You're sure you're not Torquemada reincarnated? Haven't we done enough for one day?"

"Divil the bit," Fingal said. He'd remember every word. He had a pressing reason to, but if Bob was faced with an exam question on these disorders, it was important he remember what he'd been reading. "Classify the leukaemias."

Bob lit a cigarette, pushed back his chair, and said, "Leukaemia is an abnormal increase in white blood cells which are produced in the bone marrow, but appear in the bloodstream—"

"I didn't ask for a definition. I asked—"

"For a classification. I know. Steady on, old man. The leukaemias are classified by the type of cell involved and the speed of onset and progression of the clinical course. Two types of cells may be involved: Lymphocytes, which are infection fighters, and myelogenous cells, which are immature forerunners of many blood components, including red cells, white cells, and platelets."

"So there are only two types of leukaemia?" Fingal asked.

Bob shook his head. "I said the rate of progression was important. Disease of both cell types can be acute or chronic. The chronic ones have a slow onset and can go on for many years with many patients succumbing to some other unrelated cause of death."

Fingal could hear Doctor Micks. "If it is—we must pray it is one of the chronic varieties."

"Acute leukaemias, lymphocytic and myelogenous, are swift in onset and rapidly fatal," Bob said, and grinned. "There, how did I do?"

"Top of the class," Fingal said quietly. "Absolutely right." He pulled in a deep breath and sighed.

Bob leant forward. "You all right, Fingal? I thought you were just your usual no-nonsense about work self, but now you sound, I don't know, you sound a bit low."

"I'm sorry, Bob," Fingal said. Like his love life, he didn't want to discuss family matters, not even with closest friends. Certainly not now when the tests had yet to be done and Father's diagnosis was speculative. "Just a bit tired, and worried about Part One." He slipped from his chair and pulled out his pipe. "Tell you what. Let's have that drink, a smoke, then you take the notes and grill me on the signs, symptoms, investigations, and treatment."

Fingal lit his pipe while Bob poured two Jamesons.

"Here." He handed a glass to Fingal. "Fingal," Bob said. "I've already stuck my nose into your business about Kitty. You can tell me to shut up if you like, but you're *not* yourself today. What's up?"

Fingal swallowed and felt the smoothness of the Irish whiskey. He rolled the glass between his palms, and looked at Bob. "At eleven o'clock this morning my father had blood samples taken. We'll have the results on Monday. We hope it's glandular fever." He didn't need to go on. Bob's whispered "Oh Christ" was enough for Fingal to know his friend had understood what else might be turned up.

29

The Sensation of a Short, Sharp, Shock

Describe the macroscopic and microscopic postmortem findings in a patient who had been suffering from sarcoidosis of the lungs and liver. Fingal reread the question. It didn't help. He still knew virtually nothing about the subject. Two hours ago, the invigilator had announced, "It is two o'clock. You may turn over the examination paper and begin." Moments later, Fingal had recognised his nemesis. The mine lurking in calm waters. Now, having written the other two required essays, he was glaring at the question and realising he was not going to find divine inspiration.

He sat in the back row of the hushed Examination Hall of Trinity College Dublin. Six months earlier he'd squired Kitty here to the New Year's Ball. Since Monday he'd written two three-hour exam papers each day. One before lunch. One after. The subjects were twinned. Materia medica and therapeutics, medical jurisprudence and hygeine, and pathology and microbiology. They were passed or failed in pairs, a good mark in one could compensate for a poor mark in the other. Two sets of poor marks and the student would be repeating the exam in those two subjects in December.

And the papers weren't all. Starting tomorrow would be a series of oral and practical exams. Now, on Wednesday afternoon, June

26, 1935, he was staring at the last paper of Finals Part I. Pathology. And he wasn't happy.

He'd had no trouble with two of the questions, rheumatic fever and cirrhosis of the liver. He'd learnt about the former when he'd looked after Kevin Doherty. Cirrhosis had been one of the subjects he'd missed for rugby practice, but they'd seen a patient of Hilda's on the women's ward. The poor woman had died three weeks after admission. He and Bob had spent an evening together reading the pathology. But this? This? He knew sweet Fanny Adams about sarcoidosis. He'd missed the Thursday lecture two weeks ago when Doctor Micks had come to Lansdowne Road. Fingal had never seen a case and had been too preoccupied with the blood disorders since his old chief's visit to read up on this disease. He wished to the bottom of his soul that he'd spent an hour or two on the rare inflammatory condition.

And he'd not been satisfied with his answers on this morning's microbiology paper either. A first-class answer to all three questions now should compensate for a poor showing in one question this morning. But to mess up two linked subjects? He'd be joining the chronics in December, would have to reread two vast subjects in detail to be sure of a pass, and that would mean less time to study for the all-important Finals Part II exam next June.

Damn it. He shook his head. Damn it, if he had to go down, he'd go down fighting.

On the principle that a blank sheet would garner nothing, but putting down what little he knew might collect a few critical marks, Fingal wrote, *Sarcoidosis is a rare disease of unknown causation. Collections of inflammatory cells,* but he hadn't a clue about which specific ones, *can be identified in any organ system and would be particularly numerous in the lungs and liver of the patient in this question. There is no known cure.* Just, he thought, as there is no known cure for not having prepared enough for this exam. He looked down the hall where his entire class bent over their desks scribbling. Several students from more senior years were re-sitting.

He looked up. The clock said there were fifty minutes left before time was up, but what was the point of sitting here? He held up his hand. The invigilator left his desk and walked past the ranks of desks. "Yes, Mister O'Reilly?" he said sotto voce.

"I have finished, sir." He handed his answer booklet to the lecturer. Perhaps Fingal should have said, "I am finished, sir," to convey his certainty that he had failed, but he felt an even more appropriate expression would have been, "I am bollixed."

"Once you leave the hall you will not be readmitted."

"Yes, sir."

"Very well. Good luck." He smiled.

Fingal found a bench under a sycamore tree in the courtyard. The sounds of traffic from nearby College Green were muted. The sky was overcast and he heard a distant rumble of thunder. A grey day to suit his mood. He lit his pipe feeling like a newborn taking comfort from a dummy tit. Lord knows, Fingal O'Reilly needed solace, and being certain he'd failed two subjects was the least of his troubles since Monday nine days ago. He puffed a mighty cloud and remembered.

"O'Reilly," Doctor Micks had said, "you are on time. Good." The consultant turned to his entourage. "I shall see you all back here on Saint Patrick's Ward on Wednesday."

There was a chorus of, "Thank you, sir," from the current group of clinical clerks.

He took Fingal by the elbow. "Come with me," and led him into a small room to the side of the ward. "Please sit down." He picked up a report and handed it to Fingal. "I imagine you've become quite knowledgable about leukaemia. Under the circumstances, I certainly would have read up on the subject."

"I did, sir." Fingal looked at the report. "There's no rise in the lymphocyte count so it's not glandular fever." Damn. "The platelet count is low, the red cells are low, and that explains why my father has bruises and is tired and short of breath—" Fingal looked up at his teacher and back down to the form, "but the white count isn't increased. I don't understand." He grinned. "He doesn't have leukaemia. That's wonderful."

Doctor Micks steepled his fingers and looked straight at Fingal. "That's what I thought, but blood diseases aren't my field. I asked Doctor Fullerton. He has a special interest in haematology."

Fingal's grin faded; his palms were sweating.

"I'm sorry," Doctor Micks said, "but there is a rare variant called aleukaemic leukaemia."

"It wasn't in the book I read, sir." Aleukaemic meant "without white blood." "How can anyone be suffering from an excess of white cells without having too many of them? It doesn't make sense."

"My thought exactly, but contrary to popular belief, consultants are not omniscient. My colleague explained that in this situation the abnormal cells are produced but never leave the bone marrow so they don't show up on a blood test. They do, however, interfere with the production of other blood components."

"Father's red cells and platelets are low."

"I'm afraid so." Doctor Micks leant closer. "Fingal," he said, surprising him with the familiarity, "Fingal, I very much fear it is what ails your father." He paused.

He's giving me time to digest that, Fingal thought, and it's a tough mouthful to swallow. "Will Father need a bone marrow biopsy?" he asked.

"Yes, he will. It will deny or confirm that there is leukaemia, but more importantly if there is, what cell type and whether it is chronic or acute." He touched Fingal's arm, surprising him for the second time in as many minutes. "My boy, things might yet turn out well. The condition may be chronic."

"How soon can you arrange the biopsy, sir?"

"Doctor Fullerton will do the procedure himself as a courtesy to you and to a fellow Trinity professor."

"That's very decent." It was. Even in skilled hands, driving a wide-bore instrument into the breast or hip bone to get into the marrow cavity was tricky and painful.

"Unfortunately Doctor Fullerton is leaving this afternoon for an extended visit to Saint Bartholomew's Hospital in London. He can be back on the thirtieth, do the biopsy, and read the slides first thing on Monday, July first."

That was two weeks away. Fingal was going to ask could the test not be done sooner, but his senior asked, "Where will you be at ten o'clock that day?"

"Here, sir. July first is the start of our surgical dressership at Sir Patrick's."

"I'll explain to Mister Kinnear, the senior surgeon, why you will be absent that morning. I'll talk to you here, and take you with me to your parents' house."

"Thank you very much, Doctor Micks." Fingal hesitated. If a physician of Doctor Micks's stature was comfortable with having to wait, a student should be too. But this was Father's test.

"Can we afford to wait two weeks, sir?" Fingal had been taught that in cases of cancer, speed of diagnosis and treatment were critical. To say nothing of leaving patients in a limbo of worry. Two weeks could seem like a lifetime.

"Yes."

"Two weeks?" Fingal heard his voice rise in pitch.

"I appreciate it sounds like an eternity, but if we think about it dispassionately—"

"It's not easy, sir, being dispassionate about family. This is my father."

"It's difficult for you under the circumstances, Fingal, I know." Doctor Micks inhaled deeply. "I do know."

"Thank you."

"But the harsh facts are there is no cure for leukaemia. We can try to help his anaemia with iron supplements, proper diet while we wait for the results. We'll be giving it to him regardless of the final diagnosis anyway. If he becomes very anaemic, a blood transfusion will help and for the long term—"

Fingal nodded and swallowed. "I understand, sir."

"I'm sorry, but as things stand, I think waiting so the best man in the country can do the tests makes sense. Doing them isn't going to change anything, it will only give us answers and a prognosis, and they'll be the same in two weeks as they are today. They'll not change any treatment."

"I agree." Fingal realised he was crushing the report, relaxed his grip, and smoothed out the creases in the paper. "I do understand, but the waiting's not going to be easy." He gave Doctor Micks the report.

Doctor Micks accepted the form. "Can you be free this afternoon?"

"Yes, sir."

"I promised your parents I'd call by to give them the blood results. I imagine you'd like to be there."

"Will you be able to soften the blow, sir?"

Fingal was surprised when Doctor Micks shook his head and said, "They'll need time to digest everything I'll have to tell them. I must be absolutely honest."

And he had been at Lansdowne Road that afternoon. The coming biopsy, the possible results, and the different prognoses depending upon the results had been presented factually and calmly. Father and Ma had taken the news stoically. It wasn't until Doctor Micks had left that Ma had permitted herself to cry. "It's so unfair, Connan," she said.

"Yes, it is," Father said, handing her his hanky, "but then life's not fair, and if I've understood the consultant there is a good chance I might have the fairly benign disorder."

She blew her nose.

Fingal hesitated. He didn't want to intrude. It was a time his parents needed to be together without him. "If you'll excuse me, I'll go and give Lars a ring," he said. "Let him know what's happening."

"I'd rather you didn't," Ma said. "I know you'll worry, but I think we shouldn't concern your brother until we know exactly what the future holds. You agree, Connan?"

"Completely. I'm sure I'll have the chronic sort so why upset Lars? Am I right, Fingal?" Father asked.

Fingal hesitated. For the first time ever Father, Father with a capital *F*, had asked Fingal's advice, his reassurance. "You are indeed, Dad." Dad. It seemed somehow right to call his father Dad, and by the way the man smiled, he must have thought so too. "But I'll give Lars a call anyway. I'll not worry him, just tell him you need one more test in a couple of weeks, to bide content with that and not worry." I can worry enough for all of us, Fingal thought, and Doctor Micks is right. A doctor's job is to alleviate suffering.

"Thank you," Father said. "I am relieved."

"Be a good boy, Fingal," Ma said. "I'm sure you need to get back to your hospital, but on your way out ask Bridgit to have Cook send up some tea and biscuits."

His mother had deftly protected her eldest boy for two more

weeks. And now, sensing Fingal's discomfort, she had given Fingal an excuse to leave and allow her and her husband the privacy she must know Father would prefer. She could perfectly well have rung for Bridgit.

Fingal kissed her cheek. "I'll be in touch," he said, "try not to worry too much."

The flash of a lightning bolt and nearly simultaneous thunder brought Fingal back to the present. The first drops rattled on the sycamore leaves. He scurried back to the Examination Hall, shoulders hunched against the downpour, as a second jagged strike rent the heavens and the celestial cannons roared.

Back in the shelter of the anteroom Fingal found a seat. Time for the remaining candidates would be up in twenty minutes. He'd wait for the lads. The plan had been to go for a pint after the last paper. Even if he was not enthusiastic, he'd go. Being with his friends would take his mind off his troubles.

The hall doors opened. Bob Beresford strode out, lighting a cigarette. He waved. "Fingal."

"Have a pew, Bob." Fingal nodded at the seat beside him. "You're out early."

"Huh," Bob said. "I just hope I put down enough. All that nose to the grindstone stuff with you, O'Reilly. I know I backslid for a while, but recently I've started to hope I'd make it."

"So you bloody well should. We've been telling you we'd make a doctor of you in spite of yourself, Beresford. And remember that conversation we had about making a difference—perhaps in research."

Bob nodded. "I've you to thank for that."

A group of three students left the hall, deep in discussion, no doubt having a postmortem of the paper, each anxiously seeking reassurance from his friends.

Bob said, "I think I might squeak by." He blew smoke down his nostrils. "I saw you go pretty early. You must have got the answers down in jig time."

"I hit a snag. Sarcoidosis."

"You weren't at that lecture. I remember." Bob sucked in his breath. "What about the other two questions?"

Fingal managed a weak smile. "Should be all right, but I made a hames of the microbiology paper too."

"Oh, come on, Fingal. I'll bet—"

"That's your trouble, Beresford. You'd bet on anything."

Bob laughed. "I still reckon as long as you keep your head for the rest of the week in the practical and oral exams, you'll be all right."

Perhaps he could pull himself up by his bootstraps in those next parts of the exams that would go on all week until Saturday. They'd be sitting practical tests and answering oral questions in every discipline. "I hope you're right, Bob," he said. "I hope you're right."

30

Children Casual as Birds

"Come in, Fingal." Kitty stood on the step of the Leeson Street house where she and Virginia shared a flat. "Last exams yesterday. How did it all go?" She closed the door and muffled the church bells summoning the Sunday worshippers.

He kissed her, held her at arms' length, and said, "It's very good to see you, girl." There was a clean scent in her hair. "It's been a while."

"Two weeks," she opened the door to the flat and led him in, "but you kept your promise about phoning." She frowned. "I didn't like the way you sounded on Wednesday. Do you really think you've—?"

"Ploughed path and micro?" He blew air past his upper lip. "Pretty sure."

"Here," she said, sitting on a sofa, "come and sit down. Perhaps it's not as bad as you think."

He sat beside her, feeling her warmth. "I'm happy with four subjects but—" He rocked his hand from side to side. "—there was one pathology question I couldn't answer at all and one in micro I made a very poor fist of."

"Oh dear." Fingal knew she was trying to sound cheerful. "Could you have done well enough on the other questions? The same thing happened to me once in a first-year exam, but I squeaked through."

"Maybe I have too." In his heart he didn't believe it. "I'm pretty sure I got everything right on the pathology practical. I checked my answers with Cromie and Charlie and I don't think I made too big a mess of the oral. Professor Wigham was smiling when we finished."

"When will you get your results?"

"Five o'clock tomorrow."

"It'll seem like an age."

"I can't change a thing by worrying." He forced a smile. And I've more than one cause for concern, he thought, wondering what news Doctor Micks might have tomorrow morning. "I don't want to be the spectre at the feast today." Fingal looked into her grey eyes. "It's a lovely day after last week's thunderstorms. I've not seen you for ages, and you've been very patient, so what would you like to do?"

"Take your mind off your cares," she said. She cocked her head on one side and looked at him, a smile at the corners of her mouth. "Fingal O'Reilly, from the day I met you you've been the scruffiest student ever. When was the last time you had a haircut? You look like—what's that song about Dublin Zoo?"

"Thunder and lightning is no lark. When Dublin City is in the dark," Fingal said. He didn't feel much like singing.

She chuckled. "It's the lines from the fourth verse I'm thinking of." She sang,

> —says she to me, if you don't come soon
> I'll have to get in with the hairy baboon,
> Up in the Zoological Gardens.

"That's you, O'Reilly. A great hairy ape."

He ran a hand through his mop and smiled in spite of himself. "I can't get a haircut on a Sunday."

She stood and took his hand. "Oh yes you can. Into the kitchen, boy. I'm going to trim it for you and by the time I've done I'll be sweeping up enough hair to stuff a mattress."

She sat him on a chair, wrapped a towel round his neck, took scissors from a drawer, and started. "When I've finished with this, O'Reilly"—snip—"you'll be ready to accompany a young lady for a stroll along the banks of the Grand Canal." Snip. "You'll be, in the immortal words of 'God Bless England' by Peadar Kearney"—snip—"'neat and clean and well advised.'"

Fingal chuckled. "I think that song was not one of praise for the island next door. Kearney fought with Michael Collins in the Easter Rebellion, you know."

"He did. And my uncle was in the General Post Office in April '16 too. Did two years in Kilmainham Gaol. He's still a Sinn Féiner." She laughed. "Black sheep of the family."

"Pretty socialist lot, Sinn Féin," Fingal said. "I seem to remember you felt that way too."

"I still do. Got some of it from my uncle Ruairí. He'd never use the English, Rory."

"Kitty, do you remember Paddy Keogh?"

"The wee sergeant with the pleural effusion? You told me in April you'd got him a job."

"I saw him on a tram last week. He was in great form. He'd had a pay rise to four shillings and sixpence and he's moved his family out of the tenements."

She stooped in front of the chair and kissed him, hard and long. "Jesus, O'Reilly, and I don't take His name in vain very often, that's marvellous." Her next kiss was harder.

They had the place to themselves and it was all Fingal could do to control himself.

She straightened, looked down into his eyes. "Damn you, O'Reilly, you're not just a good clinician, you give a damn about your patients, and you act on it." He heard a catch in her voice when she said, "I think that's why, even though you don't see me very often and put your work first, I haven't dated another man for nearly a year."

Tell her, Fingal. Tell her. "Kitty, I—" Wait for tomorrow until you get your results. He stood, hugged her, and kissed her hard. "Kitty, I—I could fall in love." He'd come as close as he dared and to his surprise he felt as if a load had been taken from his shoulders.

"So," she said, very quietly, "could I." She stepped back a pace. "Some things," she said, "take time to mature, like good wine."

"Do you want time, Kitty," he asked quietly.

"I don't think so—but Fingal, you do."

He looked down.

"You've a lot on your plate, waiting until five o'clock tomorrow."

And the results of Father's tests tomorrow morning.

"So let's you and me simply enjoy today."

"I'd like that."

"Let me get tidied up in here." She took a dustpan and brush and started sweeping.

Fingal sat and let his breathing and his pulse slow down.

She emptied the dustpan into a bucket, moved to his chair, stooped and kissed him. "And we're not going to have you preoccupied today."

A few more kisses like that, Fingal thought—

"You asked me what I'd like to do today. I want to walk along the Grand Canal. I'm going to take you as far as Dolphin Road."

"And what's there?"

"A restaurant. They do wonderful Sunday roasts." She tousled his hair. "Now comb it, leave your coat, it's a lovely day out and we'll head over there—and I sold a painting last week, so no arguments, O'Reilly. We're going Dutch."

"I'll not argue," he said, and if a meal out was what she wanted, fine. He didn't feel very hungry. Hadn't all week. Exams and sick fathers could steal a man's appetite quite away.

They walked hand in hand along the canal's south bank. Neither, it seemed, wanted to chatter. She'd given Fingal a lot to think about. He was in love. Yet why in the hell couldn't he spit it out? Too much his father's son? Fear of what happened to Lars with Jean Neely? That was unlikely. Kitty had as much as said she loved him too. Was it all the worry about what tomorrow might bring? Fingal O'Reilly knew the answer wasn't simple. He should stop gnawing at it like a dog at a bone.

Despite a light breeze, the day was warm and he started to sweat. Maybe he should let life bend him the way the wind tossed the weeping willows lining the bank. Their midsummer branches touched the canal like tresses falling over the heads of silver-haired women washing their hair.

Two swans glided by, white, graceful, their reflections in the calm waters blurred by a film of scum. Three drake mallard, emerald heads iridescent, squabbled and churned the waters while a dowdy duck bird stood on her head to dabble in the vegetation of the shallows. It seemed an age since he and Lars had gone wild-fowling. He'd have to be told Father's diagnosis tomorrow. Try not to think about it, Fingal, he told himself. Not now.

A high-pitched warbling distracted him. From the top of a tree, a cock linnet, red flash on his forehead, redbreasted, sang his hymn of praise, the free cousin of Paddy Keogh's caged bird. A shire horse on the towpath puffed air past its lips, making a rubbery sound. The animal leaned into its collar and strode purposefully, hauling a narrow river barge away from Dublin to a destination in the Midlands of Ireland. Smoke from the vessel's chimney curled up into the willows' filigree. Someone was making tea.

On the bank, a man in a striped shirt and corduroy trousers tied at the knees with leather thongs was using a trowel to point a retaining wall of granite blocks. He straightened and put a hand in the small of his back, grimaced at Fingal, and said, "Lord Jasus, but I've a fierce crick."

"Give your back a rest then," Fingal said with a grin, "doctor's orders."

"Are yiz a doctor, sir?" he said, kneading his back.

"Almost. You should take a break. It's a hot day for your job."

"It's as hot as the hobs of he— Sorry, miss."

Kitty smiled. "It's all right, but tell me how come you're working on Sunday?"

"It's a job dat goes all week and I've dispensation from Father Grogan to work on Sunday once I've been to Mass. Jasus, sir," the man said, giving Fingal an appraising look, "almost a doctor. I thought when I was a gossoon, young like, I'd like to be an apothecary. Instead I've been mending dis feckin' canal for twenty-five years. But I'd rather work in the sun dan the wet." He hitched one hip on the wall and pulled out a dudeen. "Doctor's orders," he said, raising the pipe with a chuckle.

"Twenty-five years," Kitty said. "That's a long time."

The man pulled off his duncher, produced a red hanky, and mopped his completely bald pate. "My family," he said, "the Lannigans, has worked on An Chanáil Mhór, the Grand Canal, since they started building it in 1757." He set his trowel on the wall and scratched his backside. "I could tell you tales all right."

The permanence and the history of this country, Fingal thought. It might be interesting to hear the man's story. He pulled out his tobacco pouch. "Like a fill?"

"You're a gentleman and a scholar, sir." He used a finger to stuff the bowl of his short white clay pipe and accepted a light. "Dis here waterway wasn't opened for forty-seven years, not until 1804, the same year the first steam engine pulled a load in England."

Kitty laughed. "I know a builder like that. It took him months to put up a garage for us in Tallaght when Dad got our first car."

The man puffed a cloud to hang in the air. "Saving your presence, miss, I don't t'ink your builder had to put up with w'at the folks who made dis did. The walls kept collapsing." He crossed himself. "I'd two relations crushed and they weren't the only ones, but the builders kept at it. They had to drain hundreds of acres of the Bog of Allen, but they did, and connected Dublin wit' the river Shannon and opened up the southwest and west of Ireland."

"You know your history," Fingal said.

"Ah sure, sir, isn't the whole feckin' country full of history? And wouldn't I be the right buck eejit if I didn't know about my own trade?"

"Thank you for telling us about it," Fingal said.

"My pleasure, sir, t'anks for the smoke, and the doctor's orders wat gave me a chance for a break." He picked up his trowel. "I'd better get on," he said.

Fingal and Kitty walked away. They had to move to make room for a sweating, beefy-faced man in red braces carrying his coat over one arm. In place of a hat, a handkerchief knotted at each corner made a sun-protector for his head. "You and your feckin', 'Wouldn't it be gas to take a stroll down by the canal?'" he said to the woman who walked beside him pushing a pram. "Fun? Jasus. I'm boiled like a feckin' lobster and the chiseller must be baked."

Fingal, who couldn't catch the wife's reply, was chuckling as he moved to be beside Kitty. "I'm warm myself," he said, and wondered was this what happened after a few years of marriage? Squabbling over trivia?

"Ah, but," said Kitty solemnly and with a deadpan expression, "at least you don't look like a feckin' lobster."

Fingal stopped and guffawed, then, other pedestrians be damned, he kissed her. "Kitty O'Hallorhan," he said, still laughing, "I love your sense of humour." If he did ask this girl to marry him, he couldn't see them bickering. She had too fine a sense of fun.

"I'm glad, Fingal," she said. "I'm glad you love my humour."

He detected a touch of wistfulness in her voice but was interrupted by a tugging at his arm. He looked down to see a naked child, beads of water clinging to his pearly skin. Fingal could count every rib. The boy shook his head and shed water like Lars's springer Barney after a retrieve. "Hey, mister . . . mister . . ."

"Gerroff," Fingal said, trying to avoid the spray.

The boy grinned. "Have yiz kicked any more arses up to the Dodder, mister?"

"Do you do that often, Fingal?" Kitty asked sotto voce and chuckled.

Fingal bent and looked at the lad's pinched face. "Enda," he said as he recognised the ex-patient. He said to Kitty, "Enda here was having a pea removed from his ear. He wouldn't hold still and he kicked my shin."

"And you offered to—? Shame." She tousled the lad's damp hair. "I'm sure he didn't mean it," she said.

"How's that ear?" Fingal asked.

"Me lug's grand now. Me mam sent me wit' a bunch of other lads from Weaver's Street to come down here for a wash. It beats sitting in a tin bat' on a Friday after me da and big brudders have used it and the water's black and cold." Enda smiled at Kitty then said to Fingal, "Last time I seen you, you'd brandy balls."

"Och," said Fingal, "I don't today." He had trouble keeping a smile from starting.

Enda turned to where half a dozen naked boys splashed in the shallows and yelled, "The big fecker doesn't have any brandy balls. He's about as much use as matches on a motorbike."

"But I have bulls' eyes. Here." He handed over a bag of black-and-white sweeties.

Enda grabbed and screeched, "I've a whole feckin' bag of bulls' eyes."

He headed for the bank where the other urchins were racing each other from the water, cheering at the tops of their voices. Enda stopped and squinted up at Fingal. "Me mam would kill me if she knew I'd not said, t'anks, mister, so t'anks very much." He frowned then said, "If you're ever on Weaver's Street, me mam'll make yiz a cup of tea." He was surrounded by his friends, leaping, grabbing, and demanding, "Me, me, me. Gimme a sweetie. I want a feckin' sweetie."

"Come on, Kitty," Fingal said, "it'll be like watching the keepers feed the lions at the zoo." He strode off forcing her to keep pace. He still wasn't very hungry himself.

"Do you always have sweeties in your pocket?" she asked.

"I do."

"Do you know, you're a big soft lump, O'Reilly," she said, and as the sounds of yelling children faded behind them kissed his cheek.

He stopped and faced her. "I've a soft spot for youngsters, and the poor wee gurriers from places like the Liberties have nothing."

She looked into his eyes. "Fingal," she said, "I think you'd be a great father."

Fingal glanced down at his boots, then faced Kitty. "I want kids one day, but—"

"But kids and medical school don't mix. I think I told you already I understand." She took his hand and they turned onto Dolphin Road. It hadn't seemed like a two-mile walk from her flat. The restaurant was three doors up. Fingal opened the door and waited for her to go in. He'd think about the future, and love and kiddies, once he knew about Father and the results of his own exams. But this morning Kitty had succeeded in making sure he wasn't preoccupied. He was going to make damn sure he'd not let his worries spoil this afternoon.

As the kitchen smells filled his nostrils, Fingal O'Reilly's mouth began to water and he realised he could do a roast beef lunch justice after all.

31

It Is Never Good to Bring Bad News

Not a vestige of a smile showed as Doctor Micks entered Saint Patrick's Ward on Monday morning. He didn't need to speak. Fingal remembered being kicked in the stomach by an opposing rugby player. He felt that way now.

"I'm truly sorry, O'Reilly," Doctor Micks said. "Please come into the office."

Fingal followed. Damn. Damn. Damn.

"Sit down please, Fingal." Doctor Micks remained standing. "I'll come to the point. Your father does have aleukaemic leukaemia—and it is acute lymphocytic."

Fingal envisioned the man wearing the red robes of a British judge removing a square of black silk from the top of his horsehair wig after pronouncing a death sentence. "I see." Fingal swallowed. His fists clenched. He wanted to scream, "No," but instead said, "I suppose there's no possibility of a mistake?" He'd been working in the hospital long enough to know that laboratory tests could be wrong.

"I'm afraid not. Doctor Fullerton is a meticulous man. He made several smears of the marrow. They show immature lymphocytes. He sent two slides over." He pointed to the brass barrel of a microscope on a nearby bench. "Would it help if you were to examine one?"

Fingal shook his head. "No thank you, sir." Fingal knew that at high magnification the malignant cells would appear as dark blue irregular circles. Wanting to peer at the harbingers of his own father's death struck him as being morbidly curious.

Doctor Micks touched Fingal's shoulder. "My boy, we can take some comfort. The lymphocytes make up less than five percent of all the bone marrow cells."

Fingal felt his hands relax. It wasn't much, but there was a glimmer. "Does that mean the disease is in remission, sir?"

"Not exactly. We'll have to be sure there's no involvement of other systems."

Fingal understood. Father had cancer of the bone marrow, but at present it was not pouring out vast numbers of cells. If the rest of the body was not affected the process was said to be in remission. It was quiescent, but only as trustworthy as a cask of powder on a burning fuse.

He wanted to ask, "How long has my father got," but that was a question for a character in a bad film. No honest doctor could ever answer that question. "You said we'd go and give them the news." Fingal stood. "Thank you for telling me first."

Doctor Micks said, "I need you, Fingal. Now that you understand, you'll show no surprise, no anger when I explain to your parents. They'll be comforted by your response if you are not visibly upset."

Moments ago, Fingal had wanted to yell, rage against the fates. Now he could at least show a façade of calmness.

The senior man continued, "I will not be prevaricating as I did at the first consultation when there was a possibility of something else. I shall be telling them the facts now. It will be hard for your parents."

Fingal bowed his head. Nine months ago he had been scornful of how Doctor Micks distanced himself from his patients, insisting that the students do the same. Yet here he was taking Fingal's feelings into consideration, asking him if he'd like to examine one of the slides, doing what he could to ease things for Father and Ma. His concern was hard to reconcile with the apparent attitude of a man who had seemed to regard human beings as mere "cases." Fingal was beginning to understand that in his teaching, Doctor Micks was trying to protect his students. He himself was a humane man.

"Now come along. I'll explain in the car what needs to be done," he said, and added, "I've already spoken to Mister Kinnear. He understands why you won't be at his rounds this morning. You will be expected this afternoon to meet Doctor Ellerker, the house surgeon, here and be instructed in your duties."

"Thank you for visiting again." Ma managed a smile when Bridgit showed Doctor Micks and Fingal into the drawing room. Ma'd had her hair done and wore her favourite cardigan and a tweed skirt. She held a lace hanky in one hand. The sun's light made her pearls shine.

"Much better day than the first time you called," Father said. "Please forgive me if I don't get up." He indicated two vacant chairs.

Fingal took one and noticed that Father had a pillow between his hip and the chair arm. His bone, the iliac crest, where the device had been thrust into the marrow cavity on Friday, would still ache.

"So, Doctor," Father said, "what have you to tell us?" His voice was flat, expression deadpan. "The blood test made it clear it wasn't a simple infection. The last two weeks have been hard on Mary." He smiled at her. "Fingal did explain why we had to wait, but I'm glad you're finally here—" He cleared his throat. "—to put us out of our misery."

Fingal glanced at Father. He was still smiling. Once more, the dark sense of humour that Father used so sparingly had caught Fingal completely off guard.

Doctor Micks smiled. "You could say that, I suppose, but you're not a horse with a broken leg and I'd make a very poor vet."

Father said, "It was, perhaps, an unfortunate choice of words, I agree, but I understand you do have a diagnosis."

Doctor Micks's smile faded, his voice became level. "I wish the news were better—"

Ma made a small sound.

"Professor O'Reilly, I am so very sorry, but you are suffering from acute leukaemia."

"I see. And that is bad, isn't it?" Father's smile had gone.

"I'm afraid so."

Doctor Micks had meant it when he'd said he wasn't going to prevaricate. Fingal wanted to get up, go to his parents, hold them, but instead he sat on the edge of his chair.

"Can anything be done?" Father asked. "We need to know."

"Very little, I'm afraid, but as I explained to your son, the results seem to show that at the moment the disease is in remission."

"I don't understand," Ma said, "I'm sorry."

"It means that while the leukaemia is not going away, it is not progressing either," Doctor Micks said.

"So I'm not getting any worse?"

"I hope not, but I will have to reexamine you and perhaps ask for some more tests before I can be sure."

"Not," Father glanced at his hip and grimaced, "not another bone marrow biopsy, I hope."

"No, but could I examine you now, Professor?"

"Certainly." Father rose awkwardly.

Fingal was well aware of the pain caued by a bone marrow biopsy. "Perhaps," he said, "Mother and I could leave and you could examine my father here, sir?"

"Rubbish," said Father. "I am perfectly capable." He limped to the door.

When he and Doctor Micks had left, Ma turned to Fingal and held up a hand before he could speak. "It's all right, son. Your father and I do understand the seriousness of his condition. He trusts your Doctor Micks implicitly, but Father has always believed that one should be as knowledgeable as possible about anything that affects one directly. We had our friend Doctor Synge round for dinner on Saturday."

"I see."

"He explained a lot about what a bone marrow biopsy—that is the correct term?"

Fingal nodded.

"What the biopsy might show so Father and I have had time to think about things, to prepare ourselves for the worst. I did have a little weep, but Father has been a tower of strength."

Fingal wondered. Certainly Father had always insisted on his boys keeping stiff upper lips. Was he practising what he preached, or had reality not sunk in?

Ma leant forward. "I'd like you to explain why your chief wants to examine Father again and what tests might have to be done."

Fingal swallowed and recalled Doctor Micks's conversation on the way here. "At the moment the leukaemia cells are in small numbers," Fingal said. "If they are only inside the bones, it is fair to say the disease is in remission."

"And that's good?"

"It is. Doctor Micks is examining Father for signs of other parts of the body being affected, particularly the nervous system and lungs. He'll then ask for some X-rays and, possibly, just possibly, the collection of some of the fluid around the brain and spinal cord."

It was the only way to detect cancerous cells in the nervous system. It was how tuberculous meningitis was diagnosed too. Fingal had become well practised in the art of lumbar puncture, slipping a wide-bore needle between two vertebrae and beneath the membranes that surrounded the spinal cord. Unless Ma asked, he'd keep that information to himself. Father had been pierced enough.

"More waiting," Ma said, and sighed. She patted his knee. "You are such a comfort to us, Fingal." She frowned. "I know we decided not to upset Lars, but I do think it's time he was told."

"I'll phone him after Doctor Micks has finished, let him know exactly what is happening, and see if he could come down for the weekend."

"Thank you. I'm sure Father would appreciate seeing both his boys. We must hope for the best, but this uncertainty is very trying," she said.

Fingal looked around the big room he'd known since he was fourteen. He'd felt safe here, protected, but he must leave this sanctuary soon and cope alone with another uncertainty, one that would only be resolved when the results of Finals Part I were posted at five o'clock.

32

Examinations Are Formidable,
Even to the Best Prepared

"Everything all right at home?" Cromie asked when Fingal arrived at the students' mess at Sir Patrick Dun's. He'd explained his first morning's absence from the surgical dressership to the lads by pleading family business and arranged to meet them before lunch.

He shrugged, avoided Bob Beresford's eye, and said, "My father's been a bit under the weather. Doctor Micks is sending him for a chest X-ray. The old man's been feeling a bit off-colour and my mother wanted him seen by a senior specialist. Our chief has visited a few times."

"Nothing serious I hope, Fingal?" Cromie asked.

"I'm sure Fingal will tell us in his own good time," Bob said, and looked straight at Fingal.

"Sorry. Of course. Just worried." Cromie clearly recognised he'd overstepped the mark. A family member's illness was nobody's business until they or those close to them chose to reveal matters.

"It's all right, Cromie," Fingal said. "I appreciate your concern." He wanted to get his mind off his family. "How did it go this morning?" he asked. "What did I miss?"

"Not much," Bob said. "Working in this discipline's going to be pretty much like our six months of medicine. Assistant professor Mister Kinnear—"

"What I'd like to know," interrupted Cromie, "is why it's called a surgical dressership?"

"Because years ago it was the students' job to change the patients' dressings," said Charlie. "The nurses do that nowadays."

"As I was saying," Bob said, fixing Cromie with a glare, "Mister Kinnear greeted us. Told us something about the history of surgery at Sir Patrick Dun's. Fitzpatrick tried to correct him—remember our first day here?"

Fingal smiled.

"'Flashing Fingers' Kinnear they call him because he once took out an appendix in six minutes flat. He looked at Fitz, remarked, 'Young man, when I want your opinion, I'll tell you precisely what it is,' and carried right on."

Charlie said, "It seems our new chief's a pretty easygoing skin, but he doesn't like to be corrected in public. Anyway," he said, "the chief dragged Sister Daly; her nurses; Harry Ellerker, the house surgeon; and us students on rounds. We saw half a dozen cases, two preoperative and four recovering. I think," he said, "I'm going to enjoy surgery better than medicine." He held up a pair of hands with fingers the size of sausages. "We're going to get a chance to assist in theatre on our days and nights on call. Might even get to do some of the simpler procedures under supervision."

"I'm looking forward to that too," Cromie said. "I've always enjoyed the carpentry on the yacht."

Fingal wondered if he could be as sanguine about cutting into human flesh as Cromie seemed. People were not made of wood. Fingal shivered and glanced at Bob. His poor ham-fisted friend would not leave the six months with a burning desire to specialise, Fingal was sure. "What happened after rounds?" he asked.

Bob said, "We were briefed by Harry Ellerker. He just graduated last week. Seems like a sound man. Geoff Pilkington's moved on to Doctor Steevens' Hospital for more training."

"It'll be the same system as the medical clerkship. One day in three with responsibilities only to the ward, see admissions, assist. Attend ward rounds every morning then two days out of three go to outpatients for the subjects like radiology and orthopaedics that we haven't covered yet."

"We'll pair off. Hilda'll be stuck with Fitzpatrick again," Charlie said, and rolled his eyes.

"Bob and I'll work together like we have done for the last three months," Fingal said, "if you and Cromie make a team, Charlie."

"Fine by me," Charlie said, and Cromie nodded.

Fingal said, "Can Bob and I have Saturday free? I've to see my brother. It's important."

Bob raised an eyebrow. He must have put two and two together and guessed things had turned out worse than the suspected glandular fever. Maybe Fingal would tell Bob his troubles. It would be a comfort not to have to be alone as the tower of strength needed by his folks. Friends were important. And they might all need each other later this afternoon. Fingal said, "Can the four of us reconvene here at quarter to five? It's only a short walk to Trinity for our results." They had to be faced.

"I'll run us over," Bob said, "and we can get away quickly afterwards. I have no doubt drink will be taken."

But will it be celebratory or to offer condolences? Fingal wondered.

Fingal, Bob, and Cromie stood at the back of a scrum of students huddled round a notice board on a wall of the Trinity Library. Charlie Greer had shouldered his way to the front. A County

Kerry man called to his friend, "Arragh, Jasus, Liam, you've ploughed it again. The whole shebang. All six subjects."

"What about you, Alfie?"

"Full house too."

"How many times is that now, altogether?"

"Four. Come on for a pint," Liam Doak said with a grin. "Next year, I'll be ten years here if I can keep this up."

"And won't your patients think you the learnèd doctor?" another student said. "I can hear them now. 'Our doctor isn't like one of those half-baked five-year ones. He spent ten years getting the learning.'"

Fingal tried to ignore the two chronics and concentrate on what Charlie was calling out as he read his way down a list of names arranged alphabetically. "Beresford, pass all six subjects."

"I don't believe it," Bob said, grinning from ear to ear. "I don't bloody well believe it, but the first two rounds are on me tonight. After I've said a couple of novenas."

"You can't say novenas, you goat," Fingal said, "you're not a Catholic."

"No matter. It's still a bloody miracle."

Fingal slapped his friend on the back. "I knew you'd do it. Our favourite chronic no more. You'll be Doctor Bob this time next year. I'm delighted for you. Well done."

"I'd not have done it without you, Fingal. Carrot and stick. Forcing me to read. Going on about doctors making a difference."

"Rubbish," Fingal said. "I didn't answer the questions. You did, and I am delighted."

Bob danced a little jig. "Begod, O'Reilly, I could get used to this passing."

"Cromie," Charlie yelled, "you've made it. So have I."

"Charlie. Charlie Greer." Fingal heard Hilda Manwell's voice. "I can't see over everybody."

"You don't need to," Charlie yelled back, "you're through, Hilda. Well done."

Fingal opened his eyes in time to see her clasping her hands above her head like a victorious prize fighter. "Good lass," he yelled. He noticed Ronald Hercules Fitzpatrick making his way from the front. His grin was oily. No prizes for guessing his results.

Charlie was pushing his way to where Fingal stood. He arrived before Fitzpatrick. Charlie lowered his voice. "I'm sorry, Fingal—"

Dear God, was that all anybody could say today? "I'm sorry." First Doctor Micks, now Charlie. Fingal stood feet planted firmly, arms hanging loosely. "Go on, Charlie, spit it out."

"You can keep four subjects—"

Fingal relaxed his still crossed fingers. "But I know I made a right hames of pathology so I'll have to repeat it and microbiology in December?"

" 'fraid so." Charlie said.

"Aye." Fingal's shoulders sagged. "Aye, well. I expected it."

"So did I, O'Reilly," Fitzpatrick said. "It's a miracle you passed too, Greer, all the classes you pair skipped for that foolish game."

"Jesus," said Charlie, "you're a ray of sunshine, Fitzpatrick. A regular, 'ever-present help in times of trouble.' Why don't you bugger off?" He turned his back.

Fingal couldn't be bothered to think of any repartée. He sighed and stared at his boots.

Charlie clapped Fingal's shoulder. "But you'll be able to stay with us. Remember what Bob said about being able to take courses? You can still do your six months' surgery from now until January, and midwifery next year."

"And a bloody great pile of extra studying now I've re-sits ahead, and if I pass them Part Two of Finals to face in June." Fingal looked up and saw Bob and Cromie watching him. Both looked solemn. Neither spoke.

Fingal took a deep breath. "So," he said. "I've had a setback. It's not the end of the bloody world—" although how Father and Ma would take it he shuddered to think. He'd not tell them yet, but his failure couldn't have come at a worse time. "You said the first two rounds were on you, Bob Beresford." Fingal forced a smile and had a fleeting image of a brokenhearted Lon Chaney in the movie *Laugh Clown Laugh*. "We'll go to the Bailey and toast your success," he said as lightly as he could manage. And I'll go easy on the drink and try to work out the best way to deal with whatever comes next.

Then he remembered. What came immediately next was a phone call to Kitty. He'd promised to let her know his results the moment he heard.

33

A Disinclination to Inflict Pain

"I admitted Mrs. CD on Monday night, two days ago," said Ronald Fitzpatrick, the familiar note of self-importance in his voice. He stood at the head of an iron bed and whipped off his pince-nez as he continued to address the assistant professor of surgery, Mister Nigel Kinnear, and the usual entourage of nurses and medical juniors. "She is forty-one and the mother of ten. She presented complaining of severe, spasmodic, right-sided, upper abdominal pain, and pain between her shoulder blades. She had experienced nausea and vomiting. The symptoms began shortly after a meal of colcannon and butter, and fried bacon. She has had previous attacks, but cannot remember exactly how many."

Fingal had made the diagnosis. The woman in the bed was two stone overweight. Her complexion was dusky yellow. Almost certainly a gallstone had lodged in her common bile duct, which had contracted forcibly trying to expel the obstruction. She was suffering from biliary colic with blockage of the duct that carried the breakdown products of red blood cells from the liver to the gut. One of those components, a yellow pigment called bilirubin, entered the bloodstream and coloured the skin. Colic was often provoked by eating a fatty meal. The condition was recurrent and most common in certain women over the age of forty who had borne many children. There was a way to remember. It was called "the five *F*s," and Fitzpatrick was spouting them while he smirked at Mister Kinnear.

"This case is fecund, female, fair, forty." He smirked. "I'll refrain from mentioning the fifth *F*, but she is that too."

Fingal nodded. Perhaps Fitzpatrick had learned a modicum of tact. Calling a patient "fat," the fifth *F*, to her face would have been unconscionable.

She struggled to sit, digging her beefy elbows into her pillows. Redness in her cheeks shone through the jaundice. "I beg your pardon, I beg your pardon, did youse call me a 'feckin female'? W'at's wrong wit' being a woman?"

Fingal could barely hide a smile. Mister Kinnear hadn't bothered to. "Come now, Mister Fitzgerald—"

"It's Fitzpatrick, sir."

"Explain to the patient what you actually said."

Fitzpatrick blushed. His wattles shook and he took an enormous breath. "I said, dear—"

"Who's dear? I'm not your dear anyroad. I'm Mrs. Colleen Donovan from Gloucester Street. My friends call me Bluebell, but I'm Mrs. Donovan 'til youse. And youse said I was a feckin' female, just dere now. Everybody heard." She looked from face to face. "Didn't yiz all?"

Fingal resisted the temptation to nod.

Fitzpatrick swallowed. "Fecund."

"Jasus," she yelled, "dere youse goes again. I'm not feckin' anything. If I was a man and me guts didn't hurt like bejasus I'd ask youse to step outside."

"Mrs. Donovan," Mister Kinnear said, "Mister Fitz—" He frowned.

"Patrick, sir."

"Used a medical word to mean you have had a number of pregnancies."

"I have. Dat's true. Far too many."

"That word is f-e-c-u-n-d. Feh-kund. Doctor talk."

"Oh." A great smile split her face. "And I t'ought— Och well, we can all make mistakes."

Use language the patient understands. Fingal could still hear Geoff Pilkington's advice, unless it's one of the unmentionables like cancer or TB.

"Continue, Mister Fitzpatrick."

"As you can see the patient is jaundiced. She is still tender in her right upper quadrant—"

"Is there a specific sign we should seek if we believe, as I am sure you do, that the gallbladder is acting up?"

"Yes, sir. If we put our hand flat on the patient's abdomen beneath the right rib margin, press in, and ask the patient to inhale, the inflamed gallbladder will be brought down onto the fingers and the pain will cause the patient to catch her breath. It's named, after an American doctor, John Benjamin Murphy, Murphy's sign. I'll demonstrate." Fitzpatrick started to turn down the bedclothes.

"More like Jesus Murphy's sign," the patient said, clinging on to the blanket. "Or Jesus, Mary, and Joseph's sign. I t'ought youse had stuck a red-hot poker in dere the other night." She looked at Mister Kinnear. "Please, sir, tell him not to do it again."

"We do believe you, Fitzpatrick." The surgeon spoke to the whole class. "Sometimes to confirm a diagnosis, as for example in this case or cases of acute appendicitis, it may be necessary to elicit pain. If so keep the number of times it is done to an absolute minimum." He smiled at the patient. "We'll not be prodding you anymore."

I'll remember that advice, Fingal thought.

Mister Kinnear continued, "Diagnosis?"

"I told Doctor Ellerker I was sure we had a case of cholelithiasis precipitating an acute attack of biliary colic, that an X-ray was indicated, and that the probable treatment would be a cholecystectomy. Sister."

Sister Henry produced an X-ray film. "Doctor McDonogh, the radiologist, says this is one of the best Roentgenograms the department has taken," she said.

The class studied it by passing it from hand to hand and holding it up to the light.

Fingal watched Colleen Donovan's gaze flit from face to face. He bent over and whispered, "It's all right, Mrs. Donovan. You're having an attack of gallstones, cholelithiasis, and a tube in your belly had a spasm."

Her face relaxed. She whispered back, "Dat's all right den. Biddy Mulligan had dat last year. She had an operation and she's been going round like a bee on a hot brick since."

"We call that a cholecystectomy. Taking out your gallbladder."

"You're a great translator, young lad. T'anks." She looked at Fitzpatrick. "I wish to Jasus that fellah'd speak the King's English."

Before he could reply, Charlie handed Fingal the X-ray film, named for the discoverer of X-rays, Doctor Wilhelm Röntgen. Fingal held it up to the light. Just under the ribs, a collection of irregular small shapes were visible, stones in the gallbladder. Beneath them was a single stone, the culprit in the common bile duct.

"O'Reilly," Mister Kinnear said, "you and Greer there are Sir Patrick's great hopes for Irish caps in rugby, I believe?"

"Charlie Greer is, sir." Fingal knew that the surgeon had played three times for his country in 1908.

"Good luck to the pair of you."

"Thank you, sir." Good of the man to be interested, but Fingal wasn't sure how much time he would be devoting to rugby football.

"Now, Mister O'Reilly. Your opinion of the case?"

Fingal rapidly summarised his thoughts.

"You're right," the surgeon said. He looked at Fitzpatrick, then to Fingal. "You both did well. Keep it up." He turned to Sister. "Put her on my emergency list for this afternoon. Now. Who's next?"

Sister started to lead the little crowd further down the ward.

Fingal bent. "You'll have your operation today." He touched her shoulder. "Don't worry. You'll be fine."

"T'anks, sir. T'anks a lot for explaining," she said, and smiled at him. "I'll not be sorry to have no more pains like dem ones I had two nights back. It was worse dan pushing out a babby, and dat's like trying to shit a feckin' football."

She looked so serious as she spoke that Fingal was able to keep a straight face. And her thanks had warmed him. He'd be lying to himself if he failed to acknowledge that being thanked and feeling he had made a difference were wonderful rewards. He was no hair-shirt-wearing saint who required no thanks. Satisfaction and contentment were important, and it was the first time Fingal had felt at ease since two weeks ago when Doctor Micks had said Father did not have glandular fever.

"Your patient's in bed 64, Fingal," Sister Daly said, and handed him a chart. "He's a sick one, so, I'm sorry to say."

"Thanks, Sister." Fingal set off down Saint Patrick's Ward. Today, Wednesday, was his first day on ward duties, and they included taking admission histories. Fingal scanned the notes.

Seamus Farrelly, aged thirty-four of Talbot Street in Monto, was a butcher by trade according to a letter sent by his local dispensary doctor.

These GPs earned a small annual salary from the government

for providing free medical care to poor patients and charged more affluent ones like Mister Farrelly a fee. Funny term Fingal thought, dispensary doctor. It signified one who practised medicine and on the same premises compounded and dispensed medications. Many practised in Dublin, and most country GPs were dispensers. Fingal was grateful to Trinity for insisting its students were well grounded in materia medica.

The GP had recorded a detailed history and the results of his examination. He had noted that the patient had started to develop upper abdominal pain and vomiting shortly after midnight three nights ago. Within twenty-four hours, the pain had moved to the right lower abdomen.

Despite advice the next day from the renowned chemist Mister Harry Mushatt of Francis Street that the patient should be brought to hospital, Farrelly had refused and taken to his bed. His granny had treated him by soaking broken-up figs in olive oil overnight, making him take the mixture in the morning, and putting bread poultices over the sorest spot.

Fingal had used poultices to treat skin abscesses. White bread was rolled in a tea towel, soaked in boiling water, wrung out, and the soggy bread-laden towel bound over the sore. The heat increased the blood flow and the rate of pus formation so the abscess came to a point and burst, releasing the pus within.

They might work on abscesses, but in Seamus Farrelly's case there had been no improvement and this morning the family had taken the butcher to see Doctor O'Gorman, who had made a diagnosis of neglected acute appendicitis and recommended immediate transfer to hospital and consultation with Mister Kinnear. By then the patient was too sick to refuse. He'd been admitted, Doctor Harry Ellerker had examined the man, and had arranged for Mister Kinnear to come from the operating theatre later today to see the butcher.

Fingal reached the bed—one of those not yet endowed. "I'm O'Reilly," he said. "I've come to examine you." He closed the screens.

The man propped up on pillows was a round, jowly person, probably one with a sense of fun when well, but today his cheeks were hectic, sweat beaded his forehead, his breath was foul, and he barely acknowledged Fingal's presence. The chart above his bed said his fever was 101.2 degrees F, his pulse 110 beats per minute.

"Not feeling so grand?" Fingal asked, sat on the bed, and took the patient's hand. It was hot and sweaty.

"Feckin' useless," the man managed in a hoarse whisper, "and I'm jacked. Utterly jacked. I can hardly bend me little finger I'm so tired."

It took little time to confirm the history as taken by the GP and the findings recorded by the nurses on the charts. "I'm going to take a look at your tummy," Fingal said, pulled down the blanket and sheet and pulled up the hospital gown. The belly was convex and moved only slightly with the man's respiration. The lower right quadrant was reddened as the result of Granny's poultices.

Fingal laid his left hand flat on the upper region and struck the middle and index fingers with the crooked first and middle fingers of his right. He repeated this procedure over all the abdomen. Everywhere his percussion produced a resonant sound, except on the lower right where all he could get was a dull thump. There was fluid or a solid mass there. Probably the latter.

A series of gurgles came up the tubing of his stethoscope as Fingal moved the bell across the belly. Good. The bowel was contracting and moving its liquid contents. It was not obstructed.

Fingal steeled himself; the next step was to palpate the entire abdomen, finishing in the right lower quadrant. If there was inflammation of the peritoneum, the examination would hurt there, but he knew the elicitation of pain was an important sign. "Sorry,

Mister Farrelly," he said, but before he could start, the screens were drawn back and Doctor Ellerker accompanied by Mister Kinnear appeared.

"So, young O'Reilly," the consultant said, "what do you reckon?"

Fingal, well practised by now in its format, trotted out the history and his findings to date.

"You agree, Doctor Ellerker?"

"Yes, sir."

"Let's assume the patient developed acute appendicitis eighty-six hours ago—untreated appendicitis now, what do you think is going on?"

Fingal struggled to remember what the Regius Professor of Surgery, Charles Ball, had said in his lecture. "If the pulse rate is under one hundred—and it isn't, it's one hundred and ten—and there's an increased white cell count, he probably has an appendix abscess. No lab tests are back yet. If there's a tender lump in the lower right abdomen and the other quadrants are pain-free—I haven't palpated yet—I'd say there was an appendix mass, a peri-appendicular phlegmon, from the Greek for inflammation, sir, that hasn't formed a pus-filled abscess yet."

"From the Greek?" Mister Kinnear chuckled. "Classical scholar, O'Reilly?"

"Hardly, sir, but we did have to do some at school."

"And your father's a professor of classics, isn't he? I've met him at college dinners."

"Yes, sir."

"Latin and Greek are useful in our trade. No question. Helps us to understand anatomy because the old anatomists were all classical scholars and named things accordingly."

Fingal remembered having to learn the name of a muscle of the face, *Levator labii superioris et alequae nasii.* Mister Kinnear was right. Knowing Latin had helped.

"Still," the chief continued, "we need a bit of science these days too. How many species have an appendix?"

"How many species?" Fingal was at a loss.

"Man, anthropoid apes, and an Australasian nocturnal burrowing marsupial, the wombat," Mister Kinnear said. "So if you're ever Down Under and find a wombat clutching its right lower belly, it probably has acute appendicitis." He chuckled.

"I'll remember that," O'Reilly said. He refrained from mentioning that he'd already been to Australia. Twice. "Should I palpate the abdomen now, sir?"

"You remember what I said this morning about the gallbladder case?"

"Mrs. CD?" The woman was Colleen Donovan, "Bluebell" to her friends, but by now Fingal was savvy enough not to mention her real names. For all he knew this patient might well know her.

"That's her, and by the way she's better off without it. It was stuffed to the gills with stones." Kinnear smiled. "She'll be right as rain in no time." His smile went. "But do you remember when your friend Fitzwhatsit wanted to demonstrate Murphy's sign?"

"Yes, sir. Don't repeat painful procedures unless you absolutely have to."

"Well done. I must examine the patient because it's ultimately up to me to decide on treatment. I'll spare you the need, and don't feel you're missing out on learning something. You'll get plenty of opportunity to feel things in theatre when it's your turn to scrub and the patient is asleep."

Fine by me, Fingal thought, and watched as his senior kneaded the patient's belly, accompanying his endeavours with a series of noncommittal grunts. By the way Seamus Farrelly's breath kept catching in his throat the examination had hurt.

Mister Kinnear straightened. "There's a bloody great lump there all right," he said. "So now it's time for a bit of Hamlet."

Hamlet? Fingal frowned but he noticed Doctor Ellerker grinning. He'd probably heard the line before.

"To cut or not to cut, that is the question," Mister Kinnear intoned. "What's your opinion, Ellerker?"

"Not, sir. That's what you taught us last year. Implement the Ochsner-Scherren conservative regime."

"Which is?"

"Special charting of pulse and temperature, draw the margins of the mass on the abdominal wall, show there with shading which areas are most tender. Nothing by mouth and pass a nasogastric tube if the patient vomits. Intravenous fluids. If things go well, the temperature and pulse will fall within twenty-four hours and the margins of the lump and areas of tenderness will shrink."

"Good lad. We'll make a surgeon of you yet," the consultant said.

Doctor Ellerker blushed.

"Of course," Mister Kinnear said, "if those things don't happen and his condition worsens we will have to operate because he'll be forming an abscess. At the moment there'll be little pus and the infection is walled off, but if it starts to spread?" He shook his head. "The adage is absolute, 'Where there is pus you must let it out.' Remember that, both of you. Under those circumstances the benefits of operating outweigh the risks."

Fingal's "Yes, sir," was echoed by the houseman's.

"And, O'Reilly, can you remember what Professor Ball told you about long-term management in cases like these?"

"If all goes well, the infection doesn't spread, and the mass shrinks, the appendix should be removed after three months. It will still be a danger to the patient that it will become infected again."

"So why wait?"

"Because now everything is inflamed. It's easy to tear bowel, cause haemorrhage. In three months the inflammation will have resolved and removing the appendix will be reasonably risk free."

"Correct." He chuckled and said, "So in three months we'll re-admit this man. I see you've been paying attention, O'Reilly, and if you've continued to impress me, in three months Doctor Ellerker will be sick and tired of doing simple appendicectomies. He'll not mind letting you do this one. Will you?"

The houseman shook his head.

"Thank you, sir," Fingal said, excited to be offered a chance actually to operate, but vividly remembering his trepidation when he'd had to tap Paddy Keogh's pleura. Perhaps it would be different when the patient was under an anaesthetic.

"And don't look so bothered, boy," the surgeon said. "I'm told by my colleagues you've been developing a good pair of hands in outpatients. Keep that up and who knows? We might make a surgeon of you too."

And after only three days working in surgery Fingal O'Reilly had to consider that it might be a professional direction worth thinking about. He liked the way most surgical conditions were relatively simple to diagnose and except for the cancers many responded well to an operation. It certainly might, but he had six months to go here and other branches of medicine to sample before he'd be sure.

34

A Time to Every Purpose Under Heaven

The heathers looked dry in the borders and several flowers on the rosebush had curled brown petals. Lars sat forward in one of the striped canvas-and-wood folding deck chairs that Bridgit had set up on the lawn in the dappled shade of the old trees. "It was a shock when you told me on the phone how sick Father is, Finn, but his X-rays were normal on Wednesday and that confirms the thing's dormant, doesn't it?"

"It does," Fingal said, and lay back in his chair. Saturday traffic murmured on Lansdowne Road, and birdsong was a descant to the clattering of the blades of a lawnmower. The air was heavy with the scent of cut grass. His pipe smoke hung like a grey phantom in the still air. "Doctor Micks was confident there was nothing involving any other system. He just wanted to be certain and the X-rays do confirm it."

"It was such a relief, to hear there's no progression," Ma said, and glanced behind her to a second-storey window. "I hope Father is having his after-lunch nap," she said. "He's a terrible man for taking a book to bed."

"Regular naps are good," Fingal said. "Help him conserve his strength."

Ma smiled. "And Cook is a wonder. She's happy to prepare the special diet Doctor Micks prescribed and fortunately Father loves her beef tea. He's not fond of the iron but will take it religiously." She looked at Lars. "Everything possible is being done."

Oh, Ma, Fingal thought, it's all stop-gap, but if it gives you comfort, who am I to spoil your hopes?

"Lars," she said, "Fingal's been marvellous arranging for the best medical advice, helping us understand what is going on. Now it's your turn to help."

"Of course."

"Father and I have been talking. He is not a man who refuses to face facts. We've made our decisions and I've something important to say." She stood, smoothed her skirt, and walked away.

Fingal frowned and looked at his brother, who shrugged.

She returned and stood where she could see both of her sons. "We understand remission does not mean cure." She straightened her shoulders. "Death," she said, "must come to all creatures."

Fingal swallowed. He'd been wrong. Ma harboured no illusions. Her eyes glittered.

"Your father and I have had a good life together, two fine sons. For him to have been granted three score years and ten would have been wonderful—but it is not to be." There was a catch in her voice. "We do understand that and we need our boys to know we do. We want no mollycoddling. No beating around the bush."

"There won't be any, will there, Lars?" Fingal said.

"Of course not."

Ma, Fingal thought, is the bravest woman I know. He wondered for a moment if Father was being so sanguine.

"Thank you. I appreciate that." She took out a hanky and blew her nose. "Father and I decided we must make the very best of what remains."

Fingal waited.

Lars said, "How can we help, Ma?"

"I don't think that you, Fingal," she said, "can do any more."
She smiled at him and turned to his brother. "Lars. You're a lawyer. Father could be the model for an absentminded professor.
He is so, so unworldly. We want you to handle his affairs, make
sure his will is in order, insurance policies up to date, that sort of
thing."

"Of course."

"Thank you. You see he wants to be sure I'll be taken care of
after—" She glanced down, stared straight up, took a deep breath,
then looked at Fingal and Lars before saying, "You may find this
odd, but we've both always wanted to view the Pyramids and the
Athenian temples. He wants to know if we can afford it."

Fingal looked at his brother. "I think it's a great idea."

"I agree."

"We have asked Doctor Micks, he concurs, and he will give us
letters of introduction to doctors in France and Greece—just in
case. We'll be making our plans as soon as we hear about our finances," she said. "I believe Thomas Cook and Son, Limited, are
very good at arranging travel."

Lord, Fingal wondered, now he'd had a moment to think, is
this Father's stiff upper lip in action or was it the kicking against
the pricks of a couple who really did not want to face the truth?
Did the answer to that question matter? No, he decided, not if it
gave them comfort. "I've heard that about Cook's," he said. "They
used the P&O steamships for long trips when I was at sea. Probably still do. I know Cook's used to run steamers on the Nile."

She sat. "Good," she said with an air of finality, "that's settled
then." She put her hanky in the pocket of her skirt and turned to
Fingal. "You were in the middle of examinations last week. I imagine you've not been in touch because you thought we had enough
to be dealing with?"

He nodded.

"I surmised that if everything had gone smoothly you would have let us know."

"I'm afraid—I'm afraid I failed two subjects." He hated having to admit failure in anything. He saw Lars's look of surprise, heard him say, "Not like you, Finn."

"Did you?" Ma asked. "That's a pity, but did you pass any?"

"Four."

She smiled. "Four out of six isn't bad," then a frown started. "Does that mean you won't be able to graduate next year as planned?"

He shook his head. "I can sit the ones I missed in December and still do my Finals next June. It's up to me to work hard enough." Wasn't that another of Father's lessons? If you wanted something badly enough, wasn't it your job to work hard enough to get it?

"Please do, Fingal. I don't think I'll mention your stumble to Father. I know how proud of you he has become. I don't want to upset him now. He very much wants to come to your convocation." Her gaze bored into him. "Don't let him down."

And how long have you been waiting to hear he's proud of you? Fingal wondered. "I will do my best, Ma," he said, and forced a grin. "I hope to see you both there." A man with acute lymphocytic leukaemia surviving for one year? Fingal was convinced that Ma had a complete grasp of the facts, was doing her best to help Father, but had he really understood the truth?

"If it's to be," she said, and patted his knee. "If it's to be, but I told you we do understand and we know it's in the lap of the gods." She tutted and stood. "Excuse me," she said, "but William who does the garden on Fridays didn't show up yesterday. Those roses over there need dead-heading." She produced secateurs from her skirt pocket. "To everything," she said, "there is a season."

"Did you enjoy the film, Kitty?" Fingal asked as they left the Savoy Cinema that evening and strolled through O'Connell Street's Saturday night crowds. Perhaps he'd been selfish. She'd wanted to see the Marx Brothers' *A Night at the Opera*, but Fingal had been in no mood for comedy. John Ford's brooding tragedy, *The Informer*, had suited him perfectly. He'd back Victor McLaglen to win an award for his portrayal of Gypo Nolan.

"It was sad," she said. "I'm not surprised the cinema was half empty. Ireland's Civil War isn't a subject that's going to appeal to many folks here. It's only thirteen years since it finished. People have long memories." She reached for his hand. "Still," she said, "with all that's going on in your life I imagine you were happy enough to get engrossed in the story for a while. Get your mind off other things. It was gripping, I'll grant you that."

"Aye. It was." They passed a closed tearoom. "I don't feel like going to a pub tonight. How about a cup of tea?"

"At this time of night? All the places will be shut."

"Not on Abbey Street. Wynn's Hotel caters to theatregoers. It's not far."

"Suits me."

Fingal still didn't feel like talking. He knew he'd been uncommunicative since he'd met her at her flat, but since he'd learned he'd failed pathology and microbiology he'd been mulling the future and his plans. This afternoon at Lansdowne Road had strengthened his resolve. He'd decided it was all a matter of how he divided his time.

He'd not skimp on attending lectures and certainly had no intention of missing a minute of the surgical experience. As long as they wanted him he'd fit in Saturday rugby matches for the Trinity team, but no more midweek practices. The rest of his time would have to be divided between studying pathology and microbiology, keeping abreast of all this year's new material, and constantly revising all the clinical stuff he'd learnt last year. He was going to graduate next June and nothing, nothing was going to interfere. That meant there were things he had to do, starting tonight.

He held open the windowed main doors, then followed Kitty into a green-marble-floored lobby beneath an ornate chandelier. "This way." He opened another door. A bell tinkled, and a waitress, whose frilly lace cap was askew, showed them to a table in the corner.

Kitty removed her hat and set it on a chair.

The waitress took out her notebook and pencil. "W'at do yiz want?"

"Pot of tea, please," he said. "Kitty?"

"I'd like some Jaffa cakes too."

"For two," he said.

The waitress licked the tip of her pencil, scribbled the order, and left.

By her accent a tenement girl, he thought, who has risen in the world because she can read and write. Good for her. He pulled out his pipe, laid it and his hands on the linen tablecloth, and looked around. The room was practically deserted. The production of J. M. Synge's *Deirdre of the Sorrows* wouldn't be finished yet in the theatre across the road. The story ended in the death of the lovers Naoise and Deidre. More death. Fingal's fist tightened.

She reached across and covered his hand with hers. "You're pretty low, Fingal. Can I help?" He looked into those grey eyes, saw how they lay beneath worry lines in her brow. "Can I help, Fingal?"

He slid his hand out from under hers. "Kitty—" God, this was hard. He cared for her. "Kitty, I've told you about my father."

"And you know how sorry I am."

"We can't tell how long he has to live."

"I've nursed people with leukaemia." Her voice was gentle.

"This afternoon my mother told me how much he wants to see

me graduate." Are you being fair to Kitty, Fingal? he thought. You know bloody well how much you yourself want it and would even if Father was fit and well. You've wanted it since you were thirteen. You shouldn't be using him as an excuse for what you're going to do. "I owe it to him to try my very hardest," he said. And it would be so sweet to keep Father proud even if he didn't make the graduation ceremony.

Kitty drummed the gloved fingers of her left hand on the tabletop. "Fingal," she said, "you're trying to tell me something, aren't you?"

He hadn't noticed the return of the waitress.

"Here yiz are." She set a tea tray on the table. "Will dere be anyt'ing else?" She scratched her left forearm. Fingal noted a row of red spots that could only be flea bites. "It's fine, thank you." He turned to Kitty. "Will you pour?"

She did, being careful to put milk into the cups before the tea. "Here." She handed him his cup and saucer. "I asked you a question, Fingal."

"I've failed an exam. I may not be able to finish by next June unless I spend an awful lot of time studying. The dressership, lectures, and outpatients gobble up the days."

"You told me on the phone on Monday you'd failed, but only two basic science exams. When it comes to working with patients? I watched you for months on Saint Patrick's Ward. I've told you before you're going to make a fine physician." She looked down at the tablecloth then back to his face. "I think the way you worked with Kevin Doherty was what made me start—" She swallowed and cocked her head. "Made me start to fall in love with you, Fingal. By the time you were worrying about Paddy Keogh, I'd got to know you much better. I was sure how I felt—even if you weren't. I was giving you time."

Christ. This was worse than he'd anticipated. He'd known he

would hurt her, but now he was going to destroy her. "Kitty, I—" He looked away.

"It's all right, Fingal," she said. Her voice trembled. "I've been waiting, hoping you'd tell me you loved me. I wasn't expecting you to ask me to marry you." She managed a tiny chuckle. "You'd have run a mile—"

She was right.

"You're trying to tell me you won't have any time for," an edge crept into her voice, "for distractions now you have to study so hard, aren't you."

He nodded.

"Let me make it easy for you, Fingal O'Reilly." Her voice cracked and a single tear ran down her cheek. "I'm going to be very busy myself for quite a while." A second tear started. "Take all the time you need." She stood, bent, retrieved her hat, and straightened. She dashed the back of her hand across her eyes. "Take all the time you want." She stiffened, then pointed at his cup. "But don't let your tea get cold."

She spun and walked, head high, handbag clutched under her right elbow. He heard the door-operated bell jingle as she passed through. His last glimpse was of the back of a maroon, mid-calf-length coat vanishing behind a closing door.

And as she left, Kitty O'Hallorhan never looked back.

35

You Can Cut That Right Out

An acrid smell of antiseptics and chloroform assailed Fingal's nostrils.

"Ready?" Harry Ellerker said, peering over his mask from where he waited on the patient's left.

Fingal stood on the patient's right and had been staring at the skylight above the operating table. As I'll ever be, he thought, and looked down. The theatre sister was beside Harry with her table of instruments. Doctor Callaghan, the GP anaesthetist, twiddled the knobs on his flowmeters, directing a gas mixture of nitrous oxide, oxygen, and carbon dioxide over chloroform and on to the patient. "Ready when you are," he said.

Fingal daren't speak. His voice might quaver.

On the operating table, Seamus Farrelly was covered in sterile white towels. Three months had elapsed since Fingal had admitted the butcher with an appendix mass that had responded to conservative treatment. He'd been readmitted last night for his appendicectomy, the operation Mister Kinnear had promised Fingal he could do. It was the last case of the afternoon list.

He took a deep breath and glanced across the room. A large window took up most of the north wall and the rest was surrounded by five tiers of steps with room for seventy-five students to stand and lean on rails observing. The gallery was deserted but for the front row. Bob, Cromie, and Charlie had turned out to offer Fingal moral support. Each had seen and assisted at several appedicecto-mies, but Fingal was the first who would operate.

"It's time," Harry said, handing Fingal a scalpel. "Make a grid-iron incision, there to there." He indicated an area of skin that had been left exposed when the patient had been draped.

Fingal took the knife, hard through his gloves. As he had suspected when he'd first seen the very sick man, he was someone with a sense of humour. He'd told Fingal, upon hearing he had a "mass" in his belly, that it was bad enough "getting dragged to church by me devout wife wit'out having a mass in me belly too. Must be feckin' small priests and altar boys in dere." He'd been a butcher for seventeen years, was married, but childless, and had been a keen hurler in his youth. The man was asleep now and his face was hidden, but there was more than a lump of diseased flesh under the sheets.

"Fingal," Harry said.

"Sorry." Fingal swallowed and drew the blade firmly along the line Harry had indicated. Blood welled and the skin gaped, the fat beneath parted. Two lips garishly painted with scarlet.

Fingal paused and glanced at Doctor Callaghan. "I didn't feel a thing," said the anaesthetist with a grin. He must have seen the look in Fingal's eyes. "It's all right, neither did the patient."

Harry swabbed. Fingal set aside the scalpel and clamped small blood vessels. Sister handed him a spool of ligature. As Fingal tied off the vessels, Harry removed the clamps and cut the ties close to the knot. There was a glistening sheet of tissue at the bottom of the wound. Now those hours of anatomy dissection were bearing fruit. Fingal recognised the fibrous tissue, the external oblique muscle's aponeurosis that attached the muscle in the midline and to the hip bone. Beneath lay the internal oblique and tranversalis, the two deeper muscles of the lateral abdominal wall.

"Slice the aponeurosis," Harry said, and Fingal did. Clamps on each side of the incision peeled the fibrous tissue back to expose maroon muscle.

"Use the handle of the scalpel. Shove it through the muscles, Fingal."

He did.

"Now put your index fingers in that hole and pull sideways."

Fingal started to sweat. He was surprised by how easily the muscle fibres separated. Blunt dissection opened far fewer blood vessels than cutting and shock from blood loss was one of the hazards of surgery to be avoided at all costs.

"Mister O'Reilly."

He half turned. Sister offered him forceps. He slid their tip into the hole in the muscles. Open. Advance. Shut. Gently pull. As he withdrew the instrument, it was followed by a pyramid of glistening peritoneum, the membrane that lines the abdominal cavity. He felt the peritoneum between finger and thumb to assure himself that no bowel had been included. It would be serious if he sliced into gut and spilled its contents into the abdomen. No bowel was palpable so a second forceps was applied and he incised the membrane between them.

"I'm in," he said, and was gratified by the firmness of his voice. "Retractor, please." Slipping the flat blade of the right-angled instrument into the incision, he pulled toward the patient's middle to give himself more room to work. "Here." He gave the handle to Harry Ellerker. "Pull on that."

Fingal accepted a large moistened swab from Sister and slipped it into the wound beneath the retractor's blade to pack loose bowel away from the field. Now came the tricky bit. He had to fish out the caecum, that bit of bowel that was the junction between the small and large intestine and from which the appendix hung, a long narrow tube. The ancient anatomists had named the organ well. Vermiform—wormlike.

"Pack." He took another gauze square and used it to grip the caecum. The smooth rubber of his gloves would have slid off the slippery bowel, but the rough gauze gave added traction. Slowly the organ emerged, and there it was. The appendix.

Fingal blew out his breath. He hadn't realised he'd been holding it and felt the dirty nurse swabbing his forehead. How did he feel inside? Certainly not as scared as he had at the start. Relief? There was that all right. He'd felt the same way when for the first time as a young deck officer he'd anchored the ship unsupervised.

Sister had given Harry a Morrant Baker forceps and was offering one to Fingal. The instrument was designed to encircle the appendix without damaging it while it was still within the abdominal cavity. Harry applied his to one end while Fingal placed his where the organ joined the caecum. He then handed his to Harry who, by pulling on both, lifted the appendix and exposed its mesentery, a thin membrane through which the blood vessels ran. It took but a moment to clamp it and the vessels firmly and divide them. The appendix was free and ready to be removed.

Fingal took a different set of forceps with ridged blades and, to facilitate its ligation and division, deliberately crushed the appendix close to the caecum, removed the forceps, and reapplied it above the crushed area to seal part of the organ that would be removed. Those days of suture duty and learning to tie knots paid off as he ligated the appendix at the crushed area then took a scalpel and divided it between the ligature and the clamp.

Harry lifted the diseased organ and dumped it and the attached forceps into a stainless steel dish.

Fingal heard the clatter of metal on metal. His feelings of

triumph were pulled up short when Doctor Callaghan asked, "Going to be much longer? Mister Kinnear would be halfway through his third case by now."

"Not long," Harry said. "Just have to suture the mesentery to secure the blood vessels, and bury the stump in the caecum."

"Let me know when you have. He's been under for a fair while—"

Fingal pursed his lips. He'd completely forgotten that a person called Seamus Farrelly lay under the towels. A childless married butcher who had been a keen hurler.

"I'd like to start lightening the dose of chloroform."

"I'll finish," Harry said. "I'm quicker."

"Fine." Fingal was happy for the houseman to speed things up and cheerfully assisted as Harry sutured the mesentery, put a purse string suture in the caecum around the base of the appendix, pushed the stump in, and tightened the loop before tying the knot.

"Closing," Harry said, pulling out the moistened swab Fingal had inserted into the belly to keep loose bowel out of the way.

"Thanks," the anaesthetist said.

Fingal was happy to cut the stitches as Harry closed the wound.

"Done," Harry said, helping Sister put on the dressing. As she tied the last knot in the bandage the patient moaned.

"That," said Doctor Callaghan, "is close to the perfect anaesthetic. As the surgeon finishes, the patient is wide enough awake to be told the fee."

Fingal laughed in relief that the surgery was over. He was startled to hear a round of applause coming from the stands, looked over and saw his three friends clapping.

Charlie Greer said, "Well done, Fingal."

Cromie added, "And we don't give a hoot about your self-imposed monastic life of study. Tonight, boyo, Hilda and Fitzpatrick are on duty so we're going to Davy Byrnes and the first pints are on you."

"I'm sorry to disappoint you lads," Fingal said, "but go away on your own. I've work to do. I've got those Part I exams in December, remember?"

"And you'll destroy them," Cromie said. "Utterly."

Fingal shook his head. "It's all right for you lot. You've only all the clinical subjects to master for Finals Part Two in June. I have them on top of repeating Part One. And I'm not going to fail this time around."

"Fingal," Charlie said. "One evening's break won't kill you. We've got our certificates of good standing in all the other clinical disciplines except the final three, midwifery, opthalmic surgery, and anaesthetics."

"That's right," Bob said. "And Mister Kinnear's bound to issue our certificates for surgery in December."

"Three months away, but that certificate will be bugger all use to me if I fail Part One. I'm studying tonight."

"I think, gentlemen," said Charlie, "we have run up against the immovable object."

"Pity," said Bob.

"Fraid so," said Fingal. "I'm going to change, have my tea, and then work. See you lot at rounds tomorrow." He strode into the surgeons' dressing room. Eejits. But he smiled. They were good lads. They meant well.

Fingal had just settled at his desk in his bedsit at Sir Patrick Dun's students' quarters and opened his pathology textbook when he heard a knock at the door. Now who the hell was that? "Come in," he roared. They'd better be quick, whoever it was. He didn't need interruptions. He had twenty-six pages to read about the pathology of cancer of the lung.

Bob Beresford stuck his head into the room. "And how is the great Lawson Tait tonight?"

"Lawson Tait? What the hell are you on about, Beresford?" Fingal scowled. "I'm busy."

"Scottish surgeon," Cromie said, pushing Bob inside and following, "who did the first appendicectomy in 1880. Clever lot, us Scots."

"I wonder," said Fingal grimly, "if he was related to the Butcher of Grand Canal Street?"

"Wasn't your patient a butcher?" Charlie asked as he brought up the rear.

"He is, but I am referring to myself," Fingal said, "the student who killed his classmates because they wouldn't let him study." But he couldn't really be angry with his friends.

"We need your help," Bob said. "And you'd never refuse to give your friends a hand. We know that." The two large brown paper bags he set on Fingal's desk clinked. "We've just come from Davy Byrnes." Bob fished out a bottle of Guinness. "You couldn't expect the three of us to put away another wheen of Mister Arthur Guinness's best by ourselves, could you? And it's not every day of the week that a pal does his first appendix."

"You lot are hopeless. Utterly bloody hopeless." Fingal laughed. "All right. All right, come in. There're glasses in the communal kitchen."

"No there's not," said Charlie, producing the tumblers. "Fill 'em up, Bob."

Bob rummaged in his pocket for a corkscrew.

Cromie and Charlie squashed onto a two-seater settee.

Bob opened the bottle with a distinct *pop* and poured. "We," he said, "are here to toast you, Fingal, aren't we, lads?"

"Indeed," said Charlie. "Pity it takes so long to pour stout." He stood, moved to the fireplace, and stared at a row of picture post-cards. "Mind if I take a look, Fingal?"

"Go right ahead."

Charlie squinted then said, "That's the Parthenon in the Athenian Acropolis, and those are the great pyramids, Cheops, Khefren—and buggered if I can remember the third, and that's the Sphinx at Giza. Napoleon's gunners made an awful mess of the poor old thing's nose in 1798. So you've friends in Greece and Egypt?"

"My folks," Fingal said. "They decided to take an extended holiday this year. They send postcards to me and my brother. Keep us posted." And Lars and I talk on the telephone once a month, he thought. It's about time I gave him a ring.

Charlie whistled. "Lucky them."

Fingal saw the sympathy in Bob's look. He was the only one of the friends who knew the truth about Father's illness. Bob had never mentioned it again since the night Fingal had told him, but always listened sympathetically if Fingal needed to talk.

Fingal said, "They left in August on their grand tour. They had hoped to take the Arlberg Orient Express from Zurich to Budapest and on to Athens, but my father felt crossing Nazi Germany would be dangerous. They went to Marseilles instead and took passage from there. They've decided to winter somewhere warm too."

"I think," said Bob, passing a full glass to Fingal, "your dad was right to keep out of—what does Adolf call it? The Third Reich? In September he banned all Jews from public life. The maniac has just announced a program to build submarines—U-boats he called them. It's got Winston Churchill's knickers in a real twist. He's been screaming in the British parliament that England must rearm."

"I wonder who the subs'll be used against?" Fingal asked, thinking of his commitment to serve in the navy.

"England," said Cromie. "There could be a war. Churchill has a point."

"I sincerely hope," said Bob, handing a glass to Charlie, "that you are both wrong."

"Your people had better not winter in Italy," Cromie said. "Mussolini's poised to invade Ethiopia. He's a fascist and he has dreams of Empire too."

"And," said Bob, "I had dreams of having a few quiet bevvies with our good friend Fingal O'Reilly tonight and for once not letting him worry about exams he's bound to pass—"

"I hope," Fingal said.

"Here." Bob gave Cromie a Guinness. "And that's enought blether too about the miserable state of the world. We can't do much about it." He pulled a silver flask from an inside pocket and opened its top. "Now," he said, "who'll propose a toast?"

"Me," said Cromie, lifting his glass. "In the immortal words of my Scottish forbears—"

"I didn't know you were descended from bears," Charlie said. "Which one? The grizzly, *Ursus horribilis,* I'll bet." He held his arms crooked above his head, hands curled into claws, and made a ferocious growling noise.

Fingal laughed.

Bob chucked a cushion at Charlie, who dodged, but managed to spill some Guinness on Fingal. "Shut up, Greer," Bob said, "and let Cromie finish." He turned to Cromie. "The floor is yours."

Cromie bowed, then said, "To Fingal's dextrous surgical fingers—"

"Sorry to interrupt," Bob said, "but would you consider being a surgeon, Fingal?"

"I might," Fingal said. "I just might. We'll see."

"Just curious," Bob said. "We're all going to have to choose pretty soon."

That, thought Fingal, is pretty promising. Bob's including himself in "all."

Bob said, "Carry on, Cromie."

Cromie pointed at Fingal. "To his forthcoming success in Finals Part One," he swept an arm wide to encompass the room and intoned, "and to us four. As us Caledonians say, 'Here's to us. Wha's like us? Damn few—and they're mostly dead.'"

Fingal had heard it before, but somehow the intense way Cromie had spoken struck a chord. Fingal was a lucky man to have these three stalwarts as friends. He lifted his glass and said, "I'll drink to that, all of it. By God I will."

36

Windy Night; a Rainy Morrow

Fingal shivered. The windows in his room clattered as another gust of the rain-sodden mid-November gale smashed against the pane and a cold draught slipped past the ill-fitting sash. The rug over his legs barely kept the chill at bay. "Dublin in the winter? Bad as the bloody Bay of Biscay," he muttered, rubbing his hands together and blowing on his fingers before he could turn the page of the book lying on the desk where he sat studying. A small paraffin heater burbled, giving off an acrid smell and precious little heat.

For a moment he mistook a knock on his door for the rattling of the window. "Come in, and shut the door behind you," Fingal called. He'd been at his books for two hours already this evening and would be grateful for a break.

Charlie Greer, who had the room across the hall in the students' quarters, came in, shut the door, and stood beside Fingal. Charlie was wearing a Paddy hat, raincoat, and carrying a hold-all. He must be going out somewhere.

"Yes, Charlie?" Fingal asked.

"Still at it? So our session here last month didn't lead your stumbling feet off the paths of righteousness." Charlie leant over and grunted. "The spleen." He read the page heading from the 1935 edition of *A Short Practice of Surgery* by Bailey and Love. "Interesting, isn't it?"

Fingal said, "It is. I try to read about any new case we see, and Bob and I were on duty last night. Fellah with a ruptured spleen came in. I assisted Mister Kinnear and Doctor Ellerker at the splenectomy. They let me close the incision."

Charlie shivered and said, "It's cold as a witch's tit in here." He asked, "Mind if I have a pew?"

Fingal shrugged. Charlie, like all Irishmen, should be used to their miserable winters. There was no point complaining. Then Fingal smiled and said, "Park yourself."

The springs gave a *twang* as Charlie flopped onto the two-seater. He said, "I'm pretty sure I'm going to be a surgeon." He grinned. "In the last five months we've removed sebaceous cysts, ingrowing toenails, repaired uncomplicated hernias, fixed abscesses, appendixes, varicose veins. I love working with my hands. I want to do more."

"I've enjoyed it too," Fingal said, "but I think of it as training for general practice. Doctors in the country are still taking out appendixes on kitchen tables."

"And speaking of which—"

"Kitchen tables?"

"No, you goat." Charlie shook his head. "Appendixes. The last time you took a break was when we descended on you with Guinness to celebrate you taking out your first one."

"No," said Fingal, holding up a hand like a traffic policeman on point duty. "Oh no. Not again." He turned in his chair and roared, "Bob and Cromie, if you're lurking out there, go 'way to hell out of it." He lowered his voice. "Charlie, I don't mind chatting with you for a while, but tonight I still want to read the pathology of pancreatitis and the bacteriology of tuberculosis. And I was just finding

out if removing the spleen was any good for cases of leukaemia."
He hoped so.

Charlie chuckled. "Don't worry. The lads aren't here. I came by
myself, and I can save you some reading. It's been tried in the past
for cases of leukaemia, but splenectomy has no curative value. It's
not done anymore."

"I see. Thanks." Fingal wasn't going to discuss his family's affairs with Charlie, so would keep his disappointment to himself.
"But I still have more studying to do tonight."

Charlie pushed his Paddy hat back and ran fingers through his
red fringe.

"You're bound to pass."

Fingal shrugged. "I shouldn't have missed so many classes."

"I wonder," said Charlie, "if all those practices last season improved our game. I've been training on Thursdays, but you haven't,
and I reckon you outplayed me last Saturday." He grinned. "Did
Bob tell you?"

"Tell me what?"

"Doctor Murray and Mister Musgrave were at the match."

Fingal spun in his chair. "Seriously? The selectors?" Rugby,
even at an international level, was an amateur game. The scouts
were volunteers who themselves had long been associated with the
sport. Since his first cap in 1927, Doctor P. F. Murray had collected
eighteen more for Ireland. To Fingal, to any serious player, there
could be no greater honour. Charlie's news made Fingal quiver.

Charlie nodded. "I reckon we both have a chance. The trial's
before Christmas. If we've been picked for it we'll hear in the next
week."

Fingal grunted. "My exam's just before Christmas too."

"Fingal," Charlie said quietly. "It's a chance to be picked to
play for your country." He waited.

Fingal said nothing.

Finally Charlie broke the silence. "You know, the rest of the lads and I, we worry about you."

"I'm fine." Fingal glanced at the page. It was time to get back to work, but Charlie was not to be put off.

"You're not the old Fingal. You're more like Mister Badger in *The Wind in the Willows*. You never leave your lair. It's not healthy. The odd night getting your mind off the books wouldn't hurt you." Charlie picked up his hold-all, unzipped it, took out a boxing glove, and tossed it at Fingal.

He caught it. "What the hell?" Without thinking he sniffed the scuffed leather and the memories came.

"Bob says you told him you'd boxed in the navy. I'd often wondered where you got those lugs."

Fingal's ears were thickened from his years in the ring at school and at sea. He laughed and nodded. "Aye, I did box a bit back then. See that?" He pointed to a scar under his left eye. "I got that in 1930 on board HMS *Tiger*. We were in Gibraltar. Referee stopped the fight early in the third." He didn't want to seem to be boasting to Charlie so didn't mention how the bout had ended.

"I go to the gym every Tuesday," Charlie said, "skip, punch the bags, spar if I can get a partner. Helps keep me trim."

"I just play rugby on Saturdays," Fingal said, "but I reckon I'm pretty fit."

"Physically," Charlie said, "but, and I mean it, you're not the old, hoist skeletal Gladys up in her knickers, stuff Fitzy's stethoscope with cotton wool Fingal. There was a time you enjoyed playing practical jokes, took a jar with the lads, went to the flicks. We reckon the odd night out of this room away from those damn books wouldn't hurt, and it doesn't have to be a night in the boozer. You're getting old before your time." Charlie grinned and said, "We'll be buying you a walking stick soon—old man."

Fingal roared with laughter. "Bugger you, Greer. Old man?

Walking stick? If you've got a second pair of gloves in that bag I'll show you who's an old man."

"Will you, by God?" Charlie laughed. "Will you? Have you guttees?"

"Gym shoes? I have." Fingal cocked his head, looked at Charlie, then back to the surgical text. Surely he could afford a couple of hours? And Fingal O'Reilly could never resist a challenge.

Charlie nodded at the hold-all. "I've three more gloves, spare trunks. Mine should fit you."

Fingal cocked his head at Charlie then marked his page. "I want to be back here at nine." He rose and chucked the glove back.

Charlie caught it, stood, and landed a deadner, a punch on Fingal's biceps.

Fingal laughed. "You, you gingernutted bollix, you have three rounds coming up. I hope you're good." He went to a coat rack and took down his overcoat and duncher, pulled gym shoes from a drawer and shoved them in his coat pockets. "I never did tell you what happened after that fight in Gibraltar was stopped, did I?" To hell with modesty. Charlie was entitled to know Fingal's boxing history. He shrugged into his coat and pointed to the scar under his eye. "After the referee restarted us in the third I KO'd my man. Knocked the tripe out of him. I won the fleet trophy." Fingal opened the door, "Just thought you should know," he said, smiling and bowing to Charlie. "After you."

Fingal walked at Charlie's side. The wind was from the southeast and blew on their backs. Never mind. A few brisk rounds would warm him up. "So you go to the gym every Tuesday, Charlie?" Fingal waited for a car to turn onto Macken Street. Since he'd teamed up with Bob for their ward duty he'd seen a lot less of Charlie

Greer than when they'd been partners during their medical clerkship under Doctor Micks.

"Unless Cromie and I are on call," Charlie said. "Come on." He led across the road. "My dad taught me to box," he said. "The old man reckoned it was a good way to get things out of your system, and it certainly came in handy if you were getting picked on at school."

Fingal laughed. "I know that," he said. "I had to learn the hard way too, but I did enjoy boxing for its own sake." He shook his head. "But ever since we started classes I couldn't fit everything in. This medicine takes up a lot of time."

"I hesitate to comment," Charlie said, "but you used to have time for other things—like Kitty O'Hallorhan."

The traffic stopped Fingal at the intersection with Holles Street. Three times since the night they'd parted he'd walked down there on his way to the flat she shared with Cromie's Virginia Treanor to try to see if Kitty would consider giving him another chance. Three times he'd turned back before he'd reached Leeson Street. "I miss her, Charlie," he said.

They crossed the road.

"The lads and I reckoned you were getting serious about her. We know you're hurting, but you're too bloody self-sufficient to tell us."

It was on the tip of Fingal's tongue to tell Charlie to mind his own business, but Charlie ploughed on, "We're worried and we'd not be if you weren't our friend. We'd help you if we could."

"Thanks, mate," Fingal said. They were his friends. "I do miss her. A lot." After nearly five years together Charlie Greer had become an easy man to trust. "I'm—I'm going to ask her for another chance after I've passed this exam, and I'll not do that if I don't study." He forced a smile. "The work on the wards, the studying keep my mind busy so I don't have time to fret over other things."

Charlie cleared his throat. "Maybe you should fret. Just a bit. Not wait too long to talk to her."

Fingal stopped. "What the hell are you on about?" He turned to face Charlie and felt the chill of the wind and rain.

Charlie stopped. "If it concerned anyone but you, Fingal, I'd not repeat this." He hesitated as if seeking permission to continue.

"Go on."

"I was having a blether with Cromie earlier. His Virginia let it slip to him last night that Kitty's seeing one of the doctors from where she's working at Baggot Street Hospital."

Not half a mile from here, just past Merrion Square, Fingal thought, and wondered who the hell the bastard was. The gobshite. He surprised himself at his vehemence.

"I see," he said very quietly. "I see." He turned from Charlie and began striding toward the gym. A trickle of frigid water slipped past his collar and Fingal O'Reilly shuddered. Seeing someone else? He jammed his hands into his coat pockets only to find them stuffed with his gym shoes. He gritted his teeth. He'd be changing into the guttees soon enough and stepping into the ring. Fingal's jaw clenched. He wished with all his heart it could be with the doctor from Baggot Street, not his friend Charlie Greer.

37

Must Often Wipe a Bloody Nose

Fingal sat in his corner at the end of the second round and inhaled the stink of sweat, dusty floors, the leather that wrapped the ring's ropes. The lights overhead glared, but the grey canvas covering the floor reflected none. The rest of the gym faded into indistinct shadow, muffled sounds of other boxers thumping bags, skipping. The only place that mattered to Fingal was an eighteen-foot-square arena bounded by four padded ropes.

What had Charlie said on the walk over? That boxing was a good way of getting things out of your system? By God it was. You'd no time to worry over other matters no matter how pressing when your opponent was trying to knock your block off. Trouble was you couldn't always control your errrant thoughts between rounds. He'd still like to have Kitty's anonymous doctor from Baggot Street in here instead of Charlie. Damn it he missed her.

Fingal willed his breathing to slow. His ribs ached. Charlie had landed a couple under Fingal's guard, but Fingal had given as good as he'd got, and more. He nudged his gum-guard in place, used his forearms to straighten his protective headgear, and stood. Charlie was good, but Fingal knew he was better. His gloved fists curled.

The referee, the gym's professional trainer, beckoned.

Fingal and Charlie left their corners, touched gloves, and crouched ready.

"Round t'ree. Last round. Box."

Fingal led with his left, circled slowly to his right. He didn't want to win on points. He wanted a knockout. Find the opening. Feint. Jab. Jab. Charlie blocked them easily. Left feint to the head. Right to the chest under Charlie's guard. Fingal felt the thump on his fist, heard breath being forced out. Charlie's helmeted features blurred in Fingal's eyes. It was no longer Charlie Greer on the receiving end, but a faceless man, an anonymous opponent. Or was he?

Fingal crouched and changed his direction of attack. Some bastard was seeing Kitty. He'd not kiss her when he had a split lip. Fingal unleashed a rapid flurry of punches all hitting home. Somehow all his anger, all his hurt were driving his fists.

He felt someone wrapping him in a tight hug, pinioning his arms. They waltzed like a pair of drunken bears.

"Fingal," Charlie gasped, and said, "we're sparring." Gasp. "It's not a title bout."

Fingal felt the referee pulling the clinch apart and dropped his left shoulder. Not a title bout? That penetrated Fingal's rage. Charlie was right. Fingal should ease up. His next couple of jabs lacked steam and Charlie's next punch, like his words, got through Fingal's guard. Once.

Damn it. Damn it. He crouched, tightened his defensive stance. Rage boiled in him. His fists clenched so tightly his gloved fingers tingled. He let his hatred focus solely on the target of all his hurt, whoever the faceless man opposite was.

Fingal let go another series of punches, stamping forward as his opponent backed against the ropes. Fingal was sure the man could be fooled with a feint to his right. He always weaved to his left and the next time, Fingal hoped, the fighter would dodge straight into a punishing right glove. That would be sweet.

Fingal feinted with his left, opened his shoulders to deliver a bone-crushing right hook, not to his friend Charlie Greer, but to all that hurt Fingal O'Reilly; the hidden, but never absent worry about Father, the constant anxiety about the exams he must pass, and—he saw the faceless man, the Baggot Street bastard kissing Kitty. His muscles knotted and his right arm became a swinging demolition ball that was going to smash—

Bone crunched as a pile-driver slammed into Fingal's nose. He tasted the copper of blood, spat, staggered, held his gloves in front of his face, and tried to backpedal. His vision was blurred, but he was aware of the referee between him and Charlie.

"Put down your gloves, sir." The referee peered at Fingal's face. "Jasus. You've a face on you like a smacked arse and your nose? It's fecked." He raised his voice. "I'm stopping the fight."

Fingal was aware of Charlie moving off the ropes. "Fingal, I'm sorry." He bent and looked. "I really am. I think I've bust your nose, but you didn't give me much choice. I had to stop you. I've never seen you like that. You went berserk."

"I t'ought youse was trying to kill Mister Greer, sir," the referee said from where he stood between them.

The jolting pain had brought Fingal to his senses. He felt his mouth fill with blood and spat. Christ, but his face was sore. And Charlie was right. Fingal was the one who should apologise. Charlie Greer had been defending himself. Fingal rocked on his heels, laid a gloved hand on his friend's shoulder. "You're right, Charlie. I got carried away. Sorry. I completely lost the bap. I'm ashamed of myself."

"It's all right," Charlie said. "No need to be. Anyone can snap in the ring." He tipped his head to one side. "Fingal?"

"Yes?"

"We're friends. All right, so you got carried away; I belted you one. That's all there is to it. Let the hare sit."

Fingal tried a lopsided smile. "Thanks, Charlie."

"Will yiz come to your corner, sir?" the trainer asked, led Fingal there, and sat him on his stool. Charlie followed.

"Dis," the trainer said, "will hurt," and without giving Fingal a moment to reflect, grabbed his nose, pulled down, and hauled the tip to the right.

"Jasus bloody Murphy," Fingal roared as what seemed like liquid fire ran over both cheeks and he heard the grating of bone on bone. Tears ran unheeded and dripped mingled with blood to the canvas below. "You've marmalised me."

"I'm sorry, sir, but when he taught me first aid the Saint John's man was insistent. Fix a broken nose at once, or you'll never get it back after it's swelled up."

Fingal blinked away the tears. The violent pain had been replaced with a constant throbbing. He nearly managed a smile. It was odd being a patient and on the receiving end. "Thank you," Fingal said, "I'm very grateful. I know how it has to be done—" Fingal managed to stop himself trying to caress his wounded nose with his gloved hand. "And I'll remember how much this hurts next time I go to treat a patient with a broken nose."

"It's the best I can do," the trainer said. "You're going to have a couple of right shiners for a week or two, and I t'ink when it heals, when the bones mend, you'll have a tilt to the left. Sorry." He turned to Charlie. "Hold out yer hands, Mister Greer. I'll get your gloves unlaced."

Fingal shrugged. Black eyes were the inevitable accompaniment of a broken nose because blood seeped into the loose tissue under the eyes. "A tilt? Well," he said, "I'm not in a competition with Ronald Coleman or Errol Flynn." He shook his head and scarlet drops flew. "Mind you," he tried a weak joke, "I could star as Captain Blood."

"True on you, sir," the trainer agreed, "but the bleeding should stop soon. I'll get you ice when we get you back to the changing room."

"Here." Fingal lifted his hands to Charlie. "Let me out."

Charlie, his hands now free, started unlacing. "Showers for us, lad, and I know I said we'd let it drop, but looking at your schnozzle I have to say again I truly am sorry, Fingal." He took off the left glove.

Fingal nudged his friend. "No need to be. It was a fair punch. And I had it coming. For a minute or two there I'd've been happy to destroy you. I was trying to," he hesitated, "trying to exorcise a ghost."

Charlie said very quietly, "I think I know her name."

"You do." Fingal used his free hand to remove his other glove. He handed them to Charlie.

"And I know you well, Fingal Flahertie O'Reilly. When you compete you always want to win, but there's no malice to you." Charlie cocked his head. "Did you lay the ghost?"

"I did not." Fingal tried to shake his head, but stopped quickly. "The exam's in a month. Once it's over I'll try to effect a resurrection. Go and see her—but not until then." Fingal lowered his head. "Thank you for telling me about Kitty. Thank you for getting me out tonight." He looked up at Charlie and offered his hand. "Friends?"

Charlie shook. "Friends." He laughed. "But you do look a sight."

Fingal opened the changing room door. "I don't feel much like studying so I'll let you buy me a pint." He managed a smile. "I couldn't read anyway. I'll hardly be able to see past this." He pointed at his nose.

"One night won't—"

"No, it won't, and I'll have all day for the next couple of Saturdays to catch up on pancreatitis and TB. I'll not be able to play rugby until this settles down." He indicated his nose.

Charlie said, "What if you're picked for the rugby trial for Ireland? Will you be able to play then?"

"Wild horses wouldn't stop me from playing in that game, Charlie Greer, and well you know it. Now come on. I want that ice for my nose, I want my shower, and by God, I want that pint."

38

I Am Disappointed

November had turned to December. The six-month surgical dresser-ship was drawing to a close. As usual at nine o'clock precisely Fingal was attending rounds conducted by Mister Kinnear, the senior surgeon. He stood at the foot of bed 85, *St. Stephen's Parish Bed. Supported by annual collection.*

Doctor Ellerker, the house surgeon, and the students were to one side, Sister Daly and and her nurses on the other. Charlie Greer had been sent on some errand.

Fingal noted that the patient, a middle-aged balding man with angular cheekbones but a bulbous nose, lay absolutely still. His breath came in shallow gasps. In contrast to the red stripes of his pyjama jacket his face was ashen. His left hand, which lay palm up on the blanket, was rough and calloused.

"Good morning, Mister Lynch," Mister Kinnear said, "and how are we this morning?"

Fingal could see what an effort it was for the man to speak. "I feel like shite. I've got a feckin' great rat gnawing at me belly." His eyelids drooped and he took shallow breaths.

"I'm sorry to hear that," Mister Kinnear said. "Give us a few minutes to talk about you, decide what to do, and we'll soon have you right."

"Dat's w'at dem doctors at Doctor Steevens' Hospital said. Fat lot of feckin' good they done me." He sniffed, swallowed, and burped noisily.

Mister Kinnear didn't even blink. "Ah but," he said, "here at Sir Patrick Dun's we're different. We will see you right."

In his five months of surgery Fingal had been impressed by the confident no-nonsense approach of his surgical seniors. One consultant was known as "Fix You Friday Finlayson." Friday was his usual operating day and his approach was consistently optimistic.

The consultant pointed at Fitzpatrick. "You admitted the patient. Give us a potted history."

Fingal felt sorry for Ronald Hercules. He looked wretched, pale with dark bags under his eyes. He and Hilda must have had a rough night. There were six new surgical patients on the wards since yesterday.

"Yes, sir." Fitzpatrick pinched the bridge of his nose. "Mister AL from Gordon Street is a forty-eight-year-old dock worker—"

That accounts for the calloused hands, Fingal thought.

"He was admitted at six this morning having experienced violent mid-upper abdominal pain and collapsed. He had not vomited. On examination he was pale, his temperature was ninety-seven degrees and pulse rate eighty. The most striking physical feature was board-like rigidity of the abdominal wall muscles." He paused for breath.

Not a tricky diagnosis, Fingal thought. An ulcer either in the stomach or duodenum had perforated, releasing corrosive stomach or duodenal contents into the peritoneal cavity. That would cause intense irritation. The body's response was to send the abdominal muscles into violent spasms.

Fitzpatrick continued, "He has a five-year history of recurrent bouts of upper abdominal pain, which comes on two hours after food. He eats biscuits at regular intervals because they relieve the pain."

"What's that called, O'Reilly?" Mister Kinnear asked.

"Hunger pain, sir." When he'd first read this technical term Fingal had been struck by its apparent trviality before he'd realised it was medical shorthand for pain being relieved when hunger was assuaged. It alone was sufficient to differentiate between a gastric or duodenal ulcer. Ulcers in the stomach acted up almost immediately after the patient ate, those of the duodenum two or more hours later and were eased by eating again.

Mister Kinnear nodded, turned to Fitzpatrick. "Any prior admissions?"

"Yes, sir. Mister AL was in Doctor Steevens' Hospital two years ago—"

"Isn't dat w'at I'm just after telling yiz? Dey told me to 'Eat little and often.' Suck feckin' chalk tablets." He coughed and both hands sought his belly. "Shite, that stings."

"Try not to talk," Doctor Ellerker said. "Just lie still."

But the patient shook his head. "Don't have a fag. No drink. For Christ's sake, no smoke, no drink?" His lip curled. "I might as well have joined a bunch of feckin' monks. Doctors? They're all a load of bollix."

Fingal had learned that not all patients were undyingly grateful, particularly those in whom treatment had been unsuccessful. Doctors had to understand and shrug off their patients' anger. The first time the class had encountered a belligerent sufferer they'd asked Doctor Ellerker later what should have been done. The houseman's reply, though blasphemous, had a ring of truth. "Don't expect all your patients to love you. The last chap everybody loved had a lousy Easter, and no doctor is Jesus Christ. We're not God. Our job is to try to understand, and give the rude ones fools' pardons."

Fitzpatrick snapped, "Don't you dare speak to Mister Kinnear like that, my good man."

The lesson about fools' pardons had gone unheeded, Fingal thought.

"Your good man? I'm not your man." A fire came into Mister Lynch's sunken eyes. "Feck off, you bollix."

Mister Kinnear bent and said, "We do understand you are in pain, worried, upset, but please try to be polite. The young doctors and I are trying to help you."

"Ah, Jasus Murphy." The patient clamped both hands tightly across his belly, gritted his teeth, then said, "I'm sorry, sir, but would youse please get on wit' it?"

"Soon, I promise," Mister Kinnear said. "Carry on, Fitzpatrick."

"Yes, sir. He was treated with six weeks' bed rest in hospital. A search was made for any factors causing stress which, as we know, is the prime cause of peptic ulcers. Initial treatment was undertaken by nursing him in a quiet room, passing a nasal tube into the duodenum and instilling milk, and giving alkalis in the form of magnesium carbonate."

"Good." Mister Kinnear turned to Bob. "And for stress what would you recommend?"

To Fingal's delight Bob didn't hesitate. "Either phenobarbitone or tincture of cannabis resin, sir."

"And cannabis's other names. Miss Manwell?"

"Hashish or marijuana, sir."

"We're just beginning to understand that particular plant. It may hold promise for the future," Mister Kinnear said, "but clearly conservative treatment has been a failure in this case." He turned to Cromie. "Diagnosis?"

"Perforated duodenal ulcer, sir."

"Right." The consultant turned to the patient. "You've got a hole in your guts."

The pain seemed to have taken the fight out of the man. "Mother of God," was all he could manage.

"Treatment, Mister Beresford?"

"Surgery, sir. Laparotomy. Close the perforation with interrupted sutures. Patch it if necessary. Wash out the peritoneal cavity. Suprapubic drainage . . ."

Fingal's eyes widened. He'd never heard Bob Beresford give such a comprehensive answer. Good for you, Bob.

"Intravenous dextrose/saline, and nurse in the Fowler's sitting-up position to encourage drainage."

Mister Kinnear smiled. "Well done, Beresford. Liking surgery, are you?"

Bob smiled. "The theory, sir, but I'm not very dextrous."

"We can't all be." Mister Kinnear turned to the patient. "I'm sure you didn't understand all that, but what it means is we're going to operate, close the hole, and make damn sure you recover postoperatively. There is one thing my young colleague forgot to mention—"

Fingal saw Bob frown.

"We'll make sure you get plenty of morphine to kill the pain, won't we, Sister Daly?"

"We will, so," she said. "I'm sure Mister Beresford only overlooked telling you because he took it for granted because it's been part of his routine for months."

Fingal saw Bob's look of gratitude.

"T'ank you, sir," the patient said, and turned his face away.

"Right," said Mister Kinnear, "who's next, Sister?" He led his entourage away from the bed.

"Bed 53, sir."

Fingal followed. While they were in the middle of the ward Charlie appeared, red-faced, breathing heavily. He was clutching something. "Excuse me, sir," he blurted, "something very important has come up. Could I speak to Fingal O'Reilly for a minute? Please?"

The consultant stopped and the little crowd with him. "If it's that important, certainly."

"Here, here." Charlie thrust an envelope at Fingal, an envelope bearing a crest and the words IRISH RUGBY FOOTBALL UNION. "Open it. Open it."

Fingal ripped the envelope open. The letter began, *Dear Mr. O'Reilly.* He had difficulty making out the words, but the gist of the first line was clear. He had been picked for the Irish trial. Fingal glanced to the bottom of the page. It was signed by Sir Samuel T. Irwin, President of the IRFU. Fingal lowered the letter and exhaled. "You too, Charlie?"

Charlie grabbed Fingal's hand. "And we're both Probables."

Fingal gasped. The trial would be between two sides. The "Probables" would go on to make up the Irish team unless injury supervened or a player on the other team, the "Possibles," massively outshone his opposite number. The cap was practically assured.

Charlie said, "Our letters say the trial's at Ravenhill in Belfast on a Saturday, so we'll have to go up the night before on the train. I'm sure Mister Kinnear'll give us the go-ahead, won't you, sir?"

"Of course you must go," the consultant said. "It's a great honour. I should know. I'll never forget my first cap. I think getting it gave me a bigger thrill than becoming a Fellow of the Royal College of Surgeons in Ireland." He shook hands with both lads. "Well done and good luck. I hope you'll both succeed."

"Thank you, sir," Charlie said. "I know we'll both try to."

Fingal's universe steadied. The shock had worn off. Lord, a trial. One last hurdle, and a low one at that, before the coveted cap. He glanced at his still not fully read letter. "Charlie," he said quietly, "what's the date of the trial?"

"Twelve days from now. Plenty of time for your nose to finish healing," Charlie said. "Saturday, December fourteenth."

"That's what I thought." Fingal's shoulders sagged. "The fourteenth." He sighed. "Do well for us, Charlie, but I'll have to decline."

"Surely not," Mister Kinnear said. "Decline a chance to gain Ireland's most coveted sporting honour? Don't be daft, man." He sounded angry.

"Why, for God's sake?" Charlie said.

"Remember the night you broke my nose and I told you wild horses couldn't stop me playing?"

"Yes."

"It's not horses, Charlie. Part One's the week of the ninth. The fourteenth's the day I'll be doing orals in bacteriology and pathology."

39

Success Is Counted Sweetest

Fingal paced up and down the corridor decorated with the portraits of previous academics. It was Saturday, December 14, and he was five minutes early for his microbiology oral. The two previous holders of the chair of pathology kept company with the first professor of bacteriology and preventive medicine, Professor Adrian Stokes. He had been succeeded in 1924 by Professor Joseph Warwick Bigger, the man who had been chosen to become dean of the faculty next year, and who, Fingal inhaled deeply, would be one of his examiners this afternoon. Not a man to be trifled with.

A door opened and a pale-faced candidate appeared. Fingal recognised Aidan Hewitt, a chronic who had started medical school even before Bob Beresford. "Prof Bigger's in a foul mood," he whispered as he passed Fingal. Hewitt had left the door open. Comfort ye my people, Fingal thought. Not long now until I'm in the lions' den. At least it was the end.

Already Fingal had sat two written examinations. Last Wednesday he'd begun the pathology paper with Question 1, *Describe the macroscopic and microscopic findings in acute pancreatitis.* Fortunately, he'd had plenty of time to devote to the intricacies of pancreatitis on the Saturday after Charlie had broken Fingal's nose. Questions two and three had both been gifts. And this morning's pathology oral hadn't been too bad at all. "Mister O'Reilly, please," a man said, and disappeared back behind the door.

Fingal used a hand to smooth down his thatch, straightened his tie, and wiped his sweating palms along the sides of his trousers. He took a deep breath and strode ahead.

"Close the door and sit," said a small man from behind a desk upon which was perched a brass-barrelled microscope. He wore a wing collar and a black tie. Fingal recognised Doctor William Jessop, assistant in the department of bacteriology. Beside him sat the redoubtable Professor Bigger. "That must have hurt," he remarked, nodding at Fingal's face. "Rugby?"

The swelling of his nose had pretty well gone and the trainer had been right, it did have a distinct list to port. There were dirty-yellow bruises fading beneath both of Fingal's eyes.

"Boxing, sir."

Professor Bigger grunted.

"I don't suppose it will stop you looking at slides," said Doctor Jessop. He pushed the microscope across the desk. "Take a look and tell us what you see."

Fingal sat, bent to the eyepiece, and spun the focussing wheels. In his mind he heard Bob Beresford saying, "Microscope: A cunningly designed optical instrument for making out-of-focus multicoloured blobs bigger." Fingal focussed and clumps of maroon rods became more defined. So the organism was "gram positive" because of its reaction to a standard colour stain and, because it was rod-shaped, a bacillus. That narrowed the search. Now. He moved the slide and noted small spheres. Those were spores. This microorganism, when threatened, protected itself by becoming encapsulated. To his knowledge there were only three spore-forming gram-positive bacilli. Two needed oxygen to develop, the aerobes. One family thrived without oxygen, the anaerobes. He looked up. "May I ask, sir, were these cultured aerobically or anaerobically?"

"Anaerobically," said Doctor Jessop.

"In that case those are *Clostridia*." Fingal thought back to his having messed up a question about the organisms on the paper in June. He'd made bloody well sure to read up about them this time. "But I'm not sure which exact one of the types." Fingal hesitated and hoped his inability to do so wasn't fatal.

"Differentiating is tricky." A faint smile played on Doctor Jessop's lips. "It's *welchii*," he said.

"It causes gas gangrene, sir." Fingal began to feel a little more at home. "*Tetani* causes tetanus, lockjaw, *botulinum* botulism, a vicious food poisoning."

He was grilled by each examiner in turn, until Professor Bigger said, "Last questions. Who first described the organism of tuberculosis?"

"Robert Koch, sir, in 1887."

"And how is it recognised microscopically?"

"The organism, *Mycobacterium tuberculosis,* is acid fast. It holds a stain even when treated with acid. Slides are prepared with carbofuchsin, acid alcohol, and methylene blue, the Ziehl-Neelsen stain, sir, and the *Mycobacteria* will appear under the microscope as red rods."

"I don't think," the great man said with a grin, "we'll be seeing you back for these exams in the warmer weather, O'Reilly. Well done."

The not-so-subtle hint that he had passed wasn't going to make waiting for the results any easier, and they would not be posted until Monday at five.

"I'll read the results again," Charlie said. "Final Part One. O'Reilly. Pathology. Pass. Seventy-eight percent. Microbiology. Pass eighty-one percent." He whistled. "Eighty-one, and the pass mark is forty." He made a low sweeping bow to Fingal. "Gentlemen," he said to Bob and Cromie, "we should be humbled in the presence of genius."

Fingal laughed at Charlie, but said, "I'm bloody relieved."

"So are we, mate," Cromie said. "Maybe we'll get a bit more of the pleasure of your company now."

"You will tonight, Cromie," Fingal said, but he wasn't going to slack off. He would like to have felt triumphant or been able to cheer, dance a jig, hurl his duncher in the air, but this was a resit. Getting the subjects he should have passed in June out of the way, that was all. He would have felt the same way after a long-nagging aching tooth had been pulled.

Bob Beresford slapped Fingal's back, Cromie pumped his hand. Hilda and Fitzpatrick were on ward duty so the lads had all been able to come to the Trinity Library.

"There you are, Fingal," Cromie said. "You've got your Christmas present nine days early and I reckon we should celebrate."

"The Bailey or Davy Byrnes?" Bob asked.

"Byrnes," Charlie said, "and it's my shout."

Fingal walked beside Charlie behind Bob and Cromie, who charged ahead through the traffic and the crowds.

The shaggy-haired man in the battered trilby who usually sat on the corner of Nassau and Dawson Streets selling newspapers and magazines was at his post and calling his wares. "*Independent, Irish Times, Pall Mall, Illustrated London News,* yer honour?" The man stank of damp underwear.

Fingal slowed, tossed a couple of coppers into the man's money satchel. "I don't want a paper," he said, "not tonight." Damn it, he had passed and he was going to celebrate.

"Don't blame you," Charlie said. "The international news is dire."

"I've not been keeping up," Fingal said. "I used to, but the last few months?" He shrugged.

Charlie said, "It's been all gloom and bloody despondency. Mussolini's forces have ripped into Abyssinia, aeroplanes and tanks against bows and spears. Last month, Japanese troops marched into Peking. I'm bloody glad we're not Germans. Hitler's declared every man from eighteeen to forty-five a Wehrmacht reservist. If he calls them up it's going to be one hell of a big army. He wants thirty-six divisions. That's 550,000 men. I'd not like to be a French *poilu* sitting in this Maginot Line they're building, and wondering when Adolf is going to come looking for revenge for '14 to 18."

"I'm glad I'm not German for more reasons than that," Fingal said. "Have you ever tried sauerkraut? And the silly buggers don't play rugby." Fingal lengthened his stride. "Bugger the Germans," he said. "I'm looking forward to my pint, and to toasting you, old friend. We're all coming out to to watch Ireland wallop England when you play the first home game in Dublin." In the stadium on Lansdowne Road, he thought, not far from home. He wondered how Father was this evening. He and Ma were on the Continent.

Charlie stopped. "I'm disappointed for you," he said. "You should be coming with me to play Wales."

Fingal shrugged. "Wasn't to be, Charlie. Not this year, unless the lad who got my place messes up, or gets hurt, and for his sake I hope he doesn't. You just play your best game ever, help Ireland win, and be sure to get a second cap for the England game." He started to walk and turned onto Duke Street. "Come on," he said. "I'm ready for that pint."

They swung into the familiar pub where Cromie was already seated and Bob leant on the long bar talking to Diarmud the barman. "Fingal O'Reilly, me oul' segotia," Diarmud called, "and Charlie Greer. Bob says the form's ninety tonight."

Fingal was pleased to be called Diarmud's old friend. And, yes, the mood was exceptional.

"We've got things to celebrate," Bob said.

"So are yiz four on the lash tonight?"

"No," Bob said, "it won't be a heavy session, but Fingal's passed his exams and Charlie's got an Irish cap."

"Jesus, Mary, and Joseph. Stop the lights. I don't feckin' believe it. Dat's gas. Bloody marvellous. Right. T'ree pints and a Jemmy."

Diarmud knew their order. A good barman should, and a good pub, and Byrnes was one, should be an extension of your living room. A place to feel at home.

"Please," Bob said. He turned to Charlie. "I know you said you'd get first shout, but it's my pleasure. Really."

"Your money's no good, Bob Beresford. Dem's on the house," Diarmud said, giving Bob his Jameson. "And when the pints are ready horse them into you for I'll have your second round on the pour. Congratulations, Fingal, and to you, Charlie." He offered a hand that was twice shaken.

"Thanks, Diarmud," Fingal said. "And I will get the first pint down in a couple of swallows." He strolled across to where Charlie and Bob had joined Cromie.

"Plant your arse, Fingal," Cromie said, and sprawled back in his chair. "And again, well done."

Fingal sat. "Before the evening gets out of hand I want to be serious for a minute."

"You, Fingal? Serious? Mother of God will wonders never cease? Can we believe that, lads?" Bob Beresford shook his head.

"He's been bugger all but serious since he failed it first time around," Charlie said.

"All right, Charlie. *Touché,* so bear with me a bit longer. I just want to thank you three for," Fingal hesitated, "for all your—"

"It's all right," Cromie said, "we understand. My father says if you can count your real friends on the fingers of one hand you're a lucky man." He grinned at them.

"True," Bob said.

"Hear him," Charlie said as Diarmud arrived with the drinks.

"Here's yer gargles," he said. "On Davy Byrnes."

"Thanks, Diarmud."

Four glasses were raised. The roared-in-unison *Sláinte*s made the other patrons stare, then, presumably because they were used to rowdy Trinity students, return to their own conversations.

After Fingal's first swallow, there was a white ring one-third of the way down his pint glass. "Your da's right, Cromie," Fingal said, and thought, Charlie, Cromie, and Bob, that was three. Fingal had become close to HMS *Tiger*'s young navagating officer, Tom Laverty, in '30, but it seemed unlikely their paths would cross again. Then there was Lars. He'd get a call later tonight to be told the exam results. "Do you reckon brothers could count as good friends?" Fingal asked.

"Don't see why not," Cromie said, "unless your names are Cain and Abel."

"Or Jacob and Esau," Charlie added, "and you'd not qualify as Esau, Cromie. You're not hairy enough." He sank a huge swallow.

Cromie ran a hand through his thinning hair. "As they say in the Liberties, Charlie, 'Feck off, you great bollix.'" His grin went from ear to ear.

"Why do you ask?" Bob wanted to know. Half his whiskey was gone.

"I've an older brother. I'll be seeing him next week. He's a really good skin. I'd count him as a friend."

"Family Christmas?" Bob asked, and inclined his head. "Things okay?"

Fingal sank another third of his pint. "Fine, Bob, but no family celebration this year." Bob knew about the leukaemia, and Fingal felt ready to tell his other friends about Father's illness, but not to-night. He'd not want to put a damper on the evening. "My folks are travelling," he said. "They'll be in Cap d'Antibes for the season. Family home's closed up except for the maid and cook, and they've been given the week off so I'll be going to my brother in Portaferry. I'm looking forward to it."

"I'm for home in Bangor," Cromie said.

"Home for me too," Charlie said.

Fingal sank the rest of his pint. "Bob? What about you?"

Bob Beresford blushed. "Seeing we have ten days off over Christmas and the New Year because the surgeons'll only be do-ing emergency cases, I'm giving myself a treat."

"Diarmud," Charlie roared.

"Right, sir. I've the pints poured."

"Tell us, Bob," Cromie demanded, and finished his first pint.

Bob coughed. "As this may be my last Christmas when dear old auntie's money's coming in, I'm having five days sking in Saint Moritz. Bette's coming too."

Charlie whistled. "Life of Riley for some," he said. "Fair play to you, Bob. Enjoy it."

"Does that mean you're going to take Finals seriously?" Fingal asked. The suggestion of Bob's inheritance stopping hadn't been lost on Fingal.

"Here's your grog." Diarmud unloaded a tray.

Bob paid. "It pains me to say it, but much against my better judgment I've actually started to enjoy seeing patients get better." He grinned at Fingal and lifted his glass in toast. "All your bloody fault, O'Reilly, making me study, keeping me at it."

Fingal hugged that thought.

"Will I take Finals seriously in June?" Bob asked. "I might."

"We'll drink to that, Bob," Fingal said. "Lads. To Doctor Beresford to be."

Glasses were raised. Their voices spoke as one and Cromie added, a little slurred, "And all who sail in her."

"That," said Charlie, "is for launching ships. Slow down, Cromie."

"Bollocks," said Cromie, "we're celebrating your cap and Fingal's pass."

They were, by God, Fingal thought. Part I was finally over and Fingal Flahertie O'Reilly was going to enjoy this evening, sink a few pints, enjoy good company—and for tonight at least pay no heed to thinking about what the next and final six months of their training would involve. "Same again, Diarmud," he roared, "and you, Cromie, sit up straight."

40

The Foxes Have Holes

Fingal tucked an Irish linen napkin into his collar and surveyed the chafing dishes on the sideboard in Lars's dining room. The scents of bacon and coffee were making his mouth water. "What time does the hunt meet?" he asked his brother. A painting above the sideboard, a Percy French watercolour of snow-covered Mourne Mountains, matched conditions outside the window.

"Eleven thirty outside Davy McMaster's at Lisbane," Lars said. "Two hours from now, so relax and enjoy your breakfast." The Portaferry Fox Hounds went out every Boxing Day, the honorary secretary was a friend of Lars's, and they'd been invited for a stir-rup cup before the hunt started. Lars poured coffee. "I'm sorry we didn't get to the dawn flight, but I never shoot if there's snow. The birds become stupid with the cold. It's too easy. You could knock them down with a stick."

The flakes had started on the morning of Christmas Eve and had made the drive to Portaferry from Belfast, where Lars had picked Fingal up from the train, tricky. The snow had stopped on Christmas Day. "Fine by me," Fingal said. "I'm sure we'll get other days fowling, and I've never seen a fox hunt."

"It'll be nippy out and we should fuel our boilers, so tuck in, Finn," Lars said.

Fingal helped himself. Myrtle, Lars's housekeeper, had left a sterling Boxing Day breakfast before going to Bangor to see her family. Servants traditionally were given their Christmas present, a "Christmas box," on December 26, hence the day's name, and they had the day off.

He chuckled and added sautéed lambs' kidneys to bacon, poached eggs, fried soda farl, and mushrooms. "At least," he said, "I didn't have to eat two Christmas dinners yesterday like last year. It's the fourth-year students who serve the patients theirs and are expected to dine at Sir Patrick's. Us fifth-years get a few days off." He wandered over and sat at the table where Lars was already tucking into rashers and eggs.

Lars said, "So, Finn, only six months to go. How does it feel?"

Fingal swallowed a mouthful of kidney. "Feel? You know bloody well I've wanted it since before you started bringing me to Strangford to shoot. Three more courses to go, one bloody great exam. How did you feel coming up to the end of law school?" Fingal used a piece of soda bread to mop up egg yolk.

Lars shrugged. "Glad that it would soon be over. Fed up I'd still more courses to take. Law's pretty dry, you know."

Fingal swallowed and attacked a rasher with all the verve of Flashing Fingers Kinnear at his work. "Medicine's not one bit dry. I've finished surgery, and I loved it, and we'll be going to the Rotunda for our midder for five months."

"Midder?"

"Midwifery. Looking after pregnant women, delivering babies, that along with a couple of other courses, it's very much the last lap." He helped himself to a cup of coffee and speared another kidney. "How do I feel? I'm champing at the bit to get on with it. Then June. Finals Part Two."

"I can imagine you'll be well prepared?"

"Bloody right. I've got to pass. Father wants to come to my graduation."

Lars hesitated, a forkful of bacon halfway to his mouth. "Do you think he will? Make it, I mean."

Fingal sighed. "Lars, I'm a final-year medical student, not a clairvoyant. I simply don't know, but I hope so. I really do." Fingal put a hand into his pocket. "At least," he said, offering a crumpled repeatedly-read telegram, "this appears to be positive." He slid the piece of paper over to Lars. Fingal now knew the words by heart.

"Congratulations—Stop—," Lars read. "Am delighted—Stop—Father well and proud as Punch—Stop—Merry Christmas—Stop—Love you and Lars—"

"I telegraphed them in Antibes to let them know I'd passed." Those six words, "Father well and proud as Punch" had meant a great deal to Fingal. A very great deal. "I think we can safely assume his leukaemia is still in remission. Ma wouldn't have said 'well' if it wasn't."

"That," said Lars, returning the telegram and pushing his empty plate away, "is the best Christmas present two sons could expect."

"So, my universe is unfolding, the folks seem to be all right, how about you, Lars?"

His brother shrugged. " 'The daily round, the common task—' "

" 'Should furnish all we ought to ask.' I know." Fingal finished a rasher. "Does it?" He looked directly at his brother.

Lars shrugged. "Pretty much. I'm well settled in here, part of the local community, I like that. It's, it's cosy. I think growing up in a wee place like Holywood makes you appreciate village life."

"It does. I'm still torn between GP and specialising, but I'll not worry about that for a while." Fingal pushed his empty plate aside. He'd decided before he came down not to broach the next subject until after Christmas Day, but he was still concerned for his brother.

"Lars, you can tell me to shut up if you like, but it's nearly exactly a year—"

"It's all right, Finn. A year since Jean Neely said no. I am well aware of that." He stared out of the window. "I still think about her. Whether the same can be said of her, I don't know. I hear she's engaged to a stockbroker now and is very happy. She always did like the good life."

And I think about Kitty and that damned Baggot Street doctor, Fingal thought.

"But, no, I don't hurt as much. Life goes on. I haven't bothered dating anybody else, and do you know? It's a lot less complicated."

"You are all right though?"

Lars laughed and yet Fingal detected a sadness in the laughter. "As rain, but thanks for asking." He glanced at his watch. "Come on," he said, "let's get these things washed up and then go and watch, in the words of your namesake, 'The unspeakable in full pursuit of the uneatable.'"

As the car neared the McMasters' the verges were filled with horse boxes parked along the Portaferry to Newtownards Road. They left Lars's car and and set off to walk the last fifty yards. Fingal trudged in tyre ruts through the ankle-deep snow, shielding his eyes against the glare of sunlight reflected from the shining hills. The air was crisp in his nostrils, but the scent of burning turf was less distinct than it had been when he'd gone shooting with Lars in February. He shrugged. His poor old proboscis would never be the same.

From around the corner ahead came the sound of iron-shod hooves on tarmacadam, an occasional whinny, and high-pitched belling as the hounds gave voice. Laughter, men's tones, women's voices.

The blackthorn hedges' ebony lattices were topped with what looked like royal icing. Small birds sat, disconsolate brown balls, their feathers fluffed against the cold, too lethargic to fly away as the two men approached. Lars was correct about the effects of cold, and right not to go shooting.

"They've got a brave day for the hunt," Lars said.

"Sound," Fingal agreed as they rounded the corner.

The road in front of Davy McMaster's farmyard was ajostle with members of the hunt, some on foot holding their horses' reins, some mounted. The horses' coats shone and their breath hung fine as gossamer in the crisp air. A woman held a chestnut gelding's bridle as the animal turned its head, twitched its ears, and watched with soft peat-brown eyes as a saddle blanket was spread and an English saddle, its surface glistening in the sun, was fitted with a slap of leather and a clink of stirrups.

Fingal overheard fragments of conversation. "The going should be good this year, not like last year's downpour."

"Perhaps young Blennerhasset won't come a cropper this year. Poor seat that boy."

And a woman's voice, offhand yet with unmistakable pride. "And so she's going to Queen's in September to study chemistry."

Another woman. "Your daughter? Little Esme? Good Lord. Girls going to university, and to read science no less? I'm sure I don't know what the world is coming to."

Hilda Manwell was taking a science, medicine, Fingal thought, and she was going to be a damn fine physician, probably a specialist. And the best of luck to her.

A joke's punch line: "I don't know about artificial respiration, but if you keep on pumping his arms and don't get his arse out of the Royal Canal you'll be at that forever," followed by a loud burst of laughter.

Davy and his wife circulated, handing out stirrup cups, which, Fingal surmised, by the steam rising from the glasses, were either hot toddies or mulled wine.

In a smaller yard behind a five-bar gate, the pack of hounds was being controlled by the huntsman and two whippers-in.

The scene was ablaze with colour. Many men wore scarlet coats, the rest black jackets. All had on pale breeches and English boots. The ladies sported navy coats, some with coloured collars. Some wore voluminous skirts and would be riding sidesaddle.

"Why the different uniforms, Lars?" Fingal asked.

"It's complicated, but the professionals, like the master and huntsman, and the gifted amateurs, wear red coats if they're men— the coats are actually called 'pinks.' And the outstanding women wear coloured collars on navy jackets. Otherwise black jackets for the men, plain navy for the women. If you're under eighteen, you've to wear tweed like young Andy Blennerhasset." He indicated a rotund young man who Fingal noticed was sorely troubled with acne, and who reputedly had a poor seat. Poor it might be, but it was certainly ample. "I wonder how long those traditions have been around." Certainly the sport wasn't Irish. It had been imported by the English aristocracy probably as long ago as the sixteenth century.

"No idea," Lars said, "but it's firmly established in this part of Ireland." He scanned the crowd. "Now, there's my friend, the secretary," Lars said, pointing to a red-jacketed man astride a large bay. "Michael." Lars waved.

"Come on over, Lars. Come and have a drink."

Davy McMaster offered a tray of drinks. Fingal took a whiskey toddy and followed Lars past other horses to where his friend sat beside a ramrod-stiff man with iron-grey hair. In his army officer's uniform with its captain's three pips on the epaulettes, and seated on a large black stallion, the man looked ready to do battle. Beside him, also mounted on a black horse, was a fine-boned woman. She had a coloured collar so must be regarded as an expert. A long chestnut ponytail escaped from under her John Bull top hat and swayed and glistened in the sun. She had full lips and pale blue eyes.

"Michael Crawford," Lars said. "Meet my brother, Fingal. Fingal, Michael Crawford."

Fingal reached up to take the proffered hand.

"How do you do, Mister O'Reilly," Michael said.

"How do you do?" Fingal replied. Idiotic greeting, he thought, and had a desire to ask instead, "How do I do what, exactly?"

"May I introduce Captain, Lord John MacNeill, First Batallion, Irish Guards and his wife, Lady Laura MacNeill?" Michael said. "Just home from India."

More how-de-do's, then the soldier said, "O'Reilly? Not Fingal O'Reilly?"

Fingal looked up and squinted against the sun. "Yes, my lord." The man's face was familiar, he was sure he'd seen pictures of it somewhere.

"I was dreadfully sorry to hear you had to turn down an Irish trial. Please accept my sympathy."

"Thank you, sir. But how did you know?"

"Sir Sam Irwin, president of the Irish Rugby Football Union, is a friend of my father, the Marquis of Ballybucklebo. Played a bit myself once too."

"I appreciate your sympathy, sir." And now he was able to place where he'd seen the man. "Played a bit"? Fingal had seen photographs in the *Irish Times* of this man scoring a try for Ireland, but he was clearly too modest to mention it.

"Perhaps next year?"

"I hope so."

"O'Reilly, forgive me, but you're a medical man, are you not?"

"Not quite, sir. Final-year student."

"I wonder if I could ask a great favour?"

Fingal nodded.

"Lady Laura had a misadventure mounting. The horse shied and she twisted her ankle."

"Please, John, don't make a fuss," she said.

Fingal was taken by the softness of her voice. She sat her mount sidesaddle with fluid grace, looking like a female centaur, her long skirt melding with the contours of the horse.

"Would you, O'Reilly, be able to assure us that my wife hasn't broken her ankle?"

Good God. Fingal had completed his orthopaedics, knew a fair bit about fractures, but still. "Well, I—"

"John, it's really not necessary."

"Laura, I don't want you riding if you've broken that ankle."

She sighed. "Mister O'Reilly." She bent, rucked up her skirt to knee level, bent her knee, hauled off her boot, and thrust her sock-encased foot at Fingal. Her calf, and a well-turned one at that, was smooth and tanned. "I think it's perfectly fine, but please have a look if you wish," she said.

A snatch of a Cole Porter song ran through Fingal's mind.

In olden days a glimpse of stocking was looked on
as something shocking.

"I wonder if you could move your horse away from the crowd, my lady?" And he followed while she walked the animal around a low wall.

"Please, proceed, Doctor," she said.

"Not quite doctor, yet," he said, and looked up to catch her returning his wry smile. "I'll have to take off your sock."

"Please carry on."

Fingal took a deep breath. He held her foot in one hand and gently peeled off the woollen sock. "I hope that didn't hurt," he said, handing it to her.

"Not at all."

It would have if a bone had been fractured. Fingal quickly examined the offending joint. She had little difficulty moving it. There was some tenderness and a good deal of swelling on the lateral side but certainly no evidence of a break. "It isn't broken, but it is sprained, my lady," he said. "You should rest it."

"I'm sure you're right, but I'll not miss the hunt for only a sprain." She smiled and there was fire in those pale blue eyes. "As long as we tell John it's not broken, everything will be fine. You'll support me in this, won't you?" He hadn't thought her smile could become any brighter, but when she asked, "Please?" Fingal was convinced her face was somehow lit from within.

He inclined his head. "Certainly, Lady MacNeill."

"Thank you." She busied herself putting on her sock and boot, but looked up to fix him with a curious look. "Queen's student, then?"

He shook his head. "Trinity."

"Trinity? Dublin?" She stopped with her boot halfway on. "I don't suppose you'd know a chap called Beresford?"

"Bob Beresford? From near Conlig? He's in my class." Hadn't Bob told him about a girl? A girl who'd married a man who was both an army captain and the son of a peer. A man called Lord John MacNeill? She was this girl with the radiant face and pale blue eyes.

"How is he?" she asked, and Fingal heard a wistful tone in her voice.

"Bob? He's fine. With a bit of luck he'll graduate this coming June."

"I do hope so," she said, rearranging her skirt. "I knew him—only vaguely, you understand." She looked up quickly, then busied herself with the reins. "But he didn't seem terribly interested in qualifying, or getting serious about anything—or anyone." She turned the horse's head sharply. "Thank you, Mister O'Reilly," she said. "I'd best rejoin John. I'll tell him your diagnosis, but not your suggested treatment." She saluted him with her crop and walked the horse away.

That is one beautiful, spirited woman, Fingal thought. He ambled back to his brother. So she was the girl from Cultra that Bob had let slip away. And she'd not asked to be remembered to him. It was a bloody good thing he'd not said how Bob had changed, was making an effort to qualify. Some hares should be left to sit. He caught up with Lars as he was finishing his drink. "Come on, brother," Fingal said as the hunting pack was let out of the yard. "Looks to me close to kickoff time. We'd better get clear of the horses." The huntsman sounded a warning on a short straight horn. Those standing began to mount. Those already mounted turned their horses to face up the road.

"Finish your drink," said Lars, "and we'll go back to the car. They'll be heading inland soon. We'll nip up a side road. There's a hill with a great view."

Fingal took the last swallow, found a wall to put his glass where Davy'd find it, and set off with his brother. Fingal's mind returned to that evening studying leukaemia with Bob Beresford. "It wasn't until she'd married an army captain that I realised I'd let a gem go." That gem was now Lady Laura MacNeill and if looks were anything to go by she was a corker. He thought of Lars and Jean Neely, and of Kitty O'Hallorhan with her soft grey eyes and soft laugh, who had been willing to wait because she understood how important his studies were. Who'd told him she loved him. Fingal inhaled. It seemed all the best people let gems go. Certainly Bob had called Kitty a jewel.

Fingal got into the car and sat quietly as Lars turned right, climbed a long hill, then parked. "Out."

They crunched through a shallow drift and stood in front of a dry stone wall. Fingal looked down. In the distance the Mourne Mountains seemed to hold up a porcelain sky so delicate it looked as if it might crack if left unsupported. High clouds drifted to the south. A skein of grey-lag geese, tiny marks against Strangford Lough, moved in a ragged vee over the wishbone-shaped Long Island. It lay beside the neighbouring Round Island. The two were white moonstones in the blue enamel of the still waters. They were owned by a wildfowling syndicate of four physicians led by a Doctor Jimmy Taylor from Bangor.

Inland the little fields were wrapped in a snowy eiderdown that rose and fell over the drumlins, the round hills of County Down. Their bordering hedges and dry stone walls were limned with white. Patches of brown bracken and dark green whin bushes were all the colour to be seen.

He heard the huntsman's horn, the belling of the pack, and in the valley not far below saw a russet blur, a fox racing across a field of unbroken snow. Fingal knew the creatures' numbers must be controlled, they ate chickens and game birds, but his heart went out to the animal running in what must be mortal terror. It vanished under a blackthorn hedge.

The hounds had the scent and tore along, noses to the ground, tails in the air, an untidy string of twelve couples, twenty-four dogs spread out over a field.

A hoarse cry of, "View Halloo." Someone had spotted the quarry in the open.

The horses, brown and chestnut, black and grey, thundered

across the field hard on the hounds' heels. He could hear the drumming, see earth and snow thrown up from the hooves. As they came nearer, the riders and steaming animals took clear shape. He had no difficulty recognising the army officer and his wife galloping side by side, Lady Laura MacNeill's ponytail a chestnut battle ensign streaming in the wind of her passage. Clearly her ankle was troubling her not one whit.

A man's black peaked hunt cap blew off. "Tally-ho." He'd seen the quarry too. Headgear forgotten, he urged his horse on.

In small groups and singly, horses and riders leapt at the hedge where Fingal had last seen the fox. Up. Seem to hang. Over. Land. But not all. Two horses wandered, reins dangling as foxhunters picked themselves up. One remounted. The other limped as he led a grey away from the hedge and clearly was heading for home. The stragglers were still attempting the hedge and now the last horse baulked and unseated its rider, who quite unaccompanied cleared the hedge and landed with an audible thump. Fingal was happy when the unfortunate picked herself up and walked to a gate.

Three up to Brer Fox. Fair play to the creature.

The sounds of the hunt died in the distance until barely audible, drifting on the still air came the cry, "Gone awaaay. Gone awaaaay."

He smiled. The hounds had lost the scent, and the fox, probably in its lair by now, was safe.

"That's it, Fingal," Lars said. "Unless you want to go and welcome them back."

Fingal shook his head. "It was quite the sight. Thanks for bringing me."

Lars smiled. "I'm glad we got a fine day for it."

Fingal laughed. " 'Half a league, half a league, half a league onward, into the valley of death rode the six hundred.' Stirring stuff this fox hunting, but my cheeks are like blocks of ice and I'm foundered. Home, James, for a hot half-un." He piled into the car.

He still carried a mental picture of Lady Laura's dancing pony-tail, her refusal to let a sprained ankle stop her from revelling in the chase. It would be better not to mention to Bob that Fingal had met her. No need to open old wounds.

Fingal swayed as the car turned a tight corner. Twigs scraped along his side and he looked out to see a blackthorn hedge like the one the fox had first taken cover under. Fingal was pleased that the animal had outwitted its pursuers. He glanced at his brother. The fox had got away from the pursuing hunt just as Jean Neely had from Lars. Just as Bob had let Laura go. And just as the fox was now safe and getting on with its life, so was Jean Neely, so was Laura MacNeill. Both women had moved on, fallen in love again.

Fingal O'Reilly stared through the windscreen and felt a great unease at the thought of Kitty O'Hallorhan marrying someone else. Did he really have to let her get away too? He'd chased her off and wished to God he hadn't. To hell with the colleague she was reportedly seeing. Fingal had told Charlie he'd ask her for a second chance after the exam results were in. They were. He'd passed. So what was holding him back?

41

From His Mother's Womb
Untimely Ripp'd

"Come on, Bob." Fingal shot to his feet. He'd been startled by the jangling of an electric bell in the Rotunda gentlemen's mess. It and other strategic sites in the hospital, like the women's common room, had bells. They were the summons for all medical students to drop everything and hurry to the labour ward. Something unusual was about to take place and they were to observe.

Cromie and Charlie were on labour ward duty so they'd be there. Hilda and Fitzpatrick would be trotting over from the antenatal clinic.

They were in the first of eight weeks of structured practical instruction in midwifery and gynaecology, the introduction to a course that would consume five months. They'd already attended the ten introductory lectures given at Sir Patrick's by the King's Professor of Midwifery, O'Donel Browne.

"What do you reckon?" Bob asked as he closed the door behind them.

Fingal shook his head. "Dunno. Could be anything. Forceps, breech—" He'd seen one breech delivery and had been impressed by the skill of the accoucheur, a skill no doubt that had taken time and experience to attain. Fingal had observed three normal confinements. All students had to watch five then conduct deliveries themselves under supervision, some in the hospital, some in the patients' homes.

He was liking midder. The women weren't sick. Well, some with complications of the pregnancy were, but on the whole this speciality was a lot more cheerful than the ones where watching the likes of Kevin Doherty die was an integral part of the work. Every woman he'd observed was happy once the baby was born. As he heard it said, "Och sure, but doesn't a babby bring its own welcome?"

And in midwifery there were techniques that could turn difficulties around and lead to excellent outcomes. Fingal lengthened his stride, pushed open the door to the labour ward, and entered a rectangular room. Beneath three large windows in the far wall was a row of enamel sinks. Electric lights hung on long flexes from a high ceiling. Even in midwifery the cornerstones of good care were light and airiness. Of the five cast-iron-framed beds in the room, one was vacant and three were occupied by labouring women.

The fourth was surrounded by the resident house officer, here called the clinical clerk; two midwives; the rest of Fingal's group of six; and ten other medical students. Some were from Trinity, but others were from the undergraduate school at the Royal College of Surgeons in Ireland and there was one Scottish chap from the University of St. Andrews. A senior obstetrician, Doctor E. Hastings Tweedy, stood at the head of the bed speaking to the group.

At regular intervals one of the three women in the other beds moaned, cried out, begged the Holy Mother for relief. One kept wanting her own mammy. Midwives and midwives in training listened to the babies' heart rates and examined each patient to determine her progress. At the appropriate time she would be delivered either by a medical student or a student midwife. Consultants like Doctor Tweedy were summoned only for complicated cases. Their private fee-paying patients who had normal deliveries were confined in nursing homes or their own beds, and not subjected to the ministrations of students.

"It stinks in here," Bob said.

There certainly was an astringent aroma. Fingal wrinkled his bent nose. "It's Dettol, a new antiseptic. Have you read the Davidson report?" he asked. "I did last night."

"Not yet. Not in detail, but I know it's about last year's outbreak of puerperal fever, postpartum infection, here. There were five maternal deaths. It's on my list." Bob grinned at Fingal. "Honestly. It is. I will read it. I promise. I know it's important. Postpartum infection is serious stuff."

"You'd bloody well better. It could be a step to the greatest advance in years. The infection's caused by the haemolytic *Streptococcus*. Doctor Davidson has three recommendations to combat it. One is using this new antiseptic, the second is wearing masks, because Davidson cultured the bacterium from throats and noses of doctors and nurses and reckons they were the source." Fingal lifted a couple of masks from a box on a table near the door, handed one to Bob and started to tie his own. "And, the third is a drug that prevents the development of streptococcal blood poisoning in mice. They'll be running a trial here."

"Honestly? I didn't think any medicine could do that."

"This stuff called Red Prontosil just might. It's a sulphonamide. Jesus, Bob, if it works for postpartum infections—remember Kevin Doherty?"

Bob nodded.

"We might finally have something to treat rheumatic fever with too, before *Streptococcus* damages the heart valves." But too late for you, Kevin, he thought. Fingal gritted his teeth, finished tying on the mask, and said through the material, "Now, let's go and see why we were summoned."

Doctor Tweedy looked over his mask at the new arrivals. "Let

me briefly recap for you two. Mrs. EL is a twenty-year-old primi-
gravida."

So it was her first pregnancy, Fingal thought, looking at a short,
thin woman. She was pale, the bags under her eyes dark and deep.
There was blood on her lower lip, probably because she had bitten
it. Her gaze never left Doctor Tweedy's face.

"Her estimated date of delivery was December twenty-eighth
so today, January eighth, she is eleven days overdue. She went into
labour at home some thirty-eight hours before she was admitted."

Mrs. EL moaned and clutched her bulging belly.

Fingal marvelled at the endurance of women. Nearly two days
in labour.

"The district midwife was summoned to the patient's home on
Railway Street early this morning, examined the patient, and concluded that the baby was lying longitudinally, vertex presentation,
right occipito anterior."

The child's spine was aligned with its mother's, it was coming
headfirst, with the back of its head turned slightly to the right and
facing the front of the mother's abdomen. This was the normal lie
and presentation.

"It was not engaged."

So the widest part of its head hadn't passed the pelvic brim.

"On rectal examination, the cervix was five shillings dilated and
the vertex two knuckles."

It was believed there was less risk of infection if the rectal route
was used for examinations to assess the progress of labour. Using
coin sizes to assess how far the cervix was dilated was routine, as
was the use of "knuckles." The midwife had described a cervix
that had only completed half its necessary dilatation and the leading edge of the baby's head was the distance between the second
knuckle of her index finger from its tip and the tip from the pelvic
floor. Both indicated poor progress.

"The midwife sensibly suggested the patient be brought here. Mrs. EL applied at the Porter's Lodge for admission. The assistant master, Doctor Edmond Solomons, as is the custom, agreed. He put her under my care. It was determined that because of her social circumstances, the six-shillings-a-day hospital fee and my own would be waived."

Fingal knew that all patients, except in these kinds of circumstances, were expected to contribute to the cost of their care. Rightly so, but money should not stand between a patient and proper help, and here, like in the twenty-five percent of beds set aside in Sir Patrick's, it clearly wasn't.

"It has taken us some time to assess her progress and have tests done. So altogether she has been in labour for forty-one hours. The adage is a true one, 'Never, never let the sun set twice on the same labour.' She has had a gruelling two days and has suffered many examinations," said Doctor Tweedy, "so I will not invite any of you to repeat anything. Instead I will tell you, there has been no change in any of her physical findings. Labour has not progressed and her contractions are becoming less frequent and less powerful. She is clearly distressed. What does all that suggest?"

"Obstructed labour, sir," Fitzpatrick called from where he stood at the front of the group, "due to a fault in one of the 'Three *P*s.'"

"Which are?" Doctor Tweedy asked.

"The powers, the passenger, or the passages."

"Very good. You," Doctor Tweedy pointed at Charlie, "what could be wrong with the powers?"

"Either the uterine contractions simply aren't strong enough, primary inertia, or more likely in this case, something else is delaying progress and the uterine muscles are exhausted trying to overcome it and are giving up. Secondary inertia."

"Assuming there is a difficulty with Mister Fitzpatrick's second *P,* the passenger, what might it be?"

Hilda Manwell said, "If the midwife is right, it is unlikely that a malpresentation could be responsible."

"You, sir," Doctor Tweedy nodded at Fingal. "Malpresentation?"

"When any part of the baby other than the head with the occiput anterior is trying to get into the pelvis. That would include—" Fingal had read up on the subject immediately after Professor Browne's lecture. How much had he remembered? "Occipito-posterior, occipito-transverse, breech, face, brow, shoulder, and transverse lie." Got 'em, he thought.

Doctor Tweedy smiled. "Been studying, I see." He turned back to the other students. "Anything else that might be wrong with the passenger?"

"Yes, sir," Fitzpatrick rushed in. "Abnormal size, malformations, double monsters—"

The patient screamed, high, piercingly, then yelled, "Jesus, Mary, and Joseph, my babby's not a monster. It's not." She burst into tears.

You are an insensitive bastard, Fitzpatrick, thought Fingal. Could you not have said teratology for malformations, conjoined twins for double monsters? We'd have understood. She wouldn't. Fingal now believed that keeping the patient in the dark often was a kindness, at least until the final diagnosis was in. That medical jargon wasn't all hocus-pocus. Sometimes it was kindly meant.

Doctor Tweedy bent to her. "It's all right, Mrs. Lannigan. I can promise you your baby's absolutely normal and it's going to be perfectly all right. I promise." He took and held her hand. "Tactless, Mister Fitzpatrick," he said levelly. "Very tactless."

Fitzpatrick stepped back from his place in the front row. Fingal saw the submissive crouch the man often assumed when chastised. Would that eejit never learn?

"As you all can see, Mrs. Lannigan is upset, so I'll come to the point. She has secondary uterine inertia, not because there is anything remotely wrong with the baby." He patted her hand and was rewarded with a smile. "But because there is something in the passages holding things up. We have carried out some investigations and decided on a course of action before you all were summoned." He turned to the resident houseman. "Doctor Milliken, please."

The junior doctor, a sandy-haired, short man tending toward chubby, stepped forward and produced an X-ray. He held it up to the light.

Fingal craned forward. The baby's skeleton was perfectly normal, as was its head.

"Please note," said Doctor Tweedy, "the distortion of the pelvic brim into a figure-of-eight shape when it should be like a fat heart. The waist of the eight is too narrow."

Fingal could see that clearly.

Doctor Tweedy bent to the patient. "It means that things are a bit tight and baby is having trouble getting through."

She nodded, her little old woman's eyes following his.

"So while I and the young doctors here have been discussing your case, the nurses have been getting things ready and we're going to do a Caesarean section. Doctor Milliken and I will operate and the young doctors will observe. And you and your baby will be fine. I promise."

So time hadn't been wasted simply to teach, Fingal thought. Good. After six months of surgery, Fingal was not squeamish about the prospect of watching a Caesarean section.

He heard footsteps and the quiet rumbling of wheels. Two masked orderlies were bringing a trolley. "We're going to take you to theatre now, Mrs. Lannigan." Doctor Tweedy let go of her hand. "You'll be fine."

Fingal waited with the rest as she was moved to the trolley and trundled out of the ward.

"Now, before we go and get ready," Doctor Tweedy said, "why do you think her pelvis is flat and contracted?"

"Rickets, sir," Fingal said. "There's never much sunlight in the tenement districts even on a good day. Pretty poor nutrition. Half the kiddies there have bow legs, twisted spines."

"And deformed pelves," the consultant said. "The tenements." He pursed his lips. "Where grannys and handy women do half the deliveries."

"Excuse me, sir," Fingal asked, "handy women?"

"Lay women who help at confinements."

Fingal frowned. "But, why wouldn't a patient send for a midwife or use the dispensary doctor? It doesn't cost anything if you don't have a lot of money."

Doctor Tweedy shook his head. "It's not the money. Dublin women have a mortal fear of hospitals and so they hope if they don't get professionals involved, things will work out all right at home. And often they do, but there can come a point when they have to come here or to one of the other hospitals and that often means the situation has become dire and, of course, if a death is involved—it's not hard to understand why other pregnant women are terrified of institutions."

"I don't understand, sir," the Scottish student said. "The patients come to us in Scotland. And Caesarean section's pretty safe."

"Until recently it wasn't," Doctor Tweedy said, "and the only safe option then for the mother was to crush the baby's head so it could be delivered. You can see the instruments called cephalotribes and cranioclasts in the museum here."

"Sounds pretty gruesome, sir," Bob Beresford said.

Fingal saw Hilda shudder. And well she might. He'd already learned that petite women, even if they didn't have rickets, were at much greater risk of obstructed labour because their pelves were small.

"And it was, if it was allowed to be done at all," Doctor Tweedy said.

"Why wouldn't it be?" Cromie asked.

"It is forbidden by the Catholic church. The mother would have been baptised and have a chance of Heaven. However, if the baby died before it could be baptised it would spend eternity in Limbo. The rule was simple. Make every effort to save the baby even if it cost the mother her life. I'm afraid I've had to do post-mortem Caesarean sections just like the ancient Romans did."

Barbaric superstitious nonsense, Fingal thought, but kept the thought to himself.

"Now, ladies and gentlemen, if you will please follow me to the theatre, I will take great pleasure in demonstrating the operation of Caesarean section."

The procedure, Fingal thought, was said to have been performed on the mother of Robert the Bruce, King of Scotland, giving Shakespeare the model for Macduff, Macbeth's nemesis.

The entourage headed off, Fingal at the rear. He'd been impressed with Doctor Tweedy. The man hadn't hesitated to reassure a terrified woman, hold her hand, and yet it was obvious he was a master of the technicalities of his discipline. It strengthened Fingal O'Reilly's resolve to be that kind of doctor—he chuckled at his own phrasing—when he grew up, in less than six months. He smiled and remembered Sister Daly using the exact words when she'd threatened to report him to Doctor Micks. "When you grow up." He had matured since then. A lot.

42

Give Crowns and Pounds and Guineas,
But Not Your Heart Away

"Good Lord, Fingal. Fingal O'Reilly? What on earth brings you here?" Virginia Treanor answered the front door of the converted three-storey house on Leeson Street. The petite blonde's head usually only reached his shoulder, but from her vantage point up a short flight of sandstone steps she looked him in the eye.

"Mostly the tram," he said, and managed a smile, "but I did walk a bit."

"Oh, very good," she said. "Incisive wit. Stunning repartée." She rolled her eyes and shook her head, but said, "I know it is a fair stretch from Parnell Square to here. Cromie's doing his midwifery there at the Rotunda so I know the other suspects including you are too." She took a pace back and folded her arms across her chest. "I suppose you came to see Kitty?"

"Please."

"I'm not sure I should let you. It's been six months since you blew her out. You hurt her, Fingal. Would you not just leave her be?"

"I can't." He tried to ignore the pelting rain that shimmered as it flew past the streetlights and trickled under his raincoat collar.

Virginia sniffed. "Wait there. I'll go and ask her." She closed the door after her.

Fingal hunched his shoulders and stepped back a couple of paces on the narrow pavement. Would she see him? He'd not blame her if she wouldn't, but he fervently hoped she'd not refuse. It might have been immediately after the foxhunt that he had decided he was going to ask her for another chance, but it had taken him until now, late January, to steel himself to do it.

Like the previous three times before Christmas when he'd headed here from Sir Patrick's, he'd almost turned back tonight. He was unsure of whether he was scared of hurting her again or terrified of rejection. There was the other man.

A motorcar sped past, chucking up from the gutter a sheet of water as big as old *Tiger*'s bow wave. He turned and roared after the driver, "Slow down, you unmitigated bollix. You're not Sir Malcolm Campbell."

"Still the same O'Reilly," he heard a familiar voice saying. "Come in, Fingal."

Fingal spun and saw her in silhouette, the light coming from the hall behind her and making a halo of her hair. "Kitty," he said. "I'm sorry."

He started forward up the steps and she stepped aside to let him into the shared hall of the building, closed the door, and said, "You look in real rag order. You're drenched. Give me your coat and cap."

"Thank you." Fingal snatched off his duncher, shrugged out of his coat, and handed them to her.

She hung them on one of a row of hooks to drip on the linoleum.

She'd changed her hairstyle. Before it had hung to her shoulders; now it was straight, parted to the left like a man's. Three rolled waves stopped abruptly just below the tops of her ears. He didn't like it and hoped it was a passing fad, not an outward sign that Kitty had decided to get rid of a lot of things from her past.

"How have you been?" he asked, and shifted from one foot to the other, the question hanging in the air.

"I'll be back in a couple of hours," Virginia said as she left their shared flat and came into the hall. "*Top Hat*'s still showing. I love Fred Astaire and Ginger Rogers." She grabbed her coat and left singing, " 'Isn't it a lovely day, to be caught in the rain?' "

"Enjoy," Kitty said.

And into that single word Fingal read volumes. Virginia would almost certainly have asked Kitty if she wanted moral support. Another's presence would have squashed anything other than small talk, at the end of which Kitty could have said good-bye without either she or Fingal having been embarrassed. But Virginia had left.

"So, Fingal, how have you been?" she said over her shoulder as she crossed to the door of the flat and turned back to him. "Good Lord," she said, "what have you done to your nose?"

He chuckled. "I didn't do anything. Charlie Greer did. We were in the gym sparring. I let my guard down for a moment." He shrugged.

"I'd have guessed you'd broken it playing rugby."

Was there a hint of bitterness that while he'd let her go he'd kept on playing? "Boxing," he said.

"Virginia didn't tell me. She's still seeing Cromie and keeps me abreast of most of the gossip. I heard from her that you passed your exam. Congratulations. You're back on course."

So she still was interested in what he was doing. "Thank you," he said as he followed her into the sitting room.

She sat in an armchair. A simple loose woollen sweater could not disguise the beautiful woman beneath. She wore no makeup. Those amber-flecked grey eyes didn't need any, nor did her full lips. "Have a seat."

He sat on the sofa facing her. He recognised that the minute she'd closed the door behind them he should have taken her into his arms, kissed her, and told her he loved her. Damnation. For all the worldliness he professed to Lars, despite his experiences in the navy, Fingal was still in matters of his own heart an overgrown schoolboy. "You're looking well," he said.

"I am well," she said. "I've been keeping myself busy. Baggot Street Hospital's a wonderful place to nurse and I've been going to night classes to improve how I use pastels." She pointed to a portrait.

No mention of the other man. Perhaps it was over. Fingal dared to hope. "That's Virginia. I'd recognise her anywhere," he said. "It's very good." We're like a couple of boxers, he thought, sparring, throwing out exploratory punches, seeking the opening. "I like the way you've caught her expression."

"It's not quite what I was after. I'm still trying for better economy of line." She stood quickly, surprising him, took two paces away and two back. Then she folded her arms and looked down on him. "Fingal," she said, "you didn't come here tonight to discuss the finer points of pastel art, did you?"

He sat forward, leaned his wrists on his knees, and stared down at his intertwined fingers before looking up into her eyes. "I came to apologise."

She cocked her head.

"Kitty, I'm sorry I pushed you away. I've regretted it ever since."

"I tried to understand. Your exams. Your father's illness. I tried, Fingal. I really did."

"Father's in France," he said. "In remission."

"I'm glad."

Silence.

She said, "If you have regrets, so had I. I broke my heart for you, cried myself to sleep. Virginia was wonderful." Kitty laughed, a short dry laugh. "Held my hand through the worst. She didn't

want me to see you tonight. Thought it would open up the wound."
She lowered her voice. "Fingal, you took away my laughter."

He hung his head.

She walked away and back again. "I appreciate your coming here
tonight to apologise. I always knew you were a gentleman. Thank
you. I accept your apology."

He looked up at her. Kitty's shoulders were braced, her stance
erect. "Kitty, I—"

She held up a hand, palm out. "Fingal, I don't want you to embarrass yourself."

"I'll not. I'll not because it's true, what I want to say. I—"

"Fingal, please don't. I've something to tell you and I want you
to hear it before you say anything." One hand plucked at a crease
in her skirt. "I think you know I've been seeing a surgical trainee."

Fingal felt his mouth drying up. Those words hit as hard as
Charlie's gloved fist.

"For more than two months. He's very sweet. A Galway City
man."

I'm sure he's very sweet, Fingal thought, but I don't give a tinker's damn if he's the duke of the whole bloody province of Con-
naught.

"Last week he asked me to marry him." The words came out in
a tumbled rush.

Fingal's mouth opened. He couldn't stifle pictures of a strange
man kissing her, caressing her, telling her he loved her, and Kitty
saying "Yes."

"I see," he said.

"Fingal, I told him I needed time to think about it." The grey
eyes looked straight into his.

Tell her, you moron, a voice yelled in his head. *Tell her you love
her.* If she needed time, that must mean she wasn't sure. Perhaps,
perhaps she still cared? But he found he simply couldn't bring

himself to ask. Fingal's words were cooler than he intended. He rose. "I'm pleased for you, Kitty. I wish you every happiness."

"Is that all you have to say, Fingal?" There was a catch in her voice. "Is it?"

"What else is there to say? You're considering a proposal of marriage." Stop being the gentleman, doing the honourable thing, the voice told him. Tell her you love her and the Galway man be damned. So what if she hadn't simply sat at home pining for Fingal O'Reilly? Swallow your pride, man, and tell her.

"All right. I understand," she said quietly.

"I don't think," he said, "there's any point in my staying. I hope you're able to make up your mind soon." He moved closer to her. She wasn't wearing her usual musk. Of course she hadn't been expecting him.

Just as he hadn't been expecting news of a marriage proposal.

"I hope, Kitty," he said, "we might stay friends." Another winner from your book of clichéd platitudes, Fingal, he thought. He extended his hand.

She took it. Her grasp was cool and firm.

He tingled at her touch.

"I know you and the lads have your big exams in five months," she said, releasing his hand. "I hope they go well for you, Fingal. I think I more than anybody know exactly how much passing means to you."

He saw how bright her eyes were. "I'll let myself out," he said. "I wish you well, Caitlin O'Hallorhan."

"And I wish you luck, Fingal Flahertie O'Reilly, I truly do."

This time it was his turn not to look back. As he closed the door he was sure he heard a sob, but he lifted his cap and coat, opened the outer door, and stepped out into the misery of a Dublin January downpour.

He wasn't surprised that his cheeks were wet.

43

To Change What We Can;
To Better What We Can

"Bugger off," Fingal yelled at a lurcher snarling at the rear tyre of his Raleigh bicycle as he wobbled along to attend a labouring patient who lived on Swift's Alley.

Fingal had ridden from the Rotunda, an institution founded in 1745, the year of Bonnie Prince Charlie's abortive Jacobite rebellion, as a "Hospital for the relief of poor lying-in women in Dublin." Proceeds from performances in the adjoining circular theatre from which the hospital had taken its name had been meant to defray the hospital's costs.

As well as its inpatient wards, the Rotunda had a busy extern department where annually 1,500 women were seen at the antenatal clinic before being delivered in their own homes. Fingal had attended to today's patient at the clinic, but he had first met her last year in Sir Patrick Dun's. As Fingal had followed the progress of Roisín Kilmartin's pregnancy, he had made sure she was taking her iron and liver extract, confirming she kept a normal level of haemoglobin.

His two-sizes-too-small bicycle had taken him across O'Connell Street Bridge, along the Quays, and now, well into the Liberties, he was bumping over the cobblestones of Francis Street, Paddy Keogh's old home territory.

Fingal pedalled harder trying to keep up with Doctor Milliken, who despite his girth crouched over his handlebars and pumped his legs like a competitor in the Tour de France. Patients who had given birth many times did not linger in labour.

Doctor Milliken cycled on, seemingly oblivious to the street urchins who cheered him along. On an April Saturday afternoon, two men from the Rotunda would be a fresh source of amusement to the youngsters. The junior medical staff and students were known by their bicycles and the midwifery bags, leather hold-alls strapped to platforms mounted over the rear wheel. They held the necessary equipment for home deliveries. Inquisitive children were told that doctors brought babies in the black bags.

"Here come the babby doctors."

Fingal recognised the gangly cigarette-smoking speaker as Jockser, who'd helped guard Bob's car when they'd come to see Sergeant Paddy last year. The lad's shirt had no collar, and his trousers, once someone else's long pants, ended halfway down his bare shins.

"Is dat feckin' great bag on your carrier the wan youse brings the snappers in?"

Fingal grinned. "Snapper" was another Dublin term for baby. Not only had he been learning medicine for the last four and a half years, he'd become fluent in the English of the tenements.

"Dey've got one bag each. Mebbe it's twins." That from Finnoula Curran of the fair shoulders, the little girl who'd directed him to Paddy Keogh's room.

Roger Milliken dismounted under a laundry-laden pole sticking out from an upper storey window. He propped his bike against a whitewashed brick wall that must last have been white before the turn of the century.

Fingal followed suit.

"Hello dere, Big Fellah." A boy in a cloth cap, clean sweater, short pants, and wearing socks and a pair of shoes got up from where he'd been sitting with his back against the wall. He grinned at Fingal. "How's the form?"

"The form? I'm grand, and hello to yourself." Fingal had to think and think hard for a name. "Declan," he said, "Declan Kilmartin. How are you?"

"Put out of me house," Declan said. "All the menfolk are, and the yougwans. There's just me granny and me mammy and the midwife in the place. Me da, him wat's workin' stackin' bricks and carryin' a hod now for his oul' pal Sergeant Paddy Keogh, the pair of dem are down at the boozer."

Brendan's income as a labourer would account for how well dressed Declan was compared with the rest of the kids here.

"De're gettin' a head start on wettin' the babby's head."

Standard practice for Irish husbands when their wives were in labour. Having babies was strictly women's work. Men had to suffer through it as best they could in the pub with their mates buying them drinks.

"Come on, Fingal," Roger Milliken said. "It's her ninth. Labour'll be short." He hefted his bag, pushed open a badly fitting plank door, and disappeared into the gloom inside.

Fingal lifted his bag and said to Declan, "Nip round to the pub. Tell Paddy Keogh I'm here and I'd like to know how he's getting on." He put his hand into his pocket. "Here's tuppence and a bulls' eye."

"T'anks, sir. You're a sound man," Declan said. "I'll tell dem and be back. It's my job, once the snapper's here, to run over to Auntie Dodie's on Dean Swift Square. Dat's where the rest of the family's at. Tell dem to come home." He trotted off.

Fingal entered the narrow communal hall and avoided a pile

of recent dog turds. Beside a rickety staircase was a broken-down pram piled high with rusty saucepans. Someone would be selling them for scrap.

He heard the familiar sounds of labour.

"Ah, Jasus, ah Jasus, *ah Jasus.*" He recognised Roisín's voice. "Feck it. Feck it. Feck it. *Feck it.*"

Another woman, whom he reckoned by her tones must be much older, kept saying, "It's all right, me darlin' girl. It's all right."

When he went into the room Fingal didn't feel the same shock he had when he'd first visited Paddy Keogh. Tattered wallpaper, no running water, open fireplace, bare floorboards, picture of the Bleeding Heart, a chipped plaster Madonna on a scarred mantel. He'd seen it all countless times. A table and four chairs looked to be in much better condition than the furniture in other places. "Me da, him wat's workin." That's what Declan had said. It looked as if Brendan Kilmartin was having a go at brightening up the room.

The floor planks had been scrubbed and the window had been washed so it let in light. Fingal remembered noting the first time he'd met Roisín that she'd kept her hair well brushed. It looked as if she tried to keep her home tidy too.

The tableau he saw was like an illustration by Fred Walker in Dickens's *Hard Times.* The patient lay on newspapers on a straw mattress near the window. She was surrounded by her mother, the uniformed district midwife, and Doctor Roger Milliken.

"Ah, Jasus, ah Jasus, *ah Jasus, Mary, and Jooooseph.*"

Delivery must be imminent.

Over the usual tenement smells to which he had become inured hung the now familiar metallic odour of amniotic fluid. He could see a large damp stain on the newspapers. Her waters had broken.

"She's nearly fully dilated, Fingal," Roger said. "Get your hands washed, there's soap and a basin of water on the table, and get over here."

Fingal chucked his coat onto a wooden chair, rolled up his sleeves, and prepared himself to deliver another baby. This time he wasn't sweating the way he had with the first five.

"Now," said Granny, "now dat's all over, who'd like a cup of tea?" She set a battered kettle on top of a small fire in the brick grate.

"Me, Ma," Roisín said weakly. "I'm gummin' for one. I'm as dry as a crop of bog-cotton."

Fingal glanced at Roger and saw the tiniest shake of his head as he said, "Very kind of you, Mrs. Butler, but Mister O'Reilly and I should be running along."

Fingal, noting a row of not-too-clean chipped metal mugs on a shelf, could understand Roger's reluctance. You could catch typhoid from drinking out of dirty cups. Fingal had lost track of the number of times he'd had to get rid of the fleas he'd collected while working in the district.

Miss Tobín, the district midwife, looked up from where she was tucking a baby under a blanket in an orange box that served as a cot. "Run on, gentlemen. I'll tidy up here." She smiled at Fingal. "I think," she said, "Mister O'Reilly, that went very well."

Fingal bowed his head, acknowledging the compliment. "Thank you."

"No," Roisín said, "t'ank you, Big Fellah."

Fingal smiled. His new nickname had stuck.

"Dat's two times youse've saved my bacon. Once wit dem neemicks, and now delivering the chiseller. And do you know?" She accepted a mug of tea from Granny Butler, "it was grand seein' a friendly face, someone you'd got to know a bit, like."

"My pleasure, Roisín," he said, and thought, my sentiments

exactly. And not just one friendly face. He'd been recognised by Jockser and Declan too.

"Ma," Roisín said, "could you make me a jam piece? I'm so hungry I could eat a farmer's arse t'rough a tennis racquet."

Fingal laughed. He'd not heard that expression before.

"You've a powerful laugh on you, Big Fellah," Roisín said, "and maybe this'll bring a smile to your face too. I asked one of the nurses at the hospital and she told me."

"Told you what?"

"Brendan and me agreed if it was a wee boy, and Lord bless us it is, we'd name him for you."

"For me?"

"Fingal Flahertie O'Reilly Kilmartin would be a powerful name," Roisín said.

Fingal glanced over to where, rosebud lips pouting and eyes closed, young Fingal Kilmartin slept. "I'm touched," he said, and his heart swelled.

Someone knocked on the door. A man's voice said, "It's Roisín's oul' wan and Paddy Keogh. Can we come in?"

"Come right ahead, you pair of bowsies." Despite having apparently insulted the two men, Granny's smile was beatific.

Fingal heard the voice outside roar, "Declan, get your arse over to your auntie's. The wean's here."

A stranger to Fingal who must be Roisín's husband Brendan came in, followed by Paddy Keogh. Paddy wore a new-looking Ulster overcoat and a bowler hat. Brendan was a heavyset man, balding, florid cheeks, broken veins in the tip of a flattened nose, piercing blue eyes that flitted from Roisín to the makeshift cot and back.

"See what the stork's brought you this time, Brendan Kilmartin," Granny said.

"Is it a boy or a child?" he asked.

"Anudder brudder for the rest."

"Jasus," Brendan said, crossing the room, kneeling, ignoring the strangers, and giving Roisín a kiss. "I love you."

Fingal glanced away. He caught Paddy Keogh's eye.

The little ex-sergeant snapped to attention, grinned, and gave Fingal a left-handed salute. "Mister O'Reilly."

"Paddy," Fingal said. "Good to see you." He noticed that Paddy swayed slightly.

"And you, sir. How's your pal wit' the motorcar?"

"Bob? Bob Beresford? He's grand." Fingal heard a cough and turned.

"Fingal, I'll need to be getting back. Can you make your own way?"

"Of course." Fingal knew Roger had understood that he would like to stay longer.

Roger lifted his bag and said to Roisín, "We'll expect you at the postpartum clinic in six weeks and bring Fingal Flahertie O'Reilly Kilmartin to the infant department."

"I will, sir."

"See you later, Fingal." Roger left.

At the other side of the room, Brendan held his new son. Roisín smiled up at them. Miss Tobín was repacking instruments.

Fingal said to Paddy, "How's the job been going? Last time I saw you on the tram you'd had a pay raise."

Paddy smiled. "Your man Willy Duggan, the builder, is a real gent. He's upped me to foreman. Me? The feckin' hat—" He tapped the bowler, which was the badge of his status and the origin of his title. "Two pounds a week, and I get to look after takin' on workers." He dropped a slow wink. "Brendan here looked after me when I was a chiseller. Helped me get into the army when I was a lad. I had to persuade the idle git to come to work, but he's got used to the idea and now he's feedin' his family better." Paddy nodded at the table and chairs. "He's buyin' bits and pieces for Roisín and she's a stranger to Uncle at the people's bank." He must have seen Fingal frown. "Dat's what we call the pawnbroker's shop and we all call him 'Uncle.'" He raised his voice, "And you can pay your own shout at the boozer too, can't you, Brendan, you great bollix?"

"True on you, Paddy," Brendan said, "true on you."

Paddy lowered his voice. "I only wish I could persuade him to move in near me on Mount Street. He can afford to get out of dis feckin' rookery, but—och," he shook his head, "I was happy to do it, but shiftin' some folks out of here? It's be easier to pull teet' wit'out an anaest'etic." He reached into his coat pocket and produced a glass bottle containing a pale liquid. "Mister O'Reilly, sir," Paddy said, "mebbe I'm talking out of turn to one of the gentry like—"

"I'm not gentry, Paddy."

"By Jasus, you are in my book, sir. A gentleman and a scholar."

Fingal blushed.

"Look what you've done."

"Me? What have I done?"

"You cured my pneumonia. Fair play. Dat's your job, but you found me, and me a feckin' cripple, you found me work. Dat wasn't charity." He made to spit, but clearly thought better of it. "I didn't mind the beggin'—much, but I hated havin' to take charity, but I'd me family. I appreciate what the folks from Saint Vincent de Paul done for us wit' dere cast-off clothes, thrown-out furniture, oul pots and pans, but Jasus I still had some pride. I used to be a sergeant for feck's sake."

Fingal thought Paddy, a little the worse for the drink, sounded close to tears.

"Findin' a man a job's not part of what doctors are meant to do. Dey're supposed to be too feckin' important. You weren't. You went looking for Willy, and you come into a place like dis lookin' for me. Because I've got dat job now the family have a good life out of the tenements. We even had a holiday to Greystones last summer. I have a job dat let me help Brendan and he's seein' to his own family now too."

"Paddy, look," Fingal said, "I spoke to a man about you, but who said to himself, 'Only one arm? Doesn't matter.' Who worked so bloody hard he got to be the foreman? Who took care of his old friends?"

Paddy looked at Fingal. "Me," he said, "but I'd not've wit'out your help, sir." He put the bottle to his mouth.

Fingal saw a large air bubble run through the liquid as Paddy took a swallow, took the bottle from his lips, and said, "Mister O'Reilly, I don't feckin' care what you say, in my book and the Kilmartins' book, in the words of the old toast, you are a feckin' gentleman, a scholar, and, if the truth be told, probably a fine judge of Irish whiskey." He wiped the neck of the bottle on his sleeve and offered it to Fingal. "Will you, sir, take a drop of the pure with me to celebrate?"

Fingal accepted the bottle, unsure if he was celebrating Paddy and the Kilmartins' change of circumstances or the birth. "I will drink with you, Sergeant Paddy, and to you," he said. *"Sláinte."* He took a mouthful and gulped it down. "Jasus Murphy." The *poitín* burned his throat, made his eyes water. He coughed and handed the bottle back to Paddy. "Grand drop that," he managed.

"If you ever want a bottle, sir."

"Thank you," Fingal said. "Thank you very much." It was an offer he was unlikely to take up. The *poitín* was firewater.

Paddy winked. "I know a fellah who can get as much mountain dew as you'd like, but I'd not want you to t'ink, sir, dat I spend my time half scuttered. I only take a drop on big days like today."

"No need to tell me, Paddy," Fingal said. He was distracted by a strident yelling. Baby Fingal Flahertie O'Reilly Kilmartin was demanding attention. He glanced over and saw Miss Tobín shooing Brendan out of the way and handing the baby to Roisín.

The door opened and Declan stuck his head round the door frame. "Can we come in?" he asked.

"Come ahead," Brendan said.

This was definitely family time, Fingal thought, as folks trooped into the cramped room. "I think," he said to Paddy, "it's time for me to be getting back to the Rotunda."

"Fair play to you, sir." He offered the bottle, which Fingal declined. "I've a bicycle to ride," he said.

Paddy laughed, then said very seriously, possibly emboldened to familiarity by Fingal's having accepted a drink, "You'll be a proper doctor soon, sir?"

"June," Fingal said, "I hope."

"You'd not t'ink—don't get cross now—you'd not t'ink of being a dispensary doctor here, in the Liberties? It's not everyone's cup of tea."

The suggestion caught Fingal off guard. He frowned. What had Roisín said about seeing a friendly face? How flattered had he been to have a baby called for him? Hadn't he been delighted to be recognised and accepted by the kids on the street? Admit it, Fingal, didn't you get a wonderful feeling seeing how successful Paddy was and knowing you'd helped?

Fingal Flahertie O'Reilly didn't surprise himself one bit when he said, "I will think about it, Paddy. I'll think hard."

44

Home and Rest on the Couch

"There," said Bridgit. "That's all done." She put one hand on a hip and peered at the pane.

"You could see your face in that," Fingal said. "It would take the light from your eyes. Well done, Bridgit." Fingal finished moving the swivel chair. From where he stood in Father's study, there was a rainbow on the recently washed and polished glass. Sunbeams danced into the room even though it was muggy outside the big house on Lansdowne Road and there was thunder in the air of the May morning.

"Thank you, Master Fingal." She flourished a yellow duster and stepped back to admire her handiwork.

"Watch out," Fingal roared as Bridgit almost stepped in a pail of sudsy water.

"Thank you, sir," she said, dodging sideways. "I'd've taken a quare purler if I'd tripped over it, so I would, and I'd've made a flood on the floor too. And after my dusting the skirting boards." She tutted and rubbed the back of her wrist against her forehead where wisps of grey hair straggled down from her centre parting. "Now, sir, if you'd just go over there." She pointed to a corner.

As soon as Fingal moved, she grabbed a Ewbank carpet sweeper and began to shove it back and forth. "I know the mistress bought me one of they Hoovers with a headlight, but, hey bye, it gulders like a bullock with the bloats. The old ways are the best."

Bridgit was still a country girl at heart, Fingal thought, with the County Antrim penchant for sprinkling her sentences with "hey bye," and her rural allusions. Dubliners would never have seen a castrated male calf with an intestine distended by wind from eating too much clover. The poor creatures certainly bellowed.

"Master Fingal."

He turned. Cook had come in. Her infrequent appearances upstairs from her kitchen were always as startling as the appeerence of the Daemon King through a stage trapdoor, but whereas he'd be accompanied by smoke and fake flames, Cook always managed to trail clouds of flour.

"Mildred," Bridgit yelled, "don't you dare get dust on my nice clean desk. I've only just polished it."

"Sorry, Bridgit," Cook shoved her hands into a large central pocket in the front of a voluminous white apron that struggled to cover her convexity, "but, I wanted to be sure that you did say they'd be here at noon, sir? Your people and your brother?"

"That's right."

"And that the specialist Doctor Micks will be here at two thirty?"

"He will. I saw him this morning."

"But he'll not need to be fed?"

"Right."

"So I'll need to have luncheon for four people ready for one o'clock and cleared away by two?"

"Right again, Cook." Fingal smiled. He'd arrived here an hour ago, at ten, to announce the imminent return of Father and Ma. It had set Bridgit racing round like a bee on a hot brick, dusting and cleaning. Cook quietly worked away in her domain. He was convinced if he'd said to her, "I'm bringing the first batallion of the Royal Iniskilling Fusiliers in an hour," she'd have said, "And would they like Denny's sausages and champ or rashers and eggs?"

Cook said, "I've phoned the butcher and he'll send round the boy on his bike to deliver pork fillets. I'll stuff and roast them." She stiffened and sniffed. "It's not like Mrs. O'Reilly, sir, to give us so little warning. Not one bit."

"I'm sorry, Cook, but I only got the telegram late last night." He fumbled in his jacket pocket. Ma had sent it from Holyhead in Wales. He read, "'Coming home—Stop—Father unwell—Stop—Tell Lars staff—Stop—Arrive noon 13—stop—Mother.' I know it's short notice for you both, but I think it was my mother's way of not wanting us to worry. It must be days since they left Cap D'Antibes. With trains, cross-channel steamers, it's quite a journey, but she waited until the last minute to tell me."

Bridgit sniffled. "The poor professor. Cook and me, we knew he wasn't well before they went away, but my own oul' ma always says, 'No news is good news, hey.' Mrs. O'Reilly sent us such lovely postcards—"

"Me too," Fingal said. Her cards and telegrams were always so cheerful it had been easy to pretend nothing was wrong over in France, but it had been.

Cook lifted her apron to dab an eye. "I hate telegrams. I remember my own ma getting one after the Somme. I was only fifteen. My big brother, Connor, God rest him. Telegrams never have good news. Your poor father. And your mother never once said he was getting worse, not until you got—"

"Don't worry, Cook." Fingal shook his head. "I swear that if my mother was up to her shoulders in quicksand she'd say nothing until it was level with her mouth because she'd not want to inconvenience anybody. Not until it was absolutely necessary."

The front doorbell rang. "That'll be my brother," Fingal said. "You two carry on. I'll let him in." He was glad of an excuse to leave Bridgit and Cook to commiserate with each other. "Thanks for coming down, Lars," Fingal said as he let his brother in. Lars was hatless and coatless. "It's good to see you." He shook Lars's hand.

"I came as quickly as I could," Lars said. "I should have been here at ten, but there was a dirty great cattle market in Drogheda and it took forever to get through."

"Don't worry. It'll be good for us both to be here to welcome them home," Fingal said, "and with your help we can have things set up before Father and Ma arrive." He opened the study door. "Bridgit and Cook have been tearing about getting the house ready, but I want a hand moving a bed. We've got plenty of time. Come on into the study and I'll tell you what needs doing."

Lars followed Fingal. "Bridgit. Cook."

"Mister O'Reilly," they said, and curtsied in unison.

"Now," said Fingal, "I've seen cases like Father's. The worst symptoms are weakness and shortness of breath." He hesitated. There were things not mentioned in front of servants, but, damn it all, Bridgit and Cook were family. "There's a toilet off the hall here on the ground floor. The folks' bedroom's up two flights of stairs. If we move a spare bed down to the study, Father wouldn't have to cope with all that climbing. And it'll be easier for Cook and Bridgit to serve his meals if he has to stay in bed." He saw Bridgit's look of gratitude. Fingal knew that lately her left knee had been troubling her with rheumatism. "We've got the desk, chair, and table over against the wall, but you and I'll need to hump the bed down, Lars, and help Bridgit make it up."

Bridgit said, "I'll go now at once and get fresh bedclothes out of the airing cupboard. They should be nice and warm, so they should."

"And I'll go back to my kitchen," Cook said. "I think tomato soup to start with and then the fillets."

"Lovely," Fingal said, "and—is the asparagus ready in the vegetable garden?"

"I'll see, sir," she said, and left.

"Let's get started," Fingal said.

Lars strode to the door.

Fingal followed. "I'm glad you're here, brother." The stairs were wide enough for them to climb shoulder to shoulder. "Sorry I couldn't explain more on the phone. I didn't know then that they'd stopped in Paris to consult a physician. Doctor Micks had given them letters of introduction," Fingal said. "I talked to him first thing this morning. Asked him to come and see Father. Doctor Micks has had correspondence from his colleague who works in the Sorbonne, a Professor Bleau. He sent all the test results and X-rays from France to my old chief. Apparently Doctor Micks had also been instructed to keep it to himself, not to worry us about it. Now he knows we've been told he says he'll be happy to discuss things with the family. He'll be here at two thirty."

"And we'll get the details then?" Lars said as they entered the spare bedroom. "I can wait." He nodded at a single bed. "Let's get this stripped. We'll be able to carry it down without taking it apart if we bring the mattress and frame separately."

Fingal pulled the eiderdown off.

"And," said Lars, "if we put the bed head close to the window, Father'll have a good view of the bird tables in the side garden. He's always loved his birds." There was a catch in Lars's voice.

"Professor and Mrs. O'Reilly," Doctor Micks continued from where he sat in Father's swivel chair, "my colleague in Paris is correct."

As soon as he'd arrived he'd been ushered to the rearranged study where Father lay in bed propped up on pilows. He'd retired there immediately after lunch.

To Fingal, who stood between Ma's and Lars's chairs, it seemed as if his father—tall, stiff-backed, always in control—had shrunk and no longer filled his pyjamas. His hair was thinner and now grey.

"I don't want to tire you, Professor, so I'll come to the point. The disease has progressed. I have reviewed results of your physical examination, laboratory findings, and X-rays. There is evidence of anaemia, large numbers of white cells in the bloodstream, and spread to the lungs."

"This does not come as a shock," Father said. "I'm weak as a kitten."

"The travelling tired you too, Connan," Ma said, stood, and plumped the pillows. "The interminable French train journeys, the English Channel, more trains, and then the Irish Sea crossing to Dun Laoghaire last night? The sea was frightfully rough."

Father took a deep breath. His cheeks were ashen, eyes sunken and dull. A cold sore disfigured his lower lip. He coughed, and lay back on his pillows. Ma patted his hand before taking her seat.

Fingal glanced at Lars, whose moustache drooped, and the wrinkles round his eyes were not laugh lines. Fingal watched his father manage a weak smile before saying, "We understood what the professor was trying to tell us, but even though my French did improve after months on the Riviera, my haematological—I believe that's the correct term—vocabulary is limited."

Doctor Micks said, "I understand, so without being too technical, the bone marrow has increased its production of immature white cells and the X-rays my French colleague took show that your left lung has been—"

Fingal knew the textbook said "invaded" and that the senior

doctor wanted a gentler way of putting it. "Invaded" sounded brutal, like the Nazi occupation of the Rhineland two months ago.

"—involved. That is one of the reasons why you are short of breath."

"There's another?" Father asked.

"There should be fourteen grams of haemoglobin, a pigment in red blood cells, per one hundred millilitres of blood. Its purpose is to carry oxygen to the tissues. I'm afraid, Professor, your value is nine. The white cells are suppressing the production of the red."

Fingal thought "invaded" was, in fact, an apt term. The forces of the white queen were crushing the defenceless reds, and there was no hope of a relieving column spearheaded by Father's doctors. The medical profession was as pathetically underarmed against leukaemia as Haile Selassie's Abyssinian tribesmen against Mussolini's armies.

"Under those circumstances I am not surprised that you are feeling exhausted," Doctor Micks said.

"Can anything be done?" Father asked.

"About the low levels of haemoglobin? Not directly," Doctor Micks said, "but we can improve them in the short term by giving you a blood transfusion."

"I don't like the sound of that," Ma said, and frowned. "I remember when I was young an aunt had a haemorrhage after childbirth. Her doctor gave her blood, but it clotted in her veins." She leaned closer to Father. "I'd not want that happening to you, Connan."

"Mrs. O'Reilly," Doctor Micks asked, "would that have been before 1901?"

Ma frowned, then said, "Why yes. I do believe it was."

"A Doctor Landsteiner made a discovery in that year. Not all humans have the same types of blood. He called them blood groups, and if we give blood of one group to a patient of the same group the clotting doesn't happen. It's perfectly safe. Karl Landsteiner was given the Nobel Prize for that work."

Father whistled. "Nobel? And of course his research will have benefitted tens of thousands. Take note of that, Fingal."

Sick as he was, Father was still trying to guide his son's career. "I will, Father," he said.

"You are sure it's safe?" Ma still sounded doubtful.

"Perfectly, but, and I must be honest," Doctor Micks said, "it will be palliative only. It will not cure, but it will give your husband back his strength and energy for a while."

"How long," Father asked "is 'a while'?"

"Between six and twelve weeks to start with."

Father looked at Ma then turned to Fingal. "When is Graduation Day?"

"July first," Fingal said. "If I pass Part Two."

"If?" Father said, and glared at Fingal. "If?" Father shook his head. "When, my boy. When you pass."

Like the Father of old, brooking no changes to his plans. "When," Fingal agreed.

"That's—that's, how long from now?" Father asked. He coughed.

"Seven weeks," Lars said.

"So, Doctor Micks," Father said, "how soon can we arrange this transfusion?"

A year ago, Ma had told him, "Your father very much wants to come to your convocation. Don't let him down." Fingal shook his head. The Lord knew he'd been studying nonstop, attending classes religiously. And yet it was an unshakable part of student lore that every year after Finals' results were announced, two questions were asked. "How the hell did he pass?" and more ominously, of a student recognised as being an ace by his fellows, "How the hell did *he* fail?" Luck always played a part. There were no guarantees.

Doctor Micks said, "Fortunately, Professor O'Reilly, we know your group is B. Professor Bleau had it determined. I must find a donor with the same group, or group O, which is acceptable to people of any blood group, cross-match the bloods—"

"Cross-match?" Ma asked.

"To make absolutely certain there is no risk of blood clotting in the veins. We mix a sample of the patient's blood with a sample of the donor's blood on a slide, leave them for a few minutes. If the cells haven't stuck together, it's safe to proceed. Sometimes we need to look through a microscope to be certain."

Fingal said, "Compatability between donor and recipient is often found in close relatives, isn't it, sir?"

"It is."

"I'm game." Fingal turned to his brother. "Lars?"

"Naturally."

Doctor Micks said, "We'll have you both tested to determine your blood groups." He turned to Father.

"How soon?" Father asked.

Doctor Micks said, "We'll do the testing tomorrow at Sir Patrick's. If either of your sons is a match, we'll take two pints at once, use some anticoagulant, refrigerate the blood, and have it into you here tomorrow afternoon."

Father said, "I thought Irishmen went out for their pints."

Even Ma managed a small laugh.

"I'll arrange with the Master of the Rotunda for Fingal to be available to help me and keep an eye on it until the transfusion's over."

"Thank you, sir," Fingal said. "It will be easier for Father here." The likes of Roisín Kilmartin would have been admitted to hospital to receive blood.

"We'll give you two bottles tomorrow and another two in a week," Doctor Micks said.

"Why wait?" Father asked.

"You really only need the red cells, but they come with a lot of fluid, the plasma. I don't want to overload your blood vessels by giving you the lot at once. Four pints will give you an extra five hundred and sixty or so grams of haemoglobin. Initially you'll feel much better."

Father took in a deep breath and said, "I shall look forward to that."

"We'll be at Sir Patrick's tomorrow, sir," Fingal said. He looked over to Lars, who caught Fingal's gaze and slowly nodded in agreement.

45

Blood Will Have Blood

"Nearly finished, Father," Fingal said. An empty glass bottle, the fourth Father'd had since Doctor Micks's consultation, hung suspended above the bed. A glass chamber that connected two lengths of red-rubber tubing was half-filled with blood, but the level was falling. No more was dripping into the chamber from the bottle. Fingal waited until the glass was empty then screwed shut a clamp on the lower length of narrow hose that led to a needle in a forearm vein. Letting air in there would not be a good idea. Air embolism was lethal. "You'll not be sorry to see the end of that."

"I'll not," Father said, "but I feel better already." He turned slightly. "Even if the blood didn't perk me up, seeing that fellow would." He smiled and pointed through the window.

Fingal looked to the bird table, which Cook covered in crumbs and tiny pieces of fat every morning. Sparrows, starlings, and a robin redbreast pecked happily, but over in one corner was a stranger. The bird was twice as large as its common cousins. It had a small head and beak, but a long tail. The back, breast, and body were dark pink, and its wings had narrow horizontal alternating stripes of blue and black. "What is it?" he asked.

"I've never seen one in town," Father said. "They prefer woodlands with oak trees. That's a jay. *Garrulus glandarius.* I wonder if it'll nest in our garden?" He smiled at Fingal. "I'd like that," Father said, "even if—" He grunted. "I'm sorry. I'm holding you up. Can you unhook me from this infernal device, please?"

"Of course." Fingal picked up a wad of cotton wool dampened with Dettol. He pressed it over Father's forearm where the needle pierced the skin. "It'll sting," he said as he pulled the needle free and pressed down with the cotton wool.

Father sucked in his breath, but smiled. "Well done," he said, "and thanks, son."

A rasping screech came from outside the window.

"The jay," Father said. "They screech and they are marvellous mimics." He laughed.

Like you, Father, Fingal thought, mimicking a man without a care in the world. Fingal didn't reply. He was too busy with sticking plaster, taping the swab to the skin, and then dismantling the transfusion set. "All done," he said when he finished. "Good thing Lars and I are both B like you."

"Chips off the old block. And thank you both," Father said. "Now that's finished, might I get up?" He inclined his head to the door of the study.

Fingal understood. After receiving so much fluid Father would want to shift some, and the toilet was across the hall. "Let me help you."

"I can manage." Father swung his legs out of bed, put on a dressing gown and walked more steadily across the floor than he had last week. "Don't go," he said. "I'll be back soon. There's something I want to say."

Fingal sat. The study was much as it had been back in '27, nine years ago. The same floor-to-ceiling shelves were packed with musty tomes. The rolltop desk was shut. Father's degrees from Queens and Oxford hung on their wall.

Through the window Fingal could see the stands of Lansdowne Road stadium against the cloudless sky. Charlie had played in three international games this season and had assured Fingal that the team captain, Jack Siggins, thought that they needed more strength in the second row and that Fingal might be the man for the job. Next season. At the moment it didn't seem important.

He heard the door open.

Father crossed the room, sat in his swivel chair, and crossed his legs. "It is very pleasant to be able to sit in a chair. Bed is so constraining."

"I hope the blood's helping," Fingal said.

"It is," Father said. "Very much." He smiled. "I never thought it would come in handy to have a doctor, well practically a doctor, in the family." He leant forward. "I was quite convinced you should study nuclear physics."

Fingal sat upright. Father wasn't going to make a last-ditch attempt to get Fingal to change careers?

Father sat back, tilted his head, and regarded his son. "I have vivid recollections of the last tête-à-tête we had in here."

Please don't go on about it, Father, Fingal thought.

"I said, 'I can't make you study nuclear physics, yet, but I will not finance your medical studies.'"

"But you have, Father, for the last two years, and I thank you for it." And for letting the barriers between us down, he thought.

"Your mother is a most persuasive woman." He smiled. "Mind you, had I still been convinced that I was right she would never have changed my mind."

Fingal had difficulty believing what he was hearing. A suggestion that Father recognised he'd been wrong?

"Fingal, I was in error. Utterly and completely and too stiff-necked to recognise it."

Fingal's mouth opened.

"Doctor Micks seems to believe you are one of the best students he's had through his hands for years, even if a bit irresponsible at times."

Fingal lowered his head then looked up and smiled. "There's a nurse at Sir Patrick Dun's, Sister Mary Daly, who would have agreed with that."

"I'm sure it's water under the bridge now, son, and I know from your mother how hard you've been working."

"Because I fai—"

"I heard about that too, but you made it up in December." Father pointed through the window at the stadium. "I can guess what it cost you."

"Rugby?" Fingal shrugged. Father didn't know about Kitty. Losing her cost a hell of a lot more.

"I've also seen you working," Father smiled, "from a very close distance. You're considerate and I believe technically skilled. Lars has told me about the patient you lost. How it hurt. How you came back. I admire that."

Fingal's eyes widened.

"At this point, Fingal Flahertie O'Reilly, I am convinced you have been right ever since you were thirteen. You were predestined for a career in medicine and you had learnt what I'd always preached. 'To thine own self be true.' Well done."

"Thank you, Father," Fingal said softly. "As you taught us I've tried to follow Polonius' advice to his son Laertes."

"To my chagrin for a while, I admit." Father inclined his head in acceptance then said, "We may only have one point of disagreement now."

"Oh?"

"I believe, and so does Doctor Micks, that you should follow the advice I was given about you by Doctors Millington Synge and Saint John Gogarty." Father leant forward and touched Fingal's knee. "Specialise, my boy. I'm still your father and it is still my responsibility to guide you."

No, Father, no it's not, Fingal thought, but I understand why you believe it is. "I might," he said. "I've nearly finished my midwifery and of all the branches of medicine I've enjoyed it most."

"Excellent," Father said. "I am glad we are in agreement. I am delighted." His smile was radiant.

It was a tiny deception, but that smile made it worthwhile. Not long after his chat with Paddy Keogh, Fingal had decided that once qualified he'd work as a locum tenens for dispensary doctors in the Liberties, but he was keeping open the thought of a specialist career later. "That's all very well, but you know that Finals start in less than three weeks. I've to pass them first."

Father said, "You will. I promised your mother I'd be at your graduation and, by God, I will. I'd have been there four years sooner with none of this to worry about." He pointed at the used transfusion equipment. "I was wrong. I'm sorry, Fingal. I was wrong. I apologise." He rose. "Stand up."

Fingal obeyed.

"I am proud of you now, boy, and when I see you up on the platform getting your degree my heart will be so full I'll be the proudest man in the hall, in all the thirty-two counties of Ireland. Make me proud, son," and with that he stepped forward and took Fingal in a gentle hug.

46

This Is the Beginning of the End

"I," muttered Bob Beresford, "I am utterly tee-bloody-totally knackered." He lit a Gold Flake.

"You, Beresford, are not alone," Fingal said. "Nobody suggested Finals would be wee buns." He shifted in his chair. Early evening sunbeams slipped into Bob's flat and highlighted the Van Gogh print. To Fingal's eye it hung skew-whiff.

"Thank God we've only today and tomorrow left to go," said Charlie Greer.

"Feels more like a lifetime," Cromie said. "It's been a desperate way to spend the start of June."

Fingal ambled over to the picture and adjusted the alignment of the frame. On Monday, ten days ago, they'd started at nine and for two days had answered three one-hour essay questions in morning and after-lunch sessions. Their knowledge of medicine, surgery, midwifery, and gynaecology had been tested at a theoretical level. Fingal's fingers still had writer's cramp. He hoped the examiners had been able to decipher his scrawl. He squinted at the whorls of painted stars. "That straight, Bob?"

"Near enough," Bob said. "I'm more worried about getting my answers straight tomorrow."

Every evening the lads congregated here for a postmortem of their day and a discussion of what the next session might hold for them.

Since writing the papers, the students had each on a daily basis been assigned to one of Dublin's teaching hospitals. There they had been doing their "clinicals" by examining a case relevant to a particular speciality, making a working diagnosis, and presenting their findings and proposed investigations and treatment options to two examiners. That completed, they were tested orally later in the day in the same discipline.

"So," Fingal said, plopping back down in his chair and pulling out his briar, "what do the inquisitors of the Trinity College School of Physic have in store for you lot tomorrow?"

"Midwifery clinical in the morning at ten, oral in the afternoon. At the Rotunda," Bob said.

"Me too," Fingal said. Getting from hospital to hospital could be a nightmare.

"I'll give you a lift. Pick you up at nine."

"Thanks, Bob." Now that all their courses were over, Fingal was living at Lansdowne Road. It gave him a base and the sustenance of Cook's meals. It also allowed him to keep an eye on Father, who still, apart from a nagging cough, seemed well. The transfusions, like the Spartans at Thermopylae, were fighting a stern rearguard action and holding fast. Ma was naturally delighted to have her grown-up boy back at home.

"You two?" Fingal asked Cromie and Charlie.

"Surgery," Cromie said, "I hear Professor Fullerton can be tough." He rolled his eyes. "I'll be at Doctor Steevens' Hospital tomorrow."

"Mental diseases," said Charlie. "I've practiced 'filling in a form to commit a lunatic to a public mental hospital' 'til I can do it in my sleep. They always ask you to do one. It's in the regulations. I had my surgery yesterday. I'd great luck. A case of gallstones in a man, but he presented exactly like that lass who thought Fitzpatrick was calling her a feckin female."

"Colleen Donovan," Fingal said. "I remember her." A heavy blonde who'd fixed Fitzpatrick with a steely glare and demanded, "W'at's wrong wit' bein' a woman?"

Bob said, "Talking of luck, did anyone hear what a jammy bugger Fitzpatrick is?"

"What happened?" Charlie said.

"Thyroid disease," Bob said.

"You mean he's got it?" Cromie said. "Nothing trivial I hope?"

Bob shook his head. "No, he's the picture of health, but the fates aren't so much smiling on the bastard as having fits of hysterical laughter. Being a betting man, I'd not like to have called the odds of it happening, but each of his cases so far, surgery, midder, and gynaecology, have all been patients with thyroid disease. A subject about which naturally he is a walking encyclopaedia."

"So," Fingal said, "he must be doing well." And despite his desire to prevent Fitzpatrick winning the prize, Fingal hadn't been able to come up with a way to stop him.

"'Doing well?' That's like saying the American sprinter Jesse Owens just ambles along. That bloody prize is guaranteed to go to Fitzpatrick," Bob said, curling his lip, "unless he really messes up on his medicine case."

"I wonder," said Fingal quietly, "if we could help that happen? I'd not want him to fail, but the thought of him getting a prize really grates."

"Don't look at me," Cromie said, "I've no ideas, but if you do come up with anything, Fingal, let us know. I'd hate to see the medal go to that arrogant gobshite."

"Hear, hear," Bob and Charlie said together.

"If I do, I'll let you know, but I'm much more interested in us. Where did you do your surgery exam, Charlie?"

"I was at Baggot Street. And I, uh, that is—" Charlie fidgeted with his fingers, then looked Fingal in the eye. "I ran into Kitty."

Fingal had a vivid recollection of an essay question in the written exam. *Discuss eclampsia.* It was a condition in which apparently healthy pregnant patients could throw an unexpected violent fit. The Greek *eklampein* literally meant "a bolt from a clear sky." Fingal, who tried to avoid remembering his disastrous meeting with Kitty in January, thought the description particularly apt at the moment. "How is she?" He was surprised when he was able to get the words out and sound unconcerned.

"She wishes us all the very best of luck. Asked me to give you her regards," Charlie said. "And seeing how she'd had to put up with us lot at Sir Patrick Dun's, she's coming with Virginia on Friday night when she holds Cromie's hand as the dean reads out the results."

"I'll take all the support I can get," Cromie said. "No impersonal list on a notice board after Finals Part Two. The examiners meet at five P.M. on Friday. Regular bloody Star Chamber. They decide who passes."

Fingal noted Cromie had omitted uttering the dreaded *F* word as if saying "fail" might portend bad luck.

"Then his high holiness, the dean, resplendent in his academic robes, will appear in the Trinity quad and solemnly read from an alphabetical list." Cromie intoned sonorously, "'Anderson—pass. Cumberland—'" He shook his head. "Strong men have been known to faint."

If Kitty had sent him a personal message and was coming on Friday, did it mean she'd turned down the marriage proposal? Wanted an excuse to see him? Fingal didn't dare hope, and yet.

As he often did when he needed time to think, he fired up his briar and hid behind a smoke screen.

Fingal sat on a hard wooden chair in the corridor outside the ante-natal ward of the Rotunda. He inhaled hospital smells. The new antiseptic Dettol overpowered most of them. Groups of midwives passed him chatting, laughing, unconcerned. He envied them their routine. In a moment he'd be summoned to examine his obstetri-cal case.

He ran over his mental checklist. Date of last period, regular-ity of cycle, estimated date of confinement, number of previous pregnancies and what had happened in each. That last was crit-ical. The teachers always stressed how much of midder practice was trying to anticipate possible complications by understand-ing antecedent events. For five months here at the Rotunda it had been, "Lord help the student who doesn't know the previous history."

In this exam Fingal would have twenty minutes to take the his-tory, examine the patient, make a working diagnosis, order tests, and suggest treatment. One examiner was none other than Doctor Bethel Solomons, Dublin's High Panjandrum of obstetrics and gynaecology.

The door opened. "Mister O'Reilly." Sister smiled at him. "Bed 6. Good luck with Mrs. EF."

"Thank you." He walked down the ward and slipped through the curtains closed round the bed. A rosy-cheeked woman sat up. She looked about forty. Her grey hair was done up in a tight bun. Her belly was distended. "Would you be my student chap?" she said, smiling at him.

"I am. Fingal O'Reilly. I'm here to examine you, Mrs.?"

"Grand, so, and it's Eithne Flynn." Her accent was pure County Cork. "It's for your exams?"

"It is. I'm going to ask you a few questions, examine you if that's all right."

"Fire away."

Fingal rapidly ran through the routine and discovered she was thirty-nine and her pregnancy was at twenty-eight weeks. She was due on September 3. She'd answered clearly and accurately. This was going to be a breeze.

He smiled and asked, "And how many's this one, Mrs. Flynn?" Five or six most certainly, he thought.

"Twenty-one." She smiled and cocked her head at him.

Fingal's jaw dropped. How in the name of the wee man was he going to get the details of twenty previous pregnancies in twenty minutes, never mind take the rest of her history, examine her, and work out a diagnosis? Twenty-one? Why him? He gritted his teeth. No help for it. Get on with it, man. "And when, when was the first?"

She frowned. Her lips moved. She ticked off the fingers of one hand with the index finger of the other. "The first was Eugene and that was in 1914."

"Any complications?"

"Oh yes."

God help me if the other nineteen were complicated too.

"The complication is that I'm wrong. The first was Ambrose and he was born in 1915." She shook her head. "Jasus, but my head's full of hobby horse shite. It was not Ambrose at all. He was 1917. It was Noreen, and she was in '15, or was it in '13?" She paused, screwed up her face, then said, "If it helps, I remember it was the year the Home Rule for Ireland Bill was thrown out by the English House of Lords, the bollixes." She looked up as if seeking inspiration.

"That was 1913," Fingal said. He imagined the cartoon character

Felix the Cat banging his head on a brick wall in frustration. Fingal glanced at his watch. Three minutes gone already. At this rate it would take an hour just to work out all twenty. He took a deep breath. Just be calm, he told himself. "Take your time, Eithne," he said. "Do your best. I'm in no rush. I'm sure it's difficult for you. I've trouble remembering things myself sometimes, and twenty's a brave wheen." But please, please try. And hurry.

She leaned across the bed. "Mister O'Reilly is it?"

"It is."

"You are in a rush, I understand, but you're not being cross with me. And you called me Eithne. That's nice. You're not like the nasty young man who came yesterday, so."

Fingal resigned himself. He'd let her chat for a few minutes then concentrate on her present problems. Perhaps the examiners would be understanding if he got that right. "Thank you." He wiped a sweaty palm on the leg of his trousers.

"A Mister Fitzpatrick." She curled her lip. "Here I was, just like I am with you, sir, and he told me I was a thick, stupid, bogtrotting woman. Just because I still have my Cork accent, so even if I have lived in the Liberties for the last thirty years. He told me to get a bloody move on. He hadn't all day to waste on an eejit. A very important and grumpy young man was Mister Fitzpatrick, bye."

Fingal could sympathise with Fitzpatrick, but there had been no need to be rude, not to an apparently simple woman who was doing her best. Fingal looked down at Eithne Flynn and then to the incomplete chart that he should have half-filled in by now. Hold on. Hadn't Bob said Fitzpatrick's midder case was one of thyroid disease? Some patients were used more than once in the exams and students didn't think it cheating to discuss what they had seen as long as they didn't identify the specific patient. Was this a bit of divine intervention? An unexpected clue to a working diagnosis?

She patted his hand and said, "And what's funny is that I was teasing him. I was *teasing* him. I've been a 'case' for exams before. I know you youngsters only have twenty minutes. He'd have got it all from me in jig time if he'd been nice like you. He still got the answers, but I made the *amadán* work for them and I thought if all you students were as bad as him, bye, I'd have a bit of fun with the next one too. And that's yourself. I reckoned I'd put the heart sideways into you and I did, didn't I?"

"I was terrified," Fingal said. "Really planking it."

"Well, don't you worry your head. First off. I've had twenty pregnancies, twenty-one if you count this one, but," and she smiled, "the Lord above was good to me. I'd one, then He took fourteen to Him before I was three months gone."

Fourteen miscarriages. And the Irish Free State had outlawed contraception in 1935? Fingal shook his head. Why the hell should any woman be treated like a brood mare?

"It was a clever doctor at Sir Patrick Dun's found out my thyroid was out of kilter and treated me. I'd five more after that. I can tell you about all my six babbies in a flash and about all else like the thyroid that ails me."

And she did. She was a walking textbook when it came to her condition. Fingal finished with five minutes to spare.

"Mrs. Eithne Flynn," Fingal said, as he made a final note, "if I wasn't in love already and you weren't wed, I'd fall for you, head over heels. Thank you."

"Go way out of that," she said, and grinned. "Now you tell the professor what you know about me and you'll be bound to pass, so."

47

Vaulting Ambition, Which O'erleaps Itself

Fingal waited on the footpath, collar turned to a persistent morning drizzle. A lorry with O'CONNOR AND SONS. FISHMONGERS TO THE QUALITY painted on its canvas sides turned off Grand Canal Street. Its solid rubber tyres rattled through the gateway of Sir Patrick Dun's. Abstaining from red meat on Fridays had been demanded by Saint Paul in his Epistle to the Corinthians. Failing to do so had been decreed to be a mortal sin by Pope Nicholas I in the ninth century. The hospital's kitchen would need fresh supplies today to prepare meals for Catholic patients.

Fingal followed the vehicle into the courtyard, skirted the outpatients building, then stopped and looked up at the inscription beneath the clock over the entrance. *Nosocomium Patr. Dun. Eq. MDCCCXIV.* It didn't seem nearly two years since Charlie had been asked to translate the Latin by Doctor Micks.

Fingal climbed the front steps. As ever, like the ones to Dublin's churches, the heavy double doors were wide open to admit those in need. He passed the brass war memorial table and skirted the Grand Staircase. Old friends now.

He headed to the ward. He had one last patient to examine there, then he'd be grilled by two examiners. The medicine oral was this afternoon and that was it. The results would be anounced sometime after five o'clock. He'd know his fate and that of his friends within ten hours. Six hundred minutes. Fingal took a deep breath. The last lap of five years' study, he hoped. Tonight he would be Doctor O'Reilly. He corrected himself. Could be. It wasn't a sure thing. In two more weeks he could be attending convocation for the conferring of his degree, watched, he prayed, by Father and Ma.

Five weeks ago the old man had said, "Fingal, I was in error. Utterly and completely," and had hugged his son, an act Fingal could but barely remember from nursery days. Thank you, Father. Thank you. It had been at that moment that Fingal had realised his father had not been the only stiff-necked one. He smiled. Perhaps, like blood groups, stubbornness ran in families?

As he turned onto Saint Patrick's Ward, he tried to close his mind to everything other than the task ahead.

"Morning, Sister Daly," he said, craning past her to read a list of this morning's candidates on her desk. He was first, Fitzpatrick was to be shortly after. Hilda would be examined here at ten.

"Bed 51, Fingal," Sister Daly said. "Mister OG. And good luck, bye." She smiled and touched his arm lightly. A change from the stern woman who eighteen months ago had held his certificate of good standing in the palm of her hand.

"Thanks, Sister."

The black-painted walls were as familiar as the flocked wallpaper in his bedroom on Lansdowne Road. In the picture over the fireplace, Saint Patrick preached on to Ossian. The floor creaked as it had always done when he passed bed 79, "The OTC Commemoration Bed," where the condition of a young man with rheumatic valvular disease, a man called Kevin Doherty, had deteriorated badly and Fingal at the start of his clinical training had overstepped his

authority and prescribed quinidine to stop Kevin's atrial fibrillation. The drug had worked. That time. If there is a Heaven, Fingal
thought, I hope you're there, Kevin Doherty.

Bed 51, named for Colonel Tench Gascoigne, had its memories too. Of a one-armed, ex-RAOC sergeant. "You mean they're
going to stick a feckin' great needle into me back?" the feisty little
man had said before Fingal had tapped his first pleural effusion.
Paddy Keogh, now out of the Liberties tenements and living in a
decent flat and working as foreman on a building site. Well done,
Paddy.

This place is full of ghosts, Fingal thought, of Doctor Micks,
the deputy professor of materia medica and therapeutics saying, "I
won't put you on probation—this time, but one more lapse." And
Geoff Pilkington, the houseman, saying, "Don't take it personally.
We can't save them all." True, Geoff. We can't.

Fingal knew he had to stifle the memories and concentrate on
the case. It and the oral this afternoon were the final hurdles. Bob
had described them last night like fences thirteen and fourteen in
the famous British Grand National horse race. A lot of tired horses
fell at number fourteen every year.

He opened the screens, glanced at the bedside table, and remembered one more ghost. A grey-eyed nurse named Caitlin O'Hallorhan
who'd washed all the old men's false teeth at once and had told him
he'd a quare brass neck for singing "Kitty My Love Will You Marry
Me?" as he'd helped her wash the dentures.

"Good morning." The man who lay on the bed was in his
midthirties with thinning sandy hair and had a scar running from
the corner of his left eye to his chin. The swelling at the base of his
throat was obvious, and had been when Fingal had last seen the
patient at medical outpatients. Not once, but twice.

Mister? Mister OG. Fingal had to dig into his memory. Oliver
Gourley. "Good morning, Mr. Gourley." The man from Boyle, far

from the sea, had a colloid goitre, an enlargement of the thyroid caused by iodine deficiency. It was often seen in people from the midlands of Ireland who ate pike or trout, but rarely bothered with sea fish, the prime source of iodine. "How are *ye,* sir—" The emphasis on the "ye" gave away his County Roscommon origin. "Nice to see ye again. Here for your exam?"

"Supposed to be." After Fingal had last examined the man, treatment had been started with thyroid extract and small doses of sodium iodide. "Did the treatment we gave you work?" Fingal asked.

The man shook his head. "Nah. 'Bout as much use as a lighthouse in a peat bog. Me lump's bigger than ever."

He was an ideal examination "case" with a clear history and obvious clinical findings. The thyroid disorder and his war wound would give a well-prepared candidate plenty to impress the examiners with.

This was a gift. Fingal knew everything about the patient, but it wasn't right. Presenting this case would be the same as answering a written question with the textbook open on your knee. "Excuse me," he said, "I have to talk to Sister."

He fled back to her desk. "Sister Daly, I need your help."

"My help?" She drew herself up and said, "You know perfectly well I'm not allowed to give hints to any candidate, Mister O'Reilly. I'm shocked you of all people would ask, so."

He shook his head rapidly. "No, Sister. No. Not that kind of help. It's Mister Gourley. I know the man. I saw him at outpatients. I know exactly what's wrong with him. Exactly what treatment he's had."

"Did you indeed, bye?" Her glare disappeared and she smiled. "You're an honest man, Fingal O'Reilly." She consulted the list. "The next candidate'll be here any minute, but go you to bed 52. I'll give Mister Fitzpatrick your case when he arrives. You can have his."

That, thought Fingal, would really give Bob Beresford's odds-calling abilities a run for their money. Fitzpatrick was going to see yet another case of thyroid disease. The gold medal was his. No question about it. Damnation. Fingal had been speculating about coming up with a way to upset Fitzpatrick's applecart. Instead he was handing him the prize on a plate. It couldn't be helped, and Fingal needed to get a move on. He'd already wasted five of his precious twenty minutes. "Thanks, Sister." He spun to go.

"Take your time, Fingal," she said. "We always tell the student nurses, only ever run in a hospital for a fire," she winked, "or a really good-looking man."

Fingal stopped and stared at her. Sister Daly had said that, and winked?

"I'll explain to the examiners why you're held up. Ask them to test Fitzpatrick first. Give you a bit of extra time."

"Bless you, Sister Daly," he said.

"Go on, Fingal. I always thought you were a sound man. Now I know it. From now on, except in front of the patients or Doctor Micks, it's not Sister. It's Mary."

"Thanks." Fingal grinned at her, and feeling a confidence he hadn't earlier, set off for bed 52.

"Mister McLoughlin, you've been wonderful." Fingal pulled his stethoscope from his ears and started to put it in his pocket.

The ginger-haired man with the high forehead and the dusky-hued cheeks said, "Ah, sure I hope yiz does well, young fellah. It'll be scary for yiz. All dem highheejins askin' questions. I'd be feckin' brickin' it if I was youse."

"I'm nervous all right," said Fingal, missing his pocket and dropping his stethoscope. He bent to pick it up and straightened.

"But I'll be fine, I'm sure. You gave me your history perfectly. I've heard your murmurs. I know what's wrong. You have mitral stenosis."

Back in '35, Ronald Hercules Fitzpatrick had been asked to report on a similar case the day the Pilgrims had visited here at Sir Patrick's to, among other things, give their blessing to the latest crop of fourth-year medical students. He'd been unable to hear the murmurs because Fingal and the lads had stuffed cotton wool in his stethoscope.

Hilda had stepped into the breach and described the symptoms perfectly. Funny, Fingal thought, how such an inconsequential event as a practical joke could fix a piece of information in a student's mind. Ronald Hercules, the butt of the joke, would certainly have remembered the nature of the murmurs he should have heard. If he had been given this case as originally intended, he'd probably have aced it too and won the bloody medal just as easily.

Fingal glanced at his watch. He'd taken only fifteen minutes, but he was confident he had made the correct diagnosis. He knew about the treatment for valvular disease, had done ever since he'd first met Kevin Doherty. Some patients, some diagnoses, would be indelibly inscribed in his memory. In five minutes the examiners would come in from outside the screens and grill him, asking him to demonstrate the clinical findings. The high cheek colour, the classic cardiac murmurs. They'd ask about treatment and what to do if heart failure supervened. Fingal could take them through that like a skilled navigating officer through charted seas, right up to the use of multiple punctures for severe leg swelling and the future hope for Red Prontosil as a curative of the original infection.

He'd been hearing conversation coming from the screened bed next door, number 51, for some time but had paid no attention. Now he was free to listen. Fingal didn't recognise two of the voices. They must be examiners, doctors he didn't know, but Fitz-patrick's high-pitched rasp was unmistakable.

"A very straightforward case. Simple goitre, treated correctly with thyroid extract and sodium iodide. The goitre is easy to see and as I am demonstrating, by deep palpation—"

Fingal heard the patient's voice. "Jasus, sir, go easy. That hurts."

"Be quiet. Strong palpation is required to delineate the regularity of the margins."

"A little more gently, please," an examiner said, "but otherwise carry on. You're doing well."

Even through the screens, Fingal could hear the smugness of Fitzpatrick's tones.

"Because the treatment has failed, the next step will be to transfer the patient to the care of a surgeon for a subtotal thyroidectomy despite its attendant risks of damage to the parathyroid glands and the recurrent laryngeal nerve."

Fingal shook his head. Would the man never learn tact? He clearly had to show the examiners what a genius he was.

"You seem to know a very great deal about the thyroid, Mister Fitzpatrick."

"I try, sir. I know you have a special interest in the disease. I read your paper in *The Lancet* last year. I thought your suggestion extremely cogent that we should stop using local anesthesia for surgery if the gland is well prepared preoperatively."

You oily bastard.

"One last question, Mister Fitzpatrick, before we let you go, and you have done extremely well—"

I hope, Fingal thought, you'll enjoy polishing your medal. Will you sleep with it pinned to your pyjamas?

"You did examine the patient thoroughly, didn't you? It is very important."

"Naturally, sir."

"You didn't just focus on the obvious thyroid disorder?"

"No, sir. Apart from it and the facial scar the patient is absolutely healthy. Absolutely. I am positive."

Fingal leant over closer to the screens. He'd seen the man six months ago and didn't want to miss what he hoped was coming next.

"Will you please turn down the bedclothes?"

Fingal held his breath and heard a rustling from next door followed by a sharp indrawing of breath and a muttered, "Oh my God."

"So if the patient is, I believe you said, 'absolutely healthy,' how do you account for the fact that his left leg has been amputated below the knee? He got the obvious facial scar then too. I'm sure if you'd not neglected to take the history of how he got it, you would have been alerted to his other war wounds. After a Somme battle in '16, I believe."

"Leuze Wood, September fifth, Royal Dublin Fusiliers, sir," Mister Gourley said.

Fitzpatrick, I could feel sorry even for you.

"Mister Fitzpatrick, I must conclude that in your desire to amaze us with your erudition about the thyroid you neglected to take a comprehensive history of his other conditions or examine the man thoroughly. Ambition, wanting to shine is natural. Trying to bluff is not, particularly when you get caught out in," he coughed, "a terminal inexactitude."

"I'm very sorry, sir."

Fingal could imagine Fitzpatrick bowing his head and wringing his hands. It was impossible to know exactly how the man must be feeling having just, euphemistically or not, been called a liar, but Fingal cringed for him.

"You should be. Now, Doctor Lyndon, do you have any more questions?"

"None."

"In that case you may go, young man."

Fingal heard the screens being pulled back, hurried footsteps growing fainter.

One voice said, "Pity about that chap," and the second voice said, "I don't think we'll have that kind of trouble with the next candidate, O'Reilly. He made Sister swap cases because he'd seen the thyroid in outpatients and didn't want an unfair advantage."

"Admirable. And if he hadn't, Fitzpatrick would have had a different case to examine and we might not have found out about him."

"Ah," said the second voice, "the Lord moves in a mysterious way. Now let's go and find out what O'Reilly has for us. He had to turn down a trial for Ireland last year, you know."

48

If You Can Meet with Success and Failure

"No thanks, Bob," Fingal shouted. "One pint's enough for me until after the results." The four friends were in Davy Byrnes and could barely hear each other over the other loud voices. Nearly every student who had taken Finals, along with two or three supporters for some of them, were crammed into the pub. Tobacco clouds blued the air. The smell of Guinness was overpowering.

A clock above the bar said five o'clock. At this precise moment the dean would be calling the examiners' meeting to order. Fingal shivered. He could imagine how an accused felon must feel as the "twelve good men and true" headed for the jury room to reach their verdict.

He'd arrived at Byrnes at four thirty after his last oral exam to find that Bob, Charlie, and Cromie had been there for an hour. As promised, Diarmud had set aside a corner table for four of his favoured regulars. Just as well, because it was standing room only and Cromie was swaying in his chair. "Don't give Cromie any more," Fingal said into Bob's ear as he headed for the bar.

"Tapeworms," Cromie said, "bloody tapeworms. How do you treat tapeworms? Last question on my medical oral. I'm as sunk as the *Lusitania*." He swallowed a mouthful of stout. "Who the hell would bother to read about tapeworms? Nasty bloody parasites.

And where's Virginia? She said she'd be here at quarter to five. Jesus, how do you treat bloody tapeworms?" Cromie shook his head.

Extract of male fern, Fingal thought, eight millilitres by mouth or, because it tastes so foul, fifteen millilitres given by duodenal tube. But he refrained from telling his friend.

Fingal's own concern was whether his answers in the oral about the diagnosis of diabetes had been good enough. The oral counted for sixteen percent of the marks in medicine. He tried to comfort himself that the clinical part of the exam—and he was sure he'd been all right with the case of mitral stenosis—counted for fifty percent.

All around him faces were creased in forced gaiety, worry lines round every eye. A man with a pint in one hand gnawed on a fingernail of the other.

Snatches heard above the tumult.

"Don't worry, Alfie. You'll be fine."

"I'm scuppered, so to hell with it, give me two gins. Both for me."

Fingal glanced at the door. No sign of Virginia or Kitty. Maybe she'd changed her mind and wasn't coming. He stuck his pipe in his mouth but couldn't be bothered to light it. He didn't want a drink, or a smoke. He wanted the waiting to be over.

Bob came back with a whiskey for himself and a pint for Charlie. "The condemned man had a hearty last jar," he said. *"Sláinte."*

"Cheers." Charlie lifted his new pint and sipped. "I dunno," he said, "but it tastes bitter today."

"Mine doesn't," Cromie said, "because you didn't get me one."

"Later, Cromie," Bob said. "After the results. Diarmud has a magnum of champagne on ice for us."

"People who don't know about bloody tapeworms don't get to drink champagne," Cromie said.

"Pity," said Bob, "it's a Dom Pérignon and probably the last I'll be able to afford if I've passed. Auntie's two hundred quid a year goes by the board once I stop being, and I quote, 'a student of medicine.'"

Fingal frowned. "Bob, exactly what does the bequest say?"

"'As long as he remains a student of medicine,' and damn you three. You've got me nearly as worried as you. I want to qualify and when I do, it's"—He sang off-key—"Lost and gone forever . . ."

Cromie and Charlie, heads together like a couple of music hall song-and-dance men, added in close harmony, "Dreadful sorry, Clementine."

Fingal paused and looked at the clock. "I can't sit here any longer." He finished his pint and stood. "Come on, drink up."

"But Virginia's not here," Cromie moaned.

"She'll know where to find you. Come on, you bowsey." He helped Cromie to his feet.

"I am not a drunkard," Cromie said primly. He swayed, righted himself like a yacht coming out of a stiff blow, and blinked. "I enjoy a jar or two, I just don't seem to have much of a—" He staggered and flopped onto a chair. "—head for alcohol."

Cromie did know his limit and it wasn't much, thought Fingal, but he would let his hair down on special occasions like New Year's Eve or, Lord help us, if he's passed the exam tonight.

Bob and Charlie stood and put empty glasses on the table. "God," said Bob, "all we need is some subaltern blowing a whistle."

"What are you on about, Beresford?" Charlie asked.

"I'm old enough to remember Pathé newsreels of troops in the trenches going over the top. There was always some poor lieutenant with a whistle. I know how the squaddies must have felt. Waiting, waiting, then H-hour and, 'Sweet Jesus, this is it.'"

Soldiers like Paddy Keogh with his amputated arm, and Fitzpatrick's medical exam case, Oliver Gourey, with his missing leg.

"I hear you, Bob," Fingal said, "but we don't have to cross no-man's-land, just walk along Duke and Dawson Streets to Trinity. And try to keep our spirits up." Fingal hoped the news would not be, for any of them, as brutal as a storm of enemy fire.

Fingal stood in the quadrangle with his friends, part of an expectant crowd in a semicircle in front of a doorway under a mackerel sky. His old shipmates believed those soft clouds foretold a shift in the weather. There certainly was going to be change in a lot of young peoples' lives tonight.

He scanned the faces, familiar after five years of classes together. Fitzpatrick was over at the far side, looking, as Fingal had once heard a depressed patient described, like a constipated greyhound. Hilda was in the front row.

The sounds of conversation were overpowered by the rumbling of traffic on College Street, but Fingal heard running feet, saw two women approaching.

"I'm sorry we're late, Cromie," Virginia Treanor said. She was panting. "We missed a tram, looked for you in the pub, and had to run to get here."

"Hello, Fingal," Kitty said. "We came to bring you four lads luck."

Not, "I came to bring you luck, Fingal." "Hello, Kitty," he said, "that was very—"

He got no further because there was a swell of gasps and mutterings of, "He's here."

From a door had appeared, resplendent in his dark red robe with its scarlet facing and matching hood, the professor of bacteriology and preventive medicine and recently appointed Dean of the School of Physic of Trinity College Dublin, Joseph Warwick Bigger. His nose was large for his square face and he wore round-rimmed spectacles. He was a man of medium height and towering academic reputation. He carried a scroll.

"Ladies and gentlemen," he barely had to raise his voice, "after due deliberation the board of examiners for the Finals Part Two examinations for June 1936 has instructed me to publish the following list of successful and unsuccessful candidates." He held the opened scroll at eye level and adjusted his spectacles.

Fingal closed his eyes.

"Aherne P. F., pass. Beresford R. St. J., pass."

It was customary not to applaud, but Fingal opened his eyes and gave his friend a massive thumbs-up. Bob Beresford, the man who had been a "chronic" for seven years before he buckled down, looked as stunned as a cow looking over a whitewashed wall.

"Brady J. H., fail."

There was a communal indrawing of breath. Fingal shook his head. Poor Jim Brady from Carrickaboy, County Cavan, was this year's "How the hell did *he* fail?" unlucky one. Or one of this year's unlucky ones. The list had a long way to go and the *O*s came so very late.

"Cromie D., pass with distinction in orthopaedic surgery—"

Fingal heard Virginia's delighted cry, saw her giving Cromie a massive hug.

"Fitzpatrick R. H., pass. Graham W., fail—"

Pass for Fitzpatrick, but no medal. The dean would have specified as he had with Cromie's distinction. Fingal could feel relief for Ronald Hercules's pass and take satisfaction knowing that the man had been deprived, no, had disqualified himself from medal consideration. "Poetic justice, with her lifted scale." Fingal frowned. He'd have to ask Father who had written that.

Charlie turned and grinned at Fingal, who returned the smile.

The dean read on and Fingal nodded with each "pass," and flinched with every "fail."

"Manwell H. A., pass—with gold medal in medicine."

There was loud applause, tradition bedamned. Everyone liked Hilda and obviously rejoiced in her success. Fingal looked at her, a good-natured short woman wearing what must be a special dress for the occasion and an out-of-date cloche hat. She was blushing, grinning, accepting handshakes and pats on the back, and probably oblivious to the tears coursing down her cheeks.

Well done, Hilda. There's the answer to Fitzpatrick's haughty, "I don't mind working with a woman," on their first day at Sir Patrick Dun's, Fingal thought, then paid closer attention. There were two *N*s, the Nolan twins who both passed, Billy O'Donahue, who didn't, and finally,

"O'Reilly F. F.—"

In cases of lockjaw, every muscle in the patient's body contracted. Fingal's were so tense he could barely breathe.

"Pass. O'Rourke—"

Pass. Mother of God. Pass. Fingal swayed, clutched his hands together. Pass. He exhaled. Round him were no shapes, only blurred colours, one running into another like the tones of a Paul Klee painting. He felt hands thumping his back, heard the slurred voice of Cromie saying, "Welcome to, to the medical profession, Doctor Fingal Flahertie O'Reilly—you oul' bollix," then sensed a gentle musk and a familiar voice saying, "Congratulations, Fingal."

His world righted itself. The dean had vanished, the crowd was breaking up.

"I believe," Cromie said, "Doctor Beresford, that you have in a certain nearby emporium of drink and strong liquors a magnum of icèd bubbles awaiting your good self and Doctors Greer, Cromie, and O'Reilly."

"You are off your face, Doctor Cromie, but come on, everybody," Bob said, and led the way.

Cromie, who, as Bob had noted, was not altogether sober, put his arm round Virginia's waist. Charlie flanked Cromie, in case petite Virginia wasn't strong enough to support her boyfriend if he teetered.

"Would you like to come too, Kitty? We're going to Davy Byrnes." She'd let her hair grow and no longer had those ridiculous waves. More like the old Kitty. For the first time he noticed silver streaks in the ebony. They complemented the amber flecks in her grey eyes.

"Yes, please." She moved beside him, her perfume stronger and filling his senses. "I'm very proud of you," she said. "How does it feel?"

"I'm numb right now. It's like—like—" Fingal groped for words. "They said in the war that some wounded soldiers didn't feel the pain for hours. I think it's going to take a while to sink in," he said, starting to walk. He wanted to reach for her hand, but he hadn't earned the right to hold it. Not yet. He wanted to ask what had happened to the proposal of marriage, tell her how happy he was to see her, sound her out, see if she'd give him another chance, but perhaps she was feeling reticent too? He glanced at her face, tried to gauge her mood, but her quiet smile told him nothing.

"Fingal, this is your evening, yours and the boys'. Let's enjoy it."

And shelve serious discussion until later. That's what you're saying, Kitty, isn't it? But at least she's not closing any doors. He didn't want to leave matters completely unspoken. "All right," he said, and moved closer to her, "but we do have things to talk about."

"I know," she said, and when she smiled up at him his heart, crammed to overflowing with relief, expanded to accept the joy.

They walked to a packed Davy Byrnes.

"Jasus," Diarmud roared from behind the bar, "by the grins on youse's faces I'd say youse've all passed. God help the sick and suffering wit' youse lot proper doctors now. Will I have to call yiz 'sir,' or 'yer honour' now, Doctor O'Reilly? Tug me feckin' fore-lock? Scrape and bow?"

"You, Diarmud Clancy," Fingal said with an enormous grin, "you can, in the words of other gurriers like you, and I ask the ladies to pardon my French, you, Diarmud Clancy, can feck right off. It's been Fingal for years and, by God, Fingal it stays." He forced his way through a throng of happy classmates to the table where the lads and Virginia sat. Cromie's head leaned on her shoulder. His eyes were shut. No chance to congratulate him on his distinction.

Fingal pulled out a chair for Kitty.

"Thank you," she said, and touched his arm.

God, but he'd missed her touch, the nearness of her.

"Nice to see you, Kitty," Bob said, turned, and roared, "Diarmud, crack that magnum."

"Right you are, Bob." He lifted the fat bottle from an ice bucket and started to unwind the wire that held the cork in place.

"So, Fingal," Bob said, "it's all over. I never thought I'd see the day, didn't want to for quite a while, but thanks. I'd not be here, but for you three. You in particular, Fingal. Making me cram for Part One. I do like the sound of 'Doctor Beresford.'"

"You worked for it, Bob. You passed the exams by yourself. You deserve it—"

"We all deserve it," Cromie muttered, and fell asleep again.

"Poor old Cromie," Bob said with a smile, "but he did well to get that distinction. He told me on the way here he wants to be a surgeon with a special interest in bone surgery."

Fingal glanced at Cromie. "I don't imagine you'll be going the surgical route, Bob."

"With my two left hands?" Bob laughed. "I'm not even sure I'd be safe in general practice. My embroidery of simple cuts leaves a certain amount to be desired."

Fingal said, "I know the dean is looking for a medically qualified research assistant."

"Are you considering that, Fingal?" Kitty asked. "I've always thought you were a people doctor." She squeezed his arm.

A *pop* from behind the bar signalled the opening of the Dom Pérignon. "Be wit' youse in a minute," Diarmud said, loading a tray with champagne coupes. "Will I bring one for your man too?" He nodded at Cromie.

"Certainly," Fingal said, "and Diarmud?"

"Yes, Fingal."

"You've been taking care of us for years. Bob won't mind. Pour one for yourself."

"Paid for with the last of Auntie's money," Bob said.

Fingal turned to him. "I've been thinking about the dean's job for you, Bob. There'd be no manual skill required and I think you could hold on to your inheritance too. We did talk about medical research before last Christmas in Neary's."

"We did. You got me interested then." Bob leant across the table. "Go on."

"It would be a job with no night work. I remember you going on strike after you'd been up all night. There'd be no suturing, no taking blood samples, Count Dracula."

Bob laughed. "That's what they called me on Saint Patrick's Ward I was so ham-fisted."

"But you can use a microscope?"

"I can."

"You'd spend lots of time in the library checking references."

"I'd enjoy that," Bob said.

Fingal hesitated. If he spoke softly nobody would overhear. He leant and put his mouth near Bob's ear. "Doctor Micks gave my father a blood transfusion recently. When he was discussing it he mentioned Doctor Landsteiner's Nobel Prize. My dad, ever the prof said, 'His research will have benefitted tens of thousands.' It's not as if you'd be doing nothing useful if you got that job."

Bob looked thoughtful. "I'm assuming your father's not getting any better?"

Fingal shook his head.

"I'm sorry, Fingal."

"Thank you, Bob. And thanks for your support. Apart from the professional people you and Kitty are the only other ones who know."

"I think," said Bob, "you would have had enough on your plate with the exams for the last year without having to worry about your dad. I don't know how you did it."

Fingal shrugged. "Having the folks away for so long helped. Out of sight out of mind." He brightened. "At least he will make it to our graduation."

Bob squeezed his friend's shoulder. "And I'll say it again. I'd not be going there, but for you and those two." He lit a Gold Flake. "And Fingal, I do believe you're right. A research career would suit me. Who knows. If I did get the job with Prof Bigger we might just find that some infection causes leukaemia. Find a cure."

"That's a good thought, Bob. Thanks," Fingal said. "Too late for my dad, but I don't think you'll regret your decision if you do apply."

Bob grinned. "You could be right. Mind you, it'll be a year or two before you lot'll have to come to Stockholm."

"Stockholm?" Kitty asked, and arched an eyebrow.

Fingal had forgotten how attractive he'd found that habit of hers. He gave her a wide smile. "Bob's going to win the Nobel," Fingal said. "They have the ceremonies there. We'll be going to watch him get his award."

She chuckled. "Good for Bob. I hear," she said, "it comes with a tidy sum of money. That would make up for your lost inheritance."

That reminded Fingal. "Bob," he said, "I think we can keep

you in Auntie's funds until the folks at the Karolinska Institute give you the cheque that goes with the medal and the diploma. I consulted the Oxford Dictionary. A student is defined as, 'one acquiring knowledge, often from books.' Seems to me you'd still be fulfilling the conditions of the bequest."

"Go 'way out of that." Bob sat bolt upright. "Fingal Flahertie O'Reilly, Doctor Fingal Flahertie O'Reilly, you *are* the Wily O'Reilly."

Fingal laughed. "It may not be legal, but I'll be seeing my brother Lars later tonight. He's a lawyer. I'll ask him if you like."

"Hang about, Fingal. Won't you be staying with us here?" Bob asked.

Fingal shook his head.

"Why the hell not?" Charlie asked. "It's 'Finals Results Night.' We're all going to get petrified." He nodded at Cromie. "He's got a head start. You can't break up the old firm, Fingal. Not tonight."

"Excuse me, folks," Diarmud said, setting a tray loaded with bubbling glasses on the table. "I'll bring the bottle in a minute."

"I'm afraid," Fingal said, "I have a promise to keep. Family." Ma wanted him home for dinner and, he thought, I want to see the look in Father's eyes when he hears my news.

"Oh, well," Charlie said. "Family? That's different." He turned away, lifted a glass, swallowed, and roared, "Diarmud. Get that bottle here quick. My glass has sprung a leak. It's nearly empty." He turned back. "Here's one for you, Kitty."

Fingal barely heard her. "Thank you."

While she was chatting to Charlie, Bob touched Fingal's sleeve. "You talked about your dad earlier."

Fingal nodded.

"I understand," Bob said just loudly enough to be heard by Fingal over the racket. "I'm going to phone my parents very soon. Yours'll be eager to hear your results. You go when you're ready.

The lads won't mind tonight and one day they'll find out about your father being so sick, but I think you're wise to keep it close tonight. Not put a damper on the *craic*."

"Thanks, Bob. Thanks a lot."

Bob shrugged and squeezed Fingal's arm.

That touch meant a great deal. Fingal looked at Kitty. In January he'd berated himself after that disastrous meeting in her flat for not hugging her and telling her he loved her. He could hear Ma's long-ago, "And is she the kind of girl you'd like to bring home to meet us?" Since he'd come home from sea that had only been the second time he'd given his mother a chance to ask that question. Only one of his brief flings before Kitty had lasted long enough, and to Fingal's embarrassment he'd be damned if he could remember that girl's surname. Angela something, but Angela what? This time was different.

"I'll head home," he said to Bob, "as soon as we've had our champagne. Get me a glass, Bob, and wake Cromie up." He turned and faced Kitty. "Kitty," he said, and looked her straight in the eye, "I was telling Bob I'll be having a glass of fizz, but then I'm expected at home for my dinner." He took a glass from Bob. "Ta."

"Oh," she said. Her shoulders slumped. "Oh dear." She let him hold her gaze as she straightened her shoulders, coughed, and said, "That's all right. I'll keep Virginia company. She's going to need help."

"Kitty." He reached across the table and touched her hand. "Kitty, I'd like you to come and meet my folks, have dinner."

She blushed. "I couldn't possibly," she said. "It would be too much trouble for them. And if your dad's as sick as he was—" She finished her champagne.

"That's one reason I want you to meet him. And Cook," he said firmly, removing his hand to give a fresh glass to Kitty, "revels in putting an extra potato in the pot." He was going to say, "I insist," but found himself asking softly, "Please."

She moved her chair closer to his, kissed him soundly, and said, "I'd love to."

Fingal took a very deep breath. He'd passed Finals. He knew by her acceptance and that kiss Kitty had forgiven him, was going to give him another chance. This time God was very definitely in His Heaven. "I know Ma's going to love you," he said, and he blushed.

Fingal was distracted by a sudden movement and saw Cromie clambering onto his chair, champagne glass clutched in a hand. Drops of champagne flew as his hand shook. Those people in the direct line of fire did not object. He stood erect, spread his arms wide at shoulder height, yelled for silence, yelled again, and when the folks in the bar were paying attention, roared, "Ladies and gentlemen, ladies and gentlemen, after five years of study, we have qualified. Raise your glasses."

Fingal did and drank to Kitty.

Cromie bowed and yelled, "We have quaf—quaf—quafilied." He hiccupped, then said, "And as far as I'm concerned, we deserve it all. *Doctors, we deserve it all.*"

At which point, Donald Cromie, Doctor Donald Cromie, M.B., B.Ch., B.A.O., pass with distinction in orthopaedic surgery, flapped his arms like wings—and fell off his chair.

49

The Wheel Is Come Full Circle

O'Reilly couldn't place the double ringing that had hauled him from sleep. He sat up and rubbed his eyes. The noise came from a telephone mounted on the chipboard wall beside his bed. He lifted the receiver.

"Doctor O'Reilly? Sister Hoey. Ward 21."

He glanced round the bedroom in the student quarters of the Royal Victoria Hospital, Belfast. "Yes, Sister." He yawned loudly. His eyes felt gritty. What the hell was he doing here?

"I'm sorry if I woke you, but it's eight o'clock and I'll be going off duty. I wanted to tell you about your patient—"

My patient?

"Mister Donnelly."

Donal. Jesus. Fragments of the day before were starting to filter back. Donal Donnelly had had a craniotomy to drain an extradural haematoma. "How is he?" O'Reilly was wide awake now.

"I've only ever seen this once before so soon after surgery, but he's been awake for the last hour."

"Thank Christ." O'Reilly's grip on the receiver lessened. "He's fully conscious?"

"Not only conscious. He's demanding to see, and forgive me if I quote," he heard her chuckle, "'that daft old goat O'Reilly.' He wants you to take him home."

"He knows where he is?"

"Very much so. He is orientated in place and time. Doctor O'Reilly, is he a betting man?"

It was O'Reilly's turn to chuckle. "He is that. He'd wager on two flies climbing a window."

"I thought so. He tried to get me to take odds of two to one on a bet of a pound that you would arrange his discharge today."

"Take his money, Sister," O'Reilly said. "Charlie Greer won't discharge him. You know that. Not yet." And, he thought, with the money Donal won at Downpatrick Races yesterday he could afford a loss. He was incorrigible, that man, but damn it, O'Reilly thought, you couldn't help loving him. First thing to be done, once he'd seen Donal, was to phone Barry at Number One Main Street and have him give Donal's wife Julie the good news. Because the Donnellys had no phone Barry would have to scoot round to their neat rented cottage on the Shore Road in Ballybucklebo.

O'Reilly saw his boots lying where he'd dropped them last night. "I'll be straight up," he said, "soon as I get a bite to eat."

"I'll have a cup of tea and some toast for you if you'd like."

"Wonderful. Thanks, Sister. I'll be as quick as I can."

He dropped the receiver in its cradle, picked up a boot, and noticed a hole in the toe of one sock. Donal was already awake, asking for his GP, and trying to make a bet? Wonderful. Anyone who regained consciousness so fully and so rapidly after brain surgery would almost certainly make a complete recovery. O'Reilly knotted the laces and looked for the other boot.

Jane Hoey was making a pot of tea for him. The first time a nursing sister had done that was when Fingal O'Reilly, fourth-year student, had been sitting with an unconscious Kevin Doherty on Saint Patrick's Ward and Sister Daly had sent a student nurse with a bite to eat.

Caitlin, known to her friends as Kitty, O'Hallorhan had been, and still was, as Kevin had described her that lunch time in 1934, "A right wee corker." And she'd be on duty on ward 21 later this morning. She'd be as delighted as O'Reilly to hear about Donal.

Jane Hoey's snack would hold him until he got home by train and had Kinky feed him a proper brunch. He fancied a brace of kippers. Maybe two brace. And a grapefruit to start with. Coffee. Lots of coffee.

O'Reilly found his other boot. It needed polishing, but bugger it. Life was too short to be worrying about having shiny boots.

He walked to the sink and splashed water over his face. His brown eyes looked back at him from a mirror. Silvering had peeled from its back and the reflection of his bent nose, which Charlie Greer had broken in 1935, vanished into a pool of black. O'Reilly needed a shave and his hair looked like a haystack after a hurricane. He held his fingers under a tap and ran them through his mop. Now, he turned and frowned, he should have a tie somewhere.

He couldn't see it. Tie bedamned. Seeing Donal was more important. He grabbed his sports jacket from the back of the door, knowing his shirt and tweed pants looked as if he'd slept in them. And he had, so why worry?

He started on the familiar walk to ward 21. In the nineteen years he'd been in practice in Ballybucklebo he'd visited this teaching hospital many times. It had been opened on its present site by King Edward VII in 1903. The building of Sir Patrick Dun's in Dublin where he'd taken much of his training had commenced exactly one hundred years earlier.

Fingal passed the cafeteria in the basement and climbed the stairs to the main corridor. They had been good times, those recently remembered student days, and his life had been eventful in the years between them and coming to Ballybucklebo.

Father, albeit in a wheelchair, had attended his son's graduation in the Examination Hall of Trinity College wearing his full academic dress of scarlet lined with blue cloth as befitted a man with a D.Phil. from Oxford University. Ma, in a bottle-green two-piece suit tailored specifically for the occasion, sported a ridiculously wide-brimmed green felt hat worn at a tilt. Her chinchilla stole sat upon three-inch shoulder pads.

The '30s, thought O'Reilly, with a smile, those years between the wars when occasions like a graduation called for ostentatious display. Graduates' fathers wore academic robes if they were on the faculty of Trinity, or morning coats, grey kid gloves, and grey top hats out of doors. Those awaiting conferral of their degrees sat in rows of chairs, the men in suits, the women in dresses under robes appropriate to their faculties. One by one they were called forward, shaken by the hand, and given their parchment.

Father's voice had been weak, but his grip firm when after the ceremony he'd shaken Fingal's hand and said, "I'm so proud, boy. So very proud."

Ma hadn't said much, just a quiet, "I knew all along you'd do it." And she'd seemed to glow. She knew that this was Fingal and Father's moment.

Professor Connan O'Reilly had died at home in his sleep three weeks later. Doctor Micks had believed his ability to hold on to life so he could keep a promise to watch his son graduate was nothing short of a miracle of willpower.

Ma, bless her, had sold Lansdowne Road, sadly let Bridgit and Cook go once she'd secured positions for them, and moved to Portaferry to be near Lars. Today he was still a bachelor, had given up shooting ducks, and of late had developed interests in wildfowl conservation and growing orchids. Every year he spent several months in Villefranche on the French Riviera. O'Reilly's big brother had volunteered when World War II broke out in 1939 but had been turned down because he had flat feet.

In the intervening years between 1936 and her death from a stroke in 1948 aged sixty-five, Ma had lived her life fully. She'd learnt to drive and had owned an Armstrong-Siddeley car, reputedly the terror of cyclists on the road of the Ards Peninsula. She'd started an aeroplane fundraising drive two weeks after Nazi Germany invaded Poland. To help she'd enlisted Laura, Marchioness of Ballybucklebo, who was bored by being alone while her husband's regiment was preparing to fight in Norway. Ma and Lady Laura had been the guests of honour when a Mark I Spitfire, bought from moneys they had raised, had been presented to 602 Squadron in time for the aircraft to fight in and survive the Battle of Britain. In 1946, in recognition of her war work and for her unfailing support of a charity for unwed mothers, she'd been awarded the Order of the British Empire. Fingal, still in Naval uniform, had accompanied her to Buckingham Palace for her investiture by King George VI.

She was buried next to Father in the family plot beneath the sombre yew trees in the cemetery on Priory Corner in Holywood, the little County Down town where Father and Ma had begun their married life and where Lars and Fingal had been born. The town where their parents had started to shape Lars Porsena and his brother Fingal Flahertie O'Reilly into the men they were today. Thank you, both, he thought. Thank you for everything.

O'Reilly strode past wards 17 and 18, the orthopaedic unit where Sir Donald Cromie worked, he who on Finals Results Night, in Davy Byrnes pub, pissed as a newt, had roared, *"We deserve it all."* And been damn lucky not to have needed a bone surgeon himself after he'd fallen off his chair. Fingal chuckled. Sir Donald must have given himself a shock that night. Since then he'd barely touched a drop, although it was reported he'd been tiddly last year at the marriage of his eldest daughter to a pathologist.

They'd grown close as students, O'Reilly, Cromie, Charlie, the three of them now working in Ulster, not keeping in touch as often as they should. They all still missed poor old Bob Beresford, MC. The Second World War had taken its toll.

Bob had volunteered for the Royal Army Medical Corps, not as a bedside physician, but as a microbiologist, and had been a captain working in Singapore on methods of preventing malaria when the Japanese overran the island fortress. He'd been awarded the Military Cross for bringing in three wounded privates under fire, the third after he'd been hit in the leg himself. Fingal believed Bob had deserved the Victoria Cross. He died in Changi prison in 1943. He'd been limping round the sick bay tending to cases of dysentery despite his own advanced malnutrition when he'd collapsed. What might have happened, O'Reilly wondered, if he'd not persuaded Bob to pursue research? His auntie's bequest had gone to Trinity to fund a scholarship for medical students.

The war had affected O'Reilly too. After graduation he'd spent one year as a locum dispensary doctor in the Liberties. He'd loved the work and he'd been able to take time for his rugby football. In 1937, he had worn the green jersey as partner to Charlie Greer in the second row of the Irish rugby team. They had beaten Scotland eleven to four and lost to England eight to nine. He kept the formal, silver tasselled green caps hidden in a locked drawer at Number One.

Father would never know, but his son had tried to take the advice of his senior colleagues and specialise. He'd spent one year as a trainee in the Rotunda but had changed his mind and moved to Ballybucklebo to general practice in 1938. His obligations to the Royal Naval Reserve had led to his call up in '39. When he'd been posted as a surgeon lieutenant commander to HMS *Warspite* he'd been delighted that the navigating officer was the same Tom La-verty who'd served with Fingal on HMS *Tiger* in 1930. Tom was to become young Barry Laverty's father. O'Reilly had seen the war out on "the grand old lady" as *Warspite* was affectionaely known in the service.

"Fingal, slow down."

That's what Kitty had asked as they were driving back to Bal-lybucklebo yesterday. He recognised today's voice, turned, and stopped. "Charlie." Fingal's smile was wide. "What the hell brings you here so early on a Sunday?"

"There's a menigioma to operate on at nine, remember? It can't wait until tomorrow. The intracranial pressure started to rise."

"Of course. You're going to let Mister Gupta do it."

"Right. And," Charlie said, "Jane Hoey phoned me. I want to have a quick look at your fellah."

"I'm heading there too." Fingal fell into stride. "It's a pretty speedy recovery, Charlie."

"It's utterly bloody amazing, and we should be grateful for the ones we win." His voice was quiet. "The astrocytoma I did yester-day?" Charlie sighed. "She was only eighteen, Fingal."

Coming down the years Fingal O'Reilly heard the voice of Geoff Pilkington, now a specialist in rheumatology in Cork City, "Don't take it personally. We can't save them all." O'Reilly knew that now. After what he'd seen during the war he certainly knew it all right. "I'm sorry," he said. "I really am." And he wondered what she'd been called, the eighteen-year-old with the brain tumour.

"Morning, Jane," Charlie said as they arrived on ward 21. "Morn-ing, Kitty."

"Morning, Mister Greer, Doctor O'Reilly," Kitty said, rising. "Sister Hoey is just giving report."

O'Reilly knew it was nursing routine at the end of each shift for the outgoing nurses to brief the incoming on the states of the patients.

"I'll be with you both in a second," she said, and smiled at O'Reilly.

"Morning, Kitty. I didn't get home last night," Fingal said, and winked at her. He'd not have got away with that in Sister Daly's day back at Sir Patrick Dun's. Kitty gave him another swift but brilliant smile and returned to her seat beside Jane Hoey.

"There's a meningioma gone to theatre for preanaesthesia with Doctor Browne," Jane was saying to Kitty, "and the astrocytoma we did yesterday." She shook her head. "I'm sorry about Molly, sir. But Mister Donnelly's raring to go." Sister Hoey handed the surgeon a chart.

He scanned it. "Take a look," and passed it to O'Reilly.

Every measurement was normal. The drain had fallen out at the last dressing change and there was no evidence of bleeding from the wound. Practically unbelieveable but the chart didn't lie. O'Reilly gave it back to Kitty. "Can we see him?"

"Just a tick," she said.

"And that's it, Kitty, so I'm off," Sister Hoey said. She rose. "Your toast and tea are ready in the kitchen," she said to O'Reilly, who thanked her.

Kitty held on to the chart. "This way." She marched off, smart in her red uniform and starched fall. That once ebony hair was tipped with silver and fell loosely to her shoulders. The modern headdress didn't cover her hair the way the ones had back in the '30s and, O'Reilly thought as he and Charlie followed her, calves like Kitty's deserved to be paid the compliment of a knee-length skirt, not hidden under the floor-length dresses of her student days. Thank you for coming back again, girl, and giving us yet another chance. You are a remarkable woman.

Donal no longer needed one-on-one nursing. He had propped himself up on pillows. His head was swathed in bandages, but they were pristine. His face was nearly as pale.

"Well, Donal," O'Reilly said. "How are you?"

"Some bugger's—" He glanced at Kitty. "Sorry, Miss Kitty. There's an eejit playing the Lambeg drums in my head, so there is."

"I'm not surprised," O'Reilly said. "You must have hit your nut a powerful whack when you fell off the motorbike."

"Is that what happened?" Donal frowned. "I've no idea how I got here." He tentatively put one hand up to his dressing. "Or how I got this."

"It's not unusual for people to be unable to remember the events immediately surrounding their accident," Charlie said.

"This is Mister Greer. He's a brain surgeon, Donal. He operated on you last night," O'Reilly said.

"Pleased to meet youse, sir." Donal frowned. "On my brain?" O'Reilly saw the brows-knotted look of concentration that flitted across Donal's face. "Did I have that operation Cissie Sloan was going on about at Sonny and Maggie's wedding?"

"Which one's that?" O'Reilly asked.

"You know, sir." Donal lowered his voice. "The one when the surgeon removes the whole brain, cleans it, and puts it back."

It hurt Fingal's jaw muscles, but he managed to keep a straight face. "Not quite. You'd bled into your head. Mister Greer stopped the bleeding. I'm not surprised you have a headache." You could have died, Fingal thought. A headache's a small price.

"Oh."

"Donal," Charlie said, "I need to examine you."

"Fire away, sir."

While Charlie made a rapid, but thorough neurological evaluation, O'Reilly said to Kitty, "I hope you'd a good night's rest."

She half shrugged. "You look a bit the worse for wear."

"I'm not cut out for sleeping in student quarters anymore."

"It's been a while," she said, "since you lived in Sir Patrick Dun's with," she nodded her head at Charlie, "and Cromie, and poor Bob."

Thirty-one years since first I met you, girl, he thought. "It has."

Charlie straightened and slipped a pencil torch back into his inside jacket pocket. "Mister Donnelly," he said, "you're close to being a medical phenomonon, but everything's pretty normal as far as I can tell."

"I'm well mended, like?"

"You're on the way to being better, but you'll need to stay in for a few days."

Donal's look at O'Reilly would have melted Pharaoh's hard heart. "Can you do nothing, Doctor O'Reilly, sir? I want for to get home. Julie'll be taking the rickets, so she will."

"Don't worry about Julie, Donal. Doctor Laverty told you he'd nip round and see her last night. Let her know where you were. Tell her not to worry."

"Is that a fact? I don't mind that at all."

"What is the last thing you do remember?"

Donal's grin was wide. "Roaring my head off at the races yesterday." He frowned. "That's about it, sir."

"Donal," Charlie said, "you're not out of the woods yet. I'll let you go to Doctor O'Reilly's care on Thursday, if you continue to improve. Your wife can visit you today. You'll be letting her know, Fingal, won't you?"

"My assistant will." When Barry gave her this morning's great news, he could tell her to come up here this afternoon and see for herself. "And," O'Reilly said, "don't worry, Donal. I'll explain to Bertie Bishop that you're sick. You'll not lose your job."

"Thanks, sir. You're a grand man for keeping an eye on things at home in the village, so you are. Keeping the wheels going round. Looking after us even when we're not sick. Like the time there now you helped me and my mates with the horse."

And wasn't that what being a GP was about? Not only treating ailments. Hadn't he learned that when he'd been able to find a job for Paddy Keogh, who still sent a Christmas card every year? Fingal Flahertie O'Reilly loved his community and his part in it.

"So that's settled," Charlie said. He looked at his watch. "I heard Jane mention tea. I'd not mind a quick cuppa before we operate." He turned back to Donal. "You go on getting better. I'll see you tomorrow."

"Thank you, sir."

"Come on, Fingal. Tea." Charlie strode off toward the ward kitchen.

"Get well, Donal," O'Reilly said as Kitty bent to straighten the bedclothes. "And Sister O'Hallorhan, I'll be having Barry run the shop on Wednesday. I'll pick you up at two at your flat." What might have happened, he mused, what if I'd had the wit to marry this wonderful girl back in the '30s? He winked at her again. "We've a ring to buy."

She stood up, and with her back to Donal, puckered and blew him a kiss.

O'Reilly's step was light as he entered the ward kitchen where Charlie had already poured two cups of tea. He handed O'Reilly a cup and an envelope. "Read that," Charlie said. "I got it on Friday. I'd like your opinion."

Australian stamps. Fingal thought he recognised the writing.

Dear Charlie,
  I am so sorry not to have kept in touch better, but my job here as consultant cardiologist at Royal North Shore Hospital in Sydney keeps me busy, that and rearing two sports-mad

boys, one of whom recently married, an Irish girl at that, from Blackrock.

It got me thinking back to Dublin and Trinity. Do you know it's nearly thirty years since we qualified? How would you and some of the lads who stayed behind feel like organising a reunion in Dublin? I'd certainly be delighted to travel home for one.

Please let me know your thoughts, and if you see Fingal O'Reilly, give The Big Fellah my regards.

> *Sincerely,*
> *Hilda Bronson (née Manwell) M.D., F.R.C.P.(I)*

"I'll be damned," O'Reilly said. "Little Hilda. I didn't know she'd gone to Oz. We've lost track of so many folks."

"So what do you think of her idea?" Charlie said.

"It's bloody brilliant. Let's do it, you, and me, and Cromie. I'd love to rehash the old days." He sipped his tea. It was time the last three of the Four Musketeers started seeing more of each other, and a reunion would take some putting together. "It would be grand to see the old faces. Well, most of them."

Charlie chuckled. "I can hear you thinking, O'Reilly, and yes I know he's practising in the Kinnegar up the road from you, but we have to invite Ronald Hercules Fitzpatrick too. Couldn't leave him out."

"Och sure, I'd not mind. I even heard him telling a joke last Christmas. He's mellowed with time." Fingal Flahertie O'Reilly took a sip of his tea. "With time," he repeated. "Who'd have thought it back in 1934 when we were dressing up Gladys in her undies then heading to Davy Byrnes for a few pints? Four youngsters full of the joys of spring. Look at us now. Cromie's bald as a coot, but he's a sober upstanding Knight of the Realm. You don't boast about it, but I know you were given the Lister Medal by the Royal College of Surgeons two years ago for outstanding contributions to the discipline."

"Well I—that is—"

O'Reilly sensed his friend's discomfort and continued. "I'll bet old Bob would have won that Nobel I teased him about, and me? Me? I've not got any gongs, Sir Fingal sounds as right to me as Lord Paddy Keogh of the Liberties, even if he was a noble wee man, but I'm happy as a pig in shite in Ballybucklebo and I'm about to settle down."

Charlie Greer took a sip of tea and smiled. "I guess Ronald Hercules Fitzpatrick isn't the only one who's mellowed with time."

O'Reilly yawned, stretched, and nodded. "Haven't we all, Charlie? Haven't we all?"

Afterword

by

Mrs. Maureen Kincaid

Hello again. It's me, Maureen "Kinky" Kincaid, so, back here at Number One. Himself, Doctor O'Reilly, has only just got home. He walked up from the Belfast train. You'd think after all the excitement of yesterday at the Downpatrick Races and him staying at the Royal Victoria Hospital all last night with poor Donal—Lord be praised he's on the mend, so—the doctor'd be content enough to get home and have his brunch.

He's done that. You should have seen the way he tucked into my freshly squeezed orange juice, a whole grapefruit, four poached kippers, toast, marmalade, and two pots of coffee.

There he was sitting at the top end of the big mahogany table with that wee dote Lady Macbeth sitting on his lap begging for scraps. You know what cats are like.

"Kinky," says he, "I'm going to ask you for a favour."

"Fire away," says I, "but I can guess what it is."

"Oh," says he, "and what might it be then?"

"You're going to tell me that Patrick Taylor fellah has spun another yarn about us folks here in Ballybucklebo, aren't you, sir?"

He shakes his head—Lord knows that man could use a haircut, but it's not my place to say so. Maybe Miss Kitty can get him to change his ways—more power to her wheel.

"This one's not about the village," says he. "It's about a bunch of medical students I once knew, back at Trinity College in Dublin." He slips Lady Macbeth a bit of kipper and pretends I didn't see him do it.

"Indeed," says I. "Rapscallions to a man, I'll bet."

He laughed. "I suppose we were rascals—then," he says, "but I think we've mellowed." He started on his fourth kipper. It gladdens the soul to see a body's cooking appreciated. "So, Kinky," he says, "it's just like I asked you to do after the last five of Taylor's stories. Could you please put some more of your recipes on paper?"

To tell the truth, it does please me to think there's folks out there trying the way I cook, mostly taught by my ma back in Beál na mBláth in County Cork, so, but sometimes I do like to try something new. "I will, sir," says I, "I have three traditional Irish dishes in mind and one for a sauce your brother Mister Lars brought back with him from Villefranche last year."

"That would be wonderful," says he.

Did you ever see the look on the face of a kiddie playing marbles with bigger boys and they've taken his last one? I swear to God that's how himself looked when he realised he'd finished the final kipper. It was an expression that would have softened Pharaoh's hard heart. "Will I do you another, sir?" says I.

"Not at all," says he, and patted his tummy, "but thanks for the notion." He buttered toast. "Kinky, when I've finished I'm going to take Arthur Guinness for a walk, drop in at the Mucky Duck, then come home. Could you maybe get the writing done while I'm out?"

"Bless you, sir," says I, brushing crumbs from his tie, "they'll be done by the time you get back."

So here I am at my kitchen table, pen in hand. Funnily enough, they'll be having tomato soup with Guinness bread, then roast stuffed pork fillets tonight for their tea when Doctor Laverty gets home. My friend who's been to America, and helps me with the differences between Irish and American measures, tells me pork fillet is called tenderloin in the U.S., and it is a tender cut. Pity sauce Béarnaise doesn't go with pork—but my apple sauce will, and I'm sure all you chefs out there know how to make that even if you can't get real Bramley apples.

TOMATO SOUP

1 tablespoon olive oil

2 medium onions, peeled and chopped

1 carrot, peeled and chopped

1 medium potato, peeled and chopped

2 pounds ripe tomatoes, skin taken off, or equivalent weight in tinned tomatoes

1 clove garlic crushed

1 teaspoon sugar

1½ pints/850 ml vegetable stock (good-quality stock cubes are grand for this)

Salt and freshly ground black pepper to taste

A little basil or parsley and cream to garnish

If using fresh tomatoes, immerse them in boiling water for a few minutes as this makes it easy to peel off the skin. When I am in a hurry, I like to use the tinned tomatoes instead. Heat the oil in a saucepan, add the onions, carrot, and potato. Cover with a lid and cook gently for about 10 minutes until softened. Add the chopped tomatoes and cook for a further 10 minutes. Then add the garlic, sugar, and stock and simmer for about 15 minutes. Blend 'til puréed, season to taste, and serve with a swirl of cream and chopped basil or parsley.

GUINNESS BREAD

280 g/10 oz plain flour
280 g/10 oz whole wheat flour
170 g/6 oz oats
50 g/2 oz sunflower seeds
4 tablespoons brown sugar
3 teaspoons salt
440 ml/15 fluid oz Guinness
2 tablespoons cooking oil
2 tablespoons treacle or molasses
300 ml/8oz/1 cup approx. milk
3 teaspoons baking soda dissolved in the milk

First prepare the baking tins by greasing them well and lining with greaseproof parchment. Turn on the oven to 200°C/400°F. Mix all the dry ingredients in a large bowl, make a well in the centre, and add the Guinness followed by the oil, treacle, and lastly the milk. You add the milk last because sometimes you may need to add more or less depending on the brand of flour used or even the weather conditions. However, what you are aiming for is a nice soft dropping consistency. Divide the mixture between 2 loaf tins (I use a large 2lb and a smaller 1lb size for this quantity of mixture and as it freezes well I always have one for an emergency). Bake in the oven at 200°C/400°F for 10 mins, then turn the oven down to 180°C/350°F and bake for a further 35 to 45 mins.

Sauce Béarnaise

6 egg yolks
75 ml/2 ½ oz white wine vinegar
200g/7 oz melted butter
1 tablespoon chopped tarragon (or ½ teaspoon dried)
Salt and freshly ground black pepper

This is probably one of the most difficult of all the French sauces to make, but I think this recipe is quite foolproof.

First you blend the egg yolks (I use the Sunbeam Mixmaster Doctor O'Reilly bought me in 1960 and it makes life a lot easier than whipping things by hand), for about one minute or so. Then with the mixer still running, add the vinegar very slowly and follow by gradually adding the butter. To finish, add the tarragon and the salt and pepper and serve immediately.

Stuffed Pork Fillet (Tenderloin)

1 pork tenderloin weighing about 450 g/1 lb
4 or 5 strips of bacon

Stuffing
25g/1 oz butter
1 medium onion, chopped finely
85g/3 oz mushrooms, chopped finely
½ teaspoon thyme (dried)
2 teaspoons parsley
110g/4 oz breadcrumbs
Pinch salt and ground pepper

Preheat the oven to 180°C / 350°F/gas mark 4.

Prepare the tenderloin by splitting it lengthwise. Then using a rolling pin or a meat mallet, batter it on both halves to flatten it.

To make the stuffing, melt the butter in a pan, then fry the onion gently for a few minutes until it is transparent and soft but not coloured. Add the mushrooms and finally the herbs. Cook for a few minutes and add the breadcrumbs and seasoning.

Spread the stuffing on one side of the pork and place the other half of the fillet on top. Wrap the strips of bacon around the pork and finally place on a piece of buttered parchment or foil and close loosely by scrunching the top and sides. Bake at the top of the pre-heated oven for about 1 hour. Open the paper or foil about 10 mins before the end of cooking time.

It will slice more easily if kept warm and left to rest for 10 mins or so.

This is very good served with apple sauce or apple fritters.

GLOSSARY

To each of the five previous Irish Country books I have appended a glossary. Judging by the letters I receive the explanations are appreciated. The English spoken in Ireland not only differs much from standard English, but the language of the regions is diverse. Belfast and Dublin dialects are as far apart as those from the Bronx, New York, and Lubbock, Texas, yet many of the expressions in Ireland are shared, so in this glossary by preceding the definition with "Dublin" or "Ulster" I have identified those more likely to be heard in Davy Byrnes pub in the city on the Liffey and those prone to crop up in the Crown Liquor Saloon near where the Lagan flows. Without those modifers, expressions are fairly universal in the Emerald Isle.

I spent October 2007 to May '10 there and frequently visited Dubh Linn, the Black Pool, or as it is properly known in Gaelic, Baile Atha Cliath, the Town of the Ford of the Hurdles, where I expanded my vocabulary. In my years in the north of Ireland I had never heard expressions like "gameball," evincing great approval. My northern versions would be "wheeker" or "sticking out a mile." "Mind your house," exhorting a sports team to be on the lookout for a tackle from behind would be translated by us roaring, "Behind, ye." A scruffy individual in Dublin would be "in rag order."

Up north they would have looked as if "they'd been pulled through a hedge backwards," or "like something the cat dragged in."

But, not all is different. North and south we'd both "go for our messages" when running errands, wonder what that "yoke" (thing-ummybob) was for and might end up "shitting bricks" (very worried) because our pal had got himself "steamboats" or "elephants" (utterly inebriated).

Our speech in the north sounds harsh and has gutturals like "och" and "lough." We often sound as if we are clearing our throats. Dubliners have a nasal accent all their own. Ordinarily I avoid attempting to render speech phonetically. The "Oim Oirish, sorr, faith and begorrah," Paddywhackery is not for me, but I have made two concessions when it comes to the Dublin dialect. The letter *G* does not exist in the syllable *ing* so I have written words like "drinking" as "drinkin'." I hope the apostrophes are not annoying. *H* (pronounced "haitch" in Dublin) is always dropped from *th* so "thing" becomes "t'ing,' "brother," "brudder." As I worked I kept hearing a Dublin friend of very long standing, Henry Galvin, saying, "Did you know, Pat, by the same token, if you divide one hundred by t'ree you get t'irty t'ree and a turd?"

And a caveat. Dublin English, like most inner-city discourse, is not for the faint of heart. Blasphemy is de rigueur, Jasus (Jesus), Mary (Holy Mother of God), Joseph, and the saints are frequently invoked. To devout Christians I apologise, but I have striven for accuracy in all things, which is why along with those exclamations a variant of the *F* word will be found in these pages.

"Feck" is a verb meaning to have intercourse, to steal, "I fecked fifty pounds," or to run away, "I fecked off in jig time." "Feck off, you eejit." It may express extreme denial. "The feck I did," and is also used as a modifier of almost anything as in "I was feckin' terrified," to the extent of being used as a hyphen. "I'd terrible dia-feckin'-rrhoea." No one who knows the true Dubliner would believe me if I left it out of the direct speech of some characters and my remit is to bring to the page people as true to life as I can make them.

So to capture the day-to-day idiom in the book I have here given definitions in this short Irish English/North American English instant translator. I hope they will add to your enjoyment.

a policeman wouldn't ask you that: A polite way of saying "Mind your own business."

acting the lig: Fooling around.

airing cupboard: Also known as a hot press. A cupboard with shelves built round and over the hot water cistern. It was a place where clothes and bedclothes could be dried and warmed. On winter days when I was a boy my mother always put my underwear in the airing cupboard so it would be warm to put on in the chill of our pre–central heating home.

all the best people: *Ulster.* Self-deprecatory expression often used when you have done something stupid. "All the best people throw up at cocktail parties."

amadán: Irish. Pronounced "omadawn." Male idiot. Contrary to popular belief men are not the only idiots in Ireland. *Óinseach,* pronounced "ushick," is the female equivalent.

anyroad: Anyway.

at myself, not: *Ulster.* Unwell.

babby: Baby.

bad bottle: *Ulster.* The putative cause of last night's inebriation. "I had sixteen pints last night and I've got the **horrors.** [*Dublin.* A bad hangover.] I must've got a bad bottle."

banjaxed: *Ulster.* Exhausted or broken.

beat Banagher/Bannagher: *Ulster.* Far exceed realistic expectations or to one's great surprise.

bee on a hot brick: Running round distractedly.

bejizzis: By Jesus. In Ireland, despite the commandment proscribing taking the name of the Lord in vain, mild blasphemy frequently involves doing just that. See also use of *"Jasus; Jesus, Mary and Joseph."*

bevvy: Alcoholic drink.

black pudding: Traditional Irish blood sausage.

blether: To talk excessively about trivia, or an expression of dismay. "What are they doing in the Senate?" "Blethering as usual." Or: "Your car has a flat tyre." "Och, blether." May be accompanied by a genteel stamping of the foot.

bloats: A disease seen in cattle who have ingested any of a number of foodstuffs which when acted on by the bacteria in the animal's rumen produce large amounts of gas, causing the animal to swell.

blow out: End a love affair. "Is Sheilah still seeing Archie?" "Nah. She blew him out."

blowout: A big night out. "Yer man put away two whole pizzas and two six-packs. Quite the blowout."

bog trotter: Pejorative. Country person (bumpkin implied).

bollix/bollocks: Testicles (impolite). May be used as an expression of vehement disagreement or to describe a person of whom you disapprove.

bollixed/bolloxed: Ruined.

bonnet: Hood (when applied to a car).

boot: Trunk (when applied to a car).

boozer: Public house or person who drinks.

both legs the same length: Standing about uselessly.

bowsey/ie: *Dublin.* Drunkard.

brandy balls: Hard, boiled, spherical candies.

brass neck: Chutzpah. Impertinence.

brave: *Ulster.* Large. Or good.

bricking it: *Dublin.* Very nervous or scared.

buck eejit: Imbecile.

bullock: Castrated male calf. Steer.

bulls' eyes: Hard, boiled, black-and-white candies.

bullshite: Bullshit.

bumper: *Ulster.* Electric rotatory floor polisher. The code word used to start the PIRA breakout from the Maze Prison in 1983.

bye: Boy.

capped/cap: A cap was awarded to athletes selected for important teams. Equivalent to a "letter" at a U.S. university.

casualty: Department of hospital. Emergency room in USA. Now A&E (accident and emergency) in Ireland and UK.

cat: *Dublin.* Ruined. Useless.

champ: A dish of potatoes, buttermilk, butter, and chives.

chancer: Untrustworthy person or one who takes unnecessary risks.

chemist: Pharmacist.

chipper: Fish-and-chip shop.

chiseller/chissler: *Dublin.* Child.

chuckin' it down: Pouring with rain.

cipher: Calculate mathematically.

clabber: Glutinous mess of mud, or mud and cow-clap.

clatter (a brave or a right): A large quantity.

codding me: Pulling my leg or deceiving me.

colcannon: Dish of mashed potatoes with bacon, cabbage, milk and cream, scallions and butter. For recipe see *Country Girl.*

confinement: Delivery of a preganant woman, or incarceration.

constipated greyhound (look like a): Be depressed and show it on your face.

Continent, the: Europe.

craic: Pronounced "crack." Practically untranslatable, it can mean great conversation and fun (the *craic* was ninety) or "What has happened since I saw you last?" (What's the *craic*?) Often seen outside pubs in Ireland: *Craic agus ceol* or "fun and music."

crick: Painful strain.

Dáil Éireann: Pronounced "Doyle Airann." Irish House of Commons.

deadner: *Dublin.* A blow to the upper arm muscles, often affectionate, but can be painful.

demob: Shortened form of demobilize or discharge troops to civilian life.

Denny's: Ireland is renowned for her pork butchers. Henry Denny started a bacon-curing plant in Waterford in 1820 and to this day it produces marvellous sausages. Its chief rival is Haffner's.

desperate: *Ulster.* Immense, or terrible. "He has a desperate thirst." "That's desperate, so it is."

dickie bird: Rhyming slang. Word.

divil: Devil.

divil the bit: None.

domiciliary: Visit at home by a specialist. GPs made home visits (house calls).

dote (n): Something adorable. "Her babby's a wee dote."

dripping: Congealed animal fat often spread on bread.

drop of the pure: A drink—usually *poitín* (see below).

drumlin: *Ulster.* From the Irish *dromín* (little ridge). Small rounded hills caused by the last Ice Age. There are so many in County Down that the place has been described as looking like a basket of green eggs.

dudeen: Short-stemmed clay pipe.

dummy tit: Baby's pacifier.

Dun Laoghaire: Port near Dublin. Pronounced "Dun Leery," literally, Leary's Fort.

duncher: *Ulster.* Cloth cap, usually tweed.

fag: Cigarette, derived from "faggot," a very thin sausage.

fair play to you: *Dublin.* To be fair or well done.

feck (and variations): Dublin corruption of "fuck." For a full discussion of its usage see the introduction to this glossary. It is not so much sprinkled into Dublin conversations as shovelled in wholesale, and its scatalogical shock value is now so debased that it is no more offensive than "like" larded into teenagers' chat. Now available at reputable bookstores is the Feckin' Book series—*The Feckin' Book of Irish Slang, The Feckin' Book of Irish Sayings,* etc.—by Murphy and O'Dea.

fist of: Attempt.

fit: *Dublin.* Of a woman. Well built.

flex: Electrical plug-in cable.

florin: Silver two-shilling piece about the size of a silver half-dollar. Worth about forty cents today. In 2010, 120 florins, about $25, would be required to purchase the same amount of goods as 1 florin would have in 1930. This must be interpreted in light of today's wild currency fluctuations.

foundered: Very cold.

Garda Síochána: Pronounced "Garda Sheekana," State Guards. National police force of the Republic of Ireland. Used to be RUC in the north. The Royal Ulster Constabulary is now PSNI, Police Service of Northern Ireland.

gargle: *Dublin.* Alcoholic drink. "The gargle's dimmed me brain." Alternate line to "The drink has dimmed my brain" from the song "Dublin in the Rare Old Times" by Pete St. John.

gas: *Dublin.* Fun.

gas man: Bit of a wit or fun to be with.

gasper: Cigarette (archaic, no longer used).

gee-gees: Horses.

gerroff: Get off, usually directed at over-affectionate animals.

git: From "begotten." Bastard, often expressed, "He's a right hoor's [whore's] git."

Glengarry: Scottish fore and aft narrow headress usually adorned with a cockade.

go and call the cows home: Be given the strength to attend easily to any task. Usually added after a big meal.

go spare: Totally lose control.

go 'way (out of that): *Dublin.* I don't believe you, or I know you are trying to fool me.

gobshite: *Dublin.* Literally, dried nasal mucus. Used pejoratively about a person.

gong: Medal.

good skin: *Dublin.* Decent person.

gossoon: From the Irish *garsún,* boy.

gub: Mouth. Also, to "dig in" one's gub is to punch it in.

gulder: To roar in anguish.

gullier: *Dublin.* The largest marble in a game of marbles.

gumming for: *Dublin.* Desperately hungry.

gurrier: *Dublin.* Street urchin, but often used pejoratively about anyone.

guttees: Canvas shoes so called because the rubber soles were made of gutta-percha.

half cut: Quite drunk. (Or someone might be simply "cut," really drunk.) Paul Dickson in *Dickson's Word Treasury* (John Wiley and Sons, New York, 1982) cites 2,660 euphemisms for "drunk." Many have come from the Emerald Isle.

half-un: Measure of whiskey. (Also served hot, with cloves, lemon juice, sugar, and boiling water added.)

hames: Testicles. Used in the sense, "Taylor made a right hames [balls] of explaining 'hames.'"

ham-fisted: Very clumsy.

hang about: *Ulster.* Wait a minute.

hat, the: Foreman, so called because traditionally he wore a bowler hat (derby).

hear him, hear him: The forerunner of "Hear, hear." A statement of complete agreement.

heel(s) of the hunt: When everything has been concluded.

heel tap: Drink much more slowly than the rest of the company, often to avoid having to pay for a round.

highheejin: Very important person. Often in the subject's own mind.

hobby horse shite: Literally sawdust. Rubbish.

horse into: *Dublin.* Drink up rapidly.

hot as the hobs of hell: Hobs are fireplace sidecasings with flat surfaces level with the grate. Those in hell would be hot indeed.

house floors: The first floor in a multistorey house in America would be called the ground floor in Ireland, thus the U.S. second floor is the Irish first floor and so on.

houseman: Medical or surgical intern. In the 1930s and '60s, used regardless of the sex of the young doctor.

how's about ye?: *Ulster.* How are you?

hurler: One playing the game of **hurling**, a fifteen-a-side ball (*sliotar*) game played with a curved stick, hurley (*camán*) and said to be the fastest team game played on dry land. The women's version is camogie.

Irish Free State: In 1922, after the Irish war of independence twenty-six counties were granted Dominion status within the British Empire and were semiautonomous. This entity was the Irish Free State, later to become the independent Republic of Ireland.

Jack/Culchie: *Dublin.* The inhabitants of Ireland are divided between those who live in Dublin, "Jacks" or "Jackeens," sophisticated city dwellers, and those who live outside the city, "Culchies," rural rubes. Both terms now are usually applied in jest and "Jack" has been superseded by "Dub."

jacked: *Dublin.* Exhausted.

jag: Jab. Usually with the needle of a hypodermic syringe.

jammy: Ridiculously lucky.

jam piece: See *"piece"* below. Slice of bread and jam or jam sandwich.

jar: Alcoholic drink.

John Bull top hat: A top hat with a very low crown as depicted in cartoons of the British personified. John Bull is to Great Britain as Uncle Sam is to the USA. Popular headgear for ladies hunting and Winston Churchill before World War I.

joking me: Teasing me.

kipper: A herring which has been split, gutted, rubbed with salt, and cured with smoke, preferably from oak shavings.

kippered: Physically destroyed.

knackered: Very tired. An allusion to a horse so worn out by work that it is destined for the knacker's yard, where horses are destroyed.

knickers: Women's underpants.

knickers in a twist: In a highly excited state.

Lambeg drum: *Ulster.* Massive bass drum carried on shoulder straps by Orangemen, and beaten with two sticks (sometimes until the drummer's wrists bleed).

let the hare sit: Leave the matter alone.

lift: A ride, or when used as a verb, to arrest.

liltie/y: Irish whirling dervish.

linnet: A small passerine bird of the finch family. Much prized for its song of fast trills and twitters and popular as a caged pet.

list (surgical): Operating slate. The names of patients and the procedures they will be having, put down in the order in which they will be performed.

lord/lady muck from clabber hill: Someone with a grossly inflated opinion of their own importance with a tendency to putting on airs and graces.

lorry: Truck.

lose the bap: A bap is a small round loaf and is used as a synonym for "head." To lose it is to become violently angry.

lough: Pronounced "lockh," as if clearing one's throat. A sea inlet or large inland lake.

lug (thick as a bull's): *Dublin.* Ear. (Very "thick," stupid.)

lummox: Big, stupid creature.

lurcher: Crossbred collie/greyhound. Frequently used by poachers.

marbles in the mouth: Speak with a very upper-class accent.

marmalise: *Dublin.* Cause great physical damage and pain.

masher: Woman chaser (archaic).

measurements: All measurements in '30s Ireland were imperial. Of those mentioned here one stone = fourteen pounds, 20 fluid ounces = one pint, one ounce = 437.5 grains. It can be seen that 1/150th of a grain was a very tiny dose and required extreme accuracy in measuring.

medals: The system of medals in the British Army was with one exception divided along class lines. Officers of the rank of major or equivalent or above might win the DSO, distinguished service order. Whereas any officer might win the MC, military cross; enlisted men, noncommissioned officers, and privates would receive the MM, military medal for deeds of equal bravery. The highest award for valour, akin to the congressional medal of honour, the VC, Victoria cross, was available to all ranks.

midder: Colloquial term for midwifery, the art and science of dealing with pregnancy and childbirth, now superseded medically by the term "obstetrics."

mind: Remember.

more power to your wheel: Words of encouragement akin to "The very best of luck."

mot/tt: *Dublin.* Girlfriend. Wife. Girl. Made famous in an eighteenth-century street song composed by blind Zozimus, "The Twang-man's [toffee maker's] Mott."

mountain dew: Illegally distilled spirits.

much use as a lighthouse in a peat bog: Useless.

not work to warm himself: *Dublin*. Bone idle.

och: Emotive multipurpose exclamation that can express anything from frustration, "Och, blether," to admiration, "Och, isn't the babby a wee dote?"

off your face: *Dublin*. Drunk.

on the lash: Dublin. A serious drinking session.

on the pour: Of Guinness. Unlike other beers, a good pint of Guinness requires skill in its preparation. Drawing one from the barrels or pump can take several minutes. One in the process of being prepared is said to be "on the pour."

operating theatre: Operating room.

OTC: Officers Training Corps. ROTC in America.

oul hand: *Ulster*. Old friend. "How's about you, Captain Hook, oul hand?"

oul ones: Old ones, usually grandparents or spouse.

Paddywhackery: Exaggerated pseudo-Irishness.

pay your shout: Buy your round of drinks.

Peeler: Policeman. Named for the founder of the first organised police force in Great Britain, Sir Robert Peel, 1788–1846. These officers were known as "Bobbies" in England and "Peelers" in Ireland.

people's bank: *Dublin*. Pawnbroker.

piece: Slice of bread or sandwich, usually qualified by its condiment. See *"jam piece."*

Pioneer: Member of a temperance organisation who will have taken "the pledge" at thirteen to abstain from alcohol.

pissed as a newt: Very drunk.

pladdy/ie: *Ulster*. Low wrack-covered reef usually only exposed at low tide.

planking it: *Dublin*. Extremely worried.

play gooseberry: Be an unwanted third at a lovers' tryst.

ploughed: Of an exam. Failed.

po-faced: Literally having a face like a bedroom chamber pot (po). Miserable looking.

poilu: French. Literally "hairy." Term of affection for First World War private soldiers. British, Tommy. American, Doughboy.

poitín: Pronounced "potcheen." Moonshine. Illegally distilled spirits, usually from barley. Could be as strong as 180 proof (about 100 percent alcohol by volume).

pork fillet: Pork tenderloin.

porter: A dark beer. It was brewed by Guinness until 1974 when it was replaced by its stronger relation, stout, which rather than being brewed from dark malts uses roasted malted barley called "patent malt."

poulticed: Pregnant, often out of wedlock.

power or powerful: Very strong or a lot. "That's a powerful smell of stout in there" or "Them pills? They done our Sally a power of good."

public school: Fee-paying private school.

purler: Heavy fall.

put in his box: Taken down a peg or two. Humbled by being humiliated.

put the heart sideways into: *Dublin.* Terrify.

quality: Upper classes.

quare: Queer. Used to mean very, strange, or exceptional. "He's quare and stupid," or "She's gone quare in the head."

quare soft hand under a duck: To be skilled or gentle.

rag order: *Dublin.* Clothes in disarray.

Raidió Éireann: Irish State radio network.

rare as hens' teeth: Very rare indeed.

rashers: Bacon slices from the back of the pig. They have a streaky tail and a lean eye.

ray: A flat cartilagenous fish of the order Batoidei, related to sharks. Prized for fish-and-chips because it is boneless.

rear up: *Dublin.* Become very annoyed and show it.

RFA: Royal Field Artillery.

rickets, near taking the: *Ulster.* Nothing to do with the vitamin D deficiency disease, but an expression of having had a great surprise or shock.

right: Very. "She's a right decent one."

rook (n): *Corvus frugilegus* is a black bird like a crow of the family Corvidae.

rook (v): *Ulster.* To cheat out of money, often all a victim possessed. "That card sharp rooked our Willie."

rookery: Term for tenement accommodation.

Saint John Ambulance Brigade: A charitable organisation dedicated to teaching and providing first aid. In Ireland it is not closely associated with the Venerable Order of Saint John.

Saint Vincent de Paul: An international Catholic organisation dedicted to fighting poverty and operational in Ireland since the mid-1800s. Their work in the tenements cannot be lauded sufficiently.

scared skinny: Terrified.

scuppered: Put an end to.

scuttered: Drunk.

segotia (me oul'): *Dublin.* My old friend. Now so overused as to be almost as clichéd as "begorrah" and "bejapers," but used tongue in cheek as self-parody.

shebeen: Irish *sibín.* Illegal drinking den.

shite/shit: "Shite" is the noun. "He's a right shite," "shit" the verb, "I near shit a brick."

shout (my, his): Turn to pay for a round of drinks.

Sinn Fein: *Irish.* Pronounced "Shin Fayn." Literally "We ourselves." Irish political movement founded in 1905 by Arthur

Griffith to support Irish Nationalism. (A **Sinn Feiner** is a member of the organisation.)

skew whiff: *Ulster.* Out of kilter (alignment).

skinful: Drunk.

skirting board: Narrow wooden strips at the base of a wall perpendicular to the floor.

slagging: Hurling of verbal abuse which can either be good-natured banter, such as "It was gas. We had a quare oul slagging match," or verbal chastisement, "Because I forgot to bring the beer home she really slagged me off."

Sláinte: *Irish.* Pronounced "Slawntuh." Cheers. Here's mud in your eye. Prosit.

snaffle: A kind of bridle bit, or to steal.

snapper: *Dublin.* Baby.

sodger man: Soldier.

sorry for your troubles: You have my deepest sympathy.

sound: Terrific. "Your horse won." "Sound."

sound man: Trustworthy, reliable, admirable. "The bookie paid up?" "Och, aye. He's a sound man."

spavined: Like a sway-backed horse.

squaddy: British Army slang for private soldier whose smallest tactical unit was the squad. In the U.S., the term would be "grunt."

steamboats: Drunk.

sticking plaster: Medical adhesive tape.

sting: Hurt.

stocious: Drunk.

stone: See *"measurements."*

stop the lights: *Dublin.* Expression of utter disbelief. "You won an Olympic medal? Stop the feckin' lights."

stunned as a cow looking over a whitewashed wall: Looking really amazed, and possibly muttering, "Stop the lights."

subaltern: Officer in the British Army below the rank of major.

surgery: Where a GP saw ambulatory patients. In the U.S., it's the doctor's "office." Specialists worked in "rooms."

sweet Fanny Adams: Verbalisation of acronym SFA. Nothing.

take the light from your eyes: Overwhelm, often by surprise and usually in a positive way. "See the diamond yer man give our Sally last night? It fair took the light from her eyes."

tanner: Sixpence. Worth about ten cents.

tea: An infusion made by pouring boiling water over *Camellia sinensis,* or the main evening meal. "I had a great steak for my tea."

terrace: Row housing, but not just for the working class. Some of the most expensive accommodations in Dublin are terraces in Merrion Square, akin to the condos on New York's Park Avenue.

there now: Now or very recently.

thon/thonder: That or there. "Thon eejit shouldn't be standing over thonder."

thruppence: Three pennies. Worth about five cents.

tightener: Very satisfying meal.

titles: In earlier times and in a more class-conscious world, titles were important. In lay society male commoners were Mister, females were Mrs. if married or widowed, and Miss if not. Better-class male children were Master. In medicine and nursing, matters were confusing. The title "Doctor" pertained to anyone who had qualified in medicine, even though in Ireland the medical degree was a bachelor's of medicine. Only medically qualified people and those holding nonmedical doctoral degrees could use this appellation. Specialist internists, in Ireland called "physicians," retained the "Doctor." Surgeons, once they had been admitted to a Royal College, reverted to the title "Mister." The historical reason would take too long to explain. Senior nurses in charge of wards (the old charge nurse, now nursing manager or nursing team leader) was called "Sister." It dated from the time when nurses were in holy orders, but in most hospitals the sisters, like Kitty O'Hallorhan, were not nuns.

toffee nosed: Stuck up.

true on you: *Dublin.* You are absolutely right.

try: Touchdown at rugby football. Was worth three points, now five.

uncle: *Dublin.* Pawnbroker.

up the builder's: Pregnant. Often out of wedlock.

urchins: Street kids, usually preteen.

walking out: Going steady.

wean: Pronounced "wane." Child.

wee buns: *Ulster.* Very easy.

wee man, the: The devil.

wee taste: *Ulster.* Small amount, and not necessarily of food. "That axle needs a wee taste of oil."

well mended: Healed properly.

wetting the baby's head: Taking a drink (or several) to celebrate a birth.

wheen: *Ulster.* An indeterminate number. "How many miles is it to the nearest star?" "Dunno, but it must be a brave wheen."

whin: Gorse or furze, a spiny shrub.

whole shebang: Lock, stock, and barrel.

WREN: Acronym derived from the initial letters of the *W*omen's *R*oyal *N*avy. Akin to WAAF or WAVE.

ye: You, singular or plural.

yiz: You, singular or plural.

you're joking me: You are pulling my leg. You're not serious.

youngwans: *Dublin.* Young ones, usually unmarried.

your man: Someone either whose name is not known, "Your man over there? Who is he?" or someone known to all, "Your man, Van Morrison." (Also, "I'm your man" as in "I agree and will go along with whatever you are proposing.")

youse: You, singular or plural.

Patrick Taylor

✧

AN IRISH COUNTRY WEDDING

*Love is in the air in the colourful
Ulster village of Ballybucklebo!*

There's a wedding to be planned, but before Dr. Fingal Flahertie O'Reilly can make it to the altar, he and his young colleague, Barry Laverty, M.B., must deal with the usual round of crises both large and small, for being a GP in a place like Ballybucklebo often means more than simply splinting broken bones and tending to aches and pains.

Much has changed in Ballybucklebo, and bigger changes are in store, but the lives and practices of these Irish country doctors remain as captivating and irresistible as ever.

"A grand read from a grand man."
—Malachy McCourt
on *An Irish Country Doctor*

✧

"A bang-up storyteller who captivates and entertains from the first word."
—*Publishers Weekly*

✧

"Taylor masterfully charts the small victories and defeats of Irish village life."
—*Irish America* magazine

FORGE®
tor-forge.com/author/patricktaylor

Take a walk through
the Irish countryside with

PATRICK
TAYLOR

and his *New York Times*
bestselling series

An Irish Country Doctor

Trade Paperback: 978-0-7653-1995-1 • Paperback: 978-0-7653-6824-9

"A grand read from a grand man."

—Malachy McCourt,
New York Times bestselling author of *A Monk Swimming*

An Irish Country Village

Trade Paperback: 978-0-7653-2023-0 • Paperback: 978-0-7653-6825-6

"Taylor's novel makes
for escapist, delightful fun."

—*Publishers Weekly*

tor-forge.com/author/patricktaylor

An Irish Country Christmas

Trade Paperback: 978-0-7653-2072-8 • Paperback: 978-0-7653-6685-6

"Has all the charm of Taylor's
previous books and adds Christmas
warmth without sacrificing credibility."

—*Publishers Weekly*

An Irish Country Girl

Trade Paperback: 978-0-7653-2073-5 • Paperback: 978-0-7653-6927-7

"A bang-up storyteller who captivates and
entertains from the first word."

—*Publishers Weekly*

An Irish Country Courtship

Trade Paperback: 978-0-7653-2175-6

"Patrick Taylor has become probably
the most popular Irish-Canadian
writer of all time."

—*The Globe and Mail*

A Dublin Student Doctor

Trade Paperback: 978-0-7653-2674-4

"Taylor masterfully charts the small victories
and defeats of Irish village life."

—*Irish America* magazine